Our *Long*

Love's Day

By Elizabeth Guider

Foundations Book Publishing
Brandon, MS 39047
www.FoundationsBooks.net

Our Long Love's Day
By Elizabeth Guider

ISBN: 978-1-64583-029-0
Cover by Dawné Dominique Copyright © 2020
Edited and Formatted by Steve Soderquist

Published in the United States of America
Worldwide Electronic & Digital Rights
Worldwide English Language Print Rights

Acknowledgements

I have many people to thank for their literary insights, reading suggestions, encouragement or criticism in the research, writing, editing or enhancement of this novel. Among those who critiqued all or part of the manuscript, offered advice about the characters or the plot, or shared pointers about their own work process were: Judi Dickerson, Raul Garza, Kenith Trodd, Gordon Cotton, Laura Hammond, Beth Harris Guider, Steve Oney, Linda Teller Parker, Gordon Steel, Giovanni Troianiello, and Virginia Steen. Among the authors whose works grounded me in similar themes, inspired me stylistically, or set a pertinent tone: Ann Beattie, J.M. Coetzee, Elena Ferrante, Elizabeth Gilbert, Francine Prose, Zadie Smith, and Meg Wolitzer. Several notable literary critics or cultural historians helped deepen my knowledge about the Late Middle Ages or Metaphysical poetry, both of which play roles in the plot: Johan Huizinga, William Manchester, Barbara Tuchman and Vicki Leon for the former period and Helen Gardner, Harold Bloom, Rosalind Tuve and Stephen Greenblatt for the latter. Special thanks to the publishers at Foundations Press, Steve Soderquist and Laura Ranger, editor Steve Soderquist, and cover designer Dawne Dominique.

And to Walter, for his good humor throughout.

In Memoriam

Despite the limitations of their time and place, these three intrepid women seized the day and left indelible literary marks. Presumably they never met—except in the imagination of this book's main character.

Christine de Pizan
(1363-1431)
Margery Kempe
(1373-1438)
Juliana of Norwich
(1342-1416)

Table of Contents

Chapter One

O ut of the blue. While she was making mayonnaise from scratch.

Deirdre Durrell Cole had not expected her husband to walk in at that hour. Of late, he had tarried at the office — *tarry* being one of those anachronistic verbs he relished. Dr. Ashton Mather Cole was, after all, an esteemed professor of Metaphysical poetry. As such, he could get away with using words like that; his wife, a lowly adjunct instructor whose specialty was the Middle Ages, could not.

At dusk, there she was, not at her desk grading papers but in the kitchen, drizzling sunflower oil and lemon juice into the egg-rich emulsion, timing the beater by the clock on the wall. Like her mother used to do in the Delta, where spreading tomato sandwiches with one's very own mayonnaise was a thing all respectable housewives did when guests awaited.

Being just an adjunct, Dr. Durrell had raised her hand during the faculty gathering to organize Klimpton's lawn picnic. Not viewed by her colleagues as domestically inclined, children notwithstanding, she had intuited that her chances of promotion depended to some obscure extent on her talents as a homemaker as well as on her ability to publish, however dense a treatise, however sparsely read. Her one notable supporter among the administrative ranks, Dr. Stella Kincaid, had nodded her approval at the raised hand when scouring for volunteers.

Thus, at the crucial moment Deirdre was completing her culinary *tour-de-force*, Ashton materialized, one arm propped against the door jamb, the other clutching his Italian leather satchel, a gift she had bestowed years before when he had been anointed with a full professorship. At the same time, she was taken on as an adjunct at the same liberal arts college in pleasantly bucolic northern Ohio. He had not thought to buy her a celebratory gift.

As for the Cole children, each had vanished as soon as they came home from school hours earlier. After a perfunctory hug and something he grabbed from the fridge, Dylan had raced upstairs to change for a touch football game. At fifteen, he mumbled more than was good for him, and his athletic skills were not his strong suit. But the weather had turned, the last traces of snow having melted and left the ground soft and grassy. His twin sister, Caitlin, on the other hand, barely nodded when she entered the house, shrugging when asked if hungry and bounding straight up the stairs.

Teenagers, Deirdre sighed, not sufficiently confident as to what that designation nowadays implied but confident enough that their offspring fell within what her husband called "normal parameters" of adolescent behavior.

What she had also intuited was that Ashton's academic standing and undisputed acumen, coupled with whatever hers counted for, did in no way make them more prepared as parents than were less gifted acquaintances of theirs. Moreover, she believed that just being alive in prior centuries—especially the calamitous fourteenth century that was her forte—was a difficult enough achievement, (life then being "nasty, brutish and short," a citation which usually drew blank stares from her students). However, being *young* had remained the most difficult patch, whatever the historical period.

She took pleasure in comparative observations like that.

While measuring out the oil and vinegar, in the proportions that her mother insisted upon as ideal, Deirdre vowed for the umpteenth time to develop better strategies to engage with her children, , especially since she interacted easily with the college kids.

Did that pass for ironic? She wasn't certain, irony being a nebulous concept, at least around the edges.

If Deirdre hesitated to discuss her inadequacy to Ashton on the question of parenting, she did intend to nudge him, however subtly, to spend more time encouraging them in this or that. Both Dylan and Caitlin had demonstrated dexterity on the clarinet, and the former had recently taken to fiddling around, as it were, on his father's prized violin.

In other ways, the siblings diverged. A couple of teachers had noted that Dylan possessed a knack for languages. (He had not, alas, made the cut for the junior football squad.) Unlike her brother's grades, Caitlin's were middling, but she was graceful, her newly long limbs a well-nigh guarantee she'd play a starring role in the upcoming revue at Mrs. Swett's Ballet Academy.

Were these differences between the twins ironic? Deirdre wasn't sure, but they were, she believed, worrisome.

"The point is, Ashton, to get into any decent college kids need to be well-rounded. Decent grades are *de rigueur*, but also, unlike in our day, they should have undertaken, if not excelled at, some athletic or artistic endeavor."

He had reacted distractedly every time she brought up a version of this subject.

"Oh, for heaven's sake, they're only fifteen, Deirdre," he had said, cutting her off not a week ago, either aggravated, or disinterested, turning back to *The Plain Dealer*, which, despite its being 2008, he preferred to read in its print version. Being able to bury his face therein was part of the paper's enduring appeal for him.

These backs-and-forths between husband and wife had been going on for months, but lately, they had an edge: so sharp an edge that Deirdre feared she had become the sole partner concerned with the hurdles the children would soon face. Ashton had redoubled efforts to complete his latest opus, a tome tentatively titled *Andrew Marvell and Ironic Intent*. Already in early draft, it was rumored by his colleagues to be the definitive interpretation of the sixteenth-century poet's oeuvre.

As a result, Deirdre acutely felt her own inertia in tackling a first ever treatise. The plan was to focus on a trio of uppity medieval women who had defied the odds by, among other things, penning their own exemplary literary works. (To her dismay, Ashton had not bothered to inquire after her proposal since the outset, his silence a rebuke, which further stymied her efforts.)

Nonetheless, she had gotten the green light from the head of the department six months ago, which news elicited a perfunctory nod from her husband but not, as she had made sure when *his* opus got the go-ahead, a bottle of *Veuve Cliquot*. A champagne toast to kick things off might have helped, Deirdre reasoned, since so far she had amassed only a folder of notes and became vague or defensive when colleagues asked after her progress.

Even the aforementioned department head, Dr. Louis Beauchamps, an avuncular type whose own tastes ran to lesser French poets no one read any more, had stopped inquiring of her efforts. His diplomatic delicacy was both a relief and an embarrassment. Every time she encountered him in staff meetings, as she had that very morning, she turned crimson, and swore to herself she'd buckle down pronto.

Or, she now told herself, as soon as the mayonnaise firmed up, the sandwiches were spread, and Saturday's college picnic was over.

Shaking off these preoccupations, Deirdre consulted one last time the smudged 3x5 card on which her mother had jotted her secret recipe and had at it.

That's when she took her eyes off the mixing bowl and glanced at Ashton in the doorway. He looked agitated.

Her spatula aloft, she flicked the beater off. "What?"

"I see you're busy."

She gestured with her free hand, palm up, as if to say *indeed*. "I'm making mayonnaise for the end-of-term party tomorrow."

He didn't seem to hear her. Instead, Ashton clasped his satchel to his chest as though it were a shield and swallowed hard. "I'm sorry, Deirdre, but this can't wait." She looked impatient but focused her gaze on her husband's face. "I've come to say that I'm leaving you...us. It's over. It's no use going on about it."

Blinking hard, Deirdre steadied herself against the counter. Confusion flickered across her face. Slowly, she wiped both hands on her apron, wadding it as she did so and pulling it up over her head,. She let it fall to the floor.

"What are you talking about?" she asked, her tone knife-sharp.

Ashton clutched his satchel closer and shifted his weight from one foot to the other. "We both know things have not been working. Between us, I mean. So, I've made up my mind."

"*Your* mind. What about mine? And no, I don't know as to 'things not working.' What the hell are you talking about?"

Despite trying to remain calm, Deirdre could feel heat rising in her chest.

"If you're going to be like that, you may as well know. I've met someone."

It took a few seconds for images of other female professors to flit through Deirdre's head. Offhand, it was hard to impugn any of them, with their bifocals and sabbaticals spent in musty libraries. Except perhaps: Roxane Johnson, the free-spirited French teacher at the children's high school who took such an interest in them.

But how on earth could he find the time to play around with *her*, or with anyone, when there was the OPUS, pages and pages of which were presumably stuffed into that satchel he was clutching?

"Who are you talking about, Ashton, and what have you gotten yourself into?"

"She's in my poetry seminar. One of my more promising students. Her name is Jennifer."

It took another few seconds for Deirdre to register that her husband—the man with whom she had fallen in love all those years ago for his brilliance, not to mention the way his arm arced so eloquently when he made a point from the lectern—had succumbed to the most banal of professorial temptations.

"Let me get this straight, you—at age, what? Fifty—have lost your marbles over a student, who is, what, twenty, twenty-one? *Only five or six years older than your own daughter!*" she screamed back at him.

"You don't have to bring the kids into this," he countered, a hint of condescension in his voice. "When you've collected yourself, we can speak about next steps."

Unable to control her anger, Deirdre picked up the bowl of the now coagulating and likely unsalvageable mayonnaise and hurled it toward the door as Ashton turned his back on his spouse. "You're a caricature, Ashton Mather Cole, whatever pretense of superiority you harbor."

She stood seething, her breathing shallow, as her cliché of a consort strode toward his private study. Shortly after, she heard a key turn and the door lock.

Chapter Two

"**N**o pedigree, but pretty enough."

That had been the verdict that her soon-to-be father-in-law, Richard Cotton Cole, had rendered when Ashton first brought Deirdre home to Beacon Hill fifteen years before. At that time, he was—(presumably or at least momentarily)—madly in love with her, as she was inordinately enamored of him.

They had met three months earlier at the annual convention of the Modern Language Association, where she had gone to network and he to deliver one of the lectures on the schedule. On the last day and after several lame attempts to introduce herself to one or another professor, pressing a business card into any hand that seemed amenable, she wandered into a half-full room at the end of the hallway, where the posted theme was, *Body and Soul: John Donne and the Poetry of Opposites*. Pacing in front of his podium, the speaker now and again gesticulated with his long arms, letting his sonorous voice rise to emphasize a point or fall an octave to recite an entire sonnet, all the while casting his fiercely dark eyes over his rapt audience.

Tired and demoralized though she was, Deirdre was transfixed, standing in the rear, not daring to take a seat nor to leave. At one point, the speaker pulled the fob of his watch out of his vest pocket and eyed the time. She chose to find the gesture endearing rather than affected. When the session wrapped, most of the attendees filed out. She lingered until the last stalwarts had shaken the professor's hand, thrust their cards upon him, or otherwise queried him on one point of contention or another.

Deirdre would not have heard her father-in-law's dismissive comment on that first visit to Boston except that she had crept down the staircase lined with the heavily, (some might say gaudily), framed ancestors on the wall to get coffee, not knowing that her fiancé and both his parents were clustered in the dining alcove overlooking the park. (Apparently, Ashton's younger sister, Adeline, who was "ailing," only ever ate in her bedroom.) Hesitating on the bottom rung, she took a deep breath, pulled her newly purchased silk robe tightly around her, and proceeded to join the threesome, a determined smile on her unmade-up face.

That such a dispiriting memory floated to the front of her mind Deirdre couldn't help. Lying in bed after her husband's revelation that April evening, she tried to martial her forces for a counterattack and not wallow in recriminations. But that withering judgment from years ago had surfaced nonetheless, followed by an equally condescending "indeed" from the only female in the room.

In short, both of Ashton's parents had from the outset disapproved of her: what she represented, (an academic groupie, a social climber, a gold-digger—or all three?), and whence she had come.

From where she had stood at the bottom of those stairs, she couldn't detect if her fiancé replied to their scathing assessment of her. In the years that followed, she often imagined that it had taken all of Ashton's wherewithal to defy his family's wishes, relegate his Puritan heritage to the back of his mind, and set about making his own way.

Up until a few hours ago, that *way* had always included Deirdre. In fact, she had helped clear that road; she had foreseen the twists and turns; she had advised when to speed up and when to slow down. And now, she was being ditched, like an unpleasant hitchhiker unceremoniously ejected from the car at the nearest rest stop.

How is it, she asked herself, that the person with whom I have shared my bed, beget children, reveled in academic pursuits and love of music and nature and books and travel, that to him all this counts as nothing, weighs little in comparison to...To what? I ask. To whom? I ask. An unformed, probably uninformed, twenty-year-old whose name is Jennifer.

Long into the night, Deirdre wrestled with images of students who might have clamored for her husband's attention or milled around at office hours to hear his comments on their papers. Or, was this Jennifer one of the chosen few who had on occasion been invited over to the house for an evening of wine and cheese and poetry in Ashton's study?

Only once had Deirdre ventured into his inner sanctum during one of these impromptu *soirées*, balancing a tray of chocolate-covered strawberries that had been left over from some event she had helped provision earlier in the day. On that occasion, Ashton was propped on the edge of his desk, a glass of chianti in one hand and a small volume bound in gold-leaf clasped in the other. His cheeks were flushed, his gaze disconcerted by her entrance.

Scrambling to their feet, the three male students mumbled an incoherent greeting; the two female guests, in their inevitable leggings and snug sweaters, remained casually arrayed on a nearby couch. They too had wine glasses in front of them.

Shifting his weight forward, Ashton slid his backside off the desk, placed his drink on a coaster and relieved his wife of the tray. "A welcome treat. We shouldn't be much longer."

From his tone, Deirdre intuited her presence was no longer required in the room, though at the time the dismissive note, as though she were a servant in the house, didn't overly bother her: she had plenty to do of her own, not the least, coming to grips with her behind-schedule research. Nonetheless, she lingered in the adjacent parlor, surprised a few minutes later to hear Ashton playing the violin and voices muddling through "Drink to Me Only with Thine Eyes."

It had been one of the first songs he had performed for her during their courtship, explaining as he proceeded to do so that "the illustrious playwright" Ben Jonson was nowadays unfairly denigrated as a lyric poet. She had nodded in agreement, drinking in all he said in those heady days with no demurral.

As those in love are wont to do.

And now? Lying awake, Deirdre pondered the subtext of her husband's poetic spiel. *With my back turned, he has been reciting, to musical accompaniment no less, the same verses to someone else, just as Jonson had long ago done to his paramour.*

Burying her head in her pillow, another recollection assailed her, an ambiguous but niggling one. She and Ashton had been at the Rivoli, the off-campus arthouse that catered to the college crowd. During the opening credits of a German picture called *The Lives of Others,* he turned to whisper he was going out to buy popcorn and sodas. A minute or two later, one of the girls across the aisle got up, but it was dark and Deirdre, trying to concentrate on the subtitles, didn't zero in on who it was. Twenty minutes elapsed before Ashton returned, no popcorn or drinks in hand. Having lost the thread of the plot, he fidgeted through the rest of the film and volunteered not a word on their way out.

"Were you feeling ill?" she had asked.

"Needed a break, that's all," he had brushed her off.

At 3 a.m. Deirdre tumbled out of bed, the sheets snarled, her pillow stained with tears, and padded her way to the bathroom. However much her marriage might be in peril, she could not afford to miss the lawn party.

Rifling through the medicine cabinet, she seized upon a prescription for Valium, now a few months out-of-date. She shook the vial; only a couple of pills remained in the wake of her wisdom-teeth extraction in Cincinnati ten months ago. She had no memory of taking any, other than one or two right after the procedure. Since the operation had been relatively painless and Caitlin had been in tow, she had extended their trip a few days, taking in the art museum and shopping for school clothes. Ashton and Dylan had been left to their own devices back home.

Perhaps it was then, Deirdre calculated, that something had developed between her husband and his student. In the very house she shared with him. She jerked on the cold tap, splashed water on her face, and gulped one of the pills.

Quietly, she glided down the hallway, cracking first Dylan's door, then Caitlin's. Both appeared fast asleep, only a sliver of light cut through the curtains from each room's sole window. For an instant, she remained in the darkened hallway, her head heavy on her shoulders. How would she tell them that their father is planning to abandon them?

Or, might she not have to say anything definitive at all: *distract, obfuscate, circumvent—until the insanity ends*, she whispered.

Once back in bed and the pill began to take effect, Deirdre strained to cast the last twelve hours in a different light. She vaunted herself to be modern, with a broad-minded perspective on how the world worked. In the twenty-first century, a sexual dalliance should not, in and of itself, derail a well-maintained relationship between kindred spirits. As a cultural historian, she understood better than most that marriage had for centuries been about the ability to assign paternity, and hence, property rights.

And yet, despite these practical purposes, the institution had, over time, accrued unto itself romantic expectations. That Ashton was susceptible to the charms of a clueless co-ed suggested that he was more self-centered than she would have liked, but surely, as soon as he applies his not inconsiderable intellect to the case, he will conclude that his wife and family mean infinitely more to him than a few nights of unfettered passion.

(And yet. Ashton had appeared in the kitchen doorway as so adamant in his ardor, Deirdre could not but turn the picture to another slant. Sex, she had to allow, had been around forever, and remains a powerful force, whereas love was a modern construct, and a fungible one at that.)

Her academic prowess would have to be mobilized as well.

The very women Deirdre would be writing about—(if she could only focus on what she had proposed to accomplish), who had lived and loved six hundred years ago—had somehow managed to rise above the dastardly things men had afflicted upon them. What strength of character, what wealth of talent, what energy must they have summoned? Having plucked them from relative obscurity, she, a mere adjunct instructor in a middling college, would posit these three as role models, shine a spotlight on their achievements and make the world, at least the academic sliver of it devoted to such interests, take note.

Surely, she could make an effort to emulate them—retain her dignity, protect her children, accomplish her literary goals—and, thereby, entice her errant husband to return to the familial fold.

The Valium had kicked in. She closed her eyes in satisfied contemplation of her next steps.

Chapter Three

A s clueless men are liable to do, Ashton banked on blueberry pancakes to leaven the atmosphere and prevent another marital skirmish, especially one in front of the twins. Although the fold-out couch was uncomfortable and the study not well-heated, he didn't dare go upstairs to rummage through the linen closet for a blanket. Rather, he pulled his tweed jacket around his shoulders and made do by wrapping both the top and bottom sheets over his exposed limbs. Funny how he had not noticed how thin that mattress was when he and Jennifer...Better not to dwell on all that; too much to get through first.

He arose early, tiptoeing to the kitchen in hopes of marshaling ingredients and setting the table before the children, and more especially before his wife, descended. Fortunately, it had become something of a ritual that he would take charge on weekends, preparing a hearty breakfast and taking the children to their music or ballet lessons, allowing Deirdre to concentrate on...well, whatever she concentrated on during her free morning.

Tilting the shutters to let in the first rays of sunshine, he surveyed the sticky floor where the mayonnaise bowl had shattered. Bending over, he picked up the shards lodged under the table and against the floor boards and dumped them in the trash. Then he snatched up a roll of paper towels, squatted on his haunches and rubbed at the greasy sheen on the affected tiles. Inadvertently, he winced at the still strong vinegary smell.

Not a person who typically raised his voice—(Boston Brahmins did not need to resort to strenuous exercise to achieve their goals)—Ashton had been stunned when his confession so visibly riled his spouse. They were, after all, academics and, by definition, more civilized than most couples who for one good reason or another decide to part company. Not only had he not bargained on such vitriolic a reaction, he had not practiced what he would say to mollify her. His only immediate solution was to utilize his children as a buffer to keep his wife's fury at bay, and give her time to realize that, as usual, he was right: his decision to leave was best for the both of them.

"Surely," he mouthed to himself as he completed one last pass over the floor and tossed the towels into the garbage.

Sighing in satisfaction, Ashton stood to regain his equilibrium, and the moral high ground. (At fifty, vigorous exercise, mental or physical, took more out of him than he thought proper or justified.) He had had six months to prepare for the rupture, and with every day that passed, it had seemed more obvious that he and Deirdre should separate.

Whatever was going on in her life (and he did occasionally allow that he had stopped noticing what that might be unless her mood negatively impinged upon, or otherwise ruined, his day), he knew that his had changed: gloriously, exhilaratingly, let it be said. He was in love, the way he had never been before, and the only place he longed to be was—so vivid the image he blushed to conjure it—inside what had surprised even him as his heart's desire. Namely, inside Jennifer, who was adored as no one, other than perhaps the fair ladies who tormented his Metaphysical poets, could be.

As was usual whenever he allowed himself to wax poetical at the memory of their sexual commerce, his blood rose. Her full lips, her narrow hips, the gate through which he entered, and found treasure, as Donne had couched it. Or was it Marvell?

Ashton had not slept as well as he might.

But he did have a pancake project to undertake.

From the freezer department of the fridge, he retrieved a bag of blueberries, shook them into a bowl, and plopped it into the microwave for sixty seconds. Scouring the pantry, he pulled out a box of pancake mix which he poured into an old, slightly cracked mixing bowl (the newer one having been smashed), and then brought out a half-dozen eggs and a quart of milk. A stick of butter had been left out overnight, half of which he smeared into a large skillet on the stove's front burner. To finish off, he set the table with four large plates, separate glasses for orange juice and milk for the kids, and two coffee cups. Eyeing the clock on the wall, which read 7:10, he pulled back a chair and sat down to wait.

On a normal day, Ashton would have gone to the porch to pick up the *Plain Dealer*, but this day being anything but normal, he ripped off a piece of paper from the writing tablet propped between the salt and pepper shakers and retrieved a ballpoint pen from his shirt pocket. Quickly, he jotted down a few things that would need to be said once the children had gone about their day. Things that his only close male friend, an English Lit professor whose specialty was the late Romantics, had advised him to equip himself with.

"When the time comes," Professor Hendricks, twice divorced and an inveterate philanderer, had intimated, "stress that the marriage has become stale and unproductive. For both of you. Don't go on about how wonderful your new squeeze is. Otherwise, your wife will go berserk."

Dr. Kincaid, who oversaw administrative functions, had been the only other person Ashton had confided in as to his relationship with Jennifer. In retrospect, it was not a helpful decision as she was fond of Deirdre, but her office was contiguous to his, so it was probable that the dalliance was as plain as day to her.

A stickler for propriety, she had endeavored to discourage the flirtation by casting severe glances the student's way every time she approached or exited Dr. Cole's office and subsequently to commend the charms of his gifted wife whenever an opportunity arose. Oblivious to the woman's unspoken censure but needing to unburden himself, he ushered the administrator into his office one Friday afternoon.

"I don't know quite how to approach this, Stella—I trust you don't mind if I call you by your first name?—but I need your advice on a delicate matter."

Now in her late fifties, the administrator had seen her share of very smart people do very stupid things. Academics, she had long ago concluded, are hardly superior to lesser mortals when it comes to screwing up their lives. "I can keep a confidence, Professor, but you may not relish my advice."

Too late to backtrack, Ashton poured out his heart to the older woman, who, predictably enough, hazarded that such an illicit relationship might well flame out, one or both parties burnt by it, usually the older, already attached, one. "No need to upset the apple cart if nothing is to come of this affair," Stella had cautioned him.

"Ah, but it's more than that, on both our parts," Ashton had energetically contended. "And, as admirable and remarkable a person as Dr. Durrell, my wife, is, our marriage is over in all but the strictest legal sense."

"It would not, respectfully, seem so, Dr. Cole, from what I have observed," she countered, adding, though he looked irritated, "her face lights up whenever—"

Scrambling to his feet, he burbled, "Be that as it may," and, without the wherewithal to flesh out his rejoinder, indicated with his own glare that the confidential colloquy had come to an end.

However, the no-nonsense Dr. Kincaid took her duties overseeing the functioning of the college seriously. Attached to the Humanities dept. for thirty years and married to the same man for twenty-five of them, she had never been seduced by the romantic notions of novelists or versifiers who were the focus of the curriculum. In particular, she had no truck with the so-called Metaphysical poets, who by their adjectival designation, she could only imagine, waxed lyrical about illicit couplings of all sorts. Otherwise, Stella had more than once had occasion to hypothesize, why would the courses devoted to them be so popular with female coeds?

Thus, her parting shot: "You might want to consider, Dr. Cole, that good people would be adversely affected by your behavior. Nothing poetic is likely to come of this," she added tartly, as she picked up her frayed pocketbook and stomped out of the professor's office.

In Ashton's case, love was not only blind but deaf.

That very weekend, after the cautionary exchange with Stella, Ashton had searched out Dr. Hendricks, finding him bleary-eyed in the faculty lounge on a Saturday afternoon, a half-empty fifth of bourbon on the adjacent table alongside a well-worn edition of *The Way of All Flesh*.

In the middle of the first item Ashton scribbled at the kitchen table—*emphasize that through no one's fault, marriage tends to imprison the soul, but that intelligent people can free themselves of its bonds, recapturing excitement that they thought lost forever*—he was distracted by the sound of shoes on the staircase, determined male steps. He stuffed the note paper in his pocket, rose from the table and flicked on the coffee pot.

"Hey, son. What do you have on tap for today?" No answer. "I'm making blueberry pancakes. Sausages too. Is your sister up as yet?"

Yawning, Dylan shrugged and headed to the fridge. "Haven't heard a peep. From Mom either."

Observed from the back, his son, Ashton noticed, was out of nowhere an inch taller than he himself. Nonetheless, he decided not to comment. His kids had become sensitive about their looks.

Dylan pulled out the orange juice and poured himself a glass, leaving the carton on the table. He brushed his auburn locks off his forehead, rubbed sleep out of his eyes and slunk into a chair.

Taking his son's arrival as a cue, Ashton swung into action, beating the eggs and pouring milk into the batter. He stirred the concoction until it was the consistency of a paste, neither too lumpy nor too runny.

"Is this the way you like it?" he asked, tilting the bowl in Dylan's direction.

"Whatever," he replied, detaching his cell phone from a holster on his belt.

In silence, Ashton arranged a half-dozen sausages in a frying pan and turned the heat up. Next, he spooned the pancake mix into the skillet, turning each one as soon as bubbles appeared and dropping berries onto each. In between, he poured himself a cup of coffee, hoping to steel his resolve. At that point, Caitlin shuffled in, thinner than Ashton had recalled from a day or two ago, and she too, he estimated, had grown taller, easily the height of her mother. He smiled at her as brightly as he could.

"I'm not going to want any sausages," Caitlin announced, taking a seat across from Dylan and flipping open her own cell phone.

"Well, good morning to you too," Ashton said, reaching around to pour his daughter some orange juice.

"Is it OK, Dad, if I bring Claudia to the picnic this afternoon? I know it's a college thing, but we're going to be studying for our math finals afterwards. She has her driver's license now, and we'll be going back to her house."

Before Ashton could register what picnic Caitlin was referring to and who on earth this Claudia was, Deirdre, stone-faced in her robe and slippers, walked in.

"If that is the plan, Caitlin, and if you promise to be home by 9 o'clock," she stepped in to reply, her voice metallic. Her tone made both children look up, and, sensing that their mother was not in a good mood, neither spoke.

Flustered by his wife's appearance, Ashton served the under-done pancakes to the twins, dished out the sausages onto a platter and placed it in the center of the table.

Deirdre poured herself a cup of coffee, gesturing with her hand to forego the usual cream and sugar Ashton offered. She took her seat at the table and speared a sausage onto her plate. "I don't care for pancakes," she declared to the room at large. The two children exchanged a glance. She consumed the sausage in two bites.

Most likely enticed by the smell of cooked meat, Caedmon padded in and positioned himself next to Deirdre's chair. She impaled another sausage with her fork and dropped it on the floor for him, something she routinely scolded the children for doing.

Turning the heat up further, Ashton soon flipped the remaining pancakes, sprinkled a few blueberries on them and, as soon as they were minimally browned, slid them onto his own plate. He poured enough syrup on the stack to drown them.

"If anyone wants any more, help yourself," he said meekly. "There's still batter in the bowl. Berries too."

Toward the end of the meal, Dylan piped up. "Mom, do I have to go to the picnic? We were thinking of getting up a game over in Silver Creek. Sammy and Jason and some of the others...," he trailed off, cowed by the tension in the air.

"You can leave right before the speeches, Dylan, but don't make a show of it," Deirdre responded. "For now, both of you are excused: clean your rooms, put out the trash barrels and take the dog out. I'll drop each of you at your lessons today as I have to be at a luncheon by noon."

Her tone brooked no dissent. The twins clambered to their feet, Caitlin eyeing her father for some clue as to what was going on in the household, but he ignored her overture.

The clock ticked more insistently than usual, Ashton noted in the long silence that settled like dust once the children vacated the kitchen. He pushed the remaining bits of pancake around the plate, mopping up the last puddles of syrup and slowly raising them to his lips. He could not bring himself to look directly at his wife, still planted at the other end of the table, still sipping the black coffee. It was a fancy brand, Ethiopian in origin, that she had acquired especially for him at one of the upscale markets that had opened in town. "It should help us get into our day, no matter what problems the students bring to bear on us," she had half-joked when unpacking the wicker basket she carried to do grocery shopping.

Perhaps, he thought to himself, if I pour myself another cup and comment on how bold and rich it is, she'll back off.

But Ashton could not muster the courage to get up out of his chair. Rather, he lay his fork across the breakfast plate in precisely the way his parents did on their fine china, wiped his chin with a napkin and cleared his throat.

"I trust that we can now discuss the matter at hand in a civilized manner," he began, unable, despite his rehearsal, to obscure the note of superiority which played in the background of his utterance. When he raised his eyes to meet hers, he could see that they were puffy, as though she had been crying. But he couldn't be certain, and he had no intention of asking.

Crucial it would be, Hendricks had advised, to remain phlegmatic, not to let past intimacy or shared experience get in the way of what had to be done. "You have to make a clean break, like an Elizabethan beheading. It really is the most humane way to sever a marriage." (Ashton had felt queasy after his session with his friend, cursing at himself for having to ask advice, and for having drunk two shots of Jim Beam at five in the afternoon.)

Deirdre downed the last of her coffee and placed the cup on its saucer with a flourish, as if to signal she had done something commendable in drinking it in its black intensity. "And what matter would that be, Ashton, that you wish to discuss so civilly?" she returned, clearly not mollified by his effort to make Saturday morning breakfast nor by his attempt to be breezy about it.

"As I thought we concurred, our marriage simply can't go on, and yes, well, as a result thereof, I am now attached to—in love with—as I think I mentioned, someone else: Jennifer, that is. She's in the graduating class, almost twenty-one."

He was trying to make his voice sound reasonable and his argument cogent. He failed.

Slowly, if not theatrically, his wife nodded, as though mulling the import of every disjointed word. "Oh, I understand now: this Jennifer is old enough for her cunt to be colonized by you, is that it?" she flung at him. "*Cry, the beloved country,*" she further threw out, though he couldn't catch the literary reference, some novel probably that he hadn't read but which she no doubt had.

Crude though her insult was, he redoubled the effort to keep his cool. "Vulgarity doesn't become you, my dear, but since you're fixated on that aspect, it's true. My relationship with this girl, this woman, that is, is no longer strictly platonic."

A quiver distended Deirdre's mouth. "I'll put it differently then. You've slyly dropped the *meta* from Metaphysical poetry. You and your student have not confined yourselves to reading Donne's 'Ecstasy.' You're actually aping every line."

This was not the direction that Ashton had intended the conversation to veer. He desperately needed to get the discussion back on track, before the kids came back down or before his wife pitched the plate of leftover sausages at him.

"I was hoping, Deirdre, that we could thrash this out like adults," he resumed reedily, then glanced up again at his wife's countenance. It was closed off, a vein in her forehead prominent. "But we appear to have reached an impasse."

Several minutes ticked over before his wife further reacted. Rising from her chair, she took the coffee cup and her own plate in her arms. Then she paused at his side, daring him to look up at her. He couldn't.

"I have a lot to do today, chauffeuring the kids, doing my part for the campus picnic. So, I won't be covering for your unconscionable behavior," she informed him. His head still lowered, Ashton blinked several times as though to acquiesce in her description of his actions, but he did not speak. "*Ergo*," she added coldly, "go *carpe diem*. And don't cross this threshold again until..."

The threat made the hairs stand up on Ashton's neck, but he remained glued to his chair until his wife had banged her dishes into the sink and flicked on the hot water tap. Without another word, she turned and left the room just as Caedmon came bounding in, demanding attention.

Numbed as he was, Ashton rallied sufficiently to clear the table, scraping three of the sausages into the dog's food dish and depositing the rest in the garbage. He washed the dishes in scalding water, rinsed, dried and replaced them on their proper shelves. With his wife's caustic words still ringing in his ears, he retrieved his satchel from his study and left the house.

Jennifer, likely back from her jog in the park, would be waiting in her off-campus apartment. Ecstasy indeed.

Chapter Four

L ike nothing is amiss, Deirdre repeated to herself, as she spread her mother's hand-crocheted blanket on the closely cropped grass of the college quad, not far from the more elaborate encampment, hand-woven picnic baskets and porcelain plates of Dr. Beauchamps and his youngish wife Berenice on one side, and on the other, a ratty-looking tarp put out by Dr. Kincaid. She nodded in both colleagues' directions, receiving in return a bemused smile from Berenice, who, rumor had it, alternated between several lovers, and a beckoning wave from Stella, who, dedicated administrator that she was, (and widow to boot), undoubtedly knew more about what went on within the college walls than anyone at Klimpton.

With neither, however, did Deirdre want to make small talk.

While the crowd was gathering and the stagehands were testing the microphones, Deirdre glanced around the lawn trying to spot Roxane, whom she had promised to introduce to a few of the language professors. It was a favor she felt obliged to return, the younger woman having gone out of her way to interest both Dylan and Caitlin in learning French. Both would be enrolled in her class the coming fall, Dylan having already demonstrated aptitude, and Caitlin, if properly encouraged, might find an interest in something besides ballet—and boys.

"Both of your kids have a good ear," Roxane had mentioned one day when she had come over for coffee. "If you'd allow, I'd be glad to engage them in conversation over the summer. That way they'd have a head start come the fall. Sophomore year is tricky for teenagers."

Deirdre had seen nothing wrong with the plan, though Caitlin couldn't be counted on to be around at the designated times, preferring to hang out with her friends or to hunker down in her room. As for what she could do to reciprocate, it didn't take the French teacher long to come up with something.

"After a few more courses, online or at the college proper, I might be able to become an instructor—somewhere else, if not here in Oakville. A recommendation from you would be so valuable, Deirdre. You know, going forward."

With alacrity, Deirdre had outlined a letter of support, leaving it un-dated so that Roxane could utilize it at a propitious time. She even tried to cajole Ashton into penning one, to no avail.

"You appeared preoccupied during the luncheon, my dear, but your tomato sandwiches were delicious. I suspect you jealously guard your recipe for mayonnaise," a voice broke in to say.

Deirdre looked up, startled, into the face of Stella, the lines around the administrator's mouth deeply etched in the sunlight. Over the woman's shoulder sat an unprepossessing young man, munching on chips.

"The recipe is my mother's. They make their own down there, each lady a little differently," Deirdre blubbered. Despite herself, she reddened. That very morning, after Ashton left and she had re-composed herself, she rifled through the pantry for a jar of Blue Plate, not bothering to blot up the goop she had thrown at her husband the evening before. (Caedmon, she reckoned, must have lapped up what was on the floor.)

"I'll be getting back then. My nephew Lou visits me so seldom. He's a music major, over at Indiana," Stella further explained, indicating the blotchy-faced young man who had by now finished off the bag of chips.

Shortly after Stella ambled back to her guest, Deirdre spotted Roxane, along with Dylan, making their way across the far side of the quad. She held up her arm and waved it back and forth.

"Guess what? We practiced a little French after his violin lesson, since, well, Caitlin must have already left her ballet class and gone off with one of her girlfriends. Right, Dylan?" Roxane volunteered, a little out of breath as they approached.

Deirdre marveled that Roxane knew her children's schedules so well but said nothing. She turned to Dylan. "What did you do with your father's violin?"

"I didn't want to drag it along, so I left it in Roxane's car," he said, then paused, absorbing the music coming from the bandshell. "Sounds like that Josquin guy. Your period, right, Mom?"

"Impressive," Roxane exclaimed, clapping her hands together in admiration. "Like father, like son—regarding your musical bonafides, I mean," she enthused.

Deirdre forced a smile and indicated a place on the outsize blanket where the two could sit.

"So, where is Dad? Isn't this obligatory for the whole college?"

"Your father had something to finish up," Deirdre ventured, determined to remain nonchalant in case Ashton were to show up.

Once the minstrels wound up their musical set, the president of the college, one Dr. Landry, made a few remarks that couldn't be heard except close to the stage, but which apparently concluded with an invitation to line up at the buffet tables for hamburgers, potato salad, and coleslaw.

About that same time, Caitlin and Claudia materialized, the two of them showing off their still reddened earlobes. An hour before, they revealed, giddy at the telling, they had had them pierced at the mall out past Silver Creek Park.

"Did it hurt?" Roxane asked.

The two girls shrugged. "They used ice. No big deal," Claudia responded.

Observing her more closely, Deirdre noticed that the girl, who at sixteen already affected a world-weary air around adults, boasted a tattoo of a butterfly on her left wrist. Suddenly, she felt overwhelmed. How would she be able to prevent her own gawky-graceful daughter from following in such ill-advised footsteps without the aid of her husband?

"Are you okay?" Roxane interjected. "Why don't I—Dylan and I—go fill plates for all of us? Then, if Ashton comes..."

"Yes, that would be helpful. And something to drink. Cokes, whatever," Deirdre quickly added, feeling more unsettled by the minute.

"Mom, do you have any gold studs I could borrow? You know, until I can buy my own," Caitlin asked.

She had taken a seat across from her mother and, unlatching her sandals, extended her long legs out into the grass. Wriggling her brightly colored toenails, she scoured the crowd, mostly clusters of students, standing and talking, families sprawled on blankets around the periphery, and the older guests, professors, emeritus, and eminent townspeople, including the mayor of Oakville, reclining in deck chairs or seated on benches close to the bandstand. Claudia had already sauntered off and was now chatting with Stella's nephew.

"I'll have to take a look in my jewelry box," Deirdre replied, her own eyes sweeping the lawn for Ashton. "However, you might have told us you were thinking of having this done. Sanitation can be an issue with such a procedure."

Caitlin rolled her eyes and looked away. Then, of a sudden, she sprung to her feet. "Back in a minute."

Deirdre tracked her daughter's movements as she scampered toward a gaggle of girls—college students, judging from their leggings and boots, their long shiny hair, their cellphones appended at their waists. They were chatting among themselves as they moved about, drinks in hand. She squinted to scrutinize the group more closely. Not her own students, but somehow vaguely familiar.

When Caitlin caught up to them, one or two paused, seemingly recognized her, and spoke. Shortly, they looked Deirdre's way, or rather one of them did, the tallest one, with golden blond hair.

From Ashton's advanced seminar on Donne and his disciples, it dawned on Deirdre. Dumbfounded by the casual camaraderie that her own daughter seemed to have with this young woman, she barely noticed that Roxane and Dylan had returned from the buffet line and were dishing out food onto half a dozen plates.

"You should eat something, Deirdre," Roxane suggested, thrusting a plateful in her direction. "You look pallid."

But before she could raise a fork, she was overcome by nausea, vomiting all over the crocheted blanket as well as onto the potato salad in front of her. Dylan looked aghast but couldn't move.

Without a word, Roxane snatched a wad of paper napkins and dabbed furiously at the mess; Stella hurried over to take stock of the scene. "Are you unwell, Dr. Durrell? I could page the campus doctor."

Several other people, including Dr. Margery Willingham, who ran the Renaissance Studies department and worked closely with Ashton, approached as well, querying Stella as to what they might assist in doing.

Swallowing the acid in her throat, Deirdre tried to reassure them. "Too much for breakfast, too much excitement," she mumbled, waving them off.

"Someone bring us a Ginger Ale," Stella called out to no one in particular.

Dizzy though she was, Deirdre looked around and caught from afar the horrified face of Caitlin, her painted mouth a gaping hole. The tall blond was standing at her shoulder, expressionless.

"I'm so sorry. I don't know what came over me," Deirdre went on, a hint of color returning to her cheeks. "Please don't make a fuss. I'll be fine. I just need..."

Claudia, still in the company of Stella's nephew, soon thrust a can of Ginger Ale in her face with her tattooed hand. "Something like this once happened to my mother in public," she regaled the group.

"When she was pregnant with my kid brother. I was twelve. It was so gross."

"If you'd like, Dr. Durrell, I can ring Ashton on his cell to come collect you, if he's not already en route," Dr. Willingham volunteered, ignoring Claudia's outburst.

"No, no. That's the last thing I would want," Deirdre retorted, more fiercely than intended. Despite glances all round, she felt too icky to care. "I have my own car. Close by."

"Understood," Stella, who was accustomed to getting things done, stated with finality. "We'll carry on regardless, wrap everything up, and if Ashton shows up—"

However unsettled, Deirdre wrung out what was left inside of her. "Actually, I'd like my children to come with me." She turned to Dylan to make sure her demand registered and then motioned in the direction of Caitlin.

"What about Dad's violin?"

"Roxane, I'm sure, will be kind enough to return it next time she's invited over," Deirdre replied.

Looking as though she had been reprimanded, however vaguely, Roxane nodded in assent.

"We're going home now, you two. Carry the basket, Dylan; leave the blanket, Caitlin," she ordered when her daughter started to put her hands on it. "It too is ruined."

Neither child objected. Both sheepishly trailed their mother along the edge of the crowd while everyone was singing along with the college anthem.

Chapter Five

"Like, what do you think is going on with Mom: is she sick or something?"

Caitlin had knocked on her brother's door an hour after they arrived home. It was not something she typically did, as each twin had lately grown more attached to their own friends and tended to bicker with more than confide in each other.

But that weekend was different. They were discombobulated.

Dylan was seated at his desk, going over the reams of notes he had taken for the upcoming history final. Unlike during earlier years, he had not volunteered to share his notes with his twin sister. When she knocked, he closed his writing tablet and swiveled toward the door.

"Come in," he had responded, just loud enough for her to hear.

She hesitated on the threshold, taking in the room as though for the first time. Her brother kept it more organized than she did her own. The bed was made, most books were on their shelves, the music stand was in the corner and a pair of barbells jutted only minimally out from under the bed.

When he didn't respond to her question, she went on. "I mean really. She seems, like, totally out of it. And then throwing up. Gross, like Claudia said."

Dylan shrugged, but rather than turn away, he gestured for his sister to close the door and prop herself on his bed.

"So, since you're the smart one, what do you think is going on?"

"I don't know, but Dad seems uptight too. Not like when he's writing a book. More like something going on between the two of them. Grown-ups sometimes grouse at each other."

"Yeah, but ours, not so much. Claudia's, well, that's all they do," Caitlin said, rolling her eyes.

"Why do you hang out with her? Always sidling up to whatever guy gives her the once-over. I don't get you at all. Not anymore."

Caitlin made a face as if to suggest she'd heard his objections before but had no intention of defending herself. Instead, she picked up the only book on the bed, an intermediate French grammar, and started to flip through it.

Dylan instinctively reached to take the book back but then didn't. Instead, he leaned back in his chair, closed his eyes, and went back over scenes from the last two days.

"Dad snapped at me when I mentioned we were supposed to go hiking. Said he had to meet someone at the faculty lounge, that he had important things to do. We'd been hiking on weekends for years, and he never said anything like that."

"Well, Mom too. Without so much as a how-de-do, she came in a while ago and put three little boxes on my dresser. I was standing at the bathroom door, practically naked. No 'excuse me,' no nothing."

"What were in the boxes?"

"All she said was, 'They're all yours now' and walked out."

Dylan gestured with his hands, not knowing what his sister was on about.

"Jewelry, dummy. She left me three pairs of pierced earrings, including the diamond ones she used to wear to parties."

Dylan looked baffled but didn't respond. They could both hear the sound of the stereo from the living room below but over the strains of a Brandenburg Concerto, (which Dylan easily recognized as No. 5), pots and pans were being banged about, presumably in the kitchen. He rose and went to the window overlooking the horse-shoe driveway. Their mother's Volvo was parked where she had left it after the campus picnic, but there was no sign of their father's Camry. Slowly, he closed the shutters and turned to face his sister. She looked up from the bed inquiringly.

"What?"

"Maybe we should try to be especially good, and helpful, to Mom, and to Dad too. What do you think?"

"That they won't notice and that we might make things worse."

Dylan shook his head to indicate he didn't buy her response but refrained from telling her how negative she had recently become, *prematurely jaundiced* being the expression Roxane had used to describe his sister's attitude toward life. He even knew the words in French.

Unsettled by so many jumbled thoughts, he crossed the room to the only armchair, plopped himself down and began to take deep breaths. Equally unnerved, Caitlin dug in the pocket of her chemise and pulled out a pack of Virginia Slims and a lighter. She lit up and held out the pack to her brother. Though he rarely indulged and disapproved of his sister's habit, he felt that the occasion required sibling solidarity. He took a long drag and reached for the ashtray on the lower shelf of his night table.

"Well, one thing we can do, so they won't be on our case, is to do well on the tests," Dylan suggested, wanting to encourage his sister without antagonizing her. In the last year, her grades had been disappointing, his had been exemplary.

Looking over at her as she smoked, he intuited a succession of emotions flitting across her face: first, irritation for being reminded of her sorry performance, then defiance, since she couldn't abide his lording it over her, and finally, sadness that she was letting everyone down, including herself. A wave of sympathy for his sibling swept over him, as why else but despondency to explain hanging around with losers like Claudia or resorting to earpiercing.

"So, how do they feel now?" Dylan asked, gesturing toward her head. She reached up to touch her lobes. As she did so, he noticed a pinkish hash mark on her inner arm.

"Can't even feel them," Caitlin said proudly.

"Good. When you wear them, Mom's earrings, don't forget to show her, and thank her. She'll like that."

Nodding, Caitlin resumed leafing through the French grammar, and back to the title page where she lingered, her thumb cracking the book open to that page. Wrinkling her nose—a gesture they each made when curiosity got the better of them—she asked her brother, "So, you and Roxane. Are you *really* good at French, or what...?"

Blowing a long, curling smoke ring, Dylan eyed his sister as though she had posed a ridiculous question. "I'm no better than you would be if you applied yourself."

"Yeah, right," she responded, clearly unconvinced.

"She thinks you have a better ear than I do...and *I* play the violin!"

"Not that well, though," Caitlin retorted. They both laughed, which prompted another thought from her. "But Dad. He's been playing it more too. Almost every time he has students over, like for Jennifer and her friends." Dylan looked unsure of who or what she meant. "You know, the blonde who sometimes stays late. I was talking to her this afternoon, right when Mom threw up all over."

Dylan took another drag on his cigarette and stubbed it out. He stood up, decisively. "We should go downstairs and offer to help. Talk to her and don't harp on Dad or anything."

Caitlin closed the grammar and uncrossed her legs, letting them dangle from the bed and into her slippers. "You go first. I'm going to put on a dress and her gold studs. Be down in ten minutes." She patted her brother on the arm and walked out, cigarette still in hand.

Propped on the edge of the bed, Dylan switched from his tennis shoes to loafers. He picked up the book and flipped it open to the

40

title page. He had forgotten what Roxane had scribbled on it: *"Pour mon petit ami exceptionnel …"* He snapped the book shut and slipped it under his pillow before heading downstairs.

Chapter Six

T hat Eydie Gormé song. Deirdre couldn't get it out of her head. She knew better, of course, that civilized people did not wallow in their misery, including women who had been thrown over for a younger version of themselves. Keeping one's dignity intact during such a trial is paramount, as, surely, she told herself, this thing with Jennifer is a momentary fling, a lapse in judgment, and an expression of vanity: this last, a characteristic with which she knew the Cole family to be amply endowed. Surely too, the interests that she and Ashton shared, such as their complementary careers, their amazing children and, dare she remind him, how seamlessly they fit together sexually, (however less frequently than before), ought to count more than cavorting with a vacuous blonde with nothing to commend her but...

She had shouted the c-word once and would not stoop to do so again.

Yet, the lyrics of the old song rang in her ears, especially at night when she thrashed about, the pillows flung hither and yon, the windows thrown open, the windows slammed shut, the radio on, the radio off. In short, the question the singer belted out: "What Did I Have That I Don't Have Now?" she, Deirdre Durrell Cole would amend to the plural *we* and, by so doing, persuade her spouse of the logic of her argument. To wit: how could he give up so much for so little?

Then there would be more tossing and turning, until another thought shattered her carefully honed argument. Youth in and of itself is an elixir. If drunk, it intoxicates, and leaves one thirsting for more.

When her mind did revert to the young woman toward whom her own daughter Caitlin had rushed that awful day of the picnic, Deirdre would become newly incensed. Her own husband, the epitome of correctitude—a descendant of Cotton Mather, for God's sake!—had succumbed to nothing more than a slit between two thighs. (She chided herself for thinking in such crass terms but couldn't escape the temptation.) How could the young woman with said *accoutrement* in her arsenal of charms imagine that it alone could inflame the ardor of such a man for more than a brief interlude?

Deirdre pondered these abiding questions throughout the week that followed Ashton's confession, alternately consoling herself that a fling could be weathered and fearing that it might not peter out any time soon.

With nerves frayed, she did not venture out except to teach her classes on Tuesdays and Thursdays or to make pit stops at the grocery. She did not go to church or attend campus functions for fear of running into Ashton or having to explain his absence. Pleading a headache or finding that she did have a plethora of papers to grade or reports to complete, she enlisted Dylan to walk the dog and mow the lawn and Caitlin to wash the dishes.

Sensing, as children do, that something serious was amiss, and that, as a result, their father was literally missing, they acquiesced without a peep.

Some ten days later, Deirdre found herself in the bathroom, fumbling in the medicine cabinet for something for her aching head.

She was shocked to catch her reflection in the mirror: dark circles under her eyes, her hair frizzy, her lips chapped. She popped two Excedrin into her mouth and downed a glass of tap water. Then she stripped. In the full-length glass opposite the shower, she studied her body, as she hadn't had occasion to do for ages. It drooped, despite regular walks and the Pilates class Roxane had dragged her to.

These things I had that I don't have now, she intoned aloud, her fingers pinching the flesh on her upper arm, it not bouncing back the way it once did. She turned on the shower, stepped into it, lathered her body, shampooed her hair, and outperformed Eydie Gormé with her own rendition. By the time she dried off, her headache had receded enough that she determined to go downstairs to her own study, switch on her computer, and take stock of what was most pressing.

First, she went through the half-dozen essays on the bubonic plague and its impact on European society from her half-dozen honors students, penned comments in the margins of each, and recorded a final grade on the last page of each printed-out composition as well as online. Next, she read through the multiple-choice quizzes she had given out two weeks before which covered the period from 1200-1550, surprised to find that all but two of her twenty pupils had managed to score better than eighty out of a hundred. Finally, around midnight, she rustled through her desk drawer for her mole-skin notebook in which she had jotted down ideas for her monograph. As yet, she hadn't come up with a title. She wanted something catchy, not something safe. Before the spring term came to an end and everyone scattered, she was determined to present Dr. Beauchamps with a proper outline.

Feeling invigorated, she leaned back in her chair and mused half aloud. Yes, most women in the Middle Ages were either dead, discarded or demented by the time they were forty. Arguably, because of that, they were hell-bent on living as fully as they could in as short a time as possible. She would make a point of that, with relevant examples. She scribbled more notes, comparing the lot of these women to her own. *Surely, after six hundred years of progress,*

I should be thankful to have resources and years ahead of me. To succumb to jealousy or to grovel would be distasteful and demeaning.

In a few minutes, she tucked her notebook away in the drawer and crossed the room to the back window. A full moon lit the branches of the red oaks in the back yard. She took in the scene, listening to the crickets and a light wind rattling the shutters upstairs. (She must get their man over to see about that; Ashton couldn't tell the difference between a nail and a thumb tack, let alone replace a window sash.)

Somehow, in getting on with things, all would come right.

Favors too Deirdre resolved to attend to, like her promise to Roxane. She would flesh out that recommendation forthwith, attesting to her friend's character and academic potential, the sort of testimonial that might help her land, say, her first ever job in a junior college or some such.

Seated before a blank screen on the computer, Deirdre realized she had less to go on than she might have wished. She racked her brain to piece together the scraps that Roxane had let fall in the course of the two years they had known each other. From out West, and a family neither too rich nor too poor; did well in school and somehow ended up in Europe; had a certificate from the Sorbonne, if she remembered rightly.

"It's framed, in my study," Roxane had said airily, "though *naturellement*, the citation is in French, in that squiggly script they're so fond of."

They were walking along Elm Street, briskly, on a frosty February morning. When Deirdre inquired further as to her course load at the Sorbonne, Roxane had diverted her attention to a store window. In fact, her friend had a habit of changing the subject whenever the conversation got too personal. Still, Roxane was likable enough, deferential to Ashton, and at ease with the children. As an added bonus, her friend spoke French with flair. (She would emphasize traits like that rather than dwell on her friend's academic degrees, or lack thereof.)

Still, a few concrete points Deirdre would need to make to whom it might concern. She began a Google search, although, with an all-too-common surname, the top entries led her only to arrest records. Even more annoying, she couldn't come up with her LinkedIn account nor any mention of her graduating from that two-year institution she had mentioned in Colorado, Patterson Junior College. Not giving up, she keyed in Hillside High and clicked on the icon devoted to staff.

The basic facts about the French teacher seemed to comport. Roxane Johnson, born in 1976 in Rockwood, Colorado, excelled at her studies at Patterson and subsequently was accepted into a two-year program in Europe. The squib said nothing about who sponsored her friend's sojourn abroad.

It would now seem impertinent to ask, Deirdre concluded. She wrote three graphs and saved her document.

Chapter Seven

From what Dylan had told Roxane, the violin had long been in his father's family in Boston, and though "not a Strad," as the teenager casually put it, it did originate in the same Italian town, Cremona, and was quite old, and valuable. The teenager had played it for her on several occasions, including recently in her L-shaped living/dining nook, its tone rich even under the touch of a novice.

Perched on a stool nearby, the French teacher had watched his long fingers slide up and down the neck, applauding theatrically when he finished the piece.

"It's Rachmaninoff, but one of his easier, earlier pieces," Dylan had mumbled, flustered by her over-the-top reaction.

"Oh, don't stop," Roxane had urged. But he desisted, saying he couldn't play anything else that well without the music in front of him. (He had not learned to be self-deprecating; he was simply shy, and unpracticed, at many things.) "Then it will be for next time—*la prochaine fois*," she responded cheerily, rising as she rattled on in

French. "I'll bring us mint tea and cookies," she announced, not waiting for a response.

Dylan returned the instrument to its case and maneuvered around an exuberant potted plant to the picture window. While Roxane was in the kitchen, he called out, "So, do you like where you live? It's close to school, so I guess that's a plus."

"It's not bad," she had replied airily, "until I find something more my style."

Not that the neighborhood was dangerous—this *was* the bucolic Ohio countryside—but from what she had picked up from other teachers a raft of robberies had taken place of late. Thieves had brazenly broken into houses and apartment dwellings, making off with computers and, this was new: the contents of medicine cabinets. A few extra police cars patrolled the area; a second security guard had been hired at the school; and, for the first time, a local detective and a doctor held forth to a student assembly on the pernicious effects of drugs and the legal punishments that awaited kids who were caught using or selling.

In the months that followed, Roxane had begun to lock her car and bolt her apartment door every time she went out.

Except for the past Saturday. So disconcerted at the picnic had she been, especially by Deirdre's curt tone with her, she had overlooked the instrument in her back seat. Once the speeches had ended and the officious Kincaid woman had headed off to corral her nephew, Roxane stuffed the smelly blanket into her tote bag, her plan being to hand-wash it and, if it came clean, return it to Deirdre without any reference to what had happened.

That evening she rifled through her medicine chest, took an Ambien and slept until 10:30 Sunday morning. A steady rain was falling and the wind had kicked up, enough to deter her from venturing out. Instead, she curled up on the sofa to read a trashy novel and then went over her lesson plans for the final three weeks of school.

Still, she couldn't focus. The distraught expression on Deirdre's face after that embarrassing incident at the college picnic kept intruding. Something unpleasant was going on in the Cole

48

household, if her own past childhood—surly stepfather, sullen mother—was any indication.

Pouring herself a glass of wine, Roxane sat and watched *60 Minutes*, but it was all about the worsening economy and what Obama was trying to do about it. Something called TARP, if she heard the acronym correctly. As the show wound down, she shut the television off and sat down at what passed for a dining room table to write to her mother. It was not a task she relished.

Dear Mother, she began, making an effort to keep her tone even-keeled, and to say nothing at all that might be construed, or misconstrued.

I know it's been a long time since I last managed to write but, as I may have told you, I am busy teaching in a high school here in Ohio. Of all places. That adventure to Europe, as you called it at the time, has paid off in that I am the closest thing to a native French speaker they could find. The students are attentive and a few have facility, which means they pick up the language with little effort. Makes it easier all around. Other than that, I am well. Have made a few friends and go out here and there.

Naturally, I trust they are still treating you decently there and that your health continues to be good.

Here, Roxane hesitated, re-read what she had written and racked her brain for anything else she might add before closing it out. She had filled only half the page. She took another gulp of wine.

Since we did not manage to connect at Christmas—I'm sure the rules there are complex, and for my part, I was out of pocket with friends—I will do my best to phone come September, on your birthday. If memory serves, it will be your fiftieth!

Anyway, I remain, as ever, your only daughter,

Roxane

After finishing the glass of chianti and munching a few crackers, she folded the cream-colored slip of Crane's stationery and slipped it into its envelope. On it, she printed the address as neatly as she could: Mrs. Winifred Perry Johnson, Farmdale Correctional Facility for Women, Boulder, Colorado, 80304. She did not include a return address.

It was only after she had deposited the envelope in the slot at the Oakville post office and headed back to her car after school that Monday afternoon that she stopped dead in her tracks. The back window on the passenger's side had been rolled half-way down, doubtless days ago by Dylan, and inside, both the Honda's leather seat and the violin case were covered in splotches from Sunday's rainfall.

So unlike her not to have noticed. When the time came, she would have some explaining to do; it would do well if Deirdre's quilt did come clean.

Once home, Roxane carefully lifted the violin case out of the back seat of her car and carried it upstairs. The last thing she wanted would be to have the instrument, be it insured or not, stolen and thus have to account for her negligence to the Coles. Fortunately, when she opened the case, the instrument appeared dry and unscathed.

Chapter Eight

Twelve days had elapsed since she had hurled the mayonnaise jar toward her husband and Deirdre had as yet not heard anything from him. As luck would have it, Ashton's mother rang up, round about dinner time, something she generally did only around holidays or birthdays. For their part, the Cole children did not automatically bother to pick up the landline as all their friends either texted or rang their cells.

But these were no longer ordinary times. Even Caedmon had assumed a more hang-dog expression, nuzzling his cold damp nose up against whichever twin appeared disposed to pay him heed.

That particular Friday evening, after a long week in which Caitlin as well as Dylan had buckled down to study for exams, Deirdre had prepared a proper meal to demonstrate to her offspring (and to herself) that she remained on top of things. When the phone rang, she was carving a pork loin into thin slices, while Caitlin had been commandeered to set the table and take the vegetable platters in.

It fell to Dylan to pick up.

From the kitchen, Deirdre soon realized it was not their father on the line, but it was a Cole. Out of the corner of her eye, she glimpsed her son in the hallway, standing stiffly and emoting distinctly into the receiver.

"Yes, Grandma. I am playing whenever I have the chance. Also, I'm learning French—Caitlin too..." After a pause,: "No, Dad's not here. On a business trip, Cincinnati, I think. But I can put Mom on." Fruitlessly, Deirdre tried to get his attention, electric knife in one hand, shaking her head in the negative, but her son had already laid the receiver down on the hall table. "It's Grandma Cole, Mom. She wants to speak to you."

Deirdre put the knife down, wiped her hands on her apron, and approached the phone. "Why don't you take the meat platter out to the table and pour the tea, or whatever you two want from the fridge. I'll only be a minute," she instructed Dylan, loud enough that her mother-in-law might overhear.

"Hello, Zenobia. How are you and Richard? And Adeline?" she inquired, turning her back to the kitchen and walking further down the hallway. Dylan duly did what he was told and joined his sister in the dining room where she was already seated, fiddling with her phone. Neither spoke; each cocked an ear for what was being said out in the hall.

"No, no, everything's fine. He should be back any day." Here there was a pause. Zenobia Cole had interrupted her daughter-in-law with some criticism, overt or veiled. "Well, I'm sure he's—actually, both of us—have been busy. The end of the school year and what-not."

Deirdre rolled her eyes, reminded yet again that her in-laws rarely inquired after her or even acknowledged that she too had a job teaching at the college—the institution, the two elder Coles believed, that was inordinately fortunate to have landed their son when Harvard or Yale should have come calling for his services.

While Zenobia chattered about the latest charity ball at the Museum of Fine Arts, something about how she and Richard were honored as long-standing patrons thereof, Deirdre's mind wandered back to that first encounter with her future in-laws. She tried to untangle what she had been told then about the Coles' complicated relationship with one or the other of both Ivy League universities. It must have been Richard, who. during her first visit to their Beacon Hill home, had given her the tour of the family portrait gallery. It was the only time her father-in-law had been so voluble, or gracious with her. Perhaps he had only done so to cow her, she now imagined.

On the phone, Zenobia had switched to a description of the current season at the Boston Symphony, and how much Ashton would have enjoyed last week's Rachmaninoff violin concerto as performed by a Russian virtuoso whose name Deirdre didn't quite get. As she hadn't quite gotten all the references Richard had thrown out during her perambulation with him through the family's pictorial history. On and on he had gone about this or that ancestor, on both sides of the family, starting with the *Mayflower* and on through the Salem witch trials.

Those unfortunate proceedings, "the burnings and what-not—the reason for it all," Richard had spluttered as she tried to formulate a suitable response to the stern visage of Cotton Mather which dominated the wall. (To her mind, all the portraits were off-putting, though she was too young and in love to extend that judgment to the present generation of Coles.) "All to do with politics, my dear, then as now. So stigmatized Cotton became after the trials, after all that his father Increase had done for the college"—here the elder Cole sucked his lip and gestured toward an even drearier visage, presumably of Cotton Mather's oddly named parent—"that he encouraged his friend Elihu Yale to give them a run for their money down in New Haven."

In recounting this obscure episode of academic one-upmanship, her host had clucked maniacally, as though the founding of a university to rival Harvard had happened only a month or so ago, and not, as Deirdre calculated, some three hundred years earlier. (Southerners, she was amply aware, were reputed to live too much in the past but these Bostonians took the cake!) She had smiled deferentially at her future father-in-law and pronounced the portraits of his Puritan forbears, "arresting." Richard had seemed gratified. But that didn't change the basic facts of the case. Neither he nor his equally daunting wife—Zenobia too descended from a formidable Puritan preacher named John Cotton—wanted their only son to marry, as they considered it, the daughter of dirt farmers from the Mississippi Delta, however successfully she may have washed off the taint.

"Undoubtedly, Ashton would have enjoyed that concert, Zenobia. And, you'll be pleased to know that Dylan is coming along nicely on the violin." (In the dining room, Caitlin gave her brother a nudge under the table. He ignored her, continuing to squirt a fresh lemon into his iced tea.) "About that, I don't know...very thoughtful of you, Zenobia, but we'll have to see. So much is going on, and with the kids..." (Losing patience and hungry, the twins both started to fidget at the table. Dylan picked up a biscuit and popped it into his mouth.)

"I will indeed," Deirdre responded to some further request, her tone less accommodating. "I do have dinner in the oven. But yes, I'm certain Ashton will be in touch. Thank you again for calling."

She re-attached the receiver and leaned her back against the wall, upset that she had to, or couldn't see a way not to, obfuscate whenever anything about her husband came up. She closed her eyes and grit her teeth. *Things cannot go on like this. He'll have to--—or else*, she silently vowed.

Marching into the dining room, she overloaded the plates and encouraged her children to eat heartily. Which they did, having lived largely on pizza and Chinese takeout for the last week, and largely in strained silence.

Until now.

"So, when is Dad coming home? What did you tell Grandma?" Caitlin soon started in, putting her fork down and staring at her plate.

Dylan jumped in to support her. "Yeah, Mom. Did you two have a fight or something?"

Deirdre took a last bite of potatoes au gratin and wiped her lips. "We're having issues, that's all. Your father will explain it when...well, whenever he gets back."

"But when *will* he be back?" Caitlin persisted, turning her gaze toward her mother. Her tone was now querulous, her thin face all acute angles.

"I—don't—know," Deirdre seethed in response, each syllable hanging in the air like a bad smell. For a long minute, the two children sat frozen, neither daring to investigate further. "Really, I don't want you two to worry. Nothing is your fault. Everything is going to work out." She looked from one to the other to make sure they absorbed her new message. "We both, your father and I, want you to be happy and successful."

Dylan and Caitlin exchanged a glance but neither spoke.

After draining her tea, Deirdre stood up. "So," she re-attacked more brightly, "who's going to want rum raisin ice cream? I know you will, Dylan." She managed an affectionate smile at each, before adding, "After that, you might want to study an hour or two for your remaining exams so that tomorrow you can do something with your friends. Make sense?"

Both children nodded, and Caitlin scrambled to her feet to help clear the table and bring in the Häagen-Dazs. Without being asked.

After dessert, the twins did as requested, retreating upstairs to their respective rooms. Deirdre could hear doors shut one after the other, but neither child apparently put on any music. Back in the kitchen, she wrapped up the leftover slices of meat, put a lid on the cauliflower casserole and finished off the ice cream directly from the carton. The dishes she rinsed haphazardly, leaving them to dry on the drainage rack.

The clock on the wall said 8:20. Now would be a good time to satisfy her curiosity, locked door or not.

For years, both Ashton and Deirdre had considered their respective studies inner sanctums, which meant that the ritual of knocking had solidified over time, neither entering the other's domain without permission, though each possessed a key for the French doors that closed them off. In addition, when they upgraded the furniture in the house ten years ago, they had acquired matching roll-top desks and a quartet of vintage Globe-Wernicke bookcases, two for each study, to house behind their glass doors the rarest of their books. And to keep the increasingly adventurous kids, then about five, from getting their hands on anything irreplaceable.

Naturally, Ashton had brought numerous tomes from Beacon Hill, including the collected sermons of his forbears, which, it could be argued, no one had read in two hundred years. The pages were yellowed, the bindings frayed, but dutiful son that he was, he arrayed them along the lower two shelves of his cases. Higher up and more accessible, he had arranged his Yale Shakespeare with their pale blue jackets and his early editions of Metaphysical poets and a few of the Elizabethans: John Donne, Andrew Marvell, John Cleveland, Robert Herrick, among the former, Ben Jonson, Sir Philip Sidney, and Edmund Spenser, among the latter.

Deirdre had helped him appoint the room, commenting as she dusted the covers about one or another poem she liked, though not mentioning that she thought the Elizabethan versifiers far outclassed their Metaphysical successors. Why risk being undiplomatic? Ashton's specialty was his life's work, and she sorely wanted her benediction of his academic pursuits to be reciprocated.

But it was not to be.

She ended up unpacking her two dozen volumes on the Middle Ages and a few treasured works from back home and displaying them as generously as she could to fill out her two bookcases. On the blank walls of her study, she hung a colorful poster of Uccello's painting of the battle of Lepanto which she had admired on her one trip to the Uffizi Gallery in Florence, and on the other, a reproduction of Jean de Meun's medieval classic, *Le Roman de la Rose*, the subject of her master's thesis at Sophie Newcomb, blown-up and gold-framed.

Ashton, meantime, busied himself hanging his family portraits, dour though they were. On the fourth wall, she helped him mount a large painting of several children disembarking a ship. Unlike what Deirdre had thought about the portrait of Cotton Mather, this canvas really *was* arresting. Even if the perspective was awkward, there was something haunting in the faces of these innocents.

She did not remember it from the Beacon Hill house.

"When the actual origin of our pilgrim forbears came to light, my parents were not keen on having it in full view," Ashton had reluctantly explained.

"Why ever not?" she had persevered, adjusting the frame on its heavy nail.

"Turns out, the four More children who made the crossing were the product of an adulterous liaison. Disavowed by the cuckolded husband, they were dispatched to the New World as punishment. Three of them died shortly after arrival. Only the fourth, *our* progenitor, survived, and eventually produced offspring."

Deirdre had nodded, intrigued.

Her husband's roots, she had decided then and there, were oddly tangled. On the one hand, there was the strong puritanical line of the Mathers and the Cottons; on the other, the sexual transgression on the More side.

Once hung, the painting added a disquieting note to the otherwise decorously appointed room.

In front of Ashton's inner sanctum that evening, Deirdre peered at the lock. In all these years, she had never ventured into that room without the formality of a knock, or making a preliminary request that she, or a servant, needed access so as to dust, or polish the floor, or water the plants. (She doubted he had ever, uninvited, ventured into hers. He did no cleaning of the household kind, nor, more to the point, did he harbor any curiosity as to what she did in her own private space.)

She listened for sounds from the children in the upstairs bedrooms. Nothing. Gripping the smooth ivory knobs, she pulled the doors apart.

The room was not as orderly as it was in her imagination. A blanket and pillowcase were thrown over the arm of the sofa, a half-full water glass sat on the adjacent side table atop a book. On the larger coffee table, a lacquered tray sat with a half-dozen wine glasses on it. In one or two, a dark red stain coated the bottom. Apparently they hadn't been washed since last used. A near-empty wine bottle stood on the floor next to a table leg, its cork nearby. She stooped to pick the two up and put them on the tray with the glasses. The bottle of cabernet sauvignon had left a faint ring on the oak floor.

Never mind, she told herself. It was not what she was there for. Rather, Deirdre turned full-circle to rake the rest of the room for something out of keeping with a collegial colloquy with students about life and art. Noticing nothing incriminating, she walked around to the front of the desk. Its roll-top had been left up, revealing a stack of ungraded essays. Though most students now worked entirely on their laptops, Ashton preferred printed-out copies, marking them up with his trademark fountain pen—in big, bold strokes, self-consciously retro, she thought, like Ashton himself.

Ignoring his comments in the margins, she flipped through a few titles: "*Irony and Insecurity in Marvell's Oeuvre*" and "*John Donne's Romance with Rhetoric.*" Among the students' names, one Jennifer Hazelton.

"Hazelton, Hazelton," she murmured aloud, not connecting the surname to anyone she had heard of. But, could this student be, she asked herself, the insouciant blonde from the picnic—the one likely screwing my husband in this very room?

Grasping the handle of the desk's top drawer, she jerked, but it was locked, or horribly stuck. So were the lower ones. In her frustration, she couldn't prevent a few hot tears from falling on the desk top, one or two staining the top-most term paper. She bowed her head and closed her eyes to get a grip. *This is not the Middle Ages; it's not even 1950. Life will go on; women cope without men.*

Was that not how her mother had put it when Deirdre's father upped and died one summer afternoon in 1990? She had so few memories of spending time with him, a small-town lawyer always caught up on a case, or hatching schemes to strike it rich.

Only once, in his latter years, she found her father on the front porch—it badly needed painting, the oppressive heat notwithstanding. Seeing her, he put the can of Sherwin Williams down, lowered himself into the swing and regaled her with stories about the river and the places he had stopped off as a boy. "When you are grown, DeeDee, you'll see the world, and have yourself a great adventure."

She was gliding back and forth in the rocking chair across from him, sipping a coke and hoping that they'd have adventures together. But, out of nowhere, his face slackened. Then he slid out of the swing onto the chipped floorboards. It was his first heart attack.

Deirdre shivered at the memory. She was twelve. The paint had seeped out all over the wooden slats of the porch.

Taking a deep breath, she turned to leave Ashton's study. Caedmon stood in the doorway, whimpering, a pool of urine at his feet.

"Did no one think to attend to you?" she asked, sympathy flooding into her voice. The dog made a gurgling sound. "Let's get your leash. We both need some fresh air." Passing him in the doorway, she grabbed up the leash but then thought better of attaching it. "Forget this thing. Let's you and I romp around any ole way, OK, Caedmon?"

The two went out the back screen door into the brisk night air toward the duck pond. Before long, the retriever spotted a couple of herons in the reeds and darted after them. Deirdre took a seat on the wrought-iron bench they had set up in a picturesque spot a decade ago. Like many things around the place, it badly needed refinishing. She made a mental note to start a list as soon as the term wrapped. With her eyes closed, she inhaled deeply, wondering why she didn't retreat to this spot more often. In a few minutes, the dog's bark startled her; she opened her eyes in time to catch a sight of bird wings flapping overhead.

"Scared those birds to death, you did." On cue, the retriever bounded over and shook out his wet fur in front of Deirdre. "Well, better here than in the house." Standing up, she patted his head and attached the leash in case the dog got it into his head to do more gallivanting.

One glance toward the house though and she set off. A light shone in the kitchen and another upstairs in the master bedroom. As soon as they got to the back porch, she released the dog, smoothed her hair and stepped into the hallway. No one, nothing. But another light was also on, the overhead fixture in her husband's study. Had she forgotten it too?

At the entrance-way, she cleared her throat. Ashton had his back to her, leaning over to stuff papers into a briefcase. A vague smell of urine rose to her nostrils.

"I rang but no one answered. Thought this would be a good time..." he said by way of explanation. His voice was matter-of-fact. He did not turn around.

"A good time for what?" Deirdre challenged him. She had tracked mud into the room and her hair was a mess. He should have alerted her before showing up, un-summoned.

"I need a few things. Shouldn't take long."

At this juncture, he did throw a glance at his wife but not one she could decipher. Fumbling in the pocket of his tweed jacket, he retrieved a loose key and inserted it into the top drawer of his desk, from which he retrieved a packet of letters and a couple of notebooks. These too he finagled into his now bulging briefcase. He re-locked the drawer, hesitated an instant and then checked to make sure the two lower drawers were locked as well.

Deirdre swallowed hard to keep a sour taste from rising in her throat. *Black bile, the humor that is taking over my body, while his juices...*

Caedmon suddenly whooshed past her and jumped up to be greeted by his erstwhile master. With his free hand, Ashton roughed the animal's still damp fur. "How you doing, fella? Been out for a swim, have you?"

His feigned interest in the dog irked her. "Aren't you going to inquire after the kids?" she demanded, throwing down the proverbial gauntlet.

"I *would* ask, though I presume not all that much has changed for them in a mere week."

"No, of course not. They're just teenagers whose father has vanished, with no explanation, as they enter upon one of the most crucial periods of their lives," she retorted, her voice thick with sarcasm. If she exaggerated the impact of their embarking on the tenth grade, so be it. Almost overnight, they had become strangers to her: Dylan, moody or overly agitated; Caitlin, inattentive, aggressive and attracted to all the wrong people.

Ashton ruffled the dog's coat again to gain a beat. He then sighed audibly to signal (so she took it to mean) that *he* was the one put upon, or put out, by the developments of the last few weeks.

"I am sorry, Deirdre. Unexpected things happen. Beyond either of our control."

His expression of helplessness in the face of uncontrollable forces only served to infuriate her further. "Oh, really?" she shot back, astounded at what platitudes could come out of her husband's mouth. "So patronizing you are, and yet when it comes down to it, the triteness of your assertions beggars belief," she fired off, enjoying the sound of her alliterative volley.

Under such unaccustomed verbal assault, Ashton turned red in the face, his lips contracting into a thin slit. But no words spilled out.

"John Donne would be turning in his grave to know to what shallow uses his poems have been put," she added for good measure. (Part of her wished she had read the poetry more closely so as to wound more deeply, but even a generic reference would likely puncture her husband's ego.)

She was right.

So insulted was Ashton by this gratuitous blow, he banged his briefcase on the coffee table, frightening the dog and rattling the wine glasses. The bottle of cabernet rolled off the tray onto the floor.

In less than a minute, a light was flicked on from the staircase. Soon Caitlin, wide-eyed and disconcerted, materialized in the doorway, her bare feet in the puddle of urine.

"Dad?" she asked, surprise and worry mingled in her voice.

"Hey, sweetie," he answered distractedly, "we didn't mean to—"

"Why are you fighting? What's going on, Mom?"

"Nothing, dear," Deirdre said. "It's a grown-up matter. Go back to bed. You have a test tomorrow."

Caitlin shook her head. "It's on Monday and then another on Tuesday," she corrected her mother. "In fact, Dad," she began again, stepping further into the room toward her father's desk, "if I do well, a C on the English test and on the History, can I try out for that summer ballet camp in Cincinnati? You know, the one in that brochure."

Ashton, looking for guidance from Deirdre, opened out his arms pleadingly. "We'll see, Caitlin. You and your brother both need to do well. Better than a C."

Looking as though she'd been knocked off track, the girl tried another tack. "Well, Dylan doesn't have to study. In case you didn't notice, he snuck out as soon as Mom took the dog out," she snitched, the accusation as much against her mother as against her brother.

Deirdre looked mildly irritated; she would talk to her son tomorrow.

"In any case, the summer camp, piano lessons, whatever. They're up to your mother," Ashton hastened to say, picking up his briefcase.

Caitlin looked crestfallen at her father's acquiescence, or indifference. "She doesn't let me do anything anymore," she wailed, beseeching her father by batting her eyes at him.

"You know that's not true, Caitlin," Deirdre replied, determined not to sound defensive.

"Well, whatever Mom says, I'm glad you're home," Caitlin then enthused, and impulsively threw her arms around her father.

Awkwardly, he patted her on her head with his free hand, the way he had the dog.

"Don't tell Dylan I told on him," she admonished them as she pranced out of the room. "Ugh. What *is* this gook on the floor?" she called out from the hallway. "Gross."

Thanks to their daughter's intrusion, the tension in the room had lifted. To Deirdre, it seemed for an instant as if nothing had come between her and her husband to alienate their affections, as though the only worries they needed to face were those they shared—their separate, if not always equal, academic aspirations and what to do with their two exasperating children. Oh, and the expectations of in-laws.

"I would have mentioned before, but your mother rang up." Ashton shot her a worried look. "They're fine. Gadding about town more than ever, from what Zenobia went on about."

"So, what did you tell her?" he asked distractedly. From the sofa, he picked up his tweed jacket and draped it over the briefcase in his left hand.

Caedmon stood expectantly, tilting his head from one to the other of his owners. They both ignored him.

"That you were away, on a business trip to Cincinnati. I was vague. *I am vague.*"

Deirdre regretted raising her voice again, but exasperation had once again started to get the better of her. She had never found it pleasant to lie, and she did not want to do so on behalf of someone else, most pertinently, her husband.

Ashton lowered his head, mumbling something inarticulate, something that sounded like a quotation. That irked her further.

"You may relish living a lie, but I swear that is the last one I'm going to tell on your behalf. So, figure out your course of action and let us know. Otherwise, my version of your treachery will become the de facto narrative of this marriage. AND YOU WON'T LIKE IT," she shouted at him.

Rather than return fire, Ashton sidestepped his irate wife, and the pool of urine, and fled through the French doors toward the front entrance. Deirdre followed him into the hallway. So rattled was he that he had to struggle to open the door, the retriever yelping at his heels. On the dimly-lit porch, he rifled in his pocket for his car keys and then pressed the remote.

"What about the dog?" Deirdre called out as he tossed his briefcase across to the passenger seat of the Camry and ducked his head to get in.

"I don't know," he mumbled, as though he had no inkling what creature she was referring to. Then, upon second thought and hoping to end on a less belligerent note, he swiveled around. "Caedmon belongs here. He's part of the family."

"So do you. So *are* you," she called after him, but he was already revving the engine and didn't catch her words.

Not that they any longer mattered to him.

Chapter Nine

D r. Margery Willingham did not mince words. As an Elizabethan scholar, she had a healthy respect for the weight of words. She was dismayed when other people did not strive for precision, especially when those other people turned out to be her colleagues, who, she firmly believed, ought especially to strive for truth-telling. Not only should these efforts be made in front of the classrooms they commanded but equally in their private lives.

Because of her reputation for rectitude and her seniority at Klimpton, the esteemed professor had been invited to the Coles' home over the years, and having been entertained pleasantly enough, she had volunteered to babysit when the couple attended conferences in Chicago or in St. Louis.

An avowed spinster, she felt entitled to judge marriages, Ashton and Deirdre's ranking as one of the more successful she had observed. Both spouses had enriching jobs in academia, two well-behaved and articulate kids, in-laws who kept their distance, enough money and enough to talk about. At the dinner table and in faculty meetings, the couple rarely interrupted each other, nor did they ignore each other. She had silently commended them for supporting each other's viewpoint, or for disagreeing in the most deferential manner.

In short, Dr. Willingham was attuned to the nuances of intimate attachments, however few such relationships she herself had enjoyed. Moreover, she had read her Shakespeare closely, and she knew it didn't take much for love to go awry, in any age.

She had noted a shift in the dynamic between the two spouses over the current school year, especially as regards Dr. Cole. He and she were ensconced in the same wing of the building, under a burnished plaque inscribed "Renaissance Studies," whereas Dr. Durrell was housed at the other end of the building under the rubric "Classical Literature and the Middle Ages."

Given their proximity, Dr. Willingham observed her male colleague's comings and goings with regularity, and with growing consternation.

To her mind, there was something "metaphysical" about Dr. Cole, as though he struggled to reconcile the devout and the dissolute within his own soul. Not that she would voice aloud such an idea, but she suspected his focus on the poetry of John Donne *et alii* was not a random choice. In years past, the professor had limited his office hours with students to Thursday afternoons, each session to fifteen minutes. Mostly, his pupils wanted to know why they received a *C* or a *D* rather than an *A* or a *B* on one or another paper, and he, like other faculty members at Klimpton, would go over the whys and wherefores that had led them to mark as severely as they had. But, given the growing pressures on tenured professors to foster a coterie of star students, ones who might go on to graduate school in said field, thereby enhancing the reputation of the undergraduate institution as well as the professor in question, Dr. Cole had begun to coddle select candidates.

A few of them were also enrolled in one or another of Margery's classes, including a couple of pretty—strikingly pretty, she was compelled to admit—coeds who had transferred from a college outside Philadelphia. A Ms. Hazelton appeared to set the tone and pace for the other, and to judge from the poise with which she performed in Margery's classes, the role did seem fitting. Intrigued by the young woman, Margery tried to come up with the Shakespearean heroine she most reminded her of: too self-possessed to be an Ophelia but not conniving enough to be a Cleopatra. More like Rosalind from *As You Like It* or Portia from *The Merchant of Venice*, the professor eventually concluded.

She wondered what Dr. Cole made of the young woman.

One afternoon, a week before Thanksgiving, Margery was leaving her office when she heard laughter spilling out from a small conference room used for seminars. She eyed her Elgin, having never bothered with a cell phone (nor aware that these new devices kept the time). It was 6:30, pitch-black outside, and the heat had been turned down in the building—some policy the school had put in place in response to austerity measures during the downturn. Or was this energy-saving measure because of students' concerns about climate change? Margery wasn't sure but she pulled her hand-knit sweater closer around her. As she passed the conference room, she glanced through the glass panel. Dr. Cole was seated at the far end of the table; a handful of students were arrayed around him, including the aforesaid Ms. Hazelton. She was flanked by several other girls, slightly less blonde, definitely less pretty, who were nibbling cookies from a platter. The less pretty girls suddenly looked up and caught a glimpse of Dr. Willingham peering in. Jennifer's eyes remained fixed on the professor.

Margery did wonder who had baked the homemade cookies.

Shortly after the Thanksgiving holiday, Dr. Cole took Margery aside to say he'd be hosting his honor students every Wednesday evening for the rest of the school year: at his home, in his study. "Too cold to do it here," he went on, "what with all this austerity nonsense." He wanted to be certain that such a schedule did not interfere with anything his colleague might have arranged. "We do share a few students, I believe?" Dr. Cole had hazarded, as though, she later figured, he was trying to elicit some pertinent comment about them.

"Admirable of you," she replied, trying not to let a hint of sarcasm, or censure, color her voice.

For an instant, he looked flustered but quickly pivoted to an unrelated subject. Was she still planning to direct the upcoming college production of *As You Like It*? "Dr. Durrell and I always enjoy your theatrical efforts."

Margery inclined her head appreciatively. "You're too kind," she murmured, as these plays, one in the fall, another in the spring, did take a toll on her, especially now that the college budget had so shrunk that no new costumes or lighting equipment could be justified. And this time around, the drama department was also tapped out, hard at work on a staging of *Wicked*. She had thus been forced to cast most of the roles from her own Shakespeare classes. Ms. Hazelton had been tasked with playing Rosalind; her friend from Philly would take on the role of Celia. She began to call the two drafted thespians by their first names, Jennifer and Kimberly.

The two performances of the comedy had come off well enough, even the vinegary Dr. Landry had attended the opening night, and duly applauded, Margery observed from the wings. As the audience and performers mingled in the foyer afterwards, she glimpsed Dr. Cole in conversation with a cluster of performers, most notably Ms. Hazelton, who had changed out of her costume but had not removed her makeup. The young woman was animated, tossing her golden locks around and batting her mascara-caked eyes. Kimberly had a knowing look on her face. Fellow students and a few faculty members wandered by to congratulate the girls, but Dr. Cole did not leave their sides until the crowd had dwindled.

Dr. Durrell was nowhere to be seen.

Hard to blame a man for taking a fancy to such a charming creature as my Rosalind—OK, Ms. Hazelton—Margery thought to herself. But surely it would pass.

During the winter term, the two amateur actresses went their separate ways. Kimberly had upped and enrolled in a drama class, dropping her Shakespeare track, while Jennifer signed on for both the Metaphysical Poets seminar (with Dr. Cole) and The Elizabethan Imagination (with Dr. Willingham). She did not, to Margery's eye, appear as focused as she had during the fall, and kept more to herself.

As for Dr. Cole, Margery did not chat with him as regularly as before; he even skipped a few of their departmental meetings.

"Always so gloomy these gatherings, so much complaining," he had allowed when she ran into him dashing out of the campus library. He appeared immaculately groomed, smelling of cologne, which scent she picked up even though they were outside on the stone steps and a light snow was falling. His eyes darted about as though looking for someone or something. His car? Jennifer Hazelton?

"We must catch up soon, Dr. Cole. I trust Mrs. Cole is doing well. Haven't of late seen much of her either."

"They do keep us busy," Ashton replied, apparently in an effort to end the exchange.

Margery patted the sleeve of his camel hair coat, and carefully made her way up the slippery steps to the library entrance.

In truth, she *had* run into Dr. Durrell, earlier in the week, not on campus but in the grocery store. She was in the produce department, comparing heads of cauliflower or broccoli, she couldn't be sure which from a distance. But from the back, Dr. Durrell looked dumpier than Margery remembered.

To be fair, it was a Saturday, and sweatpants weren't designed to be flattering. Still, she herself, albeit not that far from retirement, wore fashionably-tailored slacks and had just come from the beauty parlor down the street. However old-fashioned it might sound or politically incorrect be, Margery believed that women in academia needed to make a special effort, and not be lulled into thinking that brains, however highly valued, wholly compensated for beauty. Especially when they were surrounded by hordes of young women, most of whom were attractive, no matter how sloppily they dressed, and some of whom doubtless possessed both beauty and brains.

Dr. Willingham dawdled with her basket of fruit and vegetables until Dr. Durrell had bagged her selection. "Why, hello there. How is Dr. Cole, and the kids?"

Taken aback, Deirdre rushed to collect herself. "The kids are great, but, you know, teenagers. Their interests change so rapidly it's hard to keep up."

"Umm," Margery ventured. "Well, no doubt they keep the two of you on your toes. And Dr. Cole?"

"Oh, Ashton is—I'm sure you're aware—working on another book." She paused to lower the cauliflower into her cart. "And he has an inordinate number of students to counsel this term. I imagine you all do. The Middle Ages, well, not so much."

Margery nodded noncommittally, not wanting to engage on the subject of dwindling interest in the Dark Ages and its scant, unimpressive literature. Getting students to engage with Shakespeare was hard enough; she couldn't imagine how difficult it must be to make anyone from that earlier period enticing. "Well, I won't keep you," she said, turning away to inspect the tomatoes. But then, another thought popped into her head. "I nearly forgot. Were you ever in need, there's an excellent new hairdresser at the salon down the street. Trained in Chicago. We can't have too many good stylists here in town."

For an instant, Deirdre appeared flummoxed. "Why, thank you for the recommendation," she stammered, unconsciously clutching at clumps of her frizzy hair.

Margery inclined her head and concentrated on squeezing the heirlooms on offer. *I must not become a busybody*, she silently admonished herself. And yet, she couldn't help but think, anything illicit between her colleague and this student of theirs could not only upend a perfectly decent marriage between two professors but adversely affect the college.

If nothing else, she would make a point of feeling out Ms. Hazelton during their next student-teacher conference. Perhaps then she could properly assess the danger and, if necessary, intercede.

In the end, Dr. Willingham had more to talk about with her pretty student than she had bargained for.

Although Jennifer had been diligent in class, she had not impressed with her knowledge nor shown any originality in her thinking. But somehow, she outdid herself on her final term paper, veering off the subject at hand to discuss in detail the rhetorical tradition in which the Bard had worked. This, despite the fact that the subject to be addressed on the final pertained to the overarching themes in the plays, most notably, familial love vs lust.

"I was both pleased and puzzled by your final essay," Margery began the colloquy, hoping to ease into her probe. Jennifer toyed with an unruly lock of her hair while her left leg jiggled across the top of the right. Her ankle-high black boots were probably genuine leather, likely Italian, and nicer than most of the girls could afford, the professor observed. "I cannot quibble with the points you made, but I had concerns as to your sources," she added, her voice rising at the end as in a question.

"I don't follow," Jennifer responded, her leg suddenly stilled. She uncrossed the two and sat up straighter, leaning toward the professor's desk. Margery registered the pink gloss on her lips and a similar shade, natural or not, on her cheeks. She was, the older woman estimated, the prettiest girl she could recall ever having in her class. Unlikely that such a creature would need to know of palindromes and synecdoches, let alone what a poetic fallacy was. Some other fallacies, though...

"What I'm wondering, Ms. Hazelton—(She had reverted to the girl's surname shortly after the play in December, not wanting to appear to give preference to any one student, especially not to this one.)—is whether you were influenced by a particular work or by another professor or *personage...* (Why she introduced the Frenchified term she had no idea but instantly regretted doing so.) That is, someone who may have led you to..."

Not knowing how to finish her thought without arriving at the word *plagiarize*, the professor gestured gracefully with her arm to elicit a response.

But Ms. Hazelton appeared unwilling to give ground. She had done the required assignment, and whatever information she had absorbed from other sources, and then regurgitated, it was solely to give her essay more heft. She herself thought it was a performance to be commended rather than critiqued.

Dr. Willingham watched her student's face modulate into another key as she absorbed the insinuation. Eventually, her lips settled into what Margery interpreted as a world-weary smile, a look she thought unbecoming in one so young.

Her student's rejoinder was in fact, unequivocal. "If you're asking, Dr. Willingham, did I cheat on my exam, then I would say no."

"Oh, my dear, I wasn't so much thinking THAT," Margery batted back, putting more emphasis on the final word than perhaps it should bear.

"Well, it is your prerogative to think whatever. You are the professor," Ms. Hazelton responded evenly. "And, I believe, our time is up," she added brightly, casting her eyes at the clock on the wall. It was 6:45, though no other student had knocked at the door. (Margery had purposefully scheduled this particular *face-à-face* as her last.) Reaching for her book satchel on the floor, the girl flicked her hair out of her face and re-latched the shiny buckle on one of her boots. When she stood back up, blood had infused her cheeks, making them even rosier.

"Don't you want to know the grade I'm giving you?" Margery asked, rising from her squeaky swivel chair.

Jennifer looked as though she could take it or leave it, concentrated as she was with buttoning up her powder-blue fleece jacket.

"Well, it's a *B* on the paper, but I do trust you will peruse my comments in the margins," she stated, handing over the folder in question. Ms. Hazelton slipped it into her satchel and nodded neutrally. "Of course, final grades haven't been posted yet, but, confidentially, yours for the course is a *B+*."

Again, the girl kept her expression blank, but she did extend her arm to shake the professor's hand.

"Enjoy your end-of-term break, Ms. Hazelton."

"You too, professor," she rejoined and headed out the door.

Disappointed at how the conversation went, Margery closed her ledger and turned to look out the picture window. The Beaux Arts street lamps had come on, illuminating patches of snow clinging to the curb in front of the Humanities building. As she reached to lower the blinds, a square of blue caught her eye. It was Ms. Hazelton, who was climbing into the passenger side of a Camry, one of only three or four vehicles, including her own, left at that hour in the faculty lot. She watched until the car backed out and sped away.

"So many additional students to attend to," Dr. Willingham mouthed to herself, remembering Dr. Durrell's explanation of her husband's fraught workload. "This will come to no good," she added aloud, as she pulled the cord and shut out the scene below.

During the spring term, Margery found herself saddled with additional duties, including an extra freshman class in the modern British and American novel. "Has someone died?" she had drolly inquired of Dr. Beauchamps when he called to inform her of the scheduling change.

"Not so lucky are we, Margery dear. Our endowment, such as it was, has shriveled, and donors have stolen away like thieves in the night."

"I know. Tthe economy. So, am I being paid or is this to be done out of the goodness of my heart?"

"They are freshmen. Their minds are *tabulae rasae*. You will have the honor of filling them," the department head went on in his bantering way. (Margery considered her superior a charmer, and was duly charmed. Besides, the head of the department was cuckolded on a regular basis.) "*Mais oui*, a small stipend will be added to your monthly check." He smacked his lips and began to rifle through papers on his desk. Margery turned to leave. "By the way, I never congratulated you for giving that Hazelton girl the lead role in your play." She stopped, turned back around and looked inquiringly at Dr. Beauchamps. "Perhaps she'll merit something similar this time around as well."

"Why ever so?" Margery asked, her mind racing.

"*Rien*, but I noticed her grades are good enough. And, *entre nous*, Dr. Willlingham, her father is one of our biggest benefactors. In fact, well, never mind." He waved off whatever other considerations jostled around in his head.

Margery took a deep breath. "Poetic justice, I guess," she muttered.

Privately, she marveled at Dr. Beauchamps' uncanny ability to get his colleagues to bend the rules—not to break them, but to do things they ordinarily would not have thought necessary or seemly.

But Jennifer Hazelton in the spring term play? Not altogether a bad idea since the department had voted for *The Merchant of Venice* and she had already spent too much time to find a reasonably convincing Shylock, and thus was behind with casting. As the beautiful, intelligent Portia, Jennifer would be perfect, better than her erstwhile friend and drama major, Kimberly—and it might temporarily remove her from Dr. Cole's attentions.

She would mull the idea over that evening.

Chapter Ten

Querulous and quarrelsome the twins had become.
"You're so weird," he to her; "You're such a dork," her to him.

The bickering had reached a crescendo about the time it sank in that their father had moved out of the house. About one thing they did see eye to eye: their mother was to blame for the catastrophe.

"So, when is Dad coming back home?" Dylan demanded, at breakfast or at the dinner table, each time with more petulance.

"I truly don't know," Deirdre would let out slowly, gritting her teeth. Then she would pass the butter or refill the water glasses.

"Why did you have to yell at him, Mom? Dad didn't do anything. Like with us, you're always griping," Caitlin had piled on, before flouncing out, not waiting to be excused from the table.

Once so obliging, Dylan had taken to spending as little time as possible in his mother's company. Weather permitting, he joined Sammy and company to play football in the park, or, as often, hopped a bus over to Roxane's apartment, where they spoke French, listened to music, or watched old movies on her TV. Caitlin made herself even more scarce, eating a skimpy breakfast in a funk and refusing to come downstairs at night for dinner, let alone help with the dishes. Sometimes she didn't bother to go to school, hanging out at the mall with Claudia and her loopy male friends.

In response to her children's questions, Deirdre obfuscated. She still harbored the hope that Ashton would show up at the door, begging for forgiveness and to be reinstated in the bosom of the Cole household. Jennifer Hazelton's name would never again come up.

As April gave way to May, however, she alternated between a mania to get the house in order (she had dismissed Martha, their longtime maid), scrubbing floorboards, cleaning out closets, washing windows and depressive bouts in which she took Caedmon for long walks, allowing him, if not goading him, to antagonize any creature he came upon. Finding herself alone in the evenings, she ate out of cans or binged on Belgian chocolate. She did not have the energy or the heart to make an appointment at that beauty salon.

Left in the dark about Ashton's intentions, Deirdre toyed with the idea of accosting him in the corridors of the Humanities building and having to be forcibly removed by security. Although making a scene might satisfy her delight in the drama of it all, she, the spurned spouse, did not, however, want Ashton's lapse to become public, besmirching their image and jeopardizing job security at the college. Any scandal, she had come to believe, would tarnish her and the children as much as, if not more than, the one person who was at fault.

As it happened, she and Ashton did at times pass in the hallways, where they exchanged hasty nods or a muttered hello. In his wake, she scanned the students with their eager faces, trying to fix on the tallest, blondest, and most entitled-looking from among the females, but they moved too quickly, jostling one another, and being young. It occurred to her too that this Jennifer might not be the only one having tutorials-cum-trysts with her husband. In their identical leggings, they might be interchangeable—: like characters in Shakespearean comedies, who, to attain their hearts' desire or merely for the fun of it, (she wasn't sure which), don masks to impersonate others.

What difference do such switches make to clueless humans? (At some more serene moment, she would invite Dr. Willingham over and ask her to shed light on this theatrical convention.)

The phone in the house had rung. It must have been while she was out with the dog. It was a weeknight, around 9 p.m., when Deirdre noticed the blinking red light. She pressed the button. It was Ashton, adopting his most punctilious voice, to ask if she'd be so kind as to pull out his volume of Shakespeare's comedies and drop it off at his office. And, he hoped that the children were well.

She sat down on the stool and re-played the message, backwards and forwards, attempting to deconstruct every phrase and decipher every shift in tone—contrite, condescending, cold. So absorbed was she for an hour in this ritual she nearly forgot to retrieve the tome in question. Odd though, not his period, she mused, more like Margery's, she who dutifully mounted works from the Bard every spring and fall. Probably wasn't even paid for her efforts. *I wonder if she has any inkling...?*

The next day, a Thursday, Deirdre dropped off the requested anthology with the department's receptionist. Looking down, she noticed xeroxed fliers, advertising *The Merchant of Venice*, for two nights, in the college's Taft Theater. Perhaps she could cajole her son and daughter into coming along. Do them good; do me good, she thought.

"Will you be going to the performance tomorrow, Dr. Durrell?" the receptionist asked, appending a post-it-note to the book with Dr. Cole's name scribbled on it. "They've been practicing like crazy. Your husband's been lending a hand."

For an instant, Deirdre looked startled but caught herself up. "Quite likely. The kids too."

Without lingering, she marched down the long corridor to her own small but neatly organized office. For several hours she filled out administrative forms and wrote preliminary evaluations of the students in her classes. Then, after a quick stop in the campus canteen for a cup of coffee—she nodded at Stella Kincaid seated across the way but did not speak—she pulled out her lecture notes for her final class that day on the waning of the Middle Ages. She would summarize the merits of the great Italian writers—Dante, Petrarch and Boccaccio—and then pose a single exam question: to what extent were any one of these giants emblematic of the end of an epoch and to what extent were any one of them a harbinger of the Renaissance? They would have an hour to write up a thousand-word response on their laptops.

Invigorated by the tasks accomplished, she planned to read and grade the papers that very evening. That way she'd be freed up to attend the play the next night, whatever might be Ashton's plans. High time to take charge of the kids too, insist they come along for their own betterment. (She couldn't recall why she hadn't gone along to that other comedy back in the fall. She wondered if Margery had noticed and felt snubbed.)

By the time Deirdre got home, the sun was setting behind the pond in the back. She put her briefcase on her desk and raised the blinds to admire the deepening shades of orange as the sun sank into the water. A flock of geese circled the lake in the fading light and then disappeared behind the oaks. Then she spotted a figure, Caitlin, trotting briskly around the lake, with Caedmon on his leash. "Miracle of miracles," she said aloud, and headed to the kitchen.

"Thank you for doing that, sweetie. Taking the dog out," she said, carrying a heavy clay pot to the stove. "I'm making cheeseburgers if you and your brother are interested. Baked beans and coleslaw too. That work?"

"Whatever," Caitlin replied, but seeing her mother's face fall, added, "Yeah, that'll work. And I made a *C+* on my English test." She took the leash off the dog and patted him on his back. He was breathing heavily, his pink tongue protruding.

"Not bad. You studied," Deirdre replied, trying to sound supportive without overtly humoring her daughter. (Years ago, a *C+* would have been meant grounding, but things had become more complicated.) She unwrapped the package of ground beef and began to fashion patties. Caitlin eyed her suspiciously but said nothing; instead, she opened the fridge and fished out a platter of cheeses and a soda can.

"I like Monterrey Jack on mine. Not cheddar."

Deirdre nodded. "Is your brother home yet?"

"Don't know. Might have band practice. Final concert is next week."

"Yes, of course," Deirdre replied defensively, having forgotten the school schedule and what events parents would be expected to attend. It was as though she had been on Mars for the last three weeks and only now fallen back to Earth. Rinsing her hands off in the sink, she debated asking Caitlin to grate the cabbage for coleslaw or do it herself. Her daughter was still standing there, nibbling on a piece of cheese.

"So, Mom. Can I try out for that ballet workshop? Dad said again it was up to you."

A cloud flitted across Deirdre's face. "When did he say that?"

"When he called my cell the other day. To invite us to a play. Dylan and me, that is," she said, color rising in her cheeks.

Deirdre registered the exclusion and her own daughter's awareness of it. Willing herself not to overreact, she pulled a skillet out of the pantry, set it on a front burner and sprayed it with oil. "I believe it's another of Shakespeare's comedies," she eventually replied. "Dr. Willingham—you remember her—is in charge of staging them. You might enjoy it, Dylan, too."

"Yeah, maybe," Caitlin responded, seemingly not enthusiastic. She took another sip of coke and put down the can. Then more brightly, she added, "But Jennifer is in it. At least I'll know someone."

Stiffening, Deirdre turned the front burner off and snatched her apron off. "I need the bathroom. You could set the table and ring your brother. See if he's on his way."

"Sure," Caitlin said, wrinkling her nose in a sign of bewilderment. "Are you OK, Mom?"

Somehow Deirdre contrived to get through the meal with Caitlin and Dylan, he having shown up while she was still in the downstairs bathroom. She had tried to drown out the sound of vomiting by turning the taps full throttle, but she couldn't be sure the twins didn't overhear. She washed her face, rinsed out her mouth and stared at her spongy flesh in the mirror. Before she went back out, she pulled out an old powder compact and lipstick from the medicine cabinet and applied a little of each.

At the table, both children were considerate, passing the catsup and pouring the tea, and complementing their mother on the coleslaw, even though it was Caitlin who had concocted the latter, golden raisins included. They ate in silence except when Dylan went on about what they were practicing for the concert—the usual Sousa marches and Strauss waltzes and a medley of show tunes. All Deirdre could muster was a query about his grades. (A *B+* in English and an *A-* in biology.)

"We won't see our history grades until Monday. Old Geddings takes longer than anyone else," he explained. For once, Caitlin did not mock her twin as a smarty-pants. There was no further mention of the play, or of their father.

Later that evening, Deirdre forced herself to follow through with her plan to grade her students' final essays. Turning on her computer, she signed in with her password (Caedmon), suddenly wondering if perchance Ashton used the very same for his. Shaking off the thought, she called up the relevant subsection of the college website where the essays were posted. As she sprinkled her remarks in notes mode, she began to feel better.

One essay struck her as unusually perceptive, from student number 09 (she would only know names once grades were entered). In vivid prose, it detailed the legendary account of Petrarch's hike to the top of Mount Vanteuse in the French Alps. *"Had he simply gone up to ask for God's guidance, then yes, he would have forever been branded as medieval in his thinking. The ascent was steep, the winds unmerciful. And yet Petrarch persisted. So curious was he about the world around him, he took his time, sketching the rock formations, taking samples of strange plants. As he purportedly replied (and I for one would like to imagine he did) when asked afterwards why he had undertaken to tackle such a mountain, he replied, 'Because it was there.' In short, the poet stood on the precipice of a new age, and in so doing, helped usher it in.*

Tears came to Deirdre's eyes as she read through this paper, she too having always wanted that account of Petrarch's ascent to be verifiable. Whoever this student was, and from the syntax, she opined he might be one of her favorites, a Mr. Burnham. Jeff, if she recalled correctly. Good-looking too, with green eyes and a generous mouth, always opening doors for her or picking up dropped papers.

She leaned back in her swivel chair and took a sip of the chianti she had poured herself, thinking the wine might soothe her stomach as well as her spirit. Her thoughts meandered: *what if I had fallen for this charming young man, what if he and I...? But how could such a thing happen and why would he, at the start of his life, want—*

Out of nowhere, the doorbell rang. Three insistent times. Her watch said 9:05 p.m. However inopportune the hour, she tucked a stray wisp of hair behind her ear, smoothed her blouse, and hurried to the front door. She fumbled with the knob, finally yanking it open only to find Stella Kincaid in one of her no-nonsense knit suits and an expression to match.

"I'm intruding—you look disappointed—but I needed to catch you before bed." The older woman was clearly bent on something, speaking in short, staccato bursts.

"Come in, come in. I was finishing up some essays. Recording the grades." Deirdre stepped to the side to let Stella, who was big-boned and bulked-up, maneuver the hallway. "Why don't we go into my study? I have music on and I can pour you some wine. Helps the digestion."

"No need, no need," Stella kept repeating, holding out her thick arms to ward off whatever offer and making a beeline for the light at the end of the hall.

Once the two entered the study, Stella turned and asked, "The children? Asleep?"

"I don't know. I mean yes, upstairs, but I'm not sure what they're up to."

Without waiting for her hostess to think of it, Stella drew the French doors together and deposited herself into the armchair facing the mahogany desk. "Nice roll-top," she said. "You and Ashton both work in here?"

Deirdre pursed her lips in exasperation, figuring the visit might well last longer than she had the stamina for. "He has his own space," she replied curtly, gesturing toward the front of the house. A Beethoven string quartet was playing on the radio; she turned it down and went around to her swivel chair. "Are you sure there's not something I can get you, Stella?" (She herself could have used more alcohol but didn't dare pour herself any in front of her colleague.)

Again, the older woman brushed away the offer. "No secrets in this town, my dear. You must know that by now. The word is out—(here Deirdre blinked several times)—everyone knows about Ashton and that student. The hussy, shameless. In front of everyone, Beauchamps included."

Trying to keep her composure, Deirdre stared off at the Uccello on the far wall.

"As soon as the dress rehearsal wrapped—a misnomer really, since they don't have the budget for costumes this go-round. In any case, after the final practice last night."

"I don't know what you mean."

"Your husband. Bounded from his seat in the theater, up the steps to the stage and embraced her, like he was the director, or her father. Margery was agog, though she quickly came to the rescue, shouting last-minute instructions to the cast. And on and on, against all the rules, and with his own student no less. Some Portia she'll make."

Stella kept firing salvos in rapid succession, looking past Deirdre and out the picture window. Not knowing how to stop the barrage and feeling bombarded, Deirdre bowed her head and gripped the arms of her chair.

"It was ever thus," Stella eventually opined, wiping her brow with a handkerchief, and momentarily desisted, sensing that her hostess had been bloodied enough. She surveyed the rest of the room, letting her eyes linger on the poster of Le Roman de la Rose, which appeared to befuddle her. "Jean de Moon," she mispronounced quietly the author's name. "Anyway, my dear, I came over to supply you with ammunition."

Here, Deirdre raised her head, alarmed that there could be yet other blows to parry. "What else is there to know, Stella? I have been told the essentials by Ashton and we are, well, we will be working it out," she replied, convinced she still needed to protect her marriage and not allow others, however seemingly sympathetic, to revel in her misery. Right then, she didn't like Stella Kincaid. Not one bit.

"All very confidentially, you understand, but in my administrative capacity, it's come to my attention that Jennifer Hazelton's father—the parents are, not surprisingly, divorced—is trying to pull his donation from the college. He's some muckety-muck of a hedge fund manager. Worse, he is threatening to sue the college unless they get rid of—and these were his words to Landry—'the dastardly professor who raped my daughter.' "

Pausing to see how this revelation registered, and noting that apparently, it didn't, Stella decided it were best to empty her barrel in one blast. "Ashton is being fired—though knowing ole Landry, it'll be handled as a resignation. To avoid any further scandal, he may even decide a recommendation is in order."

"And how do you know these particulars?" Deirdre shot back, her voice hardened.

Taken aback by her colleague's peeved tone, Stella struggled to portray her own role as a bit player in this melodrama. "From what Beauchamps confided, the idea of letting Ashton go has been bubbling for a while, but only now come to a boil."

Deirdre reached over for the wine bottle and poured herself a half glass, not bothering to gesture toward Stella. Rather, she shook her head as though to indicate the conversation might as well come to an end as she was impervious to any more assaults.

For a long minute, neither woman spoke. The string quartet had been superseded by a mournful Schubert wind ensemble.

Feeling she had done her duty, however unwelcome, Stella hoisted herself out of the low-slung wingback, and determined to impart something positive.

"Whatever happens, you should protect yourself and the kids." Deirdre's eyes slowly met her guest's. "For starters, that monograph you're toying with, turn it into a book."

Deirdre arched her eyebrows, surprised at this twist in the conversation, and from someone who didn't even know who Jean de Meun was. "Why do you say that?"

"To get tenure, excel on your own merits. Especially if *he's* not going to be around."

Deirdre took in the suggestion, not having expected such unfiltered, and arguably useful, advice. She rose to accompany her guest to the door and mumbled perfunctory thanks on the porch.

Stella patted her on the arm, adding as an afterthought, "Been there myself. You will get through it," and ambled off to her car.

Watching her colleague pull out, Deirdre felt ashamed at her own rudeness. That night she finished off the chianti and slept heavily on the sofa in her study.

Chapter Eleven

The next morning, Deirdre's head felt as heavy as her heart. She took an Excedrin and went upstairs to rouse her children. If she remembered rightly, this would be the last day for the posting of grades. She'd offer to pick them up after school and take them shopping, Caitlin at least, to show how proud of them she was. "Can I make you an omelette?" she called out to her daughter in the bathroom.

"God no, Mom. Orange juice and toast. Ask Dylan," she shouted back over running water and music blasting from her radio.

Down the hall, her son was in the process of dressing, stooped over to tie his sneakers. "What about you? I can make you an omelette with ham and cheese, if you like."

"I'm fine, Mom. Sammy's father is driving us, in, like, ten minutes," he said distractedly, checking the hands on his alarm clock. When he stood up, turned and saw Deirdre though, his lips tightened. "You look really tired," he let out. "And your hair is like..." He didn't finish the sentence, but he sounded annoyed.

"I slept badly," she stuttered, disconcerted. She pulled her rumpled robe tightly around her and gave him a faint smile. Her head throbbed worse than ever.

"Whatever," he mumbled under his breath, running his hand through his own thick locks.

"At least grab some juice," she ventured, sensing Caitlin standing in front of her own room, watching them. She felt exposed, as though she were being judged, poorly, by her own children. "Anyway, I wanted to wish you both luck today. It'll likely call for celebration. We can go shopping this weekend."

The twins exchanged a glance.

"Oh, I almost forgot. If you need a ride to the college tonight, for the play, I could drop you off. I've got something to do in town but it would be on my way," she rushed to offer, Dylan standing there awkwardly, shifting his weight from one foot to the other. For the first time, she realized he was taller than she was, at least in her worn-down bedroom slippers.

"Dad's going to take us," Caitlin called out, as she started down the stairs in her sandals. "And Claudia's already outside waiting for me in her car." She continued down the stairs and to the kitchen.

Deirdre could hear the refrigerator door open and close, and shortly thereafter the front door was unceremoniously banged. Dylan, however, remained rooted in the upstairs hallway. A newly pensive look on his face further unnerved her. She wondered if he was worried about his grades, or, more likely, about his sister's.

"I was thinking, Dylan. If you two are concerned about your grades, you need to know they don't matter, or rather, they don't matter so much as you imagine." No response from her son, she plowed on. "Just know, we're always here to help you," she added, wondering if he'd grasp that the pronoun was meant as the editorial *we*, not the plural *we*.

"That's not it, Mom," her son corrected her, looking more dismayed than before. She eyed him closely. Surely her hair didn't look that bad.

"It's this Jennifer person Caitlin keeps on about. Do you like her?" Deirdre grabbed hold of the doorknob to the master bedroom so as not to crumple to the floor in front of her son. "And why is Dad mixed up with her?"

Her heart pounding, Deirdre steeled herself to come up with an adequate response. "I do not know this girl personally, Dylan, but you might want to—actually you *should*—ask your father what the story is. Only he—"

"I'm not a baby, you know," Dylan blurted out, his eyes fiercely bright.

"I know, darling," she responded, trying not to give in to tears. "We'll talk about it together this weekend. You, Caitlin and I. But you really must go. Don't be late for school."

She shooed him down the stairs, immediately retreating behind her bedroom door. The room had an empty, leftover feel about it. She flung herself across the bed and sobbed at length, barely hearing the front door open and close and a car motor backfire.

Not obliged to post her final grades online until 6 p.m. that afternoon, Deirdre let herself sleep for a couple of hours and then drew a hot bath. She poured half a bottle of something called Argan oil into the water and activated the jacuzzi jets. Within minutes suds had breached the rim of the tub and made their way onto the tiles. Unconcerned, she lay back and let her mind take her elsewhere. As far away as possible. *Have we women made so little progress, she asked herself, or is it just I?* She would get back to her notes for the monograph, list the traits her medieval heroines shared with their modern counterparts and which ones were peculiar to their time. It would be a start. Therapeutic even.

Deirdre lathered her wash rag and soaped herself front and back, gentling massaging her breasts and between her thighs. She did not allow herself to dwell on her body parts, however sore or sagging; rather, she let the pulsating water from the jets soothe her muscles, if not her spirits. Self-pity was not a trait associated with the medieval mind; it should not be one of hers.

Once toweled off, Deirdre assessed her body anew in the full-length mirror. More exercise and fewer pizzas might make a positive difference. And what couldn't be changed, she would endeavor to accept. As for her hair, Dylan could not be faulted: it was a dull, tangled mess. She would call the salon that very day.

After she took Caedmon for a walk, Deirdre cut up the leftover vegetables in the fridge and tossed them in a salad, which she ate part of, putting the rest back in the fridge, for whomever. Then, she returned to her bedroom, called the salon and got an appointment with Erica, the new hire from Chicago, for that very afternoon.

Almost as an afterthought, she rang Roxane, and got her answering machine. She left a message inviting her to go out to the movies around 7 p.m. *La Vie en Rose* was playing in town, after which they could grab something to eat. Next, she rummaged through the walk-in closet for something spring-like, settling on a pair of beige linen slacks, a floral blouse, and a matching beige jacket. Caitlin was right: warm enough for sandals. She took a deep breath, carefully applied makeup, and ran a comb through her distressed hair.

It was dusk when she parked the car in her allotted space in front of the Humanities building and raced in to post her final grades from her office computer. She had always been punctual to a fault, but the session at the hair salon had lasted several hours. Erica had convinced her that reddish-gold highlights, as well as a layered cut, would be just the thing, as she diplomatically put it, "to freshen you up." To demonstrate that she didn't feel intimidated, Deirdre opted for a manicure and a pedicure, complete with two coats of a color called *pink promise* on both her finger and toenails. Feeling revived, she left a lavish tip, and promised to return. Regularly.

As she hurried down the corridor to her office, Deirdre noticed students huddled around the video screen where various grades were already available. Several turned to watch her unlock her office door, one of the boys nudging another in the ribs. She did not hear what they said.

Once at her desk, she glanced at the marks she had scribbled on paper the night before and now weighted those scores into her overall ratings for the course. No one had failed her course or gotten a grade below *C*; only one student had merited an *A*, the one who had written about Petrarch. It was John Burnham. She hit the send button, feeling elated, both for her effort and for theirs. After printing out the essays, she put them into a folder and slipped it into her top drawer. If any student wished to contest his or her score, she'd have them at her fingertips.

While she was locking her desk, her cell phone rang. It made her jump, but it wasn't Ashton. Rather, a business-like Roxane: she would meet up in front of the Rivoli in forty-five minutes. She knew a great Chinese place nearby.

Deirdre checked her hairdo in the mirror next to the door and then turned the knob to secure the lock.

Halfway down the hall one of her students hurried to catch up to her. "Just wanted to say, Dr. Durrell," the breathless young man began, "We like your hairdo." His friends down the hallway began to titter. "Oh, and I like my grade, too. Thank you."

"You earned it, Mr. Burnham. Now go celebrate," she added, gesturing toward his fellow students. She would miss this particular bunch, she suddenly realized.

By the time she got to Elm Street and found a parking place, Roxane was pacing in front of the cinema. From a distance, Deirdre thought she seemed off-balance, but then that's how her friend always struck her, as though something had not quite come right for her.

After a quick embrace, Roxane pulled two tickets out of her jacket. "If it's okay with you, let's go right in. I often enjoy the trailers more than I do the movie. By the way, your hair looks marvelous."

When the ads came on and the lights went up, Deirdre suggested they split a bag of popcorn. Out at the concession stand, she also purchased two Diet Cokes. Fortunately, she didn't notice any students she knew or any who might be in Ashton's classes. Probably at the Taft, suffering through that threadbare production of

Shakespeare, she told herself. Her children too. *Focus on the film,* she admonished herself.

Ninety minutes later, the two friends were back on the street, both claiming they had enjoyed the picture. "They never have the oomph of American movies or, European pictures, but the songs were lovely," Roxane commented. "What did you think?"

"I'm not steeped in French cinema the way you are," Deirdre replied, "but it held my attention. I did, however, have to rely on the subtitles whenever the dialogue became animated."

Roxane did not follow up on this indirect compliment. "Hopefully you'll like this Chinese place. It's new so they seem to be making an effort," she said, leading the way down a side street toward a neon sign which flashed Shanghai Surprise in red letters.

Although Deirdre found eating out at oriental restaurants tedious—too many unknowns on the menu, too much sharing of dishes, too much effort to master chopsticks—Roxane made it easy. Within minutes, two bowls of wonton soup arrived, followed by a platter of vegetables and another of assorted fish grilled in a lemony wine sauce.

"You do know your way around Chinese menus," Deirdre threw out, hoping to draw out her friend and keep the conversation clear of her own troubles.

"Did a lot of waitressing in my time," she responded laconically, dishing out the vegetables onto a bed of rice, first Deirdre's plate, then her own. "Help yourself to as much fish as you like. And if you find it bland, we can ask for a ginger sauce."

It occurred to Deirdre that she still had no idea of Roxane's past other than her opaque references to the junior college in Colorado and to Paris. (Her Google searches had remained fruitless.) If she were to pen a proper recommendation, she would need more, and elicited offhandedly might be an effective tactic. "I was thinking, it might not be a bad idea for Dylan, Caitlin too, to hold down a summer job." Without betraying a reaction, Roxane spooned the last of her soup. "Is that essentially what you did during college?"

"A little of both," she replied neutrally, wiping her lips with her napkin and picking up her chopsticks. Deftly, she pinched a couple of snow peas and delivered them to her mouth.

Deirdre waited, forcing herself not to jump into the void. Instead, she studied the strange vegetables on her plate. Several other customers passed their table, including a couple with a whimpering child, but still, neither woman spoke.

"It would depend on what you had in mind," Roxane finally allowed, though Deirdre had no idea what she was referring to.

"I'm not following...?"

Aligning her chopsticks neatly on the rim of her plate, Roxane scooted her chair back as though to get a more encompassing view of her dinner companion. "I didn't want to bring it up, but Dylan has told me."

"Told you what?" Deirdre stammered, heat rising to her head. Her temples began to throb.

"That Ashton has embarked on an affair—that was not precisely the word your son used to describe the situation—with one of his students. I have been trying to console him, as, well, he is such a sensitive young man. And so gifted." Despite the bewilderment on Deirdre's face, Roxane became animated. "You'd be astonished at what progress Dylan's making on the violin. He insists he practices better at my place, with fewer distractions, so that's why the instrument hasn't been returned to you, not to mention the accent he now manages in French. It's almost as though—"

Here Roxane stopped abruptly, seeing Deirdre press her fingers to her forehead and realizing that she had let slip more than she had meant to about the young man who was spending so much time at her apartment, Caitlin nowhere around. "I'm sorry. I didn't mean to upset you. Drink some tea," she then offered, sliding the pot across the table.

"You mean *further* upset me," Deirdre shot back, ignoring the teapot. "What about my daughter? Have you been consoling her too?" she asked, her tone acidic. "You do teach them both, *n'est-ce pas*?"

Hearing the discordant tone, diners at the next table briefly looked over before returning to their menus. The waitress kept her distance.

"Caitlin is going through a phase," Roxane rejoined, ignoring the insinuation. "I suspect neither of us knows how to handle her moods, but your husband's behavior can't be helping matters." (Deirdre looked off into the distance to indicate that her friend was not telling her anything she didn't already know.) "Obviously, I don't know what her other teachers have said, but I'd hazard she's borderline A.D.D. and way too interested in older boys, unsavory ones, I might add. And, she's only sixteen."

"So is her brother," Deirdre muttered drily, rubbing her temples to stop the tingling and prevent another headache from taking hold.

Roxane motioned for the waitress and asked for two glasses of ice water. "Please tell me your chef does not put msg in his dishes," she demanded, loud enough for other customers to hear. The waitress shook her head in the negative and scurried off. "They all say they don't use the stuff anymore, but trust me, they do," she added, turning back to her dinner companion. "It affects some people worse than others."

Deirdre took a few swallows of water and the pain subsided. Perhaps it was the monosodium glutamate, after all, and not her marital plight. Still, it galled her that her friend had become, seemingly overnight, such a confidante of her son and an authority on her daughter. She was jealous of Jennifer for stealing her husband's affections; she did not wish to be of Roxane, for luring away her children's. Thinking she might have been too prickly, she looked up again at her companion, who was now fiddling with a piece of fish. *God knows, I will need all the help I can get in the next few months.* She drank the last of the water and tried to lower the temperature at the table.

"Since you brought it up, Roxane, who of concern is Caitlin hanging out with?"

"That floozy Claudia and her circle of dropouts or druggies. I don't know what they do all day, but attending class or turning in homework is not part of it."

"I see," Deirdre replied, trying to recall if she'd met any of this group other than the aforementioned Claudia.

"By the way," Roxane appended, apparently she too wanting to dispel the tension, "since you were beating around the bush earlier, my childhood was not exactly a bed of roses. As a teen I too was a mess, so, if you're asking, I tend to detect early signs in others. *C'est tout.*"

Had she a clearer head, Deirdre would have liked to probe her friend's past more thoroughly, but she figured that the two had exchanged enough heated words for one evening. If her children had gravitated toward Roxane—by all accounts, an empathetic teacher with good intentions—far be it from her to be dismissive, or jealous, or unduly concerned. "I appreciate what you're doing for the kids, I really do. As you can imagine, it's been a trying few weeks, with likely more to follow."

Roxane forced a smile. The teapot being still warm to the touch, she poured the remainder into their two cups. Deirdre motioned for the check. Within a minute it arrived, along with two fortune cookies.

"Shall we?" Roxane asked, picking up one and cracking it open. She read what was printed on the strip aloud: *Something you have long yearned for will happen, but patience is required.* "And yours?"

Deirdre opened hers and read the snippet to herself: *Bouncing back only happens when one has fallen from a great height.* "Well, we can read into them what we will. I think we should take them as good omens, don't you?"

"Absolutely," Roxane responded. She held open the ornately carved door of the restaurant and then accompanied Deirdre to her Volvo. "If you'll be around," she leaned in to say when her friend had put the keys into the ignition, "I will bring the violin by over the weekend. Ashton and Dylan will have to figure it out: how to share the instrument, that is."

However troubled Deirdre felt at the idea of an argument between father and son, she nodded pleasantly and started the engine.

For a change, she took the long route home, and on a whim stopped off at Scotch&Soda, a bar and grill she and Ashton had taken friends to, years ago. A nightcap after that bitter tea couldn't hurt, she reasoned. Further, she did not relish arriving home right as the kids did, chauffeured by their father, and conceivably, with his new flame in tow. The star of the damn play, she had learned, picking up one of the fliers on her way out of the Humanities building. Jennifer's name was emblazoned in bold letters right below Margery's.

A few heads turned Deirdre's way when she entered, but mercifully the light was low. She walked straight to the bar, ignoring the hostess. The bartender, a thin, middle-aged type with an equally thin mustache, soon cast his eyes her way.

"A chardonnay, please. Something light, Californian." A couple of men several stools away glanced in her direction but then went back to nursing their drinks.

"Do you want to start a tab?"

"No, no, the one glass," she specified, vaguely ruffled by what she took as an insinuation. When the drink arrived, she sipped slowly, wondering when the fashion for outsized wine goblets had set in, so awkward they were to drink from. She said nothing, no one nearby to say it to.

Eventually, she relaxed enough to swivel her stool around. A pianist in dress clothes was performing standards from the Forties and Fifties, while a surprising number of people were still eating at tables through an archway in the dining room. She could not remember who it was they had brought there to dinner as their guests, but however good the meal or the ambiance, she and Ashton had never returned, or gone out much anywhere else together in the last decade. Children. Work. Chores around the house. Trips home, to Boston or to the Delta. Course preparation, lectures out of town, faculty-student conferences. Quarrels.

Whether because of the wine or the music, Deirdre soon felt ineffably sad: something had slipped through her—*their*—fingers never to be grasped again. How could two such intelligent people let that happen, she would have turned to ask had anyone been seated next to her. Not even the bartender was near enough. He was mixing drinks at the other end, chatting away to a young couple he was serving.

While she fumbled in her purse for cash to pay for the drink, the pianist shifted to a lovely melody, one it took her a minute to identify. *How Do You Keep the Music Playing?* he sang plaintively, though no one was paying much attention. Deirdre nodded in his direction, and would have left a generous tip had it been that kind of establishment.

The bartender waved off her ten-dollar bill for the wine, jerking his head to indicate that the two men still nursing their whiskey had taken care of it. She inclined her head in their direction and left.

When Deirdre pulled into the garage shortly before midnight, the front porch lights were ablaze, though the rest of the house appeared dark. She tiptoed up the stairs, peered into the children's rooms where they seemed to be asleep, then retired to hers.

Chapter Twelve

I n Deirdre's fitful dreams that night, Ashton and Dylan tussled over the violin, struggling *mano-à-mano* before Caitlin intervened with a knife. The girl cut the case in two and flung the two pieces out the window. They made a discordant thud on the patio, which in reality turned out to be the sounds of Dylan and Caitlin rattling pots downstairs in the kitchen. She eyed the alarm clock: 9:30 on a Saturday morning; she had overslept. Once again, she dressed with care, choosing a casual but attractive skirt and blouse from Coldwater Creek and coaxing her hair back into its new style. Starting down the staircase to join the children, Caedmon at her heels, she determined to be gay, and not to inquire about the play.

That's when she heard a third voice. It was Ashton's. She could smell bacon and hear the sizzle of a skillet. Low voices too. She walked toward the kitchen, the dog, well, doggedly at her side, as though shielding her from whatever danger lurked.

"Ah, you're in time. I'm making a mushroom and tomato omelette. If I counted the eggs right, it should be enough for everyone," Ashton said in as jaunty a voice as he ever used. Clad in his chef's apron and brandishing a metal spatula, he tilted the skillet to slide the implement under and fold half the egg mixture over the vegetables. Caitlin stood next to him deep in concentration over a frying pan, a long fork in hand, turning each bacon strip over, more than once.

As soon as he saw his mother, Dylan clambered to his feet, poured another glass of orange juice, and fished a dog biscuit from his pocket for Caedmon. "You look really nice, Mom. Your hair too," he added, before opening a nearby drawer and setting another place at the table.

Turning down the burner heat under the skillet, Ashton moved to the counter and poured two cups of coffee. "I made it extra strong because you weren't up yet, but there's milk in the fridge if you want to dilute it," he explained, handing a mug to his wife.

"Thank you," she replied. "I'll have it black."

"Your skirt too, so spring-like. Is it new?"

"From the closet, waiting for the right weather."

It was almost as though nothing were out of the ordinary, this family breakfast ritual, which only unsettled Deirdre further. She sat down at her usual place and sipped the hot coffee. In the center stood a vase of daisies which she surmised her husband must have brought over that morning. She wondered if they were meant to make amends or to offset some as yet undelivered indignity.

Going around to each plate, Caitlin placed several strips of bacon on each, apparently having cooked the entire package. "I tried to make them crisp, like you do, Mom, but they came out different from yours."

"They look fine, sweetheart. Hard to ruin unless they're burnt."

Behind her, Ashton slid a portion of the outsize omelette onto each plate, and Dylan placed a basket of toast next to the flowers. Butter and jam were passed around, but only the twins helped themselves. Silence soon fell over the table, Caedmon too taking his cue from the humans. After Caitlin handed him a slice of her bacon, he curled up at her feet without a whimper.

Deirdre concentrated on the egg dish, meticulously chewing each bite. Though too salty for her taste, she did not point that out. "The bacon is excellent, Caitlin. Crisp enough but still juicy." She ate both strips, then got up to pour herself another cup of coffee. She did not offer to refill her husband's.

When she sat back down, Ashton rose and followed suit, emptying the rest of the pot into his mug. Brother and sister exchanged a furtive look but kept on eating, their heads lowered toward their plates.

To Deirdre, they both appeared cowed, as though they had been talked to, and instructed not to make matters worse. She glared at her husband, daring him to try to explain himself. She had no desire to help him out.

The clock on the wall ticked over to 10:30, more loudly than usual, Deirdre thought. Perhaps it needed a new battery, though that made no sense at all. A lawnmower started up down the street and several dogs began to howl. Caedmon came alive and sidled over to Ashton, as though expecting to be taken out for a walk. Ignoring the whining, he set his empty mug down on the table and wiped his hands with a napkin.

"So, you two," he began, looking from one to the other of his children, "what is it you have on tap for today?"

"Band rehearsal at noon. Sammy's picking me up," Dylan said, finishing up his second piece of toast.

"Riding my bike to ballet class, like in thirty minutes, and then over to Monica Ferris's," Caitlin chimed in, as if on cue. "Her mother's letting us try on costumes her older daughters wore."

Straight-forward rundowns, no hemming-or-hawing, no extraneous requests on their part. Deirdre suspected the two had rehearsed or had been rehearsed by their father—like in a Sam Shepard play about family dysfunction.

"Sounds good, right, Deirdre?" he asked breezily, finally looking his wife's way.

She ignored him. "In that case, you can take Caedmon out before you leave, Caitlin. And Dylan, please take the garbage out before you set off."

They both nodded, with no demurrals.

"So may we be excused now?" Dylan asked, unsure as to whom to address the request. Ashton crossed his arms but deferred to his wife.

"Of course. You're both excused."

However much everyone had been on their best *"Leave it to Beaver"* behavior, this had been no ordinary meal. Part of Deirdre wanted to pipe up with a plan of her own, some interesting thing to do on a weekend that in a previous existence would have enticed her husband as well. In such an instance, they would have dumped their dishes in the sink, hurried upstairs, energetically made love, taken quick showers in adjoining bathrooms, even more quickly dressed, jumped in the car and headed off for a weekend in the mountains or along the Lake Erie shore. Had this ever happened in real life? She racked her brain for a memory of such conjugal togetherness. To no immediate avail. She downed the last of her coffee and set her cup down.

"You look preoccupied and no doubt have important things to do today," Ashton hazarded (without any trace of sarcasm but irritating her nonetheless). "But I did come over expressly. Things are moving at warp speed, things you need to know about."

Deirdre darted him a look as though to say she wasn't all that enthralled by what was happening with him—and HER.

"Don't you think your own children need to be brought into this? They're not babies anymore."

"I'm well aware of that. In fact, they had the chance to visit with Jennifer last night, after the play. I believe they have absorbed what they need to know and are reconciled to..." Here Ashton twirled his hand, struggling for the appropriate characterization of the situation.

The gesture appeared so frivolous that Deirdre grew more hostile still. "Reconciled? To the implosion of our marriage and the disintegration of our family. Is that the state of affairs you were trying to summons?"

"Calm down, Deirdre. No need to be so damn dramatic," he reprimanded her, jerking his head in the direction of the back patio where Caitlin was tending to the dog. "There are complicated issues to thrash out. Once the kids are out of the way." He eyed his watch and sighed.

"Fine. Why don't you go do inventory in your study for whatever you might still need?. I'm going to rinse the dishes. Once they leave you can fill me in."

Without waiting for him to react, Deirdre began to clear the table. Ashton watched her for a moment but then quietly left to do as she had suggested.

By the time she had stacked the plates to dry of their own accord and scrubbed the two heavily encrusted skillets, Sammy's car had pulled up for Dylan. She took off her apron and brushed her teeth in the tiny bathroom adjacent to the pantry. A few minutes later, Caitlin came into the kitchen with her sports bag. Deirdre quickly wrote out a check for the monthly dance instruction fee. "I forgot it last week. Do apologize to Mrs. Swett."

"She won't mind, Mom." Caitlin stuffed it in her jeans and hoisted the strap of her bag across her shoulder. "We don't understand, Dylan and me, why Dad has to leave. You need to make him stay, you really do."

Bewildered, Deirdre didn't know how much her daughter knew or how much there was still to know herself. "Some things can't be helped, dear. But, to be clear: it's your father who is making the decision to leave. It is not I, nor you, nor Dylan."

Caitlin was biting her lip so hard a thin rivulet of blood trickled down her chin. Deirdre grabbed a napkin and wiped it away. "Everything will work out, so don't fret. Now go, go."

After she watched her distraught daughter pedal off on her English bike, Deirdre closed the front door and headed to Ashton's study. A violin concerto was playing softly on his console, Brahms, she surmised. She knocked on the closed French doors as she had always done. After what she feared might have transpired there, probably on the sofa she'd had had re-upholstered not six months ago, she no longer felt at ease in his inner sanctum, even with him there.

Ashton was rummaging through the drawers of his desk, having already amassed a pile of papers and folders on the top. "Tell me we have cardboard boxes around the house. I didn't think—"

"Unless I'm mistaken, there are a few in the attic, next to the Christmas ornaments."

"Anyway, this can wait," he concluded, tossing a couple of gold ball point pens on the desk and shutting the drawers.

"So, what is it I now need to know?"

He swallowed hard—she could see his adam's apple rise and fall—and indicated the sofa. She took a seat in the armchair; he arranged himself on the sofa.

"There's no other way to get this across, Deirdre. I'm in love with Jennifer Hazelton and she with me. We're going to be leaving here, together, and I've lined up a teaching job back in Pennsylvania, at Winslow."

A low groan escaped Deirdre. She grasped the armrests to keep her hands from shaking. Ashton tried not to be flustered by the look on his wife's face.

"I don't believe we've ever been there together but it's prestigious in its own way, Winslow is. The department is small but distinguished. In fact, Woodstone has needed help up there. It was he who—"

"I don't need to hear about your academic ascension, Ashton, nor what strings your old professor has pulled. What I've understood, no thanks to you, is that you've been fired for screwing one of your students, though Landry has been decent enough, or desperate enough, to have allowed you to resign."

Although offended by this interpretation of his career move, Ashton sucked in his breath and let his wife secrete what venom she had stored up.

"None of your behavior, needless to say, reflects well on me or our children, but I suspect you are no longer bothered by any adverse repercussions for us."

"That's not true and you know it. I came here expressly—"

"Oh yes, expressly," she said witheringly. "*Voilà* then: express yourself."

"I didn't come to gloat, Deirdre. I came because I believe in honesty. I needed to reveal that I have been transformed, drunk the elixir, as it were. I have found love, hopefully before it's too late."

Deconstructing this self-exculpatory peroration as self-serving drivel, Deirdre tossed her head in disdain. "Yes, I've seen her. Some thirty years your junior, and from what I've been told by those who assumed I already knew, or should know, her moneybags of a father is not too keen on such a—how would he couch it?—merger, and may very well have cut the purse strings."

"From whom did you hear that?" Ashton demanded, this latest rumor having not reached his ears.

"What difference does it make? If she's so in love with you, money won't matter."

"No, it won't. She's a brilliant student, *and* an amazing actress,"—(here he beamed with admiration for his lover's latest exercise of her talents)—"and from a prominent Philadelphia family. Money really isn't an issue."

"Of course not," she returned drily. "How plebeian of me. Your parents will doubtless be heartened to learn of her bloodlines. The two of you can compare portraits of your ancestors." (Part of Deirdre was enjoying this verbal firefight, at least the colorful sparks it threw off; Ashton less so.)

Although it wasn't yet noon, he scoured the coffee table and reached for a bottle of Glenfiddich. After pouring himself half a glass, he held the bottle toward his wife. She gestured with her hand to decline. He gulped almost half of the tawny liquid, causing his eyes to burn. (While he fortified himself, she turned her gaze to the bookcases, estimating that he must have accumulated well-nigh two thousand tomes during the last fifteen years. He would require a lot of cardboard boxes.)

"Dylan was right," Ashton eventually stated, his voice oddly tender. She swung her head back in his direction. "I mean, your hairdo and all. Very becoming." He took another swig of the liquor and replaced the glass on the lacquered tray.

Deirdre looked flummoxed by the compliment but did not want to be disarmed. This was war. "New girl at the salon in town," she said matter-of-factly.

He nodded almost imperceptibly and stared off into space. "Truth be told, Deirdre, finding love at our age is not a given. *The grave's a fine and private place, but none therein,*" he recited, gesturing with his hand for her to fill out the line. When she didn't oblige, he proffered his own gloss. "In other words, we must embrace what befalls us. *Carpe diem.*"

How unbearable he was becoming, Deirdre thought to herself. And she didn't enjoy Brahms, or Andrew Marvell, all that much either. "Oh yes," she eventually replied as chirpily as she could, "seize the day I should. Between cleaning the house, teaching my classes, trying to get published, monitoring the kids and making sure they stay clothed, fed and schooled, not to mention seeing to the pets, and tending to your needs, if not your wants—sure, that leaves plenty of time."

However blithely delivered, the bitterness of her words stung him. He scrambled to his feet and paced the floor. "Well, we each have to find happiness where we can. I only wish the same for you as I have been blessed with."

"So pious you are, when all you've done is have your brains fucked out, or over. Whatever the more pertinent preposition." Wielding this blow brought out beads of sweat on her brow, but it did land. In fact, seeing the dazed look on her husband's face, Deirdre momentarily regretted the coarseness of her tongue-lashing.

Murmuring to himself "no need, no need," Ashton ducked into the small bathroom right off the study and turned the faucet on. When he re-emerged, he looked less shaken.

"Perhaps it were best, Deirdre, if we let lawyers take it from here. Keep us from going at each other."

Hearing this brought tears to her eyes. "I guess this means you're asking for a divorce."

Looking contrite, Ashton nodded. "The timing will have to be worked out. But I—*we*—plan to leave town by early June. The sooner the better, or rather, the sooner the easier."

Deirdre stood still, trying to fathom the ramifications of this latest decision. "And the children?"

"I will want to see them as much as possible, but you know better than I. They're teenagers, they're in their own worlds now. They'll cope better than we think."

"Not like I," Deirdre murmured.

Eyeing his watch, Ashton pretended not to have heard her. "I have to go. We will talk during the week. The boxes can wait. All of this," he said, indicating all the furniture and the books that adorned his study.

She followed him in a daze to the door, where Caedmon had parked himself. Ashton reached down to rough the dog's ears, a gesture that to Deirdre was so redolent of the past—what was at one time the expansiveness of his affections—all of which had drawn her to him those years ago. All of which was now being obliterated.

"I heard such a haunting song last night. That restaurant out on Presidents Drive we had gone to years ago, and then never returned: *How Do You Keep the Music Playing?* A famous couple composed it, I believe. Anyway, they put their hearts into it, maybe because they were married."

"Deirdre, Deirdre," he sighed, shaking his head as though at his wits' end. He embraced her clumsily and tugged the door open.

Chapter Thirteen

During the weekend Roxane debated whether to take the violin back to the Coles or wait until Dylan next came over, at which point she would insist *he* take it home. The tense discussion at the Chinese restaurant had rattled her, leaving her convinced that Deirdre was none too pleased about her friendship with her children, especially not with her son.

All of that is behind me, she muttered, rubbing her dining room table vigorously with a cloth.

Later, moving through the apartment to water the plants and shelve books, she tried to focus on what she might do to support her friend through this difficult period—Deirdre was arguably the only female friend she had managed to cultivate in Oakville. She didn't dislike Ashton either, but he breathed more rarefied air, and kept his distance. And, Roxane was disoriented when couples broke apart. Reminded her too vividly of her mother, her stepfather and the succession of young men that followed. Not much older than her own students at Hillside High, including the twins, with whom she very much wanted to maintain a special bond.

As usual, she had not seen fit to confide in Deirdre about her own past. To describe depravity to someone so straitlaced would be pointless. Not to mention that she had asked her, in her professional capacity as an adjunct instructor, to pen a recommendation for her. *To this day*, she whispered aloud, reassured by how adroitly she had managed to assemble the pieces of a life, and to keep other people from tearing it down.

In short, the violin would have to wait.

What people don't know won't hurt them, Roxane figured out early on in life, despite what court-appointed psychologists had tried to pound into her.

"You must talk about what he did to you, Rox, honey. Don't keep things bottled up. About your mother too, all the things she did that made you uncomfortable."

Barely sixteen, she had nodded during those excruciating sessions but had clammed up when asked to describe what had gone on in that trailer park. Neither side in the trial thought it helpful to call her to testify, since neither the prosecution nor the defense was certain what she might say on the stand.

In *her* testimony, however, Mrs. Johnson argued that she had tried to defend her daughter from the assaults of her stepfather—the sole reason for stabbing him to death, she claimed—but the jury was unconvinced. The conviction put the woman away for eighteen years. As she was led away in handcuffs, she yelled for all in the crowded courtroom to hear: "You could have taken the stand, you little bitch, and defended your mama. Tried to keep him at bay, I did. Just like him, you is."

Seated in the third row, Roxane did not move a muscle nor deign to raise her head.

Whatever other facts of the case were in dispute, Mrs. Johnson had used her attractiveness to lure men and discarded them when she was done. Or, worse, when no longer interested herself, let them have a go at her daughter, starting, when was it? Around the time Roxane was thirteen. On to her own next admirer, the mother pretended not to have noticed, likely didn't care, and probably assumed her child reveled in the attention.

Sometimes, Roxane did enjoy these so-called attentions, especially as she realized her body could be a weapon, and used to her advantage.

After the spectacle in the courtroom, Roxane kept to herself, not wanting to open up to anyone. After eighteen months in foster care with a nice enough family—though given her proclivities, she spent most of it playing around with the couple's only son, at fourteen, even younger than she was. Oblivious of Roxane's conduct but concerned that their son had become inexplicably moody, they took it upon themselves to enroll their foster charge, now eighteen, in the nearest junior college.

Her life might have continued on a downward spiral, except for the fortuitous intervention of her roommate. Suzanne, a determined young woman who applied herself to her studies, while Roxane only ever racked up one-night stands and barely passable grades. Upon gaining acceptance to the U of Colorado to complete her degree, Suzanne handed her a parting gift.

"I would have used the ticket myself, but I've got to bone up before I transfer. It's nonrefundable; a trip to Paris might open your eyes—you know, to other things."

Having never been outside the state, let alone on an airplane, Roxane was dubious. But she held onto the ticket through the summer and a break-up with the only guy who seemed genuinely to like her. With no prospects and something close to a broken heart, she yearned to get away. Thus, in the aftermath of 9/11, when few Americans were venturing abroad, she rang Delta and was easily confirmed on a flight. She hopped a Greyhound across the country and on to JFK for travel on Oct. 4, 2001. It was the same day President Bush launched an attack on Afghanistan.

For Roxane, France would change everything, her time there dream-like. There she was a young, attractive American girl plopped down in a big, sophisticated city, filled with people who did big, sophisticated things—all in French. Something, her competitive juices perhaps, stirred in her. She would master the language by talking to everyone she came across, from the fishmonger in Montmartre to the salesclerks at Monoprix. She wandered into lectures at the Sorbonne by luminaries she had never heard of, but whom she applauded along with everyone else. Within six months, she had morphed, arguably, into a different person and concocted enough of a story to convince others that she was who she said she was. She even believed it herself.

By the time she returned to the States, Roxane had obtained a couple of embossed certificates attesting to her proficiency in the language and her familiarity with Gallic civilization. Enough, she figured, to land a job teaching somewhere. Anywhere but in Colorado.

After she sent out several dozen feelers and got no reply, a private high school in Ohio called her for an in-person interview.

"*Pourquoi pas?*" she asked herself.

Having learned that appearances matter, Roxane showed up in a knock-off Chanel suit and a string of fake pearls. In her handbag, she brought along a resumé (which fudged on the junior college front and exaggerated on the French front) and her certificates from Paris.

The principal and several members of the Hillside High board were impressed by the applicant's polish. Admittedly, she had no teaching experience, other apparently than private students of English in Paris, but she did speak eloquently about what efforts it took for teens to focus on learning and how important it was for teachers to empathize.

They offered her a job on the spot, starting in September 2005.

Not that Roxane hadn't performed her duties at Hillside with dedication, conducting lessons entirely in French, assigning homework on a consistent basis, and encouraging her pupils to converse among themselves in the language.

The principal was impressed enough to renew her contract the next year, and bump up her pay. Other teachers found the newcomer stand-offish, especially after she discouraged the attentions of the only unattached male instructor at the school, the biology teacher, Mr. Carrington, who doubled as the soccer coach.

"Something's a little off with her, wouldn't you say?" the longest-serving English teacher, a Miss Withers, had had occasion to opine to the junior English teacher not that long ago. This, after Roxane had shepherded a handful of pupils to a film at the Rivoli. "Wouldn't you know, a French movie even the college kids shouldn't be seeing," the elder instructor had snipped.

In the end, only Dylan, Caitlin, and Claudia, (who didn't know a word of the language but tagged along anyway), and one other boy, a senior whose parents didn't care what he did, met Roxane at the movie house for *Hiroshima Mon Amour*. None of the kids had the remotest idea what was going on in the film, though they all sat through it stoically enough. Roxane treated them to burgers thereafter, doing her best to recap what happened in France after the war, but by that hour, they had all, except for Dylan, lost interest.

A bridge too far, Roxane had had to admit, and concluded that she would be better suited to providing her insights to college kids. It was not long after that outing she approached Deirdre with the request for a recommendation.

As Roxane finished marking up her students' final exams, the doorbell rang. On the static-filled intercom was a male voice she didn't recognize. At 4 p.m. on a Saturday, she buzzed him up anyway. It was Mr. Carrington, who stood uncertainly at her opened door.

"Tryouts for the soccer team, but one of the newbies had a breakdown right on the field. Sobbing and everything," he began, jumping right in as to why he had shown up. "Said you were the only one who could vouch for her."

It didn't take long for Roxane to figure he was referring to Caitlin. "She's going through a lot, with her parents, so by extension..." She gestured to indicate enough said.

"I see. Well, not knowing whether you'd be home"—(Mr. Carrington scurried toward the front window)—"I left her down in the car." He peered through the shutters, presumably to make sure the distraught teenager was still there. "Could she come in? Says she doesn't want to go home, ever again. Maybe you can talk sense into her."

While Roxane considered this imposition, Daniel raked the room, his eyes soon alighting on the table where papers and magic markers were spread out.

"Oh, you're in the middle of grading tests. As we all should be," he added, trying for a back-handed compliment to her industriousness.

"I've practically finished. And besides, it *is* a Saturday."

He nodded in agreement. "Indeed. And a beautiful one too."

Neither knew how to proceed. Especially since he had been rebuffed before and she had other things on her mind, like a violin and a boy who played it. In any event, Daniel Carrington was way too prosaic for her taste.

"By all means, have her come up. I'll talk to her and together she and I will work it out." Roxane held out her hand. Hesitating for only an instant, he took it.

"OK, then. Thanks for doing this. She'll be up in a jiffy."

When Ashton got the call Saturday evening that Caitlin wanted him to pick her up and to stay the night with him, he glanced over at Jennifer, curled on his hotel room bed, and turned away to query Roxane. "Have you called my wife—I mean Deirdre? Why can't she do it? The child's not ill or anything, right?"

Sensing that the call might not go as she hoped, Roxane similarly turned her back to the distraught girl and declared *sotto voce*: "Your daughter expressly asked that *you* come, but, if it's inconvenient, I could drop her off. You'd need to tell me where."

After such a trying morning with Deirdre, this latest trial—a stubborn child who refuses to let things be as they are destined to be—was the last thing that Ashton wanted to contend with. Especially since Jennifer had assumed a bemused expression, as if to suggest familial entanglements were something supercilious that she was glad not to have to bother with. She reached to pour herself a glass of the sauvignon blanc her lover had ordered from the hotel's barebones room service.

Ashton shot her a sideways glance, vaguely irritated by her insouciance, and retreated further to the window. "All right, Roxane, I will drive over and take her home. What precisely is the problem?"

"I think it's clear, Dr. Cole, what is going on with the two of them. Right now they need reassurance."

"Is Dylan there too? Is that what you're saying?"

"Not right now but he has alluded to tensions at home. In my experience, children at that age are fragile creatures and seeing as a rug has been pulled out from under them, as it were."

Ashton made a face indicating helplessness, which Jennifer barely registered. She had picked up one of the hotel's promotional magazines touting Ohio's summer attractions, and was dog-earing a few pages. He sighed impatiently. "I'll be in front of your place in twenty minutes."

"I thought you and I were going out, to the movies," Jennifer said.

"Later," he replied, replacing the phone on the night table and scanning the room for his keys and wallet. "We can catch the late show. I've got to pick up my daughter and take her home."

"Something wrong with her?"

"Nothing serious. I should be back in an hour."

Jennifer picked up the remote and turned on the TV appended to the wall.

At Roxane's building, Ashton buzzed three times in rapid succession but declined to push open the door and go up. Instead, he paced out on the sidewalk, figuring she would see him and get the message. In a few minutes, she came down, violin case in hand, puffy-eyed Caitlin in her wake.

"Ah, I'm glad to get this back," he started out, reaching to take the instrument from her. Only then did he turn to greet his daughter. "You can tell me all about it in the car, sweetie, but first, thank Ms. Johnson for being so considerate."

Roxane clutched the girl by the shoulders. "Everything's going to be OK, Caitlin," she insisted, willing her to make eye contact. "You and your brother are welcome here any time. And you already have a splendid French accent," she added, trying further to encourage her.

"Sorry for the hassle, but thank you. I don't know why she...," Ashton babbled before turning to open the passenger side for his daughter. Caitlin got in.

When she got back upstairs, Roxane rang Deirdre and left a short message to the effect that Caitlin had stopped by late in the day and that Ashton was bringing her home. Oh, and that she had returned the violin to him.

As soon as familiar streets came into view, Caitlin realized that her father was driving straight to the house, not to the mysterious place where he must now be lodged. To which, maybe she really didn't want to go. She was too discombobulated to know what she wanted.

For his part, Ashton racked his brain for what might be the most persuasive thing to say to make his daughter see reason. After all, both of the twins had seemed taken with Jennifer after the play, bowled over by meeting a bonafide actress, so pretty, and so chummy with her father. He wanted the separation to proceed apace and couldn't understand why his children were making it so difficult. They would have a second woman in their lives and could come visit them often enough in Pennsylvania. He and Jennifer would lavish attention upon them, while their mother would now have more time to dedicate to their daily wants. If not ideal—and he was not prepared to say it was—it was a workable arrangement which for the kids would include extra benefits.

112

He slowed the Camry, having inadvertently exceeded the speed limit in the residential neighborhood where he himself officially lived.

"I didn't make the soccer tryout," Caitlin tossed out, like a minor hand grenade.

This was not a development that Ashton knew how to handle. *The things that throw kids for a loop*, he thought to himself. He took a deep breath at the last red light before turning onto the road toward home.

"Well, Caitlin, it's not the end of the world. Like your brother, you have other things to be involved with, in school and out."

"Like what?' she shot back, clearly dissatisfied with his response.

"I don't know. You have many talents, so focus on what you enjoy."

While she pondered this advice, Ashton pulled into the semi-circular driveway and put the car in park, but with the motor still running. He made no move to get out; she too sat there, not budging.

"So?" he eventually asked, looking her way and then to the well-lit porch.

"What I enjoy is you and Mom together in the house. More than soccer, more than ballet," she shouted, bursting into tears and fumbling with the handle to escape from the car. It only opened once Ashton turned the key off in the ignition.

Deirdre, who had been pacing the front hall, heard her daughter's voice, but it was Dylan, out walking the dog, who came running up to the car.

"What's going on, Dad? Are you back?" he asked anxiously, peering into the driver's side.

"Just dropping Caitlin off. She didn't make the soccer team. Nothing to worry about."

"Oh, I wasn't expecting that," Dylan exclaimed, opening the back door and retrieving the violin. "Thanks for bringing it. You must have stopped at—"

"We'll talk about it another time," Ashton said, unprepared to be relinquishing the family violin, even into the arms of his own son.

(Truth be told, Dylan didn't play all that well and wasn't likely to get into Harvard, but that discussion would be for another time.) Out the car window, he saw Deirdre bounding off the porch steps toward them. "I've really got to go, son. I'm late. Let her know," Ashton quickly added, revving the engine.

Disconcerted, Dylan stepped back, Caedmon started barking, Caitlin ran past her mother into the house.

On the drive back to town, Ashton tried to fight off the feeling that he was losing control of a situation which hours before he had heralded as a renaissance of the soul. Had he actually said that to his wife? Perhaps he had gone too far, his flights of fancy getting the best of him. No wonder she had tried to bring him down a peg or two.

At every stop sign and every red light back to the Elm St. Arms, Ashton sank deeper into a funk. He switched the radio on, but PBS was going on about home foreclosures. He turned it off.

Still, he reasoned, marriages—half of them—did not last, and many of those that did endure, did so only because the parties involved had no other options.

But HE? He had Jennifer and was—he saw it in his colleagues' eyes, and in those of strangers—a goddamn lucky son-of-a-bitch. *Bright hair about the bone*, he mouthed to himself. He wondered if Jennifer would be reading poetry when he entered the room or scouring the draft of his monograph he had (purposefully) left on the table. (Writing another book right now would be too taxing, he had recently determined; a pithy textual analysis of forty-odd pages would be just as useful to his fellow scholars.) Or, perhaps she was in the shower, lathering those gorgeous breasts and he could slip in right behind her...

A car honked and he lurched out of the intersection.

Still, there's a long way to go before all this is sorted out, he reflected. Deirdre's face as she approached the Camry spoke volumes. For an instant, he saw elation in it at the thought that he had come back to hearth and home; but it quickly morphed into misery as he sped off, without a word.

Ashton flinched at the idea of his own callousness.

And yet, the break-up wasn't solely because of Jennifer, he assured himself. Of its own accord, the marriage had unraveled. For longer than he cared to remember it had become—what would be the most apt word, one that stated the case without prejudice?—: *perfunctory* was the adjective that swam into view.

He looked out the window now that he had nosed into downtown and cars were bumper to bumper. Nothing to do about it except inch along, trying not to hit any of the young people crossing the street wherever and whenever they chose.

Anyway, that's what his marriage was like, had been like, for well-nigh a decade;: a monotonous routine, like cars endlessly idling on a Saturday night.

To be fair, it wasn't always thus. When they first met at that conference in Milwaukee, Deirdre had been as exhilarated by hearing him deconstruct John Donne as she had been exhilarating in describing Petrarch's ascent of some remote mountain. Her gray-green eyes lit up as they walked the streets of the city that last night, each holding forth on the merits of their respective fields, each venturing into other areas of shared artistic delight: he, quoting Keats, she, Shakespeare; he, proclaiming Brahms' second violin concerto the quintessence of music: she, that it was impossible to tire of the Brandenburg concertos; he, recalling the winter day he stood in front of Rembrandt's *The Night Watch* at the Rijksmuseum, and knew in his bones that the Renaissance meant spiritual warmth: she, conjuring the moment she came upon the medieval masterpiece by Uccello in the Uffizi. All the way to the restaurant he had chosen (having interrogated the hotel concierge for one that was elegant but casual, with good food but decent prices), where they talked nonstop over the wine and the fish, he ending on a high note. He would be writing her soon, and perhaps, depending on his job offers and her ongoing job search, they could meet up again. She had looked crestfallen. By the time he had walked her back to her hotel, she had grown quiet.

Ashton did not have vast experience with young women, other than with the students he was teaching, so he tried to make amends. "You've obviously been to Europe, but I don't know that you've ever visited Boston. At the end of the summer, you might, well, you might see fit to come up." She had brightened at this but waited for him to put into words what he had in mind. "My family is stuffy—Cotton Mather and so forth—but there is the Museum of Fine Arts and the Boston Symphony. You and I could—"

He had been tongue-tied for someone so admired as a wordsmith.

"I'd like that," she broke in, and in the middle of the lobby, planted a soft kiss on his forehead. "Thank you for a lovely evening."

If Ashton remembered rightly, he had skipped down the sidewalk toward his own lodgings. This young woman, he reckoned, must be ten or twelve years his junior, which mirrored the age difference between his parents. To his unbeknownst, they had selected one or another of their friends' progeny as possible mates for him, (albeit he had chosen to go into teaching, of all things, rather than into law or banking or the ministry).

Before he fell asleep that night in Milwaukee, all those years ago, he had composed in his head the invitation he would send the young woman, to that delightfully obscure address: Riverton, Mississippi. She had not said much about it, nor about her family, but what difference did that make? His parents would be charmed, he would work on landing a job in a place less irrelevant than the Green Mountains—he could count on his former professor, Dr. Woodstone, to pen (yet another) glowing recommendation for a professorship somewhere—and Deirdre, well, she had her own Ph.D. in hand, from somewhere in the South, so, surely, for her too it shouldn't be impossible to land somewhere contiguous, dwindling interest in the Middle Ages notwithstanding. He had fallen asleep thinking of her expressive eyes and mobile lips and other parts he hadn't had the courage to inspect more thoroughly.

(The traffic in downtown Oakville had come to a complete halt up ahead, raised voices and beer cans rolling on the asphalt could be heard. A couple of drivers had stepped out of their cars to see what all the trouble was about. Ashton glanced at the clock on the dashboard, 8:50 p.m. He could have kicked himself for not taking the back route. He did not think that to keep Jennifer waiting a good idea. He tapped his car horn, the only result being the fellow up ahead gave him the finger. Soon, he heard a police siren and saw a flashing red light up ahead. He thumped on the steering wheel and tried to remain calm.)

At a standstill, he couldn't get the image of his wife's pained expression out of his mind, so different it was from the look of admiration she had radiated in those early years. She had, as agreed, come to Boston over the Labor Day weekend in '92, and immediately upon arrival at Logan, he had whisked her off to the symphony. "Serendipitous," he had exuded, "as the soloist tonight is performing the Brahms Second." She had looked non-plussed for an instant but then burst out, laughingly, having remembered it was his favorite. He did not tell her about the family violin or that he played "rather well," if the praise of those who heard him on the instrument could be believed. He would only do so during this visit if he sensed he needed to further impress her.

They took a cab afterwards to the hotel he had reserved for her, a small one not far from his family home on Beacon Hill. "Tomorrow, when you're up and about, I'll show you around Harvard, and then you can meet my parents."

Deirdre had looked vulnerable at that latter prospect, so he took her hand and squeezed it. Her eyes were bright as she squeezed back but she didn't kiss him. "I'm tired now—(it had taken an entire day to travel from Riverton to Boston)—but you may call me any time after 9:30. Walking around the area would be splendid."

Things had gone well the following morning, as the weather was warm, and Deirdre appeared in a colorful sundress with matching jacket. The outfit looked brand new to Ashton, girlish yet conservative enough not to upset his mother. She had seemed in awe of Harvard Yard and made a point of asking that he show her where he had lodged as an undergraduate. By coincidence, they ran into Dr. Woodstone, who was on his way to one of the seminars he taught. "I say, Cole, have you heard back from any of those places? You could do worse than Ohio."

Deirdre stood demurely, without speaking, while Ashton hedged a response. "Still considering. I'll let you know when I commit. But thanks for the letter-writing."

The older professor smiled and looked approvingly at his former student's friend. "Are you a Cliffie, my dear?"

"Oh, I'm sorry. This is my friend Deirdre. She's visiting. Degrees from down south." The professor nodded absent-mindedly, and hurried on.

"He looks kindly, and distinguished," Deirdre had observed but without asking him to elaborate on the reference to Ohio, or spelling out her alma mater.

(Up ahead, cars were beginning to move, thanks to an Oakville cop directing traffic in the middle of the upcoming intersection. Several young men were being talked to by two other policemen at the curb, and a small crowd had gathered to watch. Beer cans littered the area but there didn't seem to be any broken glass. A minor ruckus in the scheme of things. As Ashton weaved through the intersection, he glanced at the brightly lit movie theater across the way, the one Jennifer had said she'd like to go to. Some picture with George Clooney she and her friends wanted to see. He didn't focus on films all that much, nor had he been to that particular cinema in years, the last time with the kids to see some Disney thing.)

Come to think of it, movies had come up that night at the dinner table at his parents, after his father had shepherded Deirdre through the portrait gallery. Once the veal roast and the vegetables had been served, Deirdre praised the concert they had attended the night before, more lavishly than she should have. "I take it you have a decent orchestra there—here Ashton's father waved his fork around trying to conjure Riverton—where you grew up?"

"It's a tiny place, I'm afraid," she had stammered, not knowing where to look. "We're lucky to have a movie theater."

118

"Oh, my," his mother had interjected, as though their guest had revealed that she had come from a distant planet with no amenities whatsoever.

Insufferable his parents were.

As he approached the Elm St. Arms, Ashton was seized by the same benumbed sensation he had felt that evening sixteen years ago. Why he had subjected his fiancée to his parents' vetting, knowing they'd clamor to get their teeth into her, he couldn't now say. Later, when she told him good night at her hotel, she didn't take his hand nor look him in the eye.

Rather, she had spelled out life's challenge to him: "I don't blame your parents. They inhabit a different world. I only hope that you're not wrapped up in theirs."

He had been newly enamored at that moment.

Still, the Coles took to dismissing Deirdre as "that poor Delta girl" whenever subsequently Ashton brought up her name, which he did less and less until eight months later. At thirty-five, he had landed an associate professor position in Ohio—and, he further announced, he would wed that June, in Riverton, which would be too remote a place and require too onerous a journey for his parents to make. The happy couple would send pictures.

After maneuvering the car into the parking garage behind the Elm St. Arms and relinquishing ten dollars and the keys to the attendant, Ashton reverted his thoughts to the woman upstairs. He suspected that Jennifer, so languidly self-confident, would acquit herself on Beacon Hill with such aplomb that his parents would be, finally, put in their place. *Far be it from her to be cowed, not by Cotton Mather himself*, he snickered.

And, if his lover still wanted to go out to the movies, then, whatever the hour, they would go.

Chapter Fourteen

B y the end of June, Caitlin had devolved into a cutter, the slices into the unsuspecting flesh of her inner thigh and her left forearm arranged into two neat hashtags. She had grown sullen when at home, spending most of her time with Claudia and Lou, the latter having dropped out of college to put together a rock band. So far, the young man had gotten only as far as his Aunt Stella's garage, where he had set up shop for the summer. When he wasn't strumming a guitar or tinkering with his rundown ride, he was smoking pot or figuring out ways to obtain more. And when he was flush, he doled it out to the chicks in his life. Caitlin was one of the flock.

Preoccupied with the breakup of her marriage, Deirdre only noticed what was happening one evening when her daughter struggled to pull off her sweatshirt over her head. Seeing the bright pink slashes, she grabbed the teen's arm. "What on earth have you been doing?" she demanded.

Caitlin wrenched her arm away. "Leave me alone. Can't you see—" and ran up the stairs, slamming her bedroom door behind her.

"It's a thing, Mom. You'd be surprised how many girls do it," Dylan interjected, trying to diffuse the situation, and defend his sister.

"Well, I don't want my daughter doing anything so awful. Worse than a tattoo," she responded, shivering at the thought of a knife edge. "What's gotten into her?"

Dylan shrugged, the question needing no answer. He too missed his father but knew it was futile, and counterproductive, to bring up anything but the occasional neutral reference to him. As a result, he had stopped weekend fishing trips or hikes in the woods—jaunts that heretofore included his dad—and devoted his energies to schoolwork or to the violin.

The only person he felt relaxed enough to confide in was Roxane, who, despite being a teacher, rarely seemed judgmental or shockable. Besides, whenever they spoke French together, which as he became proficient they did more often, he felt lifted out of himself. So much so, that one afternoon after she had read a passage to him from Marcel Proust (much of which was over his head but not all), he posed a question: Did she believe in *folie d'amour* and is that what had happened to his father with this Jennifer?

Roxane slowly put down the volume of *Swann's Way* and supported her chin in her hand, pondering. "I do believe in such a thing, Dylan, and I suspect your father was as swept away by his passion as any of the characters we've been reading about." When his face fell at this assertion, she modified her thought: "That doesn't mean he doesn't love you and Caitlin, and even your mother, but only that he couldn't resist what was happening to him."

Dylan weighed her words, sipping the hibiscus tea she favored in the afternoon. Reverting to English, he remarked: "We met her, Jennifer, I mean, a couple of times. She's hot—(he blushed, never having used such a crass word with his teacher)—you know, attractive enough, but didn't seem like our dad's type." He paused before ruefully adding, "Not so much, in any case, as to do what he did."

They were slipping into uncharted territory, Roxane realized, and rushed to inch them back onto more solid ground. "Time will tell, *mon ami*, but whatever happens, you will always be your father's son. I have no doubt but that you will make him proud."

Nodding evasively, he picked up one of her lemon cookies. She patted the arm of his chair to signal an end to the subject and stood up. "For the time being, we have to concern ourselves with your sister, *n'est-ce pas*?"

"*Justement*," he agreed. "Mom could really use some advice."

Thanks to the opinions she was now getting from Margery, Stella and Roxane, Deirdre had begun to train herself to spot behavioral changes in her children, and as her friends urged, intervene to nip anything untoward in the bud. Cutting into one's own flesh for the pleasure of it counted as untoward. After she discovered what recklessness Caitlin was up to, she began to eye her son closely too. Twins tended to do things in tandem, unwise things too.

One evening, Dylan was sprawled on the sofa, intent on a required text for his upcoming world history class in the fall. Several other volumes were piled on the table in front of him. For the better part of a month he had been studying downstairs, keeping his mother company, compensating for his sister's absence.

"You'd think she could emulate you once in a while," Deirdre stated resignedly. Dylan looked up, not comprehending. "Caitlin. Cutting herself like that."

"She'll come around, or you could tell her she can't go to ballet camp if she doesn't tow the line," he suggested. "*That*, I know she's dying to do."

Deirdre nodded, glad for the heads-up, even if it entailed another blow-up from Caitlin before getting any cooperation. She'd have to hear how her father would never have been so unfair as to prevent her from going to camp or so mean as to make her do boring things around the house. She had in a few short weeks heard enough recriminations to last a lifetime, and was just starting to grow thick enough skin not to be bruised by each assault.

Cigarettes helped. She calculated she had gotten up to a dozen Virginia Slims a day, pledging not to exceed that number.

The divorce lawyers who were brought in also helped.

Hers was a plodding sort named Howard Morrison, who had handled the college's financial matters for more than a decade but apparently found divorce proceedings more lucrative, if more stressful. Ashton's was a bouncy attorney named Willa Worthington, who had recently made partner in Oakville's leading law firm. They had instructed their respective clients that spousal communications needed to be routed through them, "for the interim."

That Deirdre was searching around for an ashtray every time they came over did not appear to faze them. Nor did the state of the house or the sullenness of the children. As far as the attorneys were concerned, keeping things civilized between husband and wife was their primary preoccupation. When Ashton came over in mid-June for a formal visit with the children, his lawyer took copious notes; Deirdre's sat quietly in his rumpled linen suit.

The encounter was nonetheless stilted.

Caitlin tugged on stray wisps of her hair and smacked gum throughout, Dylan rattled on about what he had (supposedly?) caught up on the White River, listing every exotic species that he could think of, and leaving his father visibly unsettled. The two opposing lawyers then stood sentry-like at the sliding French doors as Ashton went into his study to append blue tape to the items to have shipped to Pennsylvania: his roll-top desk, his stereo console, most of his books and the pictures on the wall, including the waifs disembarking from the *Mayflower*.

Puffing away on a Virginia Slim, Deirdre did not demur. She had become resigned.

Then, in a gesture that surprised her, her husband said, "The Globe-Wernickes should remain here. All four were acquired together and rightly belong together."

Inclining her head in gratitude, she would have spoken up, but the bouncy one beat her to the punch.

"This went well," Willa declared, clapping her hands in approbation. "Two esteemed professors behaving in such exemplary fashion. It's an honor," she further enthused, thrusting her hand toward opposing counsel and then toward his client.

For the first time in ages, Deirdre exchanged a look of complicity with Ashton. His lips curled at the edges, the closest he ever came to laughter.

Despite the buffer of lawyers and the solace of cigarettes, Deirdre did suffer relapses. When the appointed day came that the two lovers were to relocate to Pennsylvania, she drove over and parked down the street from Jennifer's apartment complex. The clock on the Volvo's dashboard flashed 11:25 a.m., and knowing how punctilious her husband was, she expected activity on the half-hour. Taking several long draws, she debated whether to get out of the car when the time came and confront her husband. But what would she say? That Caitlin was a cutter, that Dylan moped around like a whiny schoolgirl, that she herself had terminal cancer—that she wished *he* had terminal cancer.

Or, arguably, as Howard Morrison had counseled, there was nothing more to say. She'd just watch.

Right on schedule, the front doors were propped open and Ashton staggered out under the weight of a huge trunk. From a distance, he looked intent, whether also exuberant she couldn't say. Setting the thing on the pavement, he used his legs to slide it out to the curb and, taking a deep breath, hoisted it into the back of a U-Haul. And went back inside. A few minutes later, he emerged again, this time wheeling a clothes rack on which were hung countless dresses and jackets. After he made a few more trips lugging cardboard boxes, Jennifer materialized, a pet-carrying case in one hand and a handbag slung over her shoulder. Her blond hair was pulled back in a pony tail. She looked no older than Caitlin.

Back at the front door, Ashton exchanged a handshake with someone, presumably the owner of the house. He looked red in the face from over-exertion or embarrassment, or both. He wiped his forehead with a handkerchief—he was not the kind of man who approved of Kleenex—and then approached Jennifer, relieving her of the cage. A cat, Deirdre gathered, the craze for hamsters in college dorms long past. Carefully, he placed the contraption on the back seat of the car and then opened the passenger door for Jennifer. From the vantage point of the Volvo, it looked as though he threw his arms around his lover, but almost instantly she disentangled herself and ducked into the Camry. Then they were gone.

Tossing her cigarette out onto the sidewalk, Deirdre drove aimlessly around town before pulling up at an animal shelter not far from the Rivoli. Deciding then and there that Caedmon needed a companion, and competition, she selected a twitchy siamese with green eyes and pink paws. The manager told her the feline had come from a troubled home.

"Not a problem. I'm used to such," she deadpanned.

Elizabeth Guider

Chapter Fifteen

Toward the end of the summer, Deirdre did a word count of her opus. Encouraged by Margery and Stella, she had carved out three to four hours a day to write, setting a target length of 75,000 words for the completed draft. Per the computer, she had hit 69,000, and had but two more chapters to tackle. As the research started to bear fruit—especially after Dylan headed off to a camp on Lake Erie and Caitlin to an arts workshop outside Cincinnati—she narrowed her focus to one single, exceptional woman of the period, to re-examine her trajectory and track her influence. Her goal, as she expounded on it principally to Margery (who astutely raised issues Deirdre had not hitherto considered) but also to Stella and even to Roxane, was no less than to re-evaluate the much-maligned Middle Ages, so that the reader would come away appreciative of its relevance.

It was left to Margery to sound the cautionary notes, telling her friend to get her facts right first, and only then use her imagination to take the reader as far as those facts would allow.

"I know, I know, Margery. My first obligation is to contribute to the academic canon. But, I want to emphasize how this literary-inclined woman, however removed in time, handled her life challenges. Truth be told, I'm beginning to identify with Christine de Pizan. Even dream about her!"

"Now that, my dear, may very well be going too far," Margery had rejoined only half-facetiously.

Deirdre rushed to allay any concern on her colleague's part that she had become obsessed, or obsessive. "However, like Christine, I'm having to take stock of my life. Remember, I followed Ashton here, but now that he's gone, I have to ask if this will remain the place for me once the kids strike out on their own." She hesitated, then added: "For another thing, I look at you—at the top of your game—and doubt that I'll ever scale such heights."

"You exaggerate, my dear, but let me be frank," Margery replied, taking another sip of coffee and wondering suddenly what her friend did in that big house without her husband, and now without her children. "You're still a young woman, vibrant and interesting. Ashton, for all his good qualities, is hardly the only fish in the sea."

Deirdre's cheeks reddened. "So little time, and so much to attend to, I haven't—"

"Be that as it may, you may want to ponder that aspect of your life," Margery said, her tone wistful. "I didn't, and, well, here I am after forty years at the same game. Alone."

At this unexpectedly personal admission, Deirdre was at a loss for words.

"No need to go into anything now," Margery quickly halted the discussion, depositing her coffee cup in its saucer and checking the watch on her arm. "But don't forget 'time's *winged chariot.*' We must all seize the day, or it passes us by." She patted her hostess on the arm and gathered her things to leave. "Meanwhile, keep at the book. If you can write about Christine de Pizan as well as you've described her to me, it will be fine."

Deirdre took some of Margery's advice to heart.

Throughout the six weeks that Dylan and Caitlin were away, she let the house clean itself, ordered in on a regular basis, and when she did cook, invited either Roxane or Stella over to share a meal. Occasionally, she ran a theme or two from her book by them, though trying hard not to bore them or make them feel uncomfortable.

"You'd be amazed what a few of these women managed to achieve—despite having to contend with the demands placed on them by their fathers, husbands or brothers," she had enthused one evening when Roxane had come over for grilled shrimp out on the patio. "Not only was my heroine, as it were, a fearless force of nature, but she could do literary battle with the best and brightest—all men, of course!"

Roxane listened politely but had the blank look of someone out of her depth. She methodically peeled her shrimp and ate her salad, not daring to pose a question directly related to her friend's field of research. (Teaching at the college level was different from what she did at Hillside High, though she had no intention of rescinding her request for that recommendation.)

"Anyway, I hope I haven't bored you to tears, Roxane. I do get carried away sometimes."

"Not at all. And, I hope you don't mind my saying so, but you look as though a weight has been lifted, now that—well, now that things with Ashton have been more or less—you know what I mean," she had babbled, not knowing where things stood but certain that progress had been made toward finalizing the divorce.

And it had.

Deirdre no longer awoke in the middle of the night in anger or in desperation to reach over and touch her husband asleep next to her. Now, if she were suddenly awakened, she would lie quietly and think about her book, or consider how to do better by her children, or draw up lesson plans for the course in the modern novel she had taken on to stretch her budget.

In short, as the Ohio summer waned, things were going better than she had hoped.

Toward the end of August, both Dylan and Caitlin would be returning. After six weeks tooling around the house on her own, she was eager for their company, relieved that their texts had been upbeat, and that neither had mentioned their father. She did wonder how much contact they had had with him, and with Jennifer, but she had no intention of asking. There would be plenty else to talk about and get ready for: their junior year at Hillside, band rehearsals, ballet lessons, whatever other extra-curricular activities—and now that they had turned sixteen, getting their driver's licenses. No more dependence on Sammy or Claudia for rides.

On this last score, Deirdre had a surprise to spring on them: a new car. Well, not literally new, as it was second-hand, and, of all things, it was courtesy of their Boston grandparents. They were, she gathered when she got the call from them, anxious not to lose their hold on the children, whatever visitation rights Ashton might secure. She thanked her in-laws, emphasizing that their timing was impeccable and that the kids would be over-the-moon. (By her reckoning, the Honda Civic was the only extravagant gift the Coles had ever made to the family, though unspecified sums had apparently been deposited now and again to Ashton's account at Ohio Guaranty.)

The very morning of the twins' return, Deirdre was obliged to attend orientation at Klimpton, a chore she couldn't shrug off. In fact, after weeks in mostly sweats, she dressed meticulously in a silk suit and opted for her Ferragamo heels (the only designer shoes she owned). As the recently spurned spouse of a full professor, she did not want anyone to come away thinking she was so dowdy as to have deserved her fate. After feeding the pets, she sped over to the college.

Stella, in her usual take-charge manner, waylaid her in the hall, pulling her into an empty office. "You no doubt know about the cutbacks. Enrollment is off too. It appears you'll only be allotted one course this quarter, though they say things will pick up soon."

Deirdre looked flustered. "Others too? What about Margery?"

"Not sure in her case. Shakespeare is Shakespeare." Stella gesticulated to indicate the Bard would always be popular. When her colleague didn't respond, she lowered her voice further: "The good news is you should now have more time to finish your book, which you should do," she emphasized before heading back to the dean's office.

Taken aback, Deirdre suddenly thought of that funny bank error a year or so ago, $9000 deposited to her account by the Coles that, had she not said anything, Ashton would probably never have missed. She wondered to what extent his life had all along been subsidized by his parents. That he wore only the plushest of cashmere sweaters throughout the winter had always struck her as endearing rather than extravagant. She made a mental note to call Howard Morrison that afternoon to arrange a consult.

And, unfortunately, Stella was right. As an adjunct instructor in the newly streamlined department, Deirdre was assigned to a single introductory class for freshmen called *Lighting up the Dark Ages*, which title she silently deplored. (She would deal with the financial implications later.) Without waiting for a rundown on classroom assignments and scheduled holidays, she rushed home to tidy up before the children's arrival.

Only then did she notice dark clouds scudding by and wind rustling the tree branches.

Depending on whether the weather held and what else the twins might have going, she would take them out to the garage that evening or delay the surprise. While she was dusting the upstairs bedrooms, a car door slam. Hurriedly, she ran a cloth over the dresser in Caitlin's room, lifting a pair of scissors and a small pearl-handled knife with a sharp blade to dust under them. She held the knife for a moment but did not remove it.

At the front door stood her son, more filled-out, his face sun-kissed. He dropped his duffel bag and gave her a bear hug.

"Stand back and let me look at you," Deirdre exuded, breaking away and inspecting him from head to toe. "All that paddling seems to have paid off!"

Dylan laughed. "Yeah, canoeing is not as easy as it looks. But, I almost forgot. I hitched a ride with a friend. Mind if we invite him in, like, for supper and to spend the night? He doesn't want to start the drive home until morning."

"By all means," she quickly replied, glancing out the still- open door at a mud-encrusted Range Rover. She could hear the engine idling. "You two can clean up and relax. It must have been a long drive, rainy. Make yourselves a snack or show him around town. We'll wait for Caitlin before we eat."

"I'll get the rest of my things. You'll like Zach. He'll be a freshman at Penn, on an athletic scholarship. And, he plays the clarinet."

While the two young men lugged their bags upstairs, Deirdre set about peeling potatoes and cutting up broccoli spears to go with the shrimp dish and her fruit salad. She had not felt so eager to make something elaborate for months.

Zach, a strapping young man with a shock of unruly blond hair, further enhanced her mood. More poised than most young men in her classes, he looked her in the eye when speaking, and held out his hand to thank her for her hospitality.

Delighted that Dylan had made friends with someone so presentable—someone, as her mother used to say, who was "raised rather than jerked up"—she let herself imagine that her daughter might be similarly impressed, and not persist in hanging out with the addle-brained Lou, even if he was Stella's nephew.

Once she heard the upstairs bathroom shower faucet on, Deirdre took off her apron and poured herself a glass of chianti. It was 6:10 by the kitchen clock, Mrs. Swett having told her the several camp attendees from Oakville would likely be back in town by 6 p.m. She wandered into the living room, put Mozart piano sonatas on the CD player, and sat down in one of the armchairs. Cookie the siamese soon jumped into her lap, curled up and went to sleep. For a few minutes Deirdre did the same, drifting off to an *andante amabile*.

Suddenly, she was jolted awake. The phone was ringing in the hallway. The cat scampered as Deirdre got herself up and went to answer it. By the time she did, whoever it was had hung up. She turned toward the grandfather clock at the end of the hallway. It was almost 7 p.m. Had Mrs. Swett failed to specify that she'd be driving the van back to her studio rather than taking each girl home? Deirdre searched in the phone book for the number of the studio. While she was dialing, the two young men came down the stairs.

"She not home yet?" Dylan asked.

Deirdre hushed him while she listened to the answering machine at Mrs. Swett's ballet academy: a routine rundown of upcoming classes, nothing about any proposed pick-ups.

"How about I ring Caitlin on her cell?" Dylan interjected, pulling his device from his belt. Zach stood by silently as Dylan hit speed dial. The phone rang and rang. "Funny," he mumbled. "Her voicemail didn't come on. You never know with my sister," he added, more for Zach's benefit than his mother's.

"Not to worry. I've made a dip and there are crackers and cheese. You two can sit in the living room or out on the back patio with Caedmon," Deirdre suggested. Seeing Zach nonplussed, she added, "He's our golden retriever." Then, looking more determined, she said to Dylan: I'll drive over to the dance studio as I may be supposed to pick her up there."

Putting his hand on his mother's arm, Dylan tried to make her see how pointless that would be. "Mom," he said, as though remonstrating with a child, "if she were there, she'd call us to come get her. Or, if her phone were broken, someone else would call."

"He's right, Dr. Durrell," Zach chimed in. "We use our cells for everything."

Looking more anxious with every tick of the grandfather clock, Deirdre pressed her hand hard on her brow, as though to summons the best course of action. Dylan pulled out his phone again and texted his sister. It did not appear to go through. A cloud passed over his face.

"If you like, Dylan and I can go in the Range Rover and see if that's where she is. You can stay here in case she calls the home phone."

"I have a cell too," Deirdre pointed out distractedly, "but you're right. She'd ring me on this one."

Without waiting for objections, the two headed out. The rain had slacked off. "You do know where the studio is, right?" Deirdre called out, her voice high-pitched. "Be careful."

"Got it," Dylan responded, waving her off. He jumped into the passenger seat and Zach set off.

Alone again, Deirdre tried to imagine if she had gotten things mixed up—the wrong day, the wrong time, the wrong pick-up plan. She hurried upstairs to her daughter's room and rummaged around for a flyer or brochure with phone numbers for the Midwest Music and Arts Camp but found nothing. She did come across a stack of photos of her daughter, with various friends, mostly, it appeared, Claudia and Lou. No time to bother about that, she thought.

Back downstairs by the phone, she scanned the pages of the writing tablet. She had penciled in a number next to the dates July 1-August 18, which must have been the camp, a Cincinnati area code. She dialed it. A young woman eventually picked up. Indeed, camp activities had "wrapped" late the night before and yes, all the attendees had been signed out by 4 p.m. that afternoon. What was the name again she was looking for?

"Caitlin Felicity Cole," Deirdre said, pronouncing each syllable distinctly.

Yes, she and two other girls, Monica Ferris and Amber Reardon, had checked out together at 2:15 p.m. Deirdre had a fuzzy recollection of the two from past dance recitals, both high on their toes in their tutus and pink slippers, doll-like, just like her daughter, at least when on stage. She hung up the receiver without another word and paced the hall, her stomach starting to churn.

As soon as Deirdre caught sight of her son and his friend coming up the porch steps from the dance studio, she knew something terrible had happened.

"There was a wreck on the interstate and the van was totaled, Mom. The girls and Mrs. Swett have been taken to two different hospitals, depending..."

Mother and son embraced while Zach hurried to the kitchen to pour them some water. Both were sobbing when he handed them the glasses. In a minute Dylan got hold of himself. "The cops are on their way with more news," he said. "Let's wait outside on the porch."

"Do we know if Caitlin—do we know which hospital she is in?" Deirdre asked, her voice thin.

The police, a flashing red light atop their car, pulled up shortly thereafter. They did not looked pleased to be messengers. Caitlin and another girl had been transported from the scene to the regional hospital which served Oakville as well as several other localities. "We can escort you once we've alerted the other families, or you can go on your own, if you're up to it," one of the cops said.

"We can handle it," Zach told the policemen. "You just have to tell me how to get there, Dylan. Do you need to get anything from the house, Dr. Durrell?"

Deirdre shook her head as though to ward off the question but then collected herself. "My purse. It's in the study at the far end of the hall. On my desk."

They drove in silence, Zach at the wheel, Dylan in front to give directions. Deirdre sat benumbed in the back seat, trying to think of what might be needed for her daughter and any others. There had been no mention by the police of Mrs. Swett or the other two ballerinas. Nor what had happened to cause the van to flip over, nor if they were strapped in to their seat belts. She could not in her state remember what blood type Caitlin and Dylan were, though he would, of course, be the same. Not that a transfusion would be needed, but just in case...The girls had all been so beautiful in their tutus, ducklings in *Swan Lake*. She had struggled to get the costume just right, feathers and glitter and sequins. And then the big night, Caitlin so excited.

"What about Dad?" Dylan asked once they had gotten on the highway and there were no more tricky turns to navigate. His voice was low, the question barely pitched as an interrogative.

It took a minute for it to register with Deirdre.

"As soon as we know more, Dylan. No point until," she replied, her voice distant, as though dredged up from a deep well.

Chapter Sixteen

A shton was pouring over lecture notes for his first class at Winslow College when his cell phone rang. Although almost midnight, he wanted to get preparatory remarks out of the way before Sunday when no telling what was in store.

To wit: Jennifer was scheduled to return from Philadelphia early the next day—with her hedge-fund manager of a father in tow. He had already reserved a table for three at the Winslow Arms, which featured fresh fish and a plausible wine list. The meal itself he had arranged to be put on his tab, so that there'd be no quibbling over the check. He also planned to show her father around the campus, pointing out the pink limestone used for the oldest buildings, the award-winning herb garden tended by the culinary arts class, and the bell tower, which had been erected by the same firm in Philadelphia responsible for the Liberty Bell. (He would forego this last site and the contorted architectural explanation if he picked up any hint that their guest was bored.)

Over lunch, Ashton planned to steer the conversation away from his previous marriage, obviously in tatters, and toward the *Mayflower* and his formidable forbears, which rarely failed to impress. He had rehearsed lesser-known but piquant aspects of Cotton Mather's life, including contributions to the science of vaccination and to horticulture, not to mention a crucial role in the founding of Yale, which, from his own Google search, he discovered was his future father-in-law's alma mater.

What Harold Hazelton expected to get out of this encounter Ashton couldn't put his finger on. He had only Jennifer to rely on for any hint.

To hear her take on it, Mr. Hazelton had calmed down over the summer and was, albeit begrudgingly, willing to entertain the prospect that his daughter had found happiness and a viable mate. In any case, he had stopped railing about rape and was now concentrated on the financial standing of this older man she had fallen for, an academic, which, if described properly, would be an acceptable catch, even if he had assumed his daughter would end up on the arm of some hedge fund billionaire. Like himself, at least until the downturn in the market had halved his net worth.

More than these particulars, Jennifer did not feel it incumbent upon her to elaborate. In pleading her case to her parent, she had been vague about Dr. Cole's age, which she only knew because she had googled him early on during that poetry seminar she had signed up for. In truth, she had been intrigued by the word *metaphysical*, and needed just three more credits to graduate. She had not a clue who John Donne was. From the outset, though, she had admired how pleasantly the professor had called upon students, and no matter how off-base or banal their comments, he would find some nugget in the dross to burnish. Whenever she was asked to expound on an assignment, he seemed at pains to pull something arresting out of her mumbled remarks.

"If I understand you rightly—Miss, Miss Hazelton is it?—you are suggesting that Marvell's tone is more ironic than urgent when he makes his plea to the beloved. Would that be a fair assessment of how you read the stanzas?" And, yes, it would be henceforth how she read them, glancing around to note that her fellow students were impressed (except for her friend Kimberly, who knew her all too well).

Up to then, Jennifer had relied, heavily and successfully, on her pretty face but, thanks mainly to that class, it occurred to her that a functioning brain could be amusing as well. That explained her initial attraction to the relationship, and why she was so passionate about it; Ashton was passionate too but in a more basic sense. He was surrounded, if not smothered, by brainy people, starting with his wife. He craved Jennifer's body.

With so much on his mind, Ashton was more irritated than startled by the phone interruption.

"Dad? Did I wake you?"

"Not at all, son. I was just..."

He tried to imagine why Dylan would be ringing him so late on a Saturday night, when the two had only spoken a couple of times throughout the summer. Suddenly it dawned on him. "So, what do you and Caitlin think of the car?" he pivoted, having marked on his calendar weeks ago that the two would have arrived home that day from their summer camps. From Willa Worthington he had been apprised that Deirdre had taken possession of the Honda Civic from the dealership and parked it in the family garage.

"What car? I don't understand."

"The gift from your grandparents. I was assuming that's why..."

"We're at the hospital, Dad," Dylan stated as distinctly as he could. "There's been an accident."

"What are you talking about?" Ashton asked, sitting up straighter. He reached over and pressed the off button on the stereo where Julian Bream had been strumming his lute.

"Caitlin was in a van. It flipped over. She's in the OR right now, but she is one of the lucky ones."

(Dylan glanced across the antiseptic-smelling corridor to the row of blue and orange plastic chairs where Deirdre was seated. She was sipping hot coffee from a paper cup, holding it with both hands, her face mask-like; Claudia and Lou had shown up and taken seats across from Deirdre; Zach was fumbling with a packet of fig newtons from the vending machine for them to share. Several other bedraggled-looking people were slouched or sleeping on seats further down the corridor.)

Ashton stood up to take this news in, sat back down, then stood up again. He flicked the lamp on his desk off then back on. "When did this happen?"

"A few hours ago, on the way back from Cincinnati. It was raining hard. We don't know a lot as yet."

"Is she all right?" he asked impatiently. "Can you put your mother on?"

Dylan walked over to his mother, holding out the phone. "He wants to talk to you. Tell him what the doctor said."

Deirdre did, as cogently as she could. "All we know is what an emergency room doctor came out to tell us half an hour ago. She has suffered a couple of broken ribs and issues with her back. She'll be in the operating theater for a while yet—that's as precise as he would be. As soon as she's in recovery, they'll let us know more."

Ashton swallowed hard, scanning the room for a glass of water but seeing only an empty tray. He walked toward the kitchen. "Does he think she'll be OK? With the back and so forth?"

"It's too early to say," she pointed out, trying to hold herself together, stick to the known facts, and not be short with him. He was, after all, Caitlin's father and deserved to know as much as she. "The other girl transported here to Mercy, Amber somebody, suffered two broken legs. The other three, including Mrs. Swett, were airlifted from the crash site to Youngstown. They were supposedly in worse shape."

For a moment, Ashton allowed this information to seep in, without pressing for more. He wondered if anyone had died but didn't dare ask. Unsteady on his feet, he plopped down at the kitchen table. The sight of his dinner plate with a half-eaten piece of roast chicken on it, however, made him queasy. Emptying the water glass in front of him, he was suddenly relieved that Jennifer wasn't there to distract him.

"Are you still there, Ashton? Dylan can call you back in the morning with an update."

"Yes, yes. Any time there's news. And thank you," he said, trying to be sympathetic, and amenable to whatever was required of him. "You will tell her—I mean, you will know what to say—" He didn't finish the sentence and Deirdre had already passed the phone back to her son. The call was disconnected.

As to whether he needed to jump on a plane or into his car, Ashton had no idea. Nor how much to recount to Harold Hazelton of his daughter's accident. Or even to Jennifer, he further thought. Before he turned out the bedroom light, he sent a short text to his son. *"Forgot to say: text me if any developments during the night. And take care of your mom."*

Father and daughter arrived earlier than expected, the former accustomed to checking the stock markets every morning around 5 a.m., especially given how volatile they had become. Scheduled to fly out to the West Coast that afternoon, Harold Hazelton wanted to get things over with in Rolling Hills as expeditiously as possible.

As usual, Jennifer would have liked to sleep in, but this meet-up with her boyfriend, as she still referred to Ashton, was in her self-interest. So, she made the effort. One thing was if her father reneged on his pledged donation to Klimpton, the third such institution in four years to which he had helped secure his daughter's admission. It would be another thing altogether if he disapproved of her love life enough to cut off the sizable allowance deposited to her bank account each month. She had dressed soberly but stylishly to please her father, who routinely, including today, wore an understated but exquisitely tailored Brioni suit and matching tie.

Jennifer crossed her fingers that Ashton would have donned something that wasn't too tweedy. She hated to be embarrassed.

The duo arrived in Rolling Hills at 8:30 and got to the off-campus bungalow Ashton had rented at precisely 8:45 a.m. Rather than use her own key, Jennifer deferred to her father. He pressed the doorbell with authority. Several times.

"What time did you tell him we'd be here?" Harold asked his daughter, a note of impatience in his voice.

"Round about 9 or 9:30, Daddy. You drove fast."

"It's a Mercedes. They don't go slow," he said.

The door was soon opened, and Ashton held out his hand to Jennifer's father. "Come in, come in," he said. He smiled at Jennifer but did not touch her. She blushed anyway. He was wearing a tweed jacket, but one she had never seen. Fortunately, it didn't have patches on the elbows. "I was making coffee, which I'm sure you could use after your drive."

"That would be nice," Jennifer said, a little too enthusiastically, sounding more like a guest than one of the people who lived in the place.

Harold paused on the threshold, scrolling through his cellphone. "My assistant will be checking flight times for me, so I need to keep a lookout," he volunteered before slipping the phone back into his breast pocket.

At that moment, Ashton decided not to bring up the news about Caitlin. Toward dawn, Dylan had texted. She was now in the ICU, having had two vertebrae and her left ankle reset. Spinal injuries might need subsequent surgery. Deirdre, Zach (whoever he was) and he were headed home to rest but would phone around noon Sunday with another update. Hearing all this would be irrelevant to his guest, perhaps to Jennifer as well. *Let my phone not ring until he's gone*, Ashton prayed.

Once he had Harold's attention again, Ashton ushered the two through the house, without elaborating on any aspect other than how hard it was to find spacious enough accommodations so close to campus.

"This will have to do for the interim," he explained, speaking as though neither of his guests had ever been in the place.

Harold paused for a minute to scan the titles on one of the bookshelves in the study, but only let out an ambiguous "umm."

Beyond the nondescript dining area, Ashton led the two down a hallway into the kitchen, which he found himself describing with the comment: "I guess you could charitably call it old-fashioned."

When Harold's eyes came to rest on the staircase at the rear of the house, Ashton did not say anything about the two bedrooms upstairs. Nor did his guest ask for a tour. Instead, the three sat for a half-hour drinking a strong, and expensive, Ethiopian brew and eating sourdough toast with apricot preserves. Ashton did most of the talking, unable to keep from rambling about the need to have the gutters cleaned, rumored black bear in the vicinity and the cleaning woman who sang Italian arias while she tidied the place.

Harold remained inscrutable throughout, despite Ashton's attempt to entertain with these pre-rehearsed domestic details. At one point his guest reached in his pocket, took out his vibrating phone, and walked out of the room.

Jennifer sat still, quietly sipping her third cup of coffee.

"What do you think, Jen? Should we take him around the campus before heading to lunch? I did as you suggested, booking for 11:30."

"He suffers from attention deficit disorder," she said drily. "Don't go overboard about anything. He's seen it all."

"I'll try not to bore him," he replied, thinking that Jennifer might very well suffer the same syndrome. Why he hadn't alighted on that diagnosis before he did not know.

"Anyway, he'll get to the point soon enough, or over lunch. He usually eats a salad."

While they waited for Harold's call to wrap up, Ashton felt for his own cell phone. It was safely in the pocket of his slacks. He did not pull it out, nor could he, albeit they were alone, bring himself to mention Caitlin's condition to Jennifer. He did turn to look at her, the sunshine from the kitchen window catching the gold of her hair and the snow-white of her skin. Twenty-one was a beautiful age, he thought, but it was so fleeting. And she had no idea.

"You look like you want to say something," she said, though not sounding eager to hear it.

"It can wait," he returned, shaking his head. "By the way, I wasn't kidding about the bears. Apparently, two or three have come down from the mountains, prowling around, rooting in other people's garbage cans the next road over."

She looked unimpressed. "You'll just have to put the lids on tighter," she replied, picking up her cup and her father's and taking them to the sink. Ashton did the same with his. They stood awkwardly side by side, not touching. To dispel the tension, he turned the faucet on and rinsed the cups.

"Whenever you two are ready, we could head out," Harold announced from the entryway. "I've been put on an earlier flight, so a cursory drive through the campus will suffice. Then, did you say, a quick lunch?"

"Absolutely," Ashton said, grabbing his keys on the way out.

"Why don't we take the Mercedes? It's roomier," Harold suggested once he spotted the dusty Camry in the carport. "You do the driving, Ashton."

By the time they parked in front of the bell tower and got out, Ashton had decided to truncate his remarks, mentioning only how beautiful the sound of the chimes was widely reputed to be. "Shall we?" he asked, gesturing toward the narrow spiraling steps that led to the top. Checking his watch, Harold demurred. Without missing a beat, Jennifer turned and started back to the car.

"I figured the Winslow Arms would suit," Ashton said, starting the engine. "Jennifer and I have found the food there quite reasonable," he added, quickly catching himself. "The taste, that is."

Finally, over his grilled shrimp salad and a glass of imported French burgundy, Harold came to the point. "So that we are on the same page, Ashton, I wanted to emphasize that there are great expectations for my daughter." (Here, Jennifer rolled her eyes; Ashton put down his fork and eyed his guest politely.) "She is accustomed to a certain quality of life, which, well, and don't get me wrong, your being a professor of physical poetry is commendable, in its way, but unfortunately, in our society academics are not valued as they ought to be. Not like us bankers, my father, and grandfather before me..."

Ashton could have kicked himself for not having alluded to his pilgrim pedigree sooner and wondered why Jennifer hadn't (ostensibly) bothered to mention the Cole forebears herself during trips home. He took a swallow of the bone-dry wine, since he was paying for the bottle and it cost $95.

"I respect that you want the best for your daughter, Harold, but you can rest easy. My family on both sides, the Coles and the Mathers, are two of the oldest in Boston. For generations the family home has stood proudly on Beacon Hill, which I'm sure you're aware—" Irked that Harold continued to pick at his salad as though barely listening, he raised his voice. "I mean, hell, you can't get more illustrious than tracing your roots back to the *Mayflower*."

At this exclamation, Harold desisted, arranged his knife and fork across his plate and dabbed his lips with the starched linen napkin. Jennifer looked warily from one to the other.

"Not that my salary as a full professor is as paltry as one might conclude," Ashton added in a less belligerent tone, "but I will be coming into quite an inheritance. Not that I wish nor need that to happen any time soon."

Harold blew on and then slowly wiped his spectacles as he considered this information. "I am glad to hear that things are well arranged for you, Ashton, but there's another matter that concerns us."

Ashton looked up, annoyed anew by his guest's condescension, not to mention his apparently willful ignorance of the literary genre he was a leading authority on. He raised his eyebrows to invite his guest to expound further.

"I'm talking about your marriage, Dr. Cole, which, to my knowledge, has not yet been dissolved, and even when it is, will doubtless entail a considerable financial outlay on your part. You do have two teenage children, do you not?"

Ashton reddened, waved a waiter with a water pitcher off, and stole a glance at Jennifer. Her porcelain face was blank as a dinner plate. No help there. He felt additionally stymied by the enormity of what had transpired not twenty-four hours before. Caitlin was lying in an ICU hundreds of miles away, and there was a new car in the garage that she might not ever be able to drive. And these two sitting across from him were oblivious. He was about to say that

highly regarded lawyers were handling the divorce proceedings, when his cell phone rang.

"Please," Harold intoned, gesturing toward the origin of the ring tone. Ashton pulled the mobile out of his jacket pocket and saw the familiar number on the screen.

"I'll need to take this," he said defiantly, scrambling to his feet and heading out the front door of the restaurant.

No one spoke on the drive back to the bungalow, though it was obvious that Ashton had taken an important call. For his part, Harold spent the twenty-minute ride on his own phone, organizing his pick-up that evening at the San Francisco airport and confirming client meetings for the next morning. Jennifer sat upfront flicking desultorily through the radio dial, never settling on anything. Ashton would have told her to stop fiddling with the thing if he hadn't been so discombobulated by the exchange with Dylan.

Unsettled and irritated, he drove fast, without making any effort to converse about anything, though he did wonder how much Harold might have lost so far in the recession. His own relatively modest 401K had been battered.

Harold's parting words to Ashton: "Whatever you may think, I'm not one to interfere in people's lives, Dr. Cole, but presumably you now have a broader perspective on things. I'll leave it to you and my daughter to sort it out."

Without bothering to respond, Ashton held out his hand with the keys to the Mercedes. "Drives nicely," he said flatly.

The two then shook hands, clumsily, neither clear as to where the discussion had wound up. Jennifer stood apart, her mouth downturned in a pout, both men having disappointed, or bored, her. As her father revved the engine, she turned and marched into the house.

Remaining outside, Ashton dialed Deirdre's cell phone but she did not pick up. Then he unwound the hose and sprinkled the scattered wildflowers the former occupants must have planted. From what he remembered of time spent in Pennsylvania, the heat of summer would not break for another couple of weeks. A little color out front would not hurt. Might as well make something cheery of the place.

"So, what was that phone call all about?" Jennifer eventually asked as Ashton joined her in the living room. "Seemed to put you off."

She was lounging on the sofa with the cat curled up at her feet, a *Town and Country* open across her lap. She did not bother to sit up or turn toward him.

"I was already put off, if you must know, Jennifer," he responded wearily, looking around for the right chair to pull up close enough to compel her attention.

"My father can be a piece of work," she stirred herself to add, twisting a lock of hair around her index finger. "My mother too, for that matter. He's had to pay out a lot to her, alimony and all, so I guess that's why he's so hot and bothered. Not to mention the firm's losses. Now *that*, that really gets him going."

In different circumstances, Ashton would have wanted to plump the subject of the firm's financial health, specifically how severe his personal losses were and to what extent those might affect his generosity toward his daughter, but he didn't have the stomach for it now, and Jennifer seemed supremely unconcerned or unforthcoming. He dragged a wicker rocking chair across the floor and situated it a few feet from Jennifer.

She took the hint, rearranging her long body upright, ditching the magazine and re-positioning the cat in her lap. "You want to hold her, Ashton? You know, like a baby. She doesn't bite, or burp, but she does purr."

"Not right now," he replied, taking a seat and ignoring her odd remark and the sharp pain in his knees as he did so. The chair was low-slung and rickety, one of the disparate pieces of furniture left behind by the previous occupants. He regretted not claiming more things from the house in Ohio. He rocked forward. "I had wanted to tell you earlier, but," he began. Jennifer stopped petting the calico. "The thing is, my daughter Caitlin—you remember her—has been in an accident. She's in the hospital with broken ribs, which they've already dealt with. But she's going to need back surgery."

"Wow. That's awful. She wanted to be a ballerina, didn't she?" Jennifer went on, her mouth ajar. She caressed the fur behind the cat's ears. "I've never known anyone in a car crash."

A frown flitted crossed Ashton's face, but he dismissed it. All young people say banal things, he told himself.

"So, what are you going to do?" she eventually asked.

"If I can convince my wife, bring her to Philly, where the surgeons are surely better."

Chapter Seventeen

B y mid-October Caitlin was hopping around on crutches in an out-patient facility across from the hospital proper in Cincinnati, having dispensed altogether with a walker. The physical therapist told Deirdre that any further sessions were not covered by insurance and that the slight hitch in Caitlin's stride might be permanent. "If she keeps on with proper exercise and care, it might attenuate, but a career as a ballerina won't be in the cards."

Deirdre nodded, hoping the therapist had not spelled this out for his patient. "What about her pain? She doesn't complain but I see her grimace."

"In time, it should dissipate. I'm recommending, however, that the doctor renew the Oxycodone." At that point, the therapist reached into a thick binder and pulled out an invoice. Deirdre glanced at it and tried to contain her surprise.

"I'll put the check in the mail next week," she said, holding out her hand.

"You have a beautiful daughter, Mrs. Cole." Deirdre did not correct her. "But she's been through a lot." (No one, especially not Deirdre, needed to be reminded how bad the van wreck was: Mrs. Swett, who was at the wheel, and her eleven-year-old niece were killed upon impact. Of the three friends and would-be dancers in the back, Monica Ferris was thrown from the vehicle and died on the operating table; Amber Reardon suffered a crushed leg, which had to be amputated below the knee. By comparison, Caitlin escaped relatively unscathed.)

The therapist's bill was for $4800.

Part of Deirdre was glad. The part that meant she'd be sticking her husband with a bill for $2400. She was, however, more irked than angry with him, after he insisted he'd care for Caitlin in Philly but in the end, reneging on the offer. "Excellent facilities in Cincinnati. Better than here," he had told her on the phone. She imagined Jennifer standing at his shoulder in smug satisfaction. She had hung up without another word and gotten things organized. Every single insurance bill and every last item the hospital billed for, down to the Tylenol, she consigned to a designated folder and passed along to her lawyer.

Howard Morrison had told her the night he took her out to dinner that he'd keep a running tab of expenses to be shared between the spouses until the divorce became finalized. "You have enough on your plate, Deirdre," he had said over the crème caramel, laying his hand on her arm, in what she sensed was more than a strictly lawyerly gesture. "You don't need to be burdened by financial matters when you have Caitlin to see about. And yourself, of course." He had looked to her eyes, but she couldn't bring herself to return his gaze.

Too soon, she told herself, for anything like that.

Six weeks later as the cold weather set in, Caitlin was maneuvering the halls at Hillside High with barely a catch in her gait. No one had commented on her gimpy leg, at least not in front of her. She kept the pills in her locker and only popped one when the pain made her twitch, and no one was around to notice.

If Dylan bumped into his sister in the hallways at school—(they didn't share but one class as juniors)—Caitlin would feign interest in whatever he was going on about. Enthusing about this or that to get her mind off herself, he often brought up Zach, who had managed one weekend to drive to Ohio to see them both. The three of them had tooled around in the new car, both the boys insisting that she take the wheel and practice parallel parking.

"You'll have your license in no time. Then you and Dylan can come to visit me—and see your Dad too," Zach had said.

That weekend marked the first time Caitlin enjoyed herself since the accident.

Other than doing things with her brother or with Claudia, she otherwise kept to herself, going through the motions of studying and trying to keep the twinges in her legs from showing up in her face. Given how far behind she had fallen at Hillside, a private tutor came around to the school to help her play catch-up, but so far her grades were almost entirely *D*s. (Only Roxane had charitably given her a *C* on her mid-term French exam.) Caitlin didn't much care about her disappointing performance, and Deirdre had been advised by the doctors not to make an issue of it. For her, the whole idea was to get things back to normal for her daughter—and to get on with her own life, however hard being newly single might be.

Getting through the holidays was in fact its own obstacle course. Deirdre had considered taking the kids to Mississippi to check on her own mother, but the travel, she calculated, might be too much for Caitlin, and there'd be too many questions from her mother once they got there. Starting with where Ashton was and ending with how she could have let the breakup of her marriage happen. Instead, she organized a small gathering for Christmas Eve, inviting a few colleagues who hadn't left town as well as friends of the twins: Zach drove over from Penn, Claudia came with Lou in tow, and even Amber Reardon, who had been fitted with a prosthetic leg, showed up. Roxane brought a fruit cake, which she claimed she had made from scratch, but which tasted to Deirdre store-bought.

Not that it mattered. If not as carefree and crowded as earlier parties at the Coles had been, the evening came off well enough. Deirdre and Caitlin alternated on the piano, playing Christmas carols, while, encouraged by Roxane, Dylan on the violin and Zach on his clarinet improvised their accompaniment.

Howard lingered after the other guests had departed and the children had trundled upstairs. "You can put this under the tree," he quietly said, pulling a small, tastefully wrapped box out of his suit jacket.

Embarrassed, Deirdre blushed, not having thought of getting her lawyer anything, or anyone else other than her children. "So sweet of you, but you needn't have." Seeing his face fall, she hastened to amend herself. "But thank you for going out of your way."

"I didn't consider it out of my way," he rejoined, looking at her expectantly, as though it were now her move.

"Well, nonetheless," she replied, and unsure how to steer the conversation back to neutral ground, busied herself picking up plates and glasses strewn about the room.

"I should be going," Howard eventually announced, more forcefully than necessary. "It was a lovely party. I trust we'll speak sometime during the holidays."

"By all means," Deirdre replied, holding a couple of half-empty wine glasses in her hand. "Ashton will be here in a few days, for the children. There may be issues to go over..."

Reaching for his coat and muffler off the hat rack, Howard turned to face her. She held out her free hand, which he took in his and held close to his chest, longer than necessary.

Ashton did show up three days later, with Jennifer in tow. He had called ahead to invite Dylan and Caitlin to go to Chicago for New Year's. They both jumped at the idea. Since anything Caitlin was enthusiastic about needed to be encouraged, Deirdre went out the day after Christmas and bought her daughter a camel-hair coat and matching hat and gloves at the nicest department store in town. Even marked down it was pricy. (She would put half that bill in the expense folder as well.)

"You're looking well, Deirdre, especially given—everything," Ashton said, waiting in the foyer for the kids to come downstairs.

"Doesn't she want to come in?" she asked, ignoring the compliment but jerking her head to indicate the woman in the car outside.

"I left the heat on. Says she'll be fine," he replied, unease creeping up his spine. He made a smacking noise with his lips.

"How's your book coming?" she inquired, determined not to let the exchange devolve into an altercation, even though she disliked the conciliatory version of Ashton almost as much as she deplored the cavalier.

"Turning it into a monograph. Not enough material to sustain a book," he answered with studied casualness.

Deirdre tilted her head to reflect on this but said nothing.

In the silence, Ashton cast his eyes toward the top of the staircase but saw no sign of the children. He didn't dare move toward his old study, not wanting to see what had been done with the room. Nor to spot anything he might regret not having claimed at the outset, the bungalow in Rolling Hills still only partially, and so sadly, furnished. He did note the grandfather clock further down the hall, which was blithely ticking away, and which had done so for a hundred years before up in Boston. He should have taken it when he had a chance.

"So, how are things at the school?" he asked.

"If you mean at Hillside, Dylan is applying himself; Caitlin is woefully behind but too fragile for me to get after her. Keep all that in mind when..."

"I will, Deirdre. Give me some credit," he cut her off. Deirdre crossed her arms; Ashton counted to ten. "The idea," he plowed on, his pitch lower, "is to show them a good time for three days: the symphony, the Art Institute, ice-skating, anything else they might want to do."

"You can forget about the ice-skating. Caitlin's not up to that. You'll soon see."

He pressed his lips together tightly and shot another glance upstairs. A door banged and a faucet squeaked. "And things at Klimpton?" Ashton then hazarded.

"Feeling the pinch, like everywhere," Deirdre replied matter-of-factly, and, not able to resist a jab, added, "but I'm making progress on my book. Beauchamps seems pleased."

For an instant, she had the curious sensation that she had moved beyond her husband.

Chapter Eighteen

D uring the final days of the year, the book consumed Deirdre. Sitting at her roll-top, she let herself be transported back in time to a world lit, as it were, only by fire. Almost everyone around the year 1400 was young and hyped up because life was brief and hence, to be savored to the full. (As she reckoned life was even now: not as brief but equally to be savored.) Her heroine, she would stress, had made the most of what she could tease out of her circumstances, defying them or rising above them.

So absorbed did Deirdre become in her work, that she skipped her lunches, depending on Caedmon or Cookie to interrupt with their demands. Different hours of the day, she put on different music, Mozart in the mornings, Beethoven in the afternoon, Bach in the evenings. Occasionally, she opted for silence, listening only to the winter wind rattling the windows. (The shutters still hadn't been tended to.)

She felt restored in mind and spirit.

If the home phone rang, she ignored it. She kept her cell phone conversations brief, including one from Stella checking to see if she would grace the faculty hall on New Year's Eve. In the past, the Coles had celebrated with a few friends or stayed at home to watch the ball drop on TV with the children, but now a much-recovered Caitlin as well as Dylan would want to do their own thing. Her soon-to-be ex would have returned to Pennsylvania. With his paramour. Yes, she would be pleased to attend the dinner.

Once the kids left the house at 7:30 p.m. for a New Year Eve's dance at Hillside, Deirdre went upstairs to dress. She chose an off-the-shoulder eggplant-colored sheath, which could be considered either plain and unexciting or understated and elegant. For jewelry, she settled on a necklace of tiny crystals. No rings on her fingers. Studying the effect in the mirror, she reckoned it would signal—she wasn't sure what but at least that she was alive.

At 7:45 the doorbell rang unexpectedly. It was Roxane, whose expression fractured when she saw Deirdre.

"I didn't anticipate you were going out," she burbled. "So—(she held out a CD)—I brought over a movie, in French, which I thought you might like to watch."

Deirdre's eyebrows arched in vague disapproval.

"Anyway, it's one of those perfect films to get engrossed by. You can passively practice the language and it's long enough to blanket, or blank out, an entire evening." By the time Roxane had finished this spiel, she was flushed with embarrassment. "But on second thought, I can see you've got plans. You, you look amazing."

"Thank you," Deirdre returned, "for the DVD too. It'll be for another time."

"Well, I'll be headed out. I've volunteered to lend a hand at the school. That where Dylan and Caitlin have gone?"

"Yes, with friends. Keep an eye on them, if you will."

"Certainly. And enjoy yourself, wherever you're going."

For an instant, Deirdre considered asking Roxane to tag along to the Klimpton dinner, but something prevented her.

The college affair was drab, overpopulated by aging or overly lecherous associate professors and a few clerical staffers Deirdre barely knew. Anyone with any wherewithal, she quickly calculated, had gotten the hell out of Dodge. As a result, she drank too much, back-led on the dance floor, and as best she could, let the bad jokes and boorish come-ons roll off her. She would have left early but didn't want anyone to say that the new divorcée hadn't been able to stick it out.

Shortly after the countdown to 2009, Stella plopped down and proceeded to unburden herself, lamenting the state of the economy and, by extension, the finances of the college.

"It's not only the car industry that's in trouble, Deirdre. Colleges are taking a hit. Our donors, I can attest, are like rats abandoning ship."

Deirdre politely assented, preferring to hear this palaver, however worrying, than the inane jokes from the men at the table.

"The ostrich approach, my dear, isn't going to work, I can tell you that," Stella warned, waving her wine glass around as she spoke. She was beginning to slur her words. "This is a bigger bother than your husband's shenanigans, that's for sure."

Not amused by this last reference, Deirdre reached for an untouched glass of water on the confetti-strewn table. Fortunately, the other guests had gotten up to dance or to gather around the dessert table. "I appreciate your letting me know, Stella. Something to be discussed in your office. But, time now for me to go. The children, you know."

"Indeed, indeed," Stella wound up, having lost her train of thought. She waved her friend away.

Upon standing, Deirdre felt unsteady. She retreated to the restroom, where she splashed cold water on her cheeks and reapplied powder. Without returning to her table, she exited the faculty lounge determined not to draw any attention to herself.

The streets were largely deserted so soon after midnight, but she drove slowly to be on the safe side. Traffic rattled her since the van accident.

To her surprise when she let herself in, Roxane and Dylan were ensconced in the den—watching *Les Enfants du Paradis*. Something about their arrangement on the couch struck her as off-key, but she had imbibed several glasses of champagne—and off-key was something she knew her own self to be. She cleared her throat to signal her presence. They both looked startled.

"*Alors, ou est* Caitlin?" Deirdre asked, trying to keep with the theme of the moment.

"*Elle vient de s'endormir*," Roxane replied, indicating the upstairs. There was a note in her tone Deirdre couldn't identify.

"The party was a bust, Mom, and Caitlin wasn't having a good time," Dylan rushed to explicate.

"Well, I will be doing the same: going to bed. You two enjoy the film. And, if it's as long as you say, Roxane, stay for breakfast."

Reddening, her friend shook her head. "I'll be leaving when it's over, if not before," she declared, straightening up and running her hand through her hair.

"Happy New Year, Mom," Dylan called out as his mother turned to go.

"You two as well," Deirdre returned and left the room.

On Twelfth Night the Coles traditionally exchanged gifts, small ones that were supposed to inspire the recipient to reach his or her goal for the coming year, and Deirdre was determined that not everything the four of them had done as a family needed to be jettisoned. Scouring the local music shop, she bought *The American Songbook* for Caitlin and *From Bach to Bartok,* a collection of graded violin pieces, for Dylan.

"So many people commented on your voice at Christmas, Caitlin, and so many noticed how proficient you're becoming on the violin, Dylan," she told them as they unwrapped their presents.

Both seemed pleased, if mildly ashamed, since neither had gotten their mother anything. Caitlin quickly flipped through the pieces and lay the book on the piano, Dylan took his upstairs. Both had overnight plans that evening, Caitlin going to a sleepover at Claudia's, Dylan to Sammy's.

Left alone, Deirdre toyed with the idea of watching Roxane's DVD of *Children of Paradise* but didn't relish the idea of three hours sitting in front of the TV screen. At least not by herself. On a whim, she went to the hall phone and opened the address book to Howard Morrison, Attorney at Law. He might be a plodding lawyer, but he was company.

The two watched the film for an hour or so, Deirdre discovering that his French was better than hers, and that the romance of the movie whetted their own appetites. In the middle of a love scene between the main character, Garance and her poet lover, Frederick, the two retired to the master bedroom upstairs. Howard wore a back brace to support his spine. To discover that, and see him struggle to remove it, drew her to him.

PART TWO

2013

Mystical grammar of amorous glances
Feeling of pulses, the physic of love.

John Cleveland
(1613-1658)

Chapter Nineteen

D uring long drives, the radio was a godsend. On this one, Deirdre fiddled with the dial every fifty miles or so to find a stronger signal for NPR or for a station that played jazz, which she had just found out Roxane had a predilection for. Her friend never ceased to amaze (if not unsettle) her, but so far she hadn't minded her asking to come along. For the first hour, they listened in silence to the news, much of which wasn't good, especially the mass casualty shootings which seemed to pop up every month or so, not to mention terrorist attacks abroad and ongoing bloodshed in Syria.

"How serendipitous! I have things to do in New York, and besides, I haven't had the chance to see the kids for a while," Roxane had explained the day she casually rang up (though knowing full well that Deirdre would be making the trip to Penn to pick up Dylan and accompany him to Princeton)."And, if I can be of any help with Caitlin, I'd be delighted, she and I—well, we've had our ups and downs..."

"It's fine, Roxane. I could use the company on the drive, and the children would be thrilled to see you."

Deirdre wasn't sure she believed that, as even her own relationship with her daughter was fraught, but nonetheless, having someone else along might cushion any blow Caitlin had in store. When her daughter came off one of her jags, anything might happen. Better to have company as a buffer.

She finished spreading her homemade mayonnaise on the sandwiches to take along—Caitlin, while she ate like a bird, had a thing for the sloppy tomato rounds—and fried chicken always went over well on a car trip. She wrapped the sandwiches in wax paper and the pieces of chicken in tin foil and placed them in the picnic basket.

Doing so reminded her to call her own mother before setting off. As usual, she had meant to phone for weeks, but between her Klimpton classes and her research project, she had not found the time, nor had the stamina.

When she did ring at 8:30 the next morning, her mother picked up on the third ring. "Just caught me. I was headed out to get some eggs from those scrawny hens the neighbors stuck me with. Not that I'm complaining. Best layers between Memphis and Vicksburg." Her mother sounded remarkably peppy.

"Thought you'd be pleased, Mother, that I tried your recipe for mayonnaise last night, though the tomatoes up here aren't so juicy. I'm headed to pick up Caitlin and then on to Pennsylvania. Dylan's received a graduate scholarship to Princeton. Going to get a jump by auditing a class or two this summer."

"Got the smarts, huh. Takes after his dad, I guess," her mother said drily. Deirdre held her tongue and looked out the window as Roxane's car pulled up. "So, how is my granddaughter? Is she cured of all those drugs?"

"I hope so, Mother. I'll let you know."

"You could bring her down here. Maybe she's got it too easy, though I'm not one to discount what happened to her those years ago."

"Thanks for the offer. We'll be in New York City for a few days. A treat for the kids. We'll send you a postcard."

Hanging up the wall phone in the kitchen, Deirdre watched Roxane unload her car. She was dressed in a green skirt with some kind of floral pattern and a jacket that matched. The color became her, Deirdre thought. Effortlessly pretty, though what an effort others had to make to fathom what was going on with her.

"Have some coffee, Roxane. I'll be down in a jiffy," Deirdre said, opening the front door and motioning her friend in.

Roughly twenty miles from the rehab facility, Deirdre stopped at a welcome center on the outskirts of Akron. They freshened up and ambled among the fir trees in the adjoining picnic grounds. It was a perfect June day, the sun high in the sky, ribbons of clouds scudding by.

"Is there any way to prep for Caitlin? Any topic we need to avoid?" Roxane asked as she stretched her torso and let the sun warm her back.

"Like Russia, she's an enigma wrapped in a mystery and so on," Deirdre half-joked, noting that her friend did not register the reference. She changed tack. "One thing I thought we could do is play a CD I brought along. You remember Claudia and their friend, Lou, who was putting together a rock band. Anyway, they cut an album and Caitlin sings on one of the tracks. Thought that might go over well."

"Sounds like a plan," Roxane replied. "Your daughter does have a good voice. Actually, both your children..."

"Strange, isn't it, for someone so introverted to have developed stage presence. Her friend Claudia said she was a cross between Cyndi Lauper and Shania Twain, which I took to be a compliment." Roxane looked impressed. "Too bad her theatrics aren't always put to good use," Deirdre added, without further explanation.

She was thinking about all the times her daughter had pitched a hissy fit over being grounded for staying out late or leaving her room in a shambles. Caitlin had called her a tyrant on one particularly bad evening. *Bad* in the sense that her back was bothering her, and she had slapped the proffered bottle of Aleve out of her mother's hand.

"This stuff does nothing, do you hear, NOTHING. Keep it for your headaches," Caitlin had screamed, before stomping out of the house.

Howard, who was still alive then, had been chopping a salad for dinner when that altercation took place. "It's a difficult age," he offered up when Deirdre came downstairs to apologize for her daughter's outburst.

"I'm beginning to think they all are, difficult ages, that is," she responded ruefully, running her hand affectionately through his thinning hair. He had continued to dice the vegetables ever so finely.

After a few knee bends, Roxane stood up and breathed in the fresh air. "Well, it is a difficult age," she declared.

Deirdre got up from the bench and brushed the pine needles off her skirt. "That's precisely what Howard used to say about her—but that was when Caitlin was seventeen."

"So sad, about him, I mean," Roxane replied, lowering her head in apparent sympathy. Then, looking off at the surrounding park, she brightened her tone. "Why don't we take a brisk walk around the perimeter and then I'll handle the last leg. How's that?"

Deirdre did not object.

Signing off on the paperwork at Congreve Rehab took a good half hour. While Roxane desultorily paged through the institute's brochures, Deirdre scrawled her name or initials on the release forms, after which the director called over an intercom for Caitlin to join them.

"You'll be pleased to know your daughter eventually got with the program, Mrs. Cole—oh, I'm sorry, Dr. Durrell," the director corrected herself, noting the signature on the top sheet. "She even made a few friends, one of whom, I believe, has hung around an extra week so as to leave with her," she added, as she collated the various documents, and handed copies to Deirdre.

She took the stack, nonplussed but not astonished to learn that her daughter had latched on to another guy, one coming out of rehab himself.

When Caitlin knocked on the half-open door and brushed her hair back from her forehead, Deirdre was initially relieved. She looked less pasty-faced, her expression more alert (if wary) and her gangling body less concave. Oddly attractive she was, despite the tattoos and the twitchy eyes.

"Hey, Mom," she said without affect, as she stepped tentatively into the room and stood with her hands clasped behind her, awaiting instructions, almost like a prisoner would.

Roxane tried to exchange a look with Deirdre, but the latter had stood to appraise her daughter.

"You look well, sweetheart, and we're so happy you're coming with us." She held out her arms whereupon Caitlin submitted to a hug.

"Your mother's right," Roxane chimed in. "You look—(here she faltered, fishing for a fitting adjective)—*fantastique.*"

Pulling away from the embrace, Caitlin shot Roxane a look to suggest she had her former teacher's number, paused a second in thought and then asked, "My things are out here in the hall, with Ray. Can he come in, Dr. Fletcher?"

"Yes, he may. Mr. Billings needs to pick up his release packet as well."

Once back on the road, Deirdre stole a closer look at this Ray person in the rear-view mirror. Lean and hungry-looking, he had jerky eyes and thin, some might say cruel, lips. A small scar marred his left temple. She wondered if he too boasted tattoos, though none were immediately visible. Once out of traffic and on the straight-away toward the Pennsylvania border, she tried to elicit a few particulars. "So, Ray, tell us about yourself. Are you from this area?"

Having lit a cigarette, he took a few drags before responding, Caitlin apparently having to nudge him in the ribs to do so. "Grew up in Jersey. Did some gigs around Toledo. Ended up in juvvie and then this rat hole."

Neither Deirdre nor Roxane felt inspired to pursue this line of inquiry.

After a decent interval, Deirdre plunged back in.: "You will let us know when you two want to stop for lunch. We won't make it to State College until around sunset."

"Whatever," Caitlin mumbled, leaning her head against Ray's bony shoulder.

Deirdre persisted. "Which reminds me, have you heard from your brother? We'll need to alert him when we get closer."

"Got it. Will do. Over and out," she telegraphed.

Several miles passed in silence, the only sound the swoosh of long-haul trucks zipping by on the inside lane.

Eventually, Roxane jumped in. "Your mother brought along a surprise, Caitlin. It's a CD by your friends back home." She held the disc aloft and without waiting for a response slipped it into the player.

Ray and Caitlin exchanged a glance of bored resignation.

To Deirdre's and Roxane's ears the opening number was nothing short of cacophonous, the guy on drums nearly out of control and a saxophonist notably out of tune. "Jesus Christ," was all the two women heard from the back seat.

On the third track, however, Caitlin's voice soared as she sang about lost love, accompanied only by a few chords on the keyboard.

"I told you, kid, you've got it. Even if your friends are crap." This time Ray nudged Caitlin, and pulled her body closer to his. She submitted in that take-it-or-leave-it manner she had unconsciously perfected.

Before long, Roxane lowered the volume on the CD, and turned her head. "With a little training, Caitlin, a few lessons with a professional, your singing would be really special."

"Don't you worry none, Miz?, Miz...?—I forget," Ray butted in. "As luck would have it, I'm putting together a band, a real band, and Caitlin's gonna be our vocalist. So, never you mind about Carnegie Hall and shit like that," he let loose with unexpected vehemence.

Deirdre glanced in the mirror, noting that color had risen in Ray's otherwise sallow cheeks and that Caitlin had scowled. She considered calling her backseat passenger out for rudeness—(He was, after all, getting free passage back to New York City.)—but before she could formulate a reprimand, Roxane beat her to the punch.

"Well, you don't have to get your dander up, Mr..., Mr.—oh, I forget," she said, aping the sarcasm in his tone to her. "However popular your as-yet unformed band is destined to be, I would point out that Carnegie Hall is not by any stretch of the imagination shit," she countered. (As Ashton had more than once remarked, Roxane could sting like a bee.)

Unable to come up with a comparable response, Ray fumbled around in his satchel for his i-pod and earplugs. In solidarity Caitlin did the same.

For the last leg Roxane took the wheel while Deirdre tried to nap. Or at least to commune with her own thoughts.

However much Congreve Rehab, which no one would claim was cheap, might have helped ween her daughter off whatever drugs she had been on, it had not notably improved her disposition. Being around her without Dylan in the house was like walking on eggshells: so it had been at the time Ashton abandoned them, and then again for the year after the van accident, and then, just as she breathed a sigh of relief that her daughter had come through the worst of it, she discovered her stash of medicine bottles. Mostly, from what she could tell from labels that hadn't been ripped off, they were opioids. Some were clearly prescribed by Caitlin's own doctors or shrinks, others apparently were acquired from Claudia & Co., and others, either stolen or purchased.

Mother and daughter side-stepped each other for a few days in silence, Caitlin sullen or insolent, Deirdre alternately aggrieved and aloof.

Things got worse.

After eighteen months of plugging away at her manuscript, Deirdre's opus on Christine de Pizan finally saw the light of day. It merited positive reviews in three or four university press newsletters, several ho-hum mentions in European journals and a full-length, and predictably effusive, review in the Klimpton Quarterly. But, after that short-lived hoop-la, the tome was relegated to the liberal arts libraries of various colleges around the country.

"What else did you expect?" Stella had commiserated with her a month after the official publication. "It's the way of the world nowadays. You have to write like James Patterson if you wish to make a splash!"

To which Deirdre replied, "Notwithstanding all that, if getting it done helps me move up in the hierarchy here, so much the better."

Sticking her pencil behind her ear, Stella threw back her head to deliver herself of a consideration. "You scored a goal, Deirdre," Leaning forward toward her friend, she added confidentially, "but if you want to win the game, before the board forgets all about it, you should throw a launch party."

Which Deirdre did, at home, a cocktail gathering which included colleagues from Klimpton, a few friends from in town, Roxane, her hairdresser Erica, and Howard, despite his failing health. The toasts were nominally cordial—including one from Dr. Beauchamps calling Deirdre "one of our most conscientious instructors," (which she found underwhelming), and another to Christine de Pizan herself for being "a role model for all female academics," in the words of Dr. Margery Willingham, who had drunk too much but who had actually taken the time to read the afore-mentioned tome. "You made the

Middle Ages feel, Dr. Durrell, well, less like middle age!" which encomium had the effect of eliciting titters among the tweedy guests.

The only sour note to the proceedings was struck by Caitlin, who made a late entrance, glassy-eyed and sporting a new tattoo of a serpent entwined around a rose on her exposed shoulder. Teetering in too high heels, she weaved and bobbed through the last toast and up the stairs, not acknowledging any of the guests.

A hush fell over the assembled until Stella raised her glass to salute the entire department. ""To better days," she declaimed, leaving it to each guest to determine what those might consist of.

Later that night, when only Howard remained, seated at the kitchen table drying wine glasses, Caitlin crept back down to get something from the fridge. "You could have been polite, you know. Your mother was being feted tonight for all she's achieved," he reproved her. "Not to mention all she's done for you and Dylan."

Deirdre turned from the sink, sponge in hand, to observe her daughter's reaction.

"I don't give a piss about Christine de Pisser and your highfalutin friends," she hissed at her mother. "You made Dad leave and nothing's going to change that." Her jaw set in defiance, she jerked the fridge open and grabbed the first soda can inside.

"You have no right to speak like that, to me or to Howard," Deirdre called out to her daughter's back as she marched out, drink in hand.

"Let it go, Deirdre. But get help for her where you can. And, I say this as your lawyer, solicit Ashton to do his part. I'm only sorry I can't..." Howard advised, his weakened voice trailing off.

After Howard's death, Caitlin made an effort to be civil around the house, and more amenable to Deirdre's suggestions. Like enrolling at a junior college to which she would commute twice a week. For eighteen months all went well, until she fell in with the wrong crowd. Shortly before graduation, Deirdre got a call from the college provost. Her daughter, she was told, was found passed out on the floor of the band rehearsal room, a syringe nearby. She would not be allowed to graduate, despite decent grades.

However reluctantly, Deirdre did what Howard had suggested, sent Caitlin to spend the summer of 2011 with Ashton, and Jennifer. It was also the summer Dr. Beauchamps informed her that her instructor status at the college had not changed. "Another publication would help. Come up with a proposal and we'll go from there," he had counseled.

"Did I hear you are working on another book? I don't know how you find the time," Roxane was saying. They had come to a near stand-still as several highways criss-crossed and cars began to switch lanes. Shaking herself out of her reverie, Deirdre straightened up to survey the different signs. State College was another forty miles.

"Still at the proposal stage, what with one thing and another," Deirdre replied evasively, not in the mood to elaborate. Besides, talking about academic matters with Roxane made her uncomfortable, given that nothing had become of her friend's attempts to land another job. (By her own reckoning, the recommendation that she had agonized over likely had been too generic to elicit enthusiasm from prospective employers.)

Of a sudden, Roxane veered out of the left lane to take the upcoming exit, pulling into the first visible gas station. "Thought we might want to top up," she offered, "and freshen up before we get there. Caitlin, Ray...you want to get out?"

Neither of the two young people did. Deirdre retrieved the key to the washroom from the attendant and when she came back out, Roxane had already filled the tank and replaced the nozzle.

While they waited in the car, Deirdre drummed her fingers on the steering wheel, Caitlin texted her brother, and Ray smoked another cigarette. A good ten minutes went by before Roxane, her face newly made up, her lipstick brighter than before, reappeared, her walk more sinuous than before. She had changed into heels.

"We're to drive straight onto campus, Dylan says, to Campbell Hall, where he'll meet us," Caitlin read off from her phone. "I've got the directions on Google Maps."

Striding across campus, Dylan flashed the same lop-sided smile that his sister had at her disposal, on those rare occasions, that is, that she bothered to bring it out. He embraced his mother, lifted his sister off her feet, and shook hands with Ray. Only with Roxane did he skip a beat before giving her too a brief hug. In his wake came several friends, whose names he rattled off and who, following his lead, set about shaking hands with the new arrivals.

"You look great, dear, and congratulations on the degree," Deirdre said. "*Cum laude*, very impressive. I'm sure your father is as proud as am I."

"Well, I would have liked it to be *summa cum,* but we can't have everything," he responded good-naturedly. "However," he quickly shifted ground, turning to tug at the arm of one of the girls in the group, "Nasreen here did merit *summa cum laude* and, wouldn't you know, she's headed to Johns Hopkins on a full scholarship."

The dark-haired young woman, embarrassed by being singled out, turned crimson. Roxane eyed the girl closely.

"Hey, you others didn't do badly either," he threw out, poking one of the guys in the ribs. His other friends made some jocular comments which Deirdre didn't catch.

The group chatted for a few more minutes, Caitlin and Ray looking ill at ease and Roxane on edge, until Deirdre suggested they head to Dylan's lodgings where they'd all be accommodated, most of the student body having already vacated the campus.

"See you guys around. Keep in touch," Dylan turned to his fellow students to say before opening the car door for his mother and jumping into the driver's seat himself.

As they drove through the leafy campus, Dylan pointed out this or that building, the football stadium, the new arts complex, his favorite tree to study under, weather permitting. Eventually, he turned onto a tree-lined street with Victorian-era homes, pulling up in front of a gray-slated one with steep steps and a wide front porch. "We've had a lot of parties here. I'll miss that," he said, switching off the ignition and popping the trunk.

Without further ado, he carried his mother's luggage up the steps and gestured to Ray to grab the remaining bags. After he situated his mother in a large upstairs front bedroom, he escorted his sister and her boyfriend to adjoining quarters in the rear of the building. Roxane had on her own ensconced herself in an empty middle bedroom. He did not linger at her door.

Dylan's own room, which, after a cursory clean-up he invited his mother to inspect, was decently arranged, boasting a double bed and a fold-out couch as well as a window-facing desk and two now empty bookcases. Several taped-up boxes lined the sides of the room, along with two bulging suitcases Deirdre recognized as coming from home. She smiled approvingly. Only then did Dylan ask if Nasreen could come along to the family dinner booked for Friday night, since he'd offered to drive her to the City the next day.

"But of course," Deirdre said. "She seems lovely."

Lying wide awake that night in an unfamiliar bed, Deirdre couldn't get the images of her two grown children out of her mind. Dylan, newly self-possessed, Penn having polished him, academically and socially; Caitlin well-nigh unreachable, beset by demons she couldn't likely identify, let alone exorcise. He's clearly going places and she clearly isn't. Perhaps Ashton could have a heart-to-heart with her, pry her away from this succession of loser boyfriends and steer her toward someone more suitable. Like, for instance, Zach. So lovely of him to make the effort to join us in Manhattan for the weekend. A perfect friend, for the two of them...

As Deirdre began to drift off, angry voices jolted her. The sounds seemed to emanate from down the hall rather than the street. She checked her cell phone: 2:25 a.m. *It isn't what you think* was the only phrase she caught in its entirety. Must be Caitlin and Ray going at it, she surmised. If a split were in the works, so much the better. *Music my daughter can make on her own.*

The next morning, however, Caitlin and Ray were love-y-dove-y, so whatever might have created a rift between them must have gotten patched up. And unless something else got in the way, the two would peel off from the others at the end of the weekend and decamp to Jersey City, where, to hear Ray tell it, he had a pad and his mates a nearby garage where they could practice. (Bruce Springsteen has derailed the lives of many a youngster with modest musical talent, Deirdre observed to herself, but dared not suggest to those two.)

The group had coffee and toast in relative silence, Roxane the last to come downstairs, in what looked to be yet another new outfit. After gulping a cup, Dylan busied himself loading his own luggage into the trunk and stacking boxes of books on the back seat of the Honda. Without being asked, he then headed back upstairs for Deirdre's and Caitlin's things. Roxane brought down her own carry-on and lifted it into the trunk of Deirdre's rented Toyota SUV.

"You do have the address on West 12th where we'll be staying, right, Dylan?" Deirdre asked, as the travelers got into her car.

"Of course, Mom. Nasreen and I are going to pick up Zach at Grand Central, but if he and I don't connect, I'll text him your colleague's address," he replied, turning on his engine. "We'll likely be around to the place by 6 o'clock at the latest."

"I've booked the restaurant for 8:30, so that your father can join us," she called out to her son. "You too, Ray," she added, looking into the rearview mirror.

"Cool," he replied noncommittally, which Deirdre took as a yes. Without another word, he stuck his iPod plug into his ear, Caitlin soon following suit.

"Really, Deirdre, I don't need to come along to your dinner tonight. There's plenty else I should be doing there," Roxane volunteered. She had already pulled a book out of her satchel, something in French, *La Chartreuse*...something or other, which lay in her lap as yet unopened.

"Nonsense," Deirdre insisted. "You know how the children dote on you," she added, instantly thinking that *to dote* was not the appropriate verb.

"As you wish," her friend acquiesced, also noncommittally, which Deirdre took as a yes.

Which was just as well. "Other people can help keep things civil," Howard had counseled his client early on when almost anything Ashton said or did set Deirdre's teeth on edge. So eminently sensible, she mused, shifting the car into drive and pulling out into the deserted street.

As for how she now felt about her ex-husband, she wasn't entirely sure.

Mostly, and especially after Howard died and the children left home, she regretted not having a man around to talk to and to do things with. No fault of their own, but Stella, Margery, and Roxane did not wholly compensate. However, when she did communicate with Ashton, she ended up annoyed that he had remained so overbearing. Like a week ago when he had called to go over, and she had to repeat, or rather defend, the logistics of the NYC weekend.

"We're doing it to celebrate Dylan's achievements, Ashton, not yours or mine," she had pointed out as placidly as she could. "Carnegie Hall on Saturday night—Brahms' second violin concerto. How could you object to that?" she asked.

"You and I heard it together in Boston," he snipped, as though that occasion should have been enough to last a lifetime. "And, on Friday, I forget what you arranged, but it sounded touristic or over-rated."

"Again, I booked the Tavern on the Green, which you may be too snobbish for, but our children aren't," she had wound up, exasperation seeping into her voice.

In the end, Ashton had acquiesced to everything and agreed to show up. Alone.

This back-and-forth took place on the phone with the cries of a small (and either spoiled or neglected) child in the background.

Although she hated to admit it, that's what irritated Deirdre the most: what else did this Jennifer have to do than to see to her baby?

In any case, tonight's dinner, she figured, would be the trickiest part of the weekend. Outsiders—Ray, Zach, Roxane, and Nasreen— at the table might be a good thing. Without making an issue of the fact, it would be the first time she and Ashton would have had a meal together, in public, since the divorce was finalized. Four years almost to the day. Deirdre took a deep breath and looked out for signs leading to the turnpike.

Chapter Twenty

T hings became ticklish at Tavern on the Green when Ashton began to grill Caitlin about her plans, and she floundered. Deirdre attributed his persistence in that line of questioning to the wine, as his face had flushed and his hands couldn't disguise a slight tremor.

Not wanting to get into an argument with her ex, however, she looked beseechingly at the other men at the table.

To her surprise, Ray made the first stab by explaining, in reasonably complete sentences, that he and his buddies from Jersey City had well-funded plans to get their band off the ground. They had identified Caitlin as a gifted vocalist; they hoped to cut a single before the summer was out; they had meetings arranged with bookers in the area.

"My dear fellow. In the music business, it's all about the record labels. If you're not signed by one of them, you're nobody," Ashton had countered, shaking his head at the naiveté of the young.

Ray opened his mouth to object, but Caitlin kicked him under the table.

"Actually, Dr. Cole, the Internet is changing that equation. A number of musicians are going the digital route and making money at it," Zach jumped in in support of the two. Caitlin shot him a look of gratitude.

"Be that as it may, it's a hard road, my daughter is untrained and—"

"I was telling her the same thing earlier," Roxane piped up. "But with training, no telling how far she could go."

"Yeah, Dad. You haven't heard her sing, not in a long while. What's wrong with her trying to do what she enjoys?" Dylan asked.

"Nothing, nothing. Especially since the dance thing—(here Caitlin's face fell, Deirdre's grew taut). Well, what I mean is she—the two of you," Ashton rambled on, focusing for the first time on the two young people together, "need to be aware of the obstacles."

At this point he abandoned his train of thought, Ray somehow reminding him of the slack-jawed young fellows who had been coming around the house to see Jennifer before things with her fell apart. And now this one across from him, eating prime rib on Deirdre's dime, (and likely sleeping with their daughter—which is what all of them do at that age but even so—), appears as feckless as those others. And Deirdre's dime, if you really think about it, could be construed as being still his dime too. He heartily disliked this Ray fellow and resented that his ex-wife had so blithely invited him along to what was billed as a family gathering.

As for the other interlopers, Roxane had always struck him as a queer bird but harmless enough; this Nasreen was pretty and presumably shy, which was fine with him; Zach reminded him of the gifted students—too few, too few—who had over the years flitted through his courses. He wondered what the young man was studying at Princeton; for that matter, he wondered what his own son would be studying at Princeton. He should know, but if Deirdre had told him, it had slipped his mind.

Meanwhile, as Ashton ruminated, the conversation had entered even thornier territory. The talk was of Syria, and what was to be done about it. Zach's eyes had alighted on Nasreen, who until then had remained quiet, only sporadically looking up to catch something someone else said.

"Invading doesn't seem to help any situation we get involved in," she began tentatively. "However, " she continued, as everyone turned to listen, "Assad is arguably as dug-in as Saddam was, so it's going to take pressure to prod him to step down. Asylum somewhere really cushy may be the only viable solution unless—"

"Well, *you* might not be aware, but France and Britain have historical responsibilities across the Middle East," Roxane interrupted, her voice high-pitched. "They drew the lines on the map and should be the ones to lean on this tyrant."

All eyes shifted in her direction except Dylan's, who sat picking at his salad. Undeterred by his evident disinterest, Roxane went on. "To effect any real change, you need to know the back story of the region."

For an excruciating interval, no one hazarded a response, least of all Nasreen, who appeared flummoxed, if not by the argument, by the condescending tone of it.

"Actually, Nasreen does understand the history of the place. Her major was MidEast Studies. She speaks perfect Arabic," Dylan stated quietly.

Putting down his fork, Ray theatrically cocked two fingers in the direction of Roxane. "*Bang, bang,*" he shot off knowingly, which made the others at the table flinch.

To clear the air, Ashton called for the dessert menu and made an elaborate show of ordering for the entire table.

Once the waiter had brought the order, Roxane spoke up again, her tone this time bright, as though nothing awkward had taken place.

"I waited until now because I have you all together," she dove in as everyone began picking at the red velvet cake slices. At this overture, no one dared to look up except, fleetingly, Dylan, whose body tensed. "Turns out I've been hired to teach at Dorset High on the Upper West Side," she announced, scanning the faces around her for reaction.

"You mean here in the City?" Deirdre asked, stunned by the news and unsure if her own recommendation had played a part in what must be a promotion of sorts.

"Yes, right here in Manhattan. It was time for me to move on from Ohio, especially since my favorite students have graduated and gone on to greater things," she went on to say. Neither Caitlin nor Dylan raised their eyes from the plates in front of them.

"What will you be teaching, Roxane?" Zach asked, a note of challenge in his voice.

"French and Spanish. You see, I lived abroad for some time," she answered off-handedly. "*Beaucoup d'années*, in fact."

"So, you were studying, or working?" Zach persevered, not only because he was taught to fill troublesome silences but because he was puzzled by this person. (Once, she had shown up at Penn, unannounced, and he had inadvertently run into her, with Dylan. "Something of a cougar, I'd say. You'd better watch it," he remembered warning his younger friend, only half-facetiously.)

"Both, at different junctures," Roxane responded, gesturing with her hand to signal she did not wish to be further pinned down on the topic.

It was left to Ray to try to get a rise out of her. "So, Roxane, I'm asking myself, were Caitlin and Dylan among those who made you want to leave Ohio or, don't tell me, could they have been among your favorites?"

"Well, we are all here together, are we not?" she obfuscated, before turning her head toward Deirdre to say, "Enough about me. I do believe the hour has come for a toast to your son, *n'est-ce pas*?"

"Absolutely," Deirdre replied, while Ashton motioned to the nearest waiter to bring a couple of bottles of Veuve Cliquot.

When the goblets were raised, Deirdre went first: "To my—*our*—son," she corrected herself, "for achieving such an impressive milestone at Penn, for winning a coveted spot at Princeton, but mostly for being a gifted and giving person."

"Hear, hear," Ashton chimed in, providing his own gloss. "I too am immensely proud of you, Dylan. And no, I will not be asking for the violin back, so long as you promise to keep practicing!"

Had it not been for everyone's packed schedules, Ashton would have used the weekend to unburden himself of his own news, which, while not of the order of Roxane's revelation, did have bearing on the family. He had planned to make as amusing an account of it as possible, without supplying unpleasantly graphic details and without assigning blame. As it turned out, everyone, including his ex-wife, professed being tired, quickly piling into two cabs for the trip to the West Village, leaving Ashton on his own.

On Saturday the right opportunity never materialized either, what with Deirdre rushing off right after breakfast Saturday morning to Bergdorfs, followed by lunch with an old college chum and a stint at the 42nd Street library until time for the concert. (Had she so organized things that she and he would never find themselves alone? Quite possibly, he concluded.) Nor did it seem practical to bring up such a delicate matter during intermission at Carnegie Hall, what with Dylan prattling on about the violinist's performance and Deirdre and Caitlin disappearing into the interminable line for the restroom.

Thus, though he wasn't, strictly speaking, invited over to the West Village apartment for Sunday morning brunch, he would show up anyway to say his goodbyes, again, to Dylan and Zach, both headed to Princeton, to Caitlin and Ray, who would be decamping for Jersey City, to Nasreen, whose parents lived in Westchester, and to Roxane, who would be using the occasion to apartment-hunt, if he heard rightly. That way he could catch his ex-wife alone before she headed out to LaGuardia, or offer to drive her to the airport. Might make the whole sorry saga less distressful to recount and her less resentful (or gleeful?) to hear it.

Since the 59th Street Bridge was likely bumper to bumper on a Sunday, the drive to the airport would take the better part of an hour. But to broach such a painful subject while maneuvering across town, and without losing control of the narrative, appeared to be more daunting than he had bargained for. Especially since, once they started off, his ex-wife was happily people-watching from the passenger seat as they crossed from one side of the island to the other.

"Great to be reminded how invigorating this place is," Deirdre said as they headed uptown. "But who would have thought Roxane would figure that out and get herself a job here? Could you have imagined such a thing?"

"I never thought about her having any drive or ambition outside of..." Ashton responded, not sure what he was trying to articulate.

"Outside of being a teacher somewhere in rural Ohio for the rest of her life," Deirdre finished his sentence for him.

"I didn't mean it like that," he came back at her, not wanting to pick an argument and not meaning to have implied that his ex-wife was in a rut.

"Still," Deirdre went on, "Roxane has gumption," she posited, puffing now on a Virginia Slim. "Which is a word we don't hear often, probably because the quality is in short supply."

After maneuvering past a stalled truck, Ashton nodded in agreement. "I didn't know you had started up again," he remarked, opening the ashtray below the dashboard. It still had a few stubs in it with smudges of Jennifer's lipstick on them.

"Now and again," she replied vaguely, "since Howard died."

They had made their way onto the upper level of the bridge, the East River glistening in the summer sun.

"Sorry about that," Ashton said. "He did seem a decent chap, the few occasions--—well, it was a topsy-turvy time."

From his vantage point, Deirdre appeared to roll her eyes, but she did not comment. Instead, she pressed the button to lower the window. "Like Johnson said of London, who would ever tire of this city unless they were tired of life," she asked rhetorically. In a minute or two she tossed her cigarette out the window and checked the time on her cell phone. Her flight to Memphis didn't leave for two hours. "Plenty of time," she said. "No need to speed. And, in case I forget when getting out, I appreciate your doing this."

"The least I could do," he responded.

Eventually, the traffic thinned, and they made their way onto the Grand Central Parkway toward the off-ramp for the airport. Ashton realized he had missed his chance to bring up the subject at the front of his mind. It was a ticklish matter, he was devastated by it, and he now had, at age fifty-five, a three-year-old daughter to bring up. No way to make light of that.

STILL. Why ruin the camaraderie between the two of them to recount his own troubles, especially since those troubles revolved around Jennifer, whose very name his ex-wife could barely bring herself to utter. She might even gloat, right here in the car, which would spoil what had been a blessedly non-confrontational, even enjoyable, weekend.

They drove the last leg in relative silence.

Until, out of nowhere, Deirdre made herself inquire,: "So, how is the baby? I heard her crying last time we spoke." When he did not immediately respond, she free-associated. "Quite a name, Sierra. Like for someone who lives in Malibu or some other mellow enclave."

She stole a glance at her ex-husband, and was sorry for mocking the child's name. He looked disconcerted by the gratuitous jab. Older too. Hatched lines criss-crossed his forehead, his jowls sagged. Not unattractive even now, but more weighed down.

A baby will do that, she concluded.

To his credit, Ashton recovered from her jab. "Sierra is amazing. Always in motion. Certain days she reminds me of Caitlin, that is, Caitlin when she was little, before…well, before so many things happened to her. Anyway, I'm thinking of enrolling her in a French class. As you know, it's the perfect age to learn a new language, or anything else for that matter."

"What does Jennifer think?" Deirdre asked, right as they took the ramp marked *Departures* and had to make a quick choice.

"What terminal did you say you're flying out of?"

Chapter Twenty-One

To put into words what had destroyed his marriage to Jennifer did not come easily to Ashton, but he berated himself during the drive back to Pennsylvania for not having provided an account to the one person to whom he most owed one. He would have to spell it out in a letter, but only the highlights, or better, lowlights. What was it Tolstoy had said? "All happy marriages are alike, all unhappy ones unhappy in their own way…" *And boring to everyone else*, Ashton muttered. He would keep his description of the break-up brief, without wallowing in self-pity or implicitly inviting his ex-wife's moral support.

Halfway home to Rolling Hills, he found himself going over several telling incidents, each successive one more troubling than the preceding. He wasn't sure he could bear putting them in a letter.

A year into their marriage, and shortly after Jennifer became pregnant, Ashton decided to surprise his bride with tickets to a Bruce Springsteen concert in New York, reckoning that forthwith, for an indeterminate period, such jaunts would be curtailed. It was on the outskirts of the city that he dug into his pocket and flashed the tickets in her face, expecting her to squeal with delight. She didn't. Rather, she had looked crest-fallen, pointedly leafing through a stack of fashion magazines she had brought along.

Finally, she spoke up. "Springsteen's really your thing, Ash. I'll go see my dad, stay at his place tonight, hang out with friends. You know, *my* friends, from different schools. But, let's have lunch tomorrow. Cafe des Artistes or something."

So dumbfounded was he by this brush-off, as though he were a casual acquaintance she might dedicate a few hours to, he narrowly avoided side-swiping an SUV on the George Washington Bridge.

"I really don't see why you—"

"Oh, give it a rest," she had cut him off. "It's not my thing. You're—"

"What? Older, not with it enough?"

She pursed her lips, tossed her pile of magazines on the floor, and stared out the window.

Neither spoke again until they pulled up at the Warwick on 57th Street, a reservation Ashton had made believing that the hotel's celebrity guests might impress his wife. But given the chilliness between the two, he didn't bother to extol the reputation of the place. She got out and hailed a cab.

Numbed and demoralized, Ashton nonetheless took the subway to the Beacon Theater where he offloaded his extra ticket to a middle-aged woman who was overly communicative throughout the concert.

"Thunder Road" indeed.

Later on, when Sierra had turned one and Jennifer had come out of postpartum depression, Ashton went out of his way to find a nanny so that Jennifer might be freed up to do other things. After all, they were on a college campus, where, given his own status there, she could take advantage of lower tuition and other perks. He had scoured the brochure, circling courses that he thought might pique his wife's interest, and that did not sound too taxing: everything from *The Depiction of Women in the Twentieth Century Novel* to *Highlights of Western Art*. (He had long ago admitted to himself, after re-reading the term papers Jennifer had submitted in his poetry seminar at Klimpton, and comparing them to those by her friend Kimberly, that they were not notably astute. Much less so than her friend's.)

However, when he brought up the idea of enrolling in a class, she balked. Rebuffed, he dropped the subject for a time, mulling over what he might say or do to get his wife enthused about—well, anything at all. Mostly, when he returned home in the evenings, he would find her playing with her iPhone. Rarely did he walk in to find her tending to Sierra.

Brightly yet diplomatically, Ashton picked up the thread of the discussion again, this time after an elaborate dinner he had prepared (and a glass of chianti to fortify himself): "You have such opportunities here, and you're so bright, there's bound to be a field you'd like to explore." She flashed him a bored look. "Did you take a look at that brochure?"

Carefully, Jennifer folded the linen napkin he had set the table with and placed her fork on the dinner plate. Running her tongue over her lips (a gesture that used to excite him but of late unnerved him), she glared at him. "In case you're wondering, Dr. Cole— (addressing him thusly to signal her distain)—I have no desire to study further." For an instant, Ashton looked as though he had been slapped. "No way am I going to turn into another stressed-out, washed-up academic like your first wife," she further pummeled him.

"I don't believe it's the case to demean—"

"Again, in case you haven't noticed," she wound up, "I'm twenty-four. I'm not going to bury myself in a library just to make you appear to have a dutiful wife with the same dreary scholarly pretensions."

In her playpen down the hall, Sierra began to cry. Automatically, Ashton rose to see to her. "As I was saying, there's no need to drag

Deirdre into this. And I don't believe *dreary* does my ex-wife justice."

"Whatever," Jennifer mumbled, the fallback response of her generation whenever they had no ready retort, or could be bothered to formulate one.

For a while after that skirmish, the couple trundled along. Ashton did not ask his wife what she did with her days, nor did he query the high-priced nanny as to his wife's movements; for her part, Jennifer avoided all mention of the monograph Ashton was still laboring over. The two rarely ventured out together. Mostly, they communicated over the running of the house, the leaky faucet, the heating unit that needed to be replaced. Or, if he sensed his wife was in a decent mood, he'd update her on Sierra's progress—walking, talking, reading, drawing and, of late, "As her teacher hastened to tell me when I picked her up at school, she is now penning little poems to accompany her pictures."

"Must take after you," Jennifer had commented, though her tone could have been construed as caustic rather than complimentary.

Ashton decided not to hear it so. "I've been thinking, now that Sierra is at such an interesting age, your mother might enjoy meeting her only granddaughter. It wouldn't have to be a long visit but after all—"

Jennifer smacked her lips in displeasure. "There is no *after all* with her. As I indicated a long time ago, we are not in each other's lives. Period."

"But surely some part of her, or you—"

"She was jealous. That's all I'm going to say on the subject," Jennifer snapped. A dense silence fell over the dining room until Sierra toddled in and pulled at her father's pants leg.

Although it gnawed at him, Ashton did not pursue the topic of Mrs. Hazelton's estrangement from her daughter. A month or so later, Kimberly turned up, instantly realizing that her former professor had no idea her visit had been pre-arranged.

"Jen and I are going to Philly for the weekend, Dr. Cole. To a concert and other things...Old friends from the other school we attended. Before Klimpton."

"I see," he responded, eyeing her smart-looking outfit and her stylish haircut. Definitely a step up from her sloppy appearance those two years in Oakville. Or, perhaps he had unfairly compared her to the alluring figure that Jennifer cut back then. "While we're waiting for my wife to come down, would you like something?"

"No, no. I'm fine," the young woman responded, clasping and unclasping her hands as though impatient to leave. Her nails were painted a dark red as were her sandal-exposed toenails.

He ignored her fidgeting. "So, what are you doing these days, Kimberly?"

"Third year at NYU law school, Dr. Cole. I'll be clerking for a federal judge this summer."

"Impressive," he replied, not surprised that his wife had never seen fit to mention how well her former college chum was doing. "While I have you, Kimberly, I wonder if you can shed light on that rupture between Jen and her mother. You two must have talked about it—you are her best friend, right?"

Looking like she'd rather be anywhere else, Kimberly darted her eyes toward the stairs. "I really can't say, Dr. Cole. So long ago," she stammered, flummoxed either by the question or by the fact that the professor was asking it of her—out of school, as it were.

"But you must have an opinion," he pressed her.

She puffed up her cheeks and let the air out slowly. "All three of them were at fault. If Jen hasn't already told you—"

"Ah, there you are," Ashton called out brightly, his wife suddenly at the doorway, an overnight bag in one hand, sunglasses in the other. As she slipped them on, he noticed that dark red polish adorned her nails as well.

"We're running late. My fault, I know, so..." Jennifer said, flicking her wrist in a dismissive goodbye.

Intuiting the state of affairs between the two, Kimberly vigorously shook the professor's hand and mumbled her apologies. "Sorry, sir. We do need to go."

"Don't you want to let her see Sierra first?" Ashton called out as his wife headed toward the front door. "The child's asleep," she responded, without bothering to turn back around.

At the end of that weekend, Ashton realized that he no longer knew—if ever he had known—his young wife. The worst of it was that he wasn't sure he any longer wanted to know her. However beautiful she was, however much he had relished exploring her body and finding himself transported in the process and she (presumably?) satisfied thereby, however much he had imagined that her mind was as enticing—and to the extent that it wasn't yet fully formed, he could intercede to make it so—by now he knew he had erred.

He had been standing at the front window, holding Sierra in his arms so that she could admire the sunset, when a silver Infiniti drove up. It idled in front of the house for several minutes until a tall young man got out, opened the trunk and lifted Jennifer's carry-on out. At the same time, his wife emerged from the passenger side. The two spoke for a moment but Ashton couldn't make out what was said. Smiling up at the young man, Jennifer rested her hand on his arm, familiarly. Then she rolled her case to the front door. Ashton could hear her fiddle with the lock, followed by the sound of wheels on the bare floor.

"Mommy, Mommy," Sierra called out, flailing to be put down. She toddled to the hallway, but Jennifer was already halfway up the stairs.

"Down in a few," she said, impatiently enough that the child hesitated, then retreated to her father and clung to his pants leg.

When Jennifer did descend half an hour later in robe and slippers, Ashton was heating up a pot on the stove.

"Plenty of soup," he declared. "In fact, I threw in every vegetable in the house. Or, I could make you a sandwich. There's ham, cheese..., other things too."

"Mommy, Mommy, I got another blue star in school," Sierra blurted out between bites of a peanut butter sandwich. "Teacher said I did the best of anyone."

"We ate on the road," Jennifer replied, opening the fridge and retrieving an open bottle of white wine. She pulled out the cork and poured herself a glass. "What was it you did at school, Sierra, to get a star?" she asked distractedly, seating herself across from her daughter.

"I read a poem, Mommy. I mean I *re-ci-ded*—(here Ashton mouthed the correct pronunciation)—I *recited* a poem, all of it, from the beginning."

"Well, that figures, doesn't it," Jennifer replied drily, and took a sip of chardonnay. So dismayed was the child's expression that she softened her tone. "Could you do it again, sweetheart, just for me?"

"I can't remember it now," Sierra began, before bursting into tears.

Ashton came over and patted his daughter on the head. "It'll all come back to you tomorrow, Sierra. I forget poems all the time, which makes it more fun to reread them. OK? We'll do it together."

Keeping her eyes lowered, Sierra wiped her nose with the back of her hand and shook her head.

"Alright then. Let's eat some soup and then we'll try the ice cream. Perhaps your mother will have some too," he stated, regarding his wife closely for the first time that evening. There was a coldness in her eyes he had not remarked before.

After Ashton had tucked Sierra into bed and she had clung to his neck extra tight, Jennifer announced that she was leaving him, moving to New York City, on her own.

However clueless he was about women, Ashton had reflected enough on the divorce from Deirdre to admit she had, as she then claimed, almost certainly tasted "the wormwood and the gall." They had been seated across from each other in the living room, the twins having been sent upstairs. Glowering at him, she had added her own rhetorical flourish to the Biblical quotation. "To be so spurned is to taste bile. You cannot know of it unless it has happened to you."

He suspected his ex-wife might feel *schadenfreude* when he did eventually write or recount how things disintegrated with Jennifer, but he was already so demoralized that the thought of her gloating did not bother him. He would deserve it. And for what it was worth, he did now know personally about bile, having spent the last six months with stomach problems. One of the physicians at Winslow had asked what was going on at home that might account for the ailments, but Ashton couldn't bring himself to confide. "Stress, you know, doctor. Trying to finish a book, dealing with a new baby."

The doctor had scribbled a prescription for a sleep aid and a stool softener.

To little effect. Before he knew it, Ashton was drinking too much, eating erratically, still sleeping poorly and finding it hard to concentrate. Especially after Jennifer's father paid him an unexpected visit, warning him to desist in trying to contact his daughter, and hinting that if he played ball, he'd receive $100,000 in cash to hire a full-time nanny and enroll the toddler in kindergarten.

"Jennifer deserves her own life, Ashton. And wishes you and the child well. In fact, you could retain sole custody. You're going to want to continue teaching that physical poetry you're contracted for. New opportunities await you too. No hard feelings, huh?"

It was only then that Ashton sensed the threat behind his erstwhile father-in-law's words, reminding himself to tool around on Google to see what Harold Hazelton's hedge fund was really up to. "I do think your daughter and I need to discuss some loose ends. If need be, I can come the weekend to New York, whichever is more convenient for her. Bring Sierra along too."

"Not to be. Don't you get it? Not to be." With that dissuasive admonishment, Harold checked his cell phone, extended his arm to keep Ashton at bay, and took his leave.

That was four months before the family gathering at Tavern on the Green. So far, Ashton had put off saying anything definite to Sierra, but circumventing her queries was becoming more distressing by the day. He had even entertained the idea of showing up at Harold's office in Manhattan during the weekend with Deirdre and the kids but ultimately couldn't get up the courage. Besides, he couldn't risk being detained by security guards at Evermore Securities. They might call the cops.

If he did secretly hope Deirdre would be sympathetic to what had befallen him, Ashton decided as he drove the last leg back to Rolling Hills that it was for the best that the subject had not surfaced during their weekend with Dylan and Caitlin. Better, he concluded, to limit the letter to a rundown of plans for Sierra's education, and not focus on Jennifer's treachery, or his own myopia.

And written before his parents spill the beans to her. He would not mention the $100,000 cash payment he received from Harold, but he *would* set about to hire a live-in nanny.

No whiff should there be that he, the husband who had strayed and who now found himself abandoned, would like to go back to the way things were before. From what he had observed of his first wife during the New York visit, she had managed to move on with her life—the fling with that lawyer Howard, not her fault that it ended...and a book under her belt, to boot—whereas, truth be told, he could be said to have dithered.

That self-assessment pretty much dovetailed with what Ashton's parents had concluded when he rang up, and in order to forestall a visit from them, was obliged to reveal that he and Jennifer had called it quits.

They saw right through his jaunty version of the breakup.

"Looks like you've made a fool of yourself, Ash, and are now stuck—with a child no less. Who knows what college will cost by the time. Anyway, we can't help you much on that score. Adeline, as you might imagine, isn't getting any better," the elder Cole had stated flatly. "And then there's this Madoff thing. We too got bamboozled."

"Nonetheless, dear, we have continued to make gifts to Dylan and to Caitlin, which Deirdre has been gracious enough to thank us for. On multiple occasions," his mother chimed in from the upstairs phone. (Ironic, he had thought, how their allegiance had tilted toward their former daughter-in-law.) "In any case, do bring the child next time you find your way to Boston."

After a two-week search, Ashton hired the mother of one of Winslow's foreign-born students, a Syrian who had fled when hostilities broke out in that country. The woman's name was Amira. She spoke only broken English but had a kind, open face.

Chapter Twenty-Two

Once cruising altitude had been reached, Deirdre closed her eyes, determined to place the New York weekend in its proper mental folder and to bring forward a blank file in which her summer in the Delta would form the chief component. If only the things that happen could be arranged that neatly, she mused, as she pressed the button on her window seat and reclined it enough to rest her head and shoulders.

All things considered, the gathering had unspooled remarkably well: Dylan and Zach had held forth so amusingly on so many subjects it had made her head spin. Caitlin and Ray had inevitably been outshone, but even they made sporadic efforts to cast off their glumness and join in. She and Ashton had both behaved civilly, if stiltedly, but better that than an altercation in front of the kids.

Only Roxane performed off-key, as it were, trying to upstage, or put down, poor Nasreen and then springing the news about her new job.

"Never could figure her out," Ashton had commented on the drive out to LaGuardia, before trailing off with an under-the-breath comment about not figuring out much of anybody.

Something must be gnawing at him, Deirdre had surmised, though it was none of her business to wonder what. (She regretted not having shown more interest in the child, or indirectly inquiring after Jennifer, but a knot deep inside still prevented her from being charitable in regards to the woman who had stolen her husband.)

It is what it is, and I am who I am, Deirdre repeated to herself as the plane began a bumpy descent through cloud banks toward the Memphis airport. She repositioned her seat back and stared out, catching intermittent glimpses of the river. The sight of that silvery ribbon had always quickened her pulse; she would have liked to regal her fellow passengers with a few facts about the Mississippi, but those seated nearby were all glued to one screen or another.

Instead, she gathered up her unread *New Yorker* and slipped it into her shoulder bag. Time to do some calculations: the rental car counter was walkable from the arrivals area, unless the airport had been enlarged or re-arranged in the last few years; once out of local traffic, the drive down 61 South to Riverton would likely take two hours tops. Her mother should be at home and expecting her. She'd pick up steaks or chicken along the way, perhaps a bottle of wine, though Mrs. Durrell drank only rarely, to celebrate. Her own homecoming might not be such an occasion.

Driving south, Deirdre was struck by how much dust had settled on the Delta towns she passed through, how many buildings were either abandoned or in desperate need of repair. She spotted a few lonely scarecrows in unplowed or neglected fields, and barns which appeared emptied of hay or horses.

As her mother had indicated in the infrequent letters she wrote, the Great Recession had taken a toll, reducing some places to only a shadow of their former selves. Their closest neighbors, the Lormans, had picked up and moved to North Carolina to be closer to family. So too had Linda Belle, the high school beauty queen, who for years ran the town's only decent dress shop, but who boarded up the windows one night in 2010 and, as her mother put it, "skedaddled."

Dottie Hearn, a distant cousin who had partied hard through high school, finally upped and left her ne'er-do-well husband, moving upriver to Tunica to work in the casino.

Depressing her mother's letters could be, which helped explain, if not justify, why Deirdre had labored to be upbeat in hers, few though they were. In short, for more than a decade, mother and daughter, did little but write past each other, exchanging holiday greetings on the phone without ever communicating, and promising visits back and forth that never came to be.

The last time they had spoken, Deirdre phoning up to announce she was taking a sabbatical (of sorts, since she wasn't a full professor who was allowed such, but why burden her mother with that irrelevancy?) and that much of it she'd love to spend "back home."

"But of course, dear," her mother had responded, the undisguised bewilderment in her voice notwithstanding.

The pause on the line thereafter made Deirdre go a step further, promising against her own better judgment that at least one of the children, probably Caitlin, but perhaps Dylan too, would also love to come along, depending...

"Splendid," Mrs. Durrell had recovered enough to rejoin. She had not laid eyes on her two grandchildren in eight years.

As in so many instances in which she disappointed her mother, Deirdre would not be delivering on that promise either. She hadn't reckoned on Dylan's immediate transfer to Princeton and didn't have the heart to tear him away from his new adventure. Nor had she banked on Caitlin's newfound romance, if that were the proper term, and her equally newfound commitment to doing something with her music.

However disappointed Mrs. Durrell would be, Deirdre knew she wouldn't make a fuss. As of old, her mother would nod just so, as if to suggest that all was as it had to be. At the thought, she decelerated and reached for a tissue in her handbag.

While the last rays of the sun receded across the river and the highway traffic began to dwindle, Deirdre tried to conjure what she knew about her mother's current life and how she might try to enhance it, or at least not get in the way of it. Presumably, even at sixty-six, Clarissa Durrell was still teaching at the high school, English or History or both; presumably, she was still volunteering at the local library—did Riverton still have a library?—on Saturdays; presumably, she still grew tomatoes, okra and occasional herbs in the back yard; presumably, she still played bridge with the trio of friends who had not left town, or died off. Presumably, too, her mother would have come to terms with the fact that her only daughter was a forty-something divorcée with two grown kids, and that there was nothing to be done about that either.

Around sunset, Deirdre pulled into a garish gas station cum convenience store called Kangaroo, which she figured part of a regional chain and might have a grocery section. The only available produce, however, consisted of bruised red apples and three limp heads of iceberg lettuce. A couple of hens were languishing on a spit. She bought one of them for the late-in-the-day special price of $2.15, along with a Sara Lee coffee cake and a carton of Diet Cokes.

A clerk with mayonnaise-colored hair eyed Deirdre curiously from behind the counter. "You can have the other chicken for a dollar more," she said, as she rang up the tab.

"This will do," Deirdre replied, fishing in her purse for cash.

"Not from around these parts, huh?" the clerk opined.

"Not really, no," she further responded, not looking up and not wanting to prolong the exchange.

Back on the highway, Deirdre tuned the radio as best she could to whatever must be the nearest NPR affiliate, landing on the station in Greenwood. For the final forty-five minutes of her journey, she listened haphazardly to yet another debate on ObamaCare, and, in this case, what the ACA might bode for Mississippians on Medicaid. Apparently, the legislature in Jackson was balking at accepting federal subsidies, the states' rights reflex still strong in the Deep South.

She wondered what her mother thought about all this, but decided it best to wait until she brought it up. In fact, it was best that she herself not hold forth on politics, religion, marriage—or much of anything. If she did envision spending the entire year in her childhood home, she would need to respect that it was her mother's place to call the shots, even if Clarissa Durrell had never thought proper to do so when her husband was alive.

"Men rule the roost. That's all there is to it," she used to say to her daughter, dust cloth or soup ladle or watering can in hand. "You can argue with them until you're blue in the face, or, you can work around them and actually get things done."

That pretty much summed up her mother's *modus operandi* at the time, however much Deirdre as a teenager tried to convince her parents that times had changed: Stephen Quincy Durrell, a small-town lawyer set in his ways and rarely challenged, would have none of it; her mother, with a master's degree from Sophie Newcomb in New Orleans that she never did anything with, kept her own counsel.

Thinking back to their last visit, with Ashton, the kids, Caedmon too, now eight years ago, what had been a pleasant enough stay—the elder Durrells had taken them along to a community fish-fry and organized a boat trip on the river—devolved into a stand-off between the two men over the wars in Iraq and Afghanistan (which neither had heretofore ever shown much preoccupation with). Then, somehow after dinner on their last night in Riverton, Ashton and his father-in-law ended up squabbling about the war on poverty, raising voices in praise of, or impugning, that historic trip through the Delta that Robert Kennedy had taken—in the Sixties, for God's sake.

Deirdre switched off the radio and took a deep breathe.

If she had only known, or her mother had had the courtesy to tell her, that her father's heart condition had worsened, she would have butted in, insisted the two men desist, told them they were unlikely to solve the world's problems while drinking bourbon and arguing on the back porch, and instead, called upon Dylan and Caitlin to play something on their instruments, accompanied by their grandma on the upright. Mrs. Durrell's grits and pork chops did little to clear the air the next morning. Handshakes between the men were perfunctory, the kids were querulous, and Deirdre had to spend her final hour searching for the dog. Having been forgotten out on the porch the night before, and no doubt tired of hearing the two men grouse, he had wandered off.

When her father passed away fourteen months later, Deirdre flew to the Delta alone for the funeral. For several months thereafter, she had toyed with the idea of inviting her mother to come live with the family in Ohio, imagining how she would encourage her to audit a class at Klimpton, or take up quilting, not to mention babysit the kids and cook for the household now and again. But to her astonishment, Mrs. Durrell, who had only ever cleaned her house, raised a daughter, and tended to her husband's wants, was hired by the local high school to teach English and History to ninth graders. From there she rose to become in charge of the Advanced Placement courses in English, History and French for qualifying juniors and seniors.

Surely, given the extent to which her mother had spread her own wings, Deirdre thought, she will not be judgmental about my being newly on my own. After all, Clarissa Durrell had never warmed to Ashton in the first place.

As she slowed to turn off the highway, Deirdre noticed a couple of new markers, too hard to read in the dark but likely signaling one or another blues musician from the region. Zach, of all people, had been going on about this campaign over dinner at the Tavern, letting drop how much he'd look forward to accompanying Dylan, if and when he made it down there to visit his grandma. Such a visit, something to look forward to, she told herself.

It being Sunday night, traffic was at a minimum along Main Street, albeit several dozen cars were parked outside the overly-lit Baptist Church. Deirdre took a right and then a left and pulled up in front of her mother's home. Two floodlights bathed a semi-circular fern garden, and Malibu lights illuminated what was now a paved walkway from the curb to the front door. A silver Subaru stood in the driveway.

Deirdre got out, taking her shoulder bag and the wrapped chicken with her. Somewhere in her purse was a door key that might or might not still work, but rather than fumble around, she rang the bell and waited. Her mother, still in what appeared to be her Sunday church clothes, smiled as she opened the door, a cell phone in her left hand.

196

"Give me a minute, sweetheart," she whispered, putting the phone back to her ear and attempting to end a conversation. "My daughter has just arrived. But yes, over lunch sounds perfect. All right. Until then." Mrs. Durrell clicked off and held out her arms. The two embraced awkwardly, as they always had, neither being naturally demonstrative. "Sorry about that. The call. But you made excellent time. I hadn't expected you until around 9 or 10," she went on.

"Everything went smoothly, including the drive from Memphis," Deirdre replied automatically, bowled over at how well put together her mother appeared. And on a Sunday night. "You look wonderful, Mother."

"As do you, DeeDee. Your hair is becoming. But do come in. Your room's still the same and you might want to freshen up."

"I'll just put this in the kitchen. I don't know why—I bought a roast chicken, in case. Of course, well, we could go out..." she stuttered, feeling more discombobulated than she had anticipated.

Mrs. Durrell laughed. "Did you think I'd forgotten how to cook?" Deirdre looked embarrassed. "Not to worry. Put the bird in the fridge for tomorrow. I had the butcher—you'll remember old Mr. Stevens, well, now it's his son Seth who's taken over—cut up two filet mignons and I've made your favorite vegetables." (Deirdre had no clue as to this Mr. Stevens, nor any idea what vegetables had apparently been her favorites.)

"Sounds great," she replied, determined to be appreciative whatever her mother came up with. She headed to the kitchen, now updated and enlarged with a granite-top island in the center, and wedged the bag with the chicken into the well-stocked fridge. Her mother remained in the hallway, scouring her messages on a pad next to the phone. "I'll get my suitcase from the car and take it upstairs. You'll let me know what I can do to help."

"Not a thing. Relax for a while. If it suits, we'll eat in forty-five minutes or so."

During dinner Deirdre tried to entertain her mother with updates on the children, launching energetically into an account of Dylan's accomplishments and minimizing Caitlin's challenges. Mrs. Durrell listened attentively, posing questions, trying to form a less fuzzy portrait of the two kids she hadn't seen in years. From her face, however, Deirdre could sense more puzzlement than pride, which made her rush to emphasize her children's achievements.

"Not that many college graduates get a grant to Princeton," she enthused. "Plus, he has a good friend who's already enrolled there—his name's Zach, doing economics—and I only discovered this weekend, a girlfriend."

"Ah," Mrs. Durrell responded, pausing the cutting of her steak. "Is it serious?"

"I don't know quite what you mean by that," Deirdre rejoined, though instantly regretting the implied criticism. "But yes, they do seem attached to each other. She'll be studying at Johns Hopkins. Hers is a full scholarship as well."

"I see," Mrs. Durrell remarked, not clear as to where the other university was.

In the pause that followed, Deirdre took a few bites of the asparagus casserole, ostensibly one of her favorite vegetables. Funny, she thought, how her mother had a way of coloring her silences, making them disconcertingly revelatory in their own way.

The two ate in silence for several long minutes, Deirdre ravenous after her long day and amazed at how tasty the lady peas and fried okra were. Her mother took a long sip of her iced tea and then held out the basket of homemade biscuits for her daughter to take another.

Eventually, Mrs. Durrell came up with another question. "So, dear, are they still playing the clarinet?"

"They?"

"Dylan and Caitlin. They are still twins, are they not?"

"Of course. As a matter of fact, Caitlin wants to break into the music business, as a singer. You know, with a rock band, that sort of thing," Deirdre explained as best she could. She did not refer to the unprepossessing Ray or the pad in Hoboken, just the thought of which made her uneasy.

"Stephen always said the child had a beautiful voice. Didn't do much singing in front of me, but it must have registered with him." Mrs. Durrell looked away toward the window, her eyes bright.

"Nor with Ashton and me," Deirdre rushed to add. "Always wanted to be a ballerina, until her accident, that is."

Mrs. Durrell nodded uncertainly, not having been apprised of the details of the car wreck, only that her granddaughter had undergone physical therapy. "Such a pretty child she was. Photogenic too, from the pictures you've sent."

"Still is, Mother. Quite beautiful."

"That never hurts," Mrs. Durrell said, her voice wistful, before rising to bring out a key lime pie from the fridge.

As the light caught her mother's face, Deirdre observed her high cheekbones and full lips, arresting traits very much like Caitlin's. She would have said so except that her cellphone started to vibrate in the pocket of her skirt. She pulled it out, an unknown number but from the local 601 area code. She clicked the icon.

"Hello? Yes, this is Deirdre Durrell." A pause followed as the caller identified herself. "Oh, yes. Rose. How lovely of you," Deirdre continued, raising her eyes to meet her mother's.

Later, Mrs. Durrell explained that she had run into several of her daughter's childhood friends, the ones, she specified, "who didn't move away or lose touch with home. I thought you might be pleased to reacquaint yourself, now that you're newly..."

She let her voice fall off, not needing to finish the sentence. The subject of the divorce from Ashton had been skirted throughout the meal. If Mrs. Durrell had never warmed to the aloof Bostonian who had married her daughter, neither did she approve of couples who separated when children were involved. She had expressed her regret over the breakup at the time, inviting her daughter to pay a visit, and offering to send a check to help out. She had not been taken up on either count.

As far as Deirdre was concerned, she had no desire to re-hash the details of the split nor to recount the accommodations she had made in the aftermath. Had she ever mentioned Howard, and how much he had helped her feel better about herself? No point now. Better, she quickly deduced, to focus on the academic work she planned to do and to show polite interest in meeting up with an old friend or two. To humor her mother, if nothing else. Especially if she stayed for any considerable time. Again, the nature and duration of the visit had not been spelled out by either woman, neither knowing as yet how she felt about the prospect of a prolonged visit.

"So, Mother, how exactly is Rose?"

"Still running Kleinfeld Collectibles. Fixed it up real nice, she has," Mrs. Durrell said admiringly. "Always knew she had the smarts, that girl. Like you, and Dennis, Elwood's son Hank too," she went on, finishing up her pie and eyeing Deirdre's plate. "If you'd like another slice later, hon, help yourself. You're thinner than ever."

"Thanks, Mother. It's delicious. Everything, in fact. But I'll likely go to bed early. Had to be up at dawn this morning, what with the kids setting off." She did not mention Ashton or Roxane or anything else about the weekend in New York City. The fewer chances for her mother to be judgmental, the more likely they would get along.

The two washed and dried the dishes in silence, neither having struck the right chord during the evening, but each consoled by the thought that the skittishness would dissipate as the days went on.

"Sleep as late as you want, dear," Mrs. Durrell finally suggested, warmth stealing into her voice. "I have to go over to the school early for a couple of parent consults. So, make yourself at home, I mean, well, it is still your home, in a matter of speaking."

Deirdre wanted to hug her mother but resisted the impulse. Strange how they had never been overtly affectionate with each other when her father, by contrast, had been all hands. Especially during that last visit, when he mussed her hair at the slightest opportunity, though at the time she had no idea of his worsening condition. A wave of sorrow swept over her, leading her to dry every last fork and spoon with special care.

"That's enough, dear. The dishes can take care of themselves," Mrs. Durrell said, stealing a glance at her daughter's stricken face. "I'll fix the coffee pot, and if, by chance, you're up first, simply press the button."

Lying in bed that night, the sound of cicadas almost deafening, Deirdre marveled at the changes around her. If the town, what little of it she had seen so far, appeared down-on-its-luck, her widowed mother appeared to stand straighter, shine brighter. What would Roxane have commented? "Your mother has an amazing *presence*," doubtless pronouncing the noun in her exaggerated French accent.

So unexpected, and so ironic, Deirdre thought. When Stephen Q. Durrell, attorney at law, was around and holding forth, his wife faded into the background. But now, the renovated house reflected her mother's newfound confidence—: bright colors had been applied to the walls, new furniture alongside the family antiques came across as effortlessly elegant rather than incongruous. Her own room had been done in a soft mauve, but her cherrywood desk was still tucked under the windowsill and the rose-colored canopy still hung over her childhood bed.

Then there was what she saw when she came downstairs for another slice of pie at 2 a.m. Wandering into the living room, she spotted a brochure on the marble-topped table, an open letter stuck inside. From Viking Cruises, inviting a Ms. Clarissa Dupree Durrell to consider another "memorable" trip with a companion, like the one two summers ago down the Danube. Why not venture further, to the Far East or South America, the personalized letter went on.

Deirdre put her dessert plate down and studied the room. On the far wall was a painting she had never seen before. She tiptoed over. It was a view of Budapest, the river snaking through the middle. She felt disoriented, as though in front of a gaping hole. Years of her mother's life had unspooled, and she had not only not been a party to them but had not been told about them. Moreover, her own life had been arranged at a vast remove from her mother's gaze, limiting their ability to empathize one with the other.

Quid pro quo, Deirdre murmured. She took her plate back to the kitchen and stole back up the stairs.

By the time she tumbled out of bed the next morning, it was 9:30. A note left on the kitchen table read: *Hope you slept well, DeeDee. Do whatever with yourself as I likely won't get home until late afternoon. Don't know what your plans are for the rental out front, but these keys are to your father's Buick. Still runs like a top, so feel free to take it over. Also, Pattie Lee rang up as I was walking out the door. Word gets out around here. Phone number's on the pad. Mother*

Pattie Lee?

Deirdre remembered her as the wildest girl in high school, the one who went all the way with several of the football players and openly bragged about it. But she had undergone some sort of conversion later on, if memory served.

Anyway, after the heaviest, albeit delicious, evening meal she had consumed in ages, Deirdre decided to get her bearings by walking around town. Except, by the time she had gone two blocks, she was sweating as she never did in that Pilates class Roxane dragged her to. She had forgotten how sticky June could be in the Delta. Sunscreen, deodorant and a pair of sunglasses were all in order, she calculated, though it appeared the Rexall on Main Street had been repurposed as a Rite-Aid. She popped in, picked up a dusty spray can of Coppertone, an Arrid roll-on stick, a packet of kleenex, and a pair of tortoise-shell sunglasses for $9.99.

At the only manned check-out counter she heard her name called out. Loudly.

"Why Deirdre Ann Durrell. Is it really you, or do my eyes deceive me?!" Before she could swerve around, she was clutched by a gardenia-scented arm belonging to the aforementioned Pattie Lee, who quickly let it be broadcast that she was now married to Swifty

Patterson. "You remember him. The receiver on the '83 squad—the only time Central High ever, well, what does it matter now, right?"

Here, Pattie Lee released her hold and stepped back to survey her erstwhile school chum full-length.

"Right," Deirdre stammered, disconcerted by the outburst, though no one else was nearby other than the bored-looking clerk. She placed her purchases on the counter and fumbled with the latch on her purse. "Great to see you again, Pattie Lee. You're looking well."

"Way too fat, you mean, but naturally you wouldn't say that. Wouldn't be PC," she prattled on, smacking her fire-engine red lips together to indicate she was perfectly pleased with her body weight as well as everything else about her persona. "Rang your mom earlier—truth be told, she practically runs the school now. Smart like you, I declare." (She chuckled at her own lame joke and scrutinized Deirdre more closely.) "You sly thing, you look thirty-five, if that. But so thin. All that bad food up north, right? No one wants to eat it, I suppose."

At a loss for words against this cascade of inanities, Deirdre turned toward the clerk and handed her a credit card. Two other customers had by now joined the check-out line.

"We could fatten you up over at the church, if you like. Wednesday evening is fellowship time. You should come, get back to your values as well as to the mashed potatoes and gravy."

A flicker of irritation swept over Deirdre's face, but she forced a polite smile. "Appreciate it, Pattie Lee, but I'll be spending most of the time with Mother, and getting on with a project I'm working on."

"Slipped my mind, it did. You're a big-shot professor now, with a book out and everything," Pattie Lee went on, opening her blue eyes ever wider and batting her lashes. The gesture made her round face look like some ludicrously painted doll's head.

"I wouldn't use the word big-shot to describe my role at the college and I've never been a Baptist, but thanks for the offer," Deirdre managed to interject, and in a tone to signal that she was taking charge of the conversation and trying to end it. She swiveled back around to sign the Amex receipt, but she could feel Pattie Lee's eyes laser into her back.

"But your husband was, correct? A big-shot, I mean. You and he got divorced, I do believe." Pattie Lee puckered her lips, noisily, in mock sympathy. "Happens, I guess."

Deirdre waited until the clerk finished stuffing her purchases into a plastic bag and tearing off the credit card receipt. A fleeting glance of commiseration passed between the two. Cattiness, Deirdre suddenly thought, had gone out of style among women almost everywhere but apparently not in the Delta. But here she was; she couldn't resist scoring a point. "Yes, divorce does happen, Pattie Lee. Though you're unusually blessed, married to someone as renowned as Swifty Patterson," she lobbed over the net, as it were, out of reach of her opponent.

"Are you two done yapping?" the man right behind them in line carped. He was carrying a basket with fig newtons and a carton of soft drinks. Likely from out of town, he looked to be in a hurry.

"Why yes, sir, we are now," Pattie Lee snipped, reproving the stranger, and then making an elaborate show of stepping aside to allow Deirdre to pass in front of her toward the exit.

"I'm sure I'll see you around, Deirdre. Don't just closet yourself at home."

"Wouldn't dream of it. And nice to see you, Pattie Lee."

Back out on the hot pavement, Deirdre took a deep breath, trying to remember what else her mother had mentioned about the redoubtable Pattie Lee. Something about her having become the region's biggest Tea Party organizer. She pulled a tissue from the plastic bag and wiped her forehead. Then she peeled off the sticker from the sunglasses, put them on and proceeded to stroll down Main Street, browsing the shop windows while keeping to the shadier side of the street. No one else spoke to her, though several people eyed her curiously. She smiled back at everyone and began to feel better, despite the stifling heat.

As she circled back toward the busiest commercial block, she paused in front of Kleinfeld's Collectibles. Something for her mother's house would be a thoughtful gesture. Plus, she had always liked Rose, however widely their paths had diverged after high school.

The door clanged as she entered; a faint but oddly familiar smell of cinnamon rose to her nostrils. At the cash register to the left, a woman was paying for a purchase being gift-wrapped by the clerk. Deirdre walked past the two and began to wander the aisles—: the shelves were laden with wax candles, china figurines, silk flowers, wicker baskets, wall decor and an assortment of cookbooks, inspirational poetry and miniature New Testaments. Glass casements held more expensive-looking porcelain and ceramic vases, jewelry and silver ornaments. She squinted to read the price tags on a few of the vases.

Eventually, a voice behind her called out pleasantly: "May I help you, madame? I'll be glad to open the case if you're interested in something."

Deirdre turned her head, tilting it quizzically to take in an un-made-up face, a kindly one with comforting gray eyes. "Rose? It's Deirdre. Deirdre Durrell." Embarrassed, she held out her hand.

"Oh, my word. I knew you were expected but I didn't think—" Without finishing her sentence, the store owner hobbled a step closer and clasped her old friend's arm. ""It's my diabetes. Acts up now and again. *Ergo*, the crutches. But come on over to the counter."

As they made their way back to the front of the store, Deirdre noticed the wisps of gray in her friend's bob. Clearly, she didn't bother to color her hair nor, despite her still slender frame, to dress in anything more becoming than loose slacks and looser blouses.

"I don't want to interrupt, but I hoped I'd find you. Other than the foot, are you well?"

"Doing right fine, all things considered," Rose answered, casting her eyes around the store apparently to see if anyone else was about. "But tell me, Deirdre. You're here for a while, your mother implied. We must get together. All these years have passed," Rose went on, some muscle constricting in her face.

At a loss to know if she should offer condolences to her old friend—(When had the elder Kleinfelds finally succumbed? She couldn't recall if her mother had told her.)—she racked her brain for something pleasant to inquire of. "Indeed. *Tempus fugit*, as Mrs. Stone would have remarked. Remember her?"

"How could we not!" Rose agreed, shutting her eyes to conjure their long-ago Latin teacher. "And if that phrase didn't strike a chord with us, she would have added in that deep-throated voice of hers—(which Rose now feebly attempted to imitate):—'*carpe diem, pueri et puellae, carpe diem.*' "

The two chuckled at the memory, Deirdre hastening to recall how brilliantly Rose had performed not only in Latin but in every other subject the two had tackled together.

Without a doubt, Deirdre reckoned, her friend would have ended up as valedictorian of the class of 1986, had it not been for the family tragedy. Their senior year, both of Rose's parents were diagnosed with cancer—he with lung, she with breast—and their only daughter dutifully turned down multiple scholarship offers to look after them, insisting that her older brother stay the course and not leave engineering school on their behalf. Against all odds, she kept both parents alive for years, taking charge of the store as their condition deteriorated, and somehow managing to marry and give birth to a son.

More prudent to ask after children than after spouses, especially of older women, Deirdre had discovered. Thus: "So, how is your son? Did he too graduate from Central?"

Rose let out a deep breath. "Finally. He's nineteen now. And a handful."

Right then, the door clanged and another customer ambled in. Rose nodded her way. "Be right with you, Arlene." Turning back to Deirdre, she added, "Anyway, my brother's going to step in to help. But do stop by again. We'll have lunch. The diner gets seafood from the coast every Thursday, or we could have drinks at the Park."

"I'll make a note of it. Take care, Rose."

Once back out in what was now the scorching noonday heat, Deirdre realized she hadn't inquired after the vase that had caught her fancy, and that she was sure would please her mother. It would give her another excuse to see Rose, and next time she would be armed with the name of the son, the brother too, for that matter.

Chapter Twenty-Three

On their way to Jackson for shopping and a concert by the Mississippi Symphony, Deirdre pulled in to the only full-service pump in town, her mother already rummaging in her handbag for cash. It had taken a month for her boxes of books and note tablets to arrive, so in the meantime she had concentrated on getting her father's Buick back into working order, washing and polishing the exterior, dusting the interior and updating the contents of the glove compartment. Earlier that morning, she had packed an igloo with sodas, tomato sandwiches, and two green apples.

"You'd think we were headed to Alaska," her mother had remarked, though not at all displeased by her daughter's efforts.

This would be the first time the two had ventured out together beyond the city limits of Riverton as well as the first time Deirdre had taken the Buick on the open road. She did not want anything to go wrong. She unscrewed the cap, lifted the nozzle and pressed the lever for the most expensive gas, something she rarely did even for her Volvo back home.

While standing there, shifting her weight from foot to foot and wondering if she had brought along her sunglasses, a dark SUV slithered up alongside. A nicely dressed man got out to fill his tank from the only other functioning pump. He was big-framed, and authoritatively, if off-handedly, appeared to take up a lot of space.

For an instant, she thought his eyes snagged on her, but he quickly began to fill up what looked to be a company rental. Having replaced the nozzle and the Buick's cap, Deirdre went inside the station to pay. Soon, the other customer entered and stood behind her.

"Looks like your Buick is more of a gas guzzler than my Escalade," the stranger said, eyeing the $38.86 rung up on the cash register.

"It was literally on empty—and besides, I splurged on premium plus."

"How lucky they must be if you treat all your friends that well," he added, his tone bemused.

As she turned, Deirdre flashed the man a smile. He reminded her of someone, but she couldn't think of whom.

While the clerk rang up the man's bill, $25.00 even, Deirdre lingered, scouring the rack of assorted snacks. Perhaps her mother would like something during the drive. She settled on mints and returned to the cashier. The other customer had walked out.

Outside, the stranger had already opened the door of the Escalade, but his attention was focused elsewhere, at something close to the ground. As she approached her own car, Deirdre couldn't help but follow his gaze.

He pointed. "Your right rear tire is low. Take a look."

She walked over and studied the tire, not entirely convinced but not wanting to be impolite. Besides, she liked the sound of the man's voice, assured but not overbearing. "If you say so. I'm no expert."

"If you pull up over there," he advised, indicating a dilapidated-looking contraption at the side of the station, "I'll top it up. Won't take a minute."

She nodded and tapped on the passenger window. Her mother eyed her curiously. "That man says our back tire is low. He's going to fill it," Deirdre said, trying to sound neutral.

"How very helpful," Mrs. Durrell replied, also trying to sound neutral.

While he fumbled in his pockets for quarters for the machine, Deirdre noticed the Vicksburg plates on the SUV and a sticker on the windshield. "Whatever does ERDC stand for?" she asked as he bent over to attach the air hose to the tire valve.

"They should have left well enough alone: Waterways Experiment Station, it used to be called, part of the Army Corps of Engineers." He glanced up at her face. She looked puzzled. "I take it you're not from around here, despite the plates on your Buick."

"No, I mean yes. I *am* from around here. But been away for many years."

"Hmm. Same here." He got up from his haunches and re-looped the air-hose onto the machine. When he turned around to face her, she was looking straight at him.

"Thank you for doing that," Deirdre said, extending her hand for him to shake. He did so briefly, she thinking that somehow, despite the nondescript surroundings, they were on a stage and this was a crucial scene.

"My name's Rowan," he inadvertently revealed. "I'm here for a few days to deal with a family matter. My sister's son needs to be recovered, and she can't take off." Deirdre's mouth fell open, but no words spilled out. "I'm sorry. I didn't mean to waylay you as though..." There was a dense pause. Another car had pulled up behind the Escalade, its motor still running. "Anyway, did I mention? You have amazing eyes. In the sunlight, they appear to shift from olive to green."

"Thank you," she said, blushing. "This may sound odd, but I know who you are: Rose Kleinfeld's brother. My name's Deirdre. Deirdre Durrell."

It was Rowan Kleinfeld's turn to be flabbergasted. He darted his eyes toward the Buick, noticing that the older woman had rolled the passenger side window down. She was watching the two of them.

On the spot, he made a mental calculation and took a chance. "If you're back from wherever you're headed by Tuesday, come have a drink with me, Deirdre Durrell. At the Park Hotel, say, around 6:00. We can compare notes on the hometown we left."

Deirdre looked dubious and moved to get back in the car, fumbling for the car keys in her purse. Rowan subtly inclined his head at the older woman as he headed back to his. Mrs. Durrell watched until the SUV revved up and headed out of the station.

"You left the keys with me, dear, remember?" Mrs. Durrell said, picking up the key chain from her lap and handing it over. "Well, I must say. That man cuts a figure..."

Without a word, Deirdre started the engine.

Rarely had Deirdre been so keyed up about what, in theory, was an innocuous encounter with a man as she was about having a drink with Rowan Kleinfeld. Ever since she and her mother returned Sunday evening from Jackson, she had walked around with her head in the clouds. She had not mentioned the man's name to her mother, let alone that she had been invited for drinks at the town's only reputable hotel, reputable being a fungible word. On Monday she could barely sit still at her desk, jotting a few notes about life at the medieval court of Charles VI of France but otherwise staring out the window at the crepe myrtles.

Although it might have made eminent sense, she had resolved not to phone Rose for particulars about her brother, facts that might help her make an informed decision about whether to show up at the Park Hotel. Specifically, she would not stoop to asking her friend what his marital status was—single, engaged, married, divorced, widowed, estranged, separated, gay, bisexual, or, as Facebook had obligingly conjured, "complicated." Nor would she revert to googling him.

She lay in bed wide awake that night, calculating whether her new acquaintance had bothered to mention to his sister that he had run into one of her former schoolmates, and that they would be having a drink together. Finally, as 2 a.m. ticked over, she reckoned that he had not bothered to do so, which, to her mind, would have made their encounter that much more intriguing. Nor had she managed to tell her mother what it was that would keep her out for part of the evening on Tuesday. Keeping things to herself would make the get-together less encumbered with expectation—if she chose to show up.

What would her friends advise? For that matter, did she even have any friends outside of her former married life or her staid academic circle in whom she could confide such a thing—: the *thing* being that she was infatuated with a man she had met in front of a gas pump and with whom she had exchanged not more than a hundred words. Lying in the darkness, it occurred to her that Roxane was the only insouciant enough creature to encourage her to embrace the unknown. *Mais oui, mon amie. Il faut vivre sa vie pleinement*, she would likely say, gesturing with her meticulously manicured nails.

On Tuesday Mrs. Durrell, whose routines unwound like clockwork, left for her regular beauty parlor appointment at 9 a.m., to be followed by her bi-weekly bridge club, then lunch with the school principal, leaving Deirdre to her own devices. The house to herself, she spent the morning trying on the different outfits she had bought at Macy's in Jackson, ultimately settling on a silky green sundress with spaghetti straps and a matching jacket with long sleeves. Hotels are typically icebox-cold, she reasoned, but, if not, and only if she felt relaxed, she could remove the jacket. The dress itself had a built-in bra which enhanced her already sufficient cleavage. (*Why hide a perfectly decent bosom*, Roxane would no doubt contend.)

However unlike her to devote such inordinate attention to her appearance, Deirdre was enjoying for the first time in years—or EVER, if she were inclined to admit such a thing—the prospect of being flirted with by someone as unexpected (and good-looking) as this Rowan Kleinfeld was. And, if things progressed beyond chit-chat, she would not make a big deal about whatever status he cared to claim, as she hoped he wouldn't look askance at, or be stymied by, hers.

Although she could have easily walked to the Park Hotel, Deirdre backed the Buick out of the garage and cruised around town in order not to arrive before her date did. At 6:15 she parked several spaces away from the hotel entrance, checked her loosely (but painstakingly) styled hair and lipstick in the rearview mirror and got out, making an effort to appear unhurried. The July heat was still so relentless at that hour, however, she moved rapidly to the entrance and pushed open the heavy brass door.

Inside, she blinked several times to adjust to the light coming through slatted shutters. A couple of guests looked up from the leather armchairs scattered about the lobby but soon went back to checking their phones. A uniformed young woman behind the reception was typing away on a computer. It was so quiet Deirdre could hear the click, click click of the keys. A grandfather clock in a far corner chimed the quarter hour.

Unless it had been relocated, the bar was tucked into an alcove toward the rear of the establishment. She and Ashton had years ago had a drink there with her one remaining male friend from high school, Dennis Tremayne, the valedictorian to her salutatorian, and to whom she imagined her fiancé might spark. He hadn't, as she recalled, alcohol notwithstanding. How could she have imagined that he would? Her betrothed, a Boston-bred, Harvard-educated professor of poetry, far outshone, in theory at least, her friend, a would-be teacher with a degree from Delta State tucked away in a drawer.

She shook off the memory of that long-ago encounter and eyed the only two men in the place, the bartender and a man on a stool wearing a linen sports jacket. Their chatter abruptly ceased and the man swiveled around.

"Ah, I was about to conclude you weren't coming. But here you are," Rowan began, hastening over to greet her. "And you look so—so summery," he added, beaming. He gestured toward a small table in the corner.

Deirdre could feel the heat rising in her cheeks. "Thank you," she burbled. "You look well yourself, especially considering the heat outside."

"I'm accustomed to it but you're right. July never fails to be brutal around here." The bartender meanwhile had discreetly turned away and busied himself arranging liquor bottles on the shelves behind him.

Deirdre nodded in agreement, feeling more self-conscious than she had bargained on and unable to dredge up anything amusing to say or un-intrusive to ask. Suddenly, she wondered if Rowan was staying at the hotel or had merely chosen it as the only viable venue in town for a tryst. That was not a line of inquiry she could possibly go down. Taking a deep breath, she scoured the room to alight upon something worthy of comment.

Rowan's gaze remained on her face. "I had been thinking all weekend it wasn't just the color." Deirdre looked flummoxed. "Your eyes. It came to me they were thoughtful eyes, which also makes them reassuring to look at," he said. Deirdre smiled faintly and turned back toward her companion. "So," he sped up in a more business-like tone, "what would you like? Allen here can mix a mean margarita or there are a couple of wines to choose from."

"A chardonnay or whatever," she replied, not wanting to appear hard to please.

Rowan motioned to the bartender, settled on a Kendall Jackson for her and a gin&tonic for himself. They did not clink their glasses, but Deirdre took a few substantial sips to steady her nerves.

"You chose well," she eventually said to break the silence.

"Yes, I did," he returned, observing her more intently.

Meanwhile, several other customers had slipped into the bar, including a man who nodded in Rowan's direction. In a few minutes, the bartender placed a bowl of salted nuts and black olives in front of them and then on the other tables, three of which were now occupied. The sound of other voices made Deirdre relax a little. She un-scrunched her toes but did not take her jacket off.

"So," they both began at once to speak, which made them both chuckle. She deferred to him.

"My sister tells me you're here for an extended visit, and that the other lady in the car was likely your mother. Is she well?"

"Quite. A force of nature, in fact. She's been teaching at Central almost since my father died. It's done her a world of good."

"Still, she must be happy to have you around," Rowan persisted.

"To be honest, it's my first extended stay in many years," she confided, though kicking herself for priming the obvious question of what she had been doing in the interim, which she didn't (yet) want to deal with. She tacked in another direction. "So, how is Rose, and more to the point, your nephew? I can't recall his name."

Rowan took in air to fill his cheeks and slowly let it out. "Jason's his name. Too much now for Rose to handle on her own, as competent as she is. Together, we're determined to get him off whatever he's on and then back on his feet." Deirdre slowly shook her head. "Be glad you've never had to deal with anything like this," he continued, not pausing long enough for her to disabuse him. "Did you ever imagine that our hometown—not that different from Mayberry when you think about it—would be ravaged by drugs or that youngsters would be running guns in order to get their hands on the stuff...?" He took a swallow of his drink and set his glass down. The muscles of his jawline had tightened. He looked out past her, at the rest of the room, as though bewildered by the presence of others or the changes in the world.

"A sad state of affairs," Deirdre concurred, thinking of Caitlin and trying to calculate how long it had been since they had spoken on the phone. Her daughter's last text had been a couple of weeks prior: *Got a part-time waitress gig. Ray's band is awesome. Love the City. Say hello 2 Grandma.* Part of her wanted to blurt out that she did understand Rowan's burden and would be glad to help but something held her back. She also could have reached out and touched his hand, which lay inert on the table, but she didn't.

"Can I get you two another round?" the bartender interrupted to ask while on his way to a nearby table, a tray with various drinks balanced in his left hand.

"I'm fine, really," she said, swirling the last of her chardonnay.

Rowan waved Allen away. "I didn't mean to saddle you with such a depressing story," he recommenced, picking up his thread and spinning it forward. "Still, there's one good thing about it all." Deirdre's eyebrows went up in a question mark. "It's going to take more time than I estimated to get Jason into rehab. I'll have to be around for a couple of weeks."

"Rose will be delighted," she lobbed over, the wine having loosened her tongue.

Rowan paused long enough for the corners of his lips to crinkle into a smile. "I was hoping she would not be the only one."

A couple of days later, Rowan rang Deirdre on her cell, inviting her to go on "a ramble" to find an old watering hole. "The real kind, that is," he said laughingly, "grapevines on the overhang and smooth rocks in the stream." It's where he and his friends used to hang out at the height of summer, he further explained, his tone enthusiastic, boyish even. "We'll have a picnic. And don't forget to bring a bathing suit."

By that time, she could not say no.

Despite having now googled Rowan Kleinfeld and finding he boasted a B.S. from Mississippi State, an M.S. from Georgia Tech and a Ph.D. from CalTech, she also discovered he was married, with a daughter at MIT, and (judging from the sparse but vivid photos on his Facebook page) two black labradors. Further, he resided in St. Louis, where his wife was civic-minded and photogenic, and given to wearing fancy ball gowns. In a few of the shots, he looked bored, or so Deirdre intuited. His LinkedIn profile indicated that Dr. Kleinfeld regularly traversed the country on behalf of ERDC, fixing dams and bridges and riverbeds.

After twenty minutes on the Internet, Deirdre flicked the computer off and sat another ten minutes benumbed. She theorized he might have done the same, since Rose's information about her would be necessarily sketchy, looking her up on LinkedIn or Facebook to find out that she too had advanced degrees, children, a dog, a published book and another in progress, and an ex-husband.

Might make things easier if everything were out in the open. That way they could talk gaily about Caedmon and his two labs and not have to dwell on anything too private or painful.

Thus, having determined not to fret about their respective pasts, she fasted for an entire day, cleaned her mother's house, weeded the garden, and took a brisk walk, hoping in the process to shed a pound or two. At forty-five, she had not worn a bathing suit in public since a family outing on Lake Erie when the twins were ten.

She needn't have worried overmuch. In the end, none of them ventured into the water.

To begin with, Deirdre had been disappointed when the SUV stopped in front of the house around 11 a.m. that Saturday. Peering down from her bedroom window, she quickly changed her mind and decided to wear an old but still sufficiently elasticized one-piece underneath her navy blue bermudas and short-sleeved blouse.

"I think your friend is here—two of them," Mrs. Durrell had called out from downstairs. Shortly thereafter the doorbell rang. The voices at the door carried into her bedroom.

"Do come in. Deirdre should be down in a jiffy," her mother said.

"Mrs. Durrell, I presume," Rowan responded, a hint of bemusement in his tone. "I'm Rowan Kleinfeld, Rose's brother, and this is my nephew, Jason."

"Nice to meet you, both of you."

There might have been a murmured response from the nephew, but Deirdre wasn't sure. She stuffed the Coppertone in her straw purse and made her way downstairs.

Rowan smiled as she approached. Jason kept his head lowered, unruly locks of charcoal black hair in his face. Worse even than Caitlin's demeanor those years ago, she thought, quickly shaking off the image of her sullen teenage daughter. "So, you're Jason. Nice to have you on this outing in case we get lost. You probably know the area better than your uncle or I do."

The youngster shrugged. "Not really," he managed to mumble, looking up enough for Deirdre to note his sandpaper complexion. Like Rowan's and Rose's, his eyes were gray, but they had no luster.

"Well, we should be going," Rowan declared, eyeing his wristwatch. "Unless you too would like to come along, Mrs. Durrell?"

"Mercy no," Deirdre's mother replied, gesturing with her hands but clearly pleased by the offer. "However, I did fry up a chicken last night. The bag's in the fridge, DeeDee," she added, darting a glance toward the kitchen.

"Again, lovely to officially meet you, Mrs. Durrell. And for the food. Never too much for a picnic."

"Right you are about that," Mrs. Durrell said.

"Oh, I almost forgot," Rowan added, dropping his voice an octave. "I did meet your husband, Stephen, briefly, years ago. Helped us with the estate, when our parents passed away. A godsend he was. So many issues to sort through."

In the kitchen, Deirdre's heart skipped a beat. She and her mother rarely brought up her father's name. She wondered what was writ on her mother's face hearing that unexpected compliment. Hurriedly, she retrieved the bag of chicken and returned to the foyer. Jason was now fidgeting; he didn't seem to know what to do with his outsized hands.

"OK. I think that's everything. Love you," Deirdre said, leading the way out of the house, hoping her parent didn't ascribe too much to what was a harmless outing with the brother and son of a former classmate. Perhaps she too shouldn't ascribe too much to the jaunt. She opened the passenger side door without waiting for either of the two men to oblige.

Once beyond the city limits, Rowan switched the radio on but suggested Deirdre tune to whatever station might appeal. "You know how they all are," he added cryptically, glancing in the rearview mirror at his nephew. Jason had stuck his earplugs in and appeared to be zoned-out.

"Yes, I do," Deirdre replied, busying herself with the FM dial until she alighted on what must be the NPR station in Greenwood. A symphony was in full swing, tempestuous, oboes and horns to the fore. Hard to talk over. Probably Brahms and likely to endure a good forty-five minutes. Just as well. She eyed the intermittent stretches of cotton and corn fields out the window and tried not to worry about the passenger in the back seat. She had no idea what to say to Rowan, but her heart went out to him. No easy task dealing with someone who has a drug problem.

As the SUV turned off the state highway and onto a badly pocked back road, Rowan finally spoke. "There's a novel called *Aimez-vous Brahms?*' which my sister kept on her nightstand for years. Her French period, I guess." He smiled at his own witticism.

Deirdre nodded but did not supply him with the French author's name or go on about how closely she and Rose had studied together during high school, reading aloud trashy (but to them sophisticated) Gallic novels like those of Françoise Sagan as well as devoting themselves more seriously to Latin and history and whatever else teachers threw at them. Nor did she claim that his sister, not she or Dennis Tremayne, would likely have been valedictorian or salutatorian and would now boast a framed doctorate on her wall if fate hadn't intervened. She wondered if Rowan saw it that way or if, being a man and far away at the time, he had been oblivious to the unfortunate timing that hindered the upward trajectory of his sibling's life.

After a pause during which Rowan slowed the Escalade to a crawl and headed down a gravel road with steep gullies on each side, he added: "By the way, I didn't mean to suggest Rose was frivolous. Smarter and more conscientious than I ever was."

"I remember well. She was gifted."

"The foreign airs she put on had something to do with the boy she had a crush on. They studied together and he went about quoting Baudelaire. I recall a beret of some sort." Deirdre looked flummoxed, believing he must be mistaken about this element. She threw him a glance to encourage him to elaborate. "Problem was, this Dennis person was smitten with someone else in their coterie. He went on to become a professor but doesn't come home much, so she says."

Deirdre racked her brain but couldn't recall an incident in which any of this made sense. Rose had never mentioned a secret crush; nor had Dennis Tremayne—a French-sounding name, if one thought about it, but no one back then did—gone about quoting Gallic poets. If he had done so, they surely would have all laughed at him. But in love? Something to ask about, if she ever happened to visit him at Delta State.

By that time, Rowan had stopped the car in front of a tree trunk laying across the road. "This looks like the end of the trail, but I think we're close enough." He turned and smiled at Deirdre. Jason meanwhile unplugged and hopped out with the picnic basket over his arm. Following his lead, Rowan brought along the igloo and binoculars, Deirdre, another basket with a tablecloth and cutlery.

It took only a short walk down what remained of the graveled path to find the pond. It was almost perfectly round and was fed by a creek that snaked down from the hillside and culminated in a feeble attempt at a waterfall. A few wood ducks took flight on the far side at their arrival. They dropped what they were carrying in a grassy area overhung with shade trees. The green of their leaves was intense. Once they had looked briefly around, Deirdre spread the tablecloth and handed out cold Dr. Peppers.

Jason set off uphill toward a copse of beech trees and disappeared from view. With his soda in hand, Rowan walked down the incline toward the edge of the pond. Close up, the water had a purplish sheen to it. A dilapidated fishing boat with two huge drums in it bobbled at the shoreline. The drums were rusted but seemingly air-tight.

But there was a smell.

"You need to see this, Uncle Rowan. You too, Miss Deirdre," Jason suddenly shouted, waving his arms from up on the hillside. He had spotted a rotted board attached to a tree twenty yards to the west. *Swim at your own risk. Industrial waste sight*, the warning read. When the two adults approached, he added, "With spelling like that, can they be trusted?" he asked, demonstrating more wit than Deirdre had assumed he possessed. Like Caitlin, she thought, the young man could surprise to the upside.

"Well, I'll be damned," Rowan responded, shaking his head. "That explains the odor down there."

"But it doesn't explain who's responsible for it. Such a shame," Deirdre added.

"Does this pond have a name, Uncle Rowan? If it does, I can check it out on the Internet. There are sites devoted to this shit."

"Jason, watch your language."

"Yeah, sorry."

"I am too, Deirdre, for having dragged you here and we can't even take a dip. A lot has changed in thirty-five years. The pond got much smaller as well as polluted," he sighed.

She smiled at the sentiment, thinking that there was, despite the polluted pond and whatever else, an exquisite pleasantness being in the company of this man. "Yes, *tempus fugit*. However, we still must eat. Don't know about you two but I'm famished. Afterwards, you can show us the bridge you built upstream on the creek."

Rowan nodded. "Yes, my first engineering feat. With a friend. We were fifteen and it took a month, but in the end, you could walk across without crashing into the water below."

"Cool," Jason commented. Over lunch, he became more animated, and under persistent questioning, talked about computers and the environment.

"Perhaps, after your rehab, you can take a course or two. It helps to focus your mind on something you're interested in," she suggested. Both men looked her way curiously. She plunged in. "Like with my daughter, Caitlin. She too had a problem as a teen. Several problems, in fact."

"Like drugs or what?" Jason asked.

"That and a car accident. But after a lot of hurdles, she's found a good path. Wants to be a professional singer—: needless to say, she has a beautiful voice. Anyway, she's performing with a rock band around New York."

"Cool," Jason said again, looking both abashed and impressed.

Deirdre concentrated on her tomato sandwich. "Enough of these," she added, passing the bag of chips over to Jason. He managed the faintest of smiles and took them.

For what seemed a considerable interval no one spoke. Sitting cross-legged, Rowan leaned over and fetched a knife from the picnic basket with which he set about peeling a couple of apples. He had long fingers and well-trimmed nails, and what looked like a Rolex on his left wrist. He took off the peeling of each apple in one pale-green scalloped ribbon. He then cut the fruit into slices and placed the plate in the middle of the tablecloth.

"And what of your son?" he asked casually, picking up a slice himself and purposefully keeping his eyes off of Deirdre. "Is he similarly talented?"

Google does have its uses, Deirdre thought. "Dylan's in graduate school at Princeton. International Studies. But he does play the violin, and the clarinet, like his sister," she telegraphed, as cogently as she could. "They're twins, though sometimes..." Her eyes darted from one to the other of the two men, relieved to have unburdened herself but unsure if she had made any sense.

"He sounds cool, too," Jason said, further endearing himself to Deirdre.

Only a part-time zombie, she decided. Otherwise, a sensitive kid.

Rowan meanwhile busied himself by unscrewing a thermos of coffee and retrieving a small carton of milk from the igloo. "I'm thinking the two, meaning your Caitlin and Dylan, are about the same age as Jason and my Connor," he said, having quickly done the necessary math. "She's at MIT, studying, well, things I have not a clue about," he further said, self-deprecatingly.

Deirdre noted his flushed face and held out her paper cup for him to fill with coffee. She drank it black. Jason snapped the cap off another Dr. Pepper and upended the bottle. She did not ask about Rowan's wife, nor he about her husband.

Later, the three hiked a half-mile along a barely discernible path that skirted the creek from on high. Eventually, they looked down as the stream curved away from them and saw it: a wooden bridge, rickety and without a railing on one side, but still standing.

"Why, it's amazing. Must be twenty feet across. How ever did you do it?" Deirdre exclaimed, unabashedly impressed.

Rowan beamed. "We were young. And my dad hauled the timber to us in an old Ford pick-up. Took some doing putting it together, but afterwards, we had a lot of friends show up to celebrate. Beer and dancing to somebody's boom box. Nobody drowned, that I recall."

"I bet your parents were proud," Deirdre said.

Rowan shrugged. "I suppose. They encouraged us to apply ourselves to practical things. That's probably why my dad dubbed it, 'the bridge to nowhere,' and did so, mind you, long before the expression targeted politicians who spend money foolishly."

While the grown-ups were admiring the structure from afar, Jason made his way down the overhang and approached the structure. The creek flowed swiftly below but gurgled loudly enough to be heard.

He hollered back up the hill. "Hey, you two. I'm going to cross over and back."

"Slowly, don't shake it and watch your step," Rowan yelled back. Tensing, Deirdre grabbed her companion's arm. He stiffened but did not pull away. She could hear her own heart beating, his too.

After taking an exaggerated bow on the far side of the bridge, Jason started to make his way back across. As he approached the near bank, he looked up at Rowan and Deirdre and waved in triumph, but, in so doing, he took his eyes off the planks. He stepped on a loose board, which made the slats beneath him creak and come apart. He jumped just as several planks snapped loose and upended, landing half in the water below, half on the muddy bank.

When they scrambled down to him, Jason was wincing in pain—between howls of laughter. "The best time I've had in ages," he avowed. His ankle immediately began to swell and blood oozed from a scratch on his leg, but other than that. "Now I really do need one of those painkillers," he deadpanned. They all laughed.

At the urgent care center, a harried-looking doctor gave Jason a tetanus shot, put three stitches in his calf and sent him on his way with an ice pack for the ankle and a prescription for high-dosage Tylenol. Out of earshot of the patient, Rowan, backed up by Deirdre, told the physician that Oxycontin would be overkill.

The doctor didn't object. "In our day, you sucked it up when stuff happened, but you wouldn't believe what people expect us to prescribe nowadays. Glad to see the young man has got sensible parents."

Neither Rowan nor Deirdre disabused the doctor.

During the next week, Deirdre buckled down to her research, taking notes on pertinent passages from the original writings of Julianna of Norwich and Margery Kempe, the other two medieval women she planned to focus on in her next book. Along with Christine de Pizan, they had to contend with difficult circumstances yet somehow they had risen above them—and immortalized themselves through their writings.

Typically, she rose early, breakfasted with her mother, texted Dylan and Caitlin to see how they were getting on (often not hearing back until the next day), ran errands and then closed herself in her room for five or six uninterrupted hours. She tried not to let her mind wander, especially not to thoughts of Rowan, but the Thursday after their outing, he having not phoned her, she called Rose to check on Jason.

"Ah, Deirdre. We were just talking about you," Rose exclaimed, her voice unusually gay.

"I hope I haven't interrupted your supper," Deirdre stuttered, "but I wanted to make sure Jason was recovering apace."

"He's better. Been extolling your virtues, said that you kept your *sang froid* throughout his ordeal. In truth, he didn't use the words *sang froid*, but you get the drift."

"I'm glad to hear that. He's a good kid, and not so much a kid anymore. I do hope all goes well in Jackson, and beyond."

"Amen to that. They're headed over there tomorrow."

"Great," Deirdre replied, feeling her heart sink. Rose, she feared, was deliberately withholding anything pertinent about Rowan. She wondered if he were in the room, listening to his sister. "Well, I'll let you go."

"Don't forget. When your schedule permits, you and I must have lunch."

"Absolutely."

For the rest of the evening, Deirdre replayed every scene from their Saturday escapade, wondering if she had failed to pick up some signal Rowan had given her, or whether the mention of her children, and everything their existence implied, had done enough to dissuade him from—whatever he needed to be dissuaded from.

So be it, she kept repeating. She would not dwell on what should not be: she had her project to work on, her kids to interact with on social media, Ashton to keep in the family loop, her mother to spend quality time with, and a few local friends to reconnect with. Unfortunately, Pattie Lee had quickly become irritating, best to be avoided, but what about Dennis? Albeit being brought up in a trailer park, he had made something of himself. Her mother would doubtless know more.

Much-needed rain fell for the next two days, keeping both women house-bound, Mrs. Durrell undertaking to organize her lesson plans for the coming school year, Deirdre taking copious notes on her trio of women heroines and their very different gifts as writers. By Sunday morning the storm had moved out; the air felt crisp and cool. Mrs. Durrell went to early church at 8:30, leaving Deirdre to sleep in. When she returned, her daughter was at the kitchen table, flipping through the *Commercial Appeal*.

"You seem down in the dumps, DeeDee. Why don't you take a walk? When you get back, we'll attack that shrimp casserole I have in the freezer."

Deirdre set off at a brisk pace, happy to be out in the fresh air, not having yet found anything as rigorous to do or anyone to do it with since Roxane cajoled her into trying Pilates. As she walked along, she had automatically put her hands on her back to allay the stiffness. She did a couple of knee bends and then lengthened her spine as best she could, wondering how her friend was settling in to New York City. She had heard nothing; only Dylan had mentioned in passing that she had come once to Princeton "to see the place."

Along the main street of town hardly anyone was about, it being the hour of most church services, including the Baptists, where, she noticed, their parking lot overflowed with cars. She hurried past the red-brick façade, not wanting to risk an encounter with Pattie Lee. Further on, in front of Kleinfeld's Collectibles a sign read *MIDSUMMER SALE*, all in florid caps, likely Rose's doing. Perhaps that vase she had admired would be marked down. She had zeroed in on the perfect spot for it in the living room. She sped up again, not wanting to keep her mother waiting.

She could smell the bubbling casserole as soon as she turned the key and went inside.

"There was a phone call while you were out," her mother called out from the kitchen. Deirdre dropped her shoulder bag on the hat rack.

"Oh?"

"From Rowan Kleinfeld. Something about a movie. His number is on the pad out there."

During lunch, Deirdre let her mother do most of the talking, limiting her own remarks to compliments on the casserole and a mention of the sale at Rose's store—: "She does carry a number of lovely things, vases and all"—but her mother did not take her up. Instead:

"Charming man, Rowan. I understand he's married, travels a lot and so forth."

For an instant, it crossed Deirdre's mind that her mother had also seen fit to search for Rose's brother on the Internet, but she was too stunned to ask. "Seems so," she mumbled, reaching for another helping of creamed corn and a biscuit. "He has a daughter, at MIT."

"Hmm. Impressive, and gratifying, I imagine."

After dessert, Deirdre offered to do the dishes, but her mother shooed her off. "Return your call. There's not much to do here. And you've been eating like a bird."

Back in her room, she clicked on Rowan's cell number.

If she didn't mind the late notice, they would meet up 5:30-ish, at the Park Hotel again, and then drive to Greenville. If, that is, she was at all keen to see a remake of *"The Great Gatsby."* They could have dinner before or after, whichever she preferred.

For thirty minutes they sipped their drinks at what had tacitly become their table, talking about the only safe subject they so far had in common: Jason. Seems the young man had submitted well enough to the rehab center, shook hands with his assigned roommate and dutifully followed his case worker—a former Marine, who didn't appear to tolerate insubordination, which, Rowan explained, might be a plus. "Never really had much of a father, and Rose, indefatigable though she is, couldn't always keep tabs on him."

He swirled the ice in his gin&tonic, looking away at the few other guests who were congregated at the bar. One of them, a pudgy man in an ill-fitted suit, gave the two a long look before turning back to his companion and whispering in her ear.

Rowan pretended not to notice; Deirdre, feeling vaguely on edge, kept her eyes lowered.

After a discrete interval, she said, "I suspect you've done all you can for Jason. And, even when both parents are around and involved with their children, there are things they don't pick up on." He brought his eyes back to Deirdre's face, inviting her to go on. "With

Caitlin, it was one thing after another, not all of which were her fault." He nodded pensively. "But, as far as I can tell from afar, she's now on a better path."

Deirdre finished her wine and put her glass down as though to indicate she would be ready to leave if he were. He took the hint, leaving a tip on the table.

The grandfather clock in the empty lobby chimed the half- hour as they walked past. The eyes of the clerk behind the desk appeared to follow them out the door, or perhaps, Deirdre thought, she was feeling the effects of the wine.

Once in the SUV and, alone with Rowan, she felt ebullient, glad too that she had spent the afternoon showering and restyling her hair. He had noticed, his gaze more than appreciative. He drove in silence for a good ten minutes, pointing out a few homes where friends of his had lived and the now vacant lot where the local drive-in had been. "It was pretty run down by the time I left Central, so I doubt you and Rose ever went there."

"A few times. A whole bunch of us in somebody's car. I can only remember seeing *Back to the Future* there. Nothing else has stuck."

Out on the highway, they rode along in silence, Deirdre watching the huge sun, purple and orange, as it sank toward the western banks of the Mississippi. "Such a glorious sunset today. I had forgotten how spectacular they can be down here."

"In that case, I have something to show you. Up ahead is a perfect overlook, if I can still get to it."

About ten minutes later, Rowan turned off at an unmarked exit, crossed over railroad tracks and took a dirt road through a fallow field toward the river. They passed an abandoned house and barn off to their left and soon arrived at a grassy knoll overlooking the river. As soon as they parked, the sun slipped below the horizon on the far side of the river.

"This is a glorious spot. How did you ever come across it?" she inquired, her voice soft.

"I'm an engineer, remember," he laughed. "At one time or another, we've mapped or monitored or otherwise intervened along every inch of the river." He looked closely at her as he spoke.

"Though this has always been a special place." She smiled back at him, meeting his gaze. "Still is, special, that is," he added quietly.

Embarrassed, Deirdre fiddled with the car door. "Shall we get out?"

They made their way to the edge of the drop-off, an undergrowth of brambles and an outcropping of rocks below them. Rowan stood so close she could smell his scent, something tart but subtle. He pointed to landmarks across the river, such-and-such a town to the north, a landing place for Union troops during the Civil War not far to the south, and so on. Before she knew it, her body was leaning for support against his. A light breeze had kicked up, bringing goosebumps to her arms.

"Your skin is cool to the touch," he remarked, running his hand over her arm. His voice sounded fragile. "Perhaps we should get back to the car."

Once inside, Rowan reached to start the engine but of a sudden held the keys aloft. "We do have choices. We could go on to Greenville or we could go back to the hotel—or we could stay here, the two of us alone."

Deirdre's heart fluttered in her chest. For too long, no suggestion like this had been made to her. Dried up she did not wish to be. "I would have come to my senses by the time we got to either place, so no. Here is fine," her voice as firm as she could hold it.

Without another word, Rowan cracked the windows to let in the fresh air and then reclined the front seats to create a nearly flat bed. The checkered tablecloth from their picnic had been left in the back seat. They spread it out.

At first tenderly and then with ferocity, they made love, deep into the evening, with only his moans and her cries breaking the silence. Deirdre was lifted out of herself by Rowan's caresses; responding in kind, she did not want them to end. Nor, apparently did he. Around 11 p.m. by the dashboard clock, thirst and exhaustion overcame them. They got out of the car on opposite sides, to dress, and to clear their heads.

The sound of indeterminate night creatures was deafening in the darkness.

During the drive back, neither spoke until they saw the lights of town.

"There's much to say, Deirdre, but right now I don't feel the need. I want only to savor what has happened."

"*World enough, and time,*" she murmured. ""Let us not worry about it," she added, brushing his arm.

In front of her mother's house, Rowan kissed her and held her face in his hands. "I have to leave on Tuesday, but we will be in touch," he said. She smiled faintly, faintly disbelieving. "We will *have* to be in touch," he repeated, more emphatically.

When asked over coffee the next morning, Deirdre was noncommittal about the movie. Studying her daughter's face, Mrs. Durrell sighed audibly, but did not persist.

Chapter Twenty-Four

R owan did keep in touch with Deirdre, as best he could, given that work took him from the Russian River in California to Chesapeake Bay as well as to hotspots in-between. Those trips bracketed occasional social events his wife Sophie obliged him to show up for, ones that required a bonafide husband in attendance as opposed to one or the other of her male admirers. The Kleinfelds' of St. Louis had been for a decade or more an open marriage, which was another way of saying dispiriting except for the daughter they both adored. But now that Connor was enrolled at MIT and poised to make her own way in the world, there was less reason for the couple to stick it out.

Some of this Rowan recounted to Deirdre during the few times he managed to get back to Riverton that fall of 2013. They barely left the Park Hotel during those rendezvous, eliciting smirks from the clerks and setting tongues wagging amongst those small-town biddies who lived for such gossip.

For her part, Rose was not amused, nor did Mrs. Durrell approve. Nonetheless, the two women held their tongues. Rowan appeared more exhilarated when he came to town than Rose could rightly recall, and he encouraged Jason to stick with the rehab. It was hard to fault her own brother for coming around more often. For her part, Deirdre had acquired a lilt to her step. How could her own mother not be pleased?

Truth be told, after fifteen years of marriage and another five to move beyond its wreckage, Deirdre found that she preferred that the love affair was intermittent and uncertain in its prosecution. She relished the trysts, but being on her own had in unobtrusive ways freed her: she no longer had to ask permission, as it were. In addition, she had other things to wrap her arms around. Her research was proceeding apace without being all-consuming, keeping company with her mother, satisfying without being onerous, and following her children's progress up North, absorbing without being angst-inducing.

Regarding the twins, the basics were reassuring. Dylan was sharing a rambling house off-campus with Zach and several other graduate students, and weekend parties aside, was coming to grips with his course load. Caitlin had cycled through waitressing jobs before moving up to hostess at one place, the raise allowing her to take singing lessons in the City. Weekends were taken up with gigs in the area, arranged by Ray but often involving other bands than his.

Deirdre tried to tease out the nuances in her children's text messages, but the medium defied her analysis. She opted for phone calls to each, which usually caught Caitlin in high spirits, but Dylan subdued, which she decided was befitting a doctoral student at Princeton.

It was Mrs. Durrell who brought up the idea of a year-end gathering in Riverton.

"Why don't we have Dylan bring his friend Zach and that girl he's seeing, Nasreen something-or-other?" she suggested one evening. "Caitlin can bring that Ray fellow you mentioned. And, you should let Rose know both she and her son, and for that matter, her brother too, are invited for a toast on New Year's Eve."

To Deirdre's surprise, both Dylan and Caitlin agreed to make it down for the holidays, bringing along for part of the time Zach, Nasreen, and Ray.

"What about Roxane?" Deirdre thought to ask her son during the call.

"Don't, Mother," he had urged, his voice brooking no dissent. In a lighter key, he added, "She's got other plans, anyway."

"How do you know: have you spoken to her recently?"

"Last week. And it wouldn't work, her going down there. OK?"

Deirdre felt disturbed after that exchange and ashamed that she hadn't kept up with Roxane herself. She would make reconnecting one of her New Year's resolutions. As for the Kleinfelds, she dropped by the store the next day, bought the green vase, and invited Rose, Jason, and Rowan for the get-together. Her friend appeared touched by the gesture, and vouched for Jason too, as he'd have finished up his detox program by year's end.

Then this: "I can't speak for Rowan, but I'll inquire. As you can imagine, he and Sophie socialize a lot in St. Louis, especially at holidays. They are important patrons of the arts, as I understand it." Deirdre tried to keep a straight face. ""Though seeing as you and he... Anyway, I'll ask."

Rose carefully wrapped the vase, keeping her eyes bent on the task.

Deirdre would have liked to declare that, even if the Kleinfelds weren't unhappy being shackled to each other, she herself was content to enjoy Rowan's company, as he hers, whenever they got the chance. The other part of her said it was no one else's business what she and he did, and likely no one cared all that much anyway, Sophie least of all.

That Christmas was one of the happiest for Deirdre since the twins received their first bicycles back in Ohio.

Although on pins-and-needles as to what impression Caitlin might make on her grandmother, she needn't have fretted. Now twenty and drug-free, she arrived wearing stylish boots and a below-the-knee wool dress, her tresses trimmed, her expression alert. In tow was an unrecognizable Ray, clean-shaven and ramrod-straight, though still oblivious to social graces: he juggled two cell phones, texting or taking calls without regard to anyone around him. If Caitlin was annoyed, she managed to disguise it, though at one point Deirdre heard her whisper to him to turn the damn things off.

Fortunately, Dylan showed up a few hours after his sister, with Nasreen on his arm, both of whom bowled Mrs. Durrell over with their perfect manners. Zach flew in on the 24th, bringing gifts, including a beautifully bound anthology of Renaissance songs for Caitlin and an offbeat tome called *The New York Nobody Knows* for Deirdre.

On Christmas Eve, Deirdre and her mother alternated at the piano, with Zach on the clarinet, Dylan on the violin and Caitlin and Nasreen in full throat. Even Ray, who couldn't but notice how chummy his girl friend was with Zach, joined in, taking up Stephen Durrell's old fiddle. Their rendition of *O Holy Night* was wobbly, but they nailed *O Little Town of Bethlehem*.

Just as they wound up the evening's festivities, the phone rang. Deirdre picked it up, hoping it might be Rowan.

"Ah, I figured you'd all be around about now. *Bon Noel,*" a female voice, slightly accusatory, began.

"Hello, Roxane. To you too. Merry Christmas." During the pause at the other end, Deirdre shot a glance toward Caitlin and Dylan. The latter's face fell.

"I wanted to make sure everyone got there OK and what-not."

It occurred to Deirdre that her friend might have imbibed more than an eggnog or two.

"Yes, it's wonderful to have them here. And it's lovely of you to check in with us, Roxane. I trust it's not too cold up there, or if it is, that's it's a white Christmas and not just sludge. As you can imagine, snow in the Delta is unthinkable." Deirdre heard herself throw out these anodyne comments but couldn't help it. The call had discombobulated her.

Roxane ignored the platitudes. "Is Dylan nearby? I'd like to wish him a propitious 2014," she declared, her tone sharper.

Deirdre shot her son another glance. He frantically shook his head, and slunk as best he could between Zach and Nasreen.

"I'm afraid they've gone out, but I'll be sure to tell them both." Silence. "Anyway, do take care and thanks for calling. We'll be in touch."

"It's late there too," she persisted, as if the two grown children had no business being out and about at such an hour.

"Yes, but you know how it is: they're young. Catching up with old friends. As I said, we'll speak again soon."

"Good-bye, Deirdre. Let him—them—know I rang."

There was a strained silence in the parlor as Deirdre hung up the receiver. She noticed Zach pat Dylan's arm; Nasreen looked irritated but didn't say anything. The interruption amounted to the only sour note of the evening, though everyone pretended not to have heard it.

For New Year's Eve, Mrs. Durrell invited a couple of her fellow teachers, one a widow named Mrs. Stennis, the other a spinster named Miss Dearborn, as well as the principal of the school, Elwood Harrison.

A balding man with sympathetic eyes and a ready smile, Mr. Harrison took Deirdre's hand in both his, and said how much he enjoyed knowing that Central alumni had gone on to great things. "Your mother couldn't be prouder," he concluded, as though that were an incontestable fact. (Deirdre was flummoxed, as he seemed to know much more about her career than she did about his tenure at the high school, or how far back it went.)

Behind him came Rose, who had dressed in a billowing purple outfit, which had the effect of swallowing her up and accentuating her walking cane. She shepherded into the living room not only Jason, who was cleaned up and sported a red tie, but also an oddly familiar man in a tweed jacket with the inevitable elbow patches.

"So long as none of you mind?" he politely inquired, pulling out a meerschaum and a lighter. Only then, from his voice, did Deirdre recognize Dennis Tremayne, their erstwhile high school study partner, who, Rose was quick to announce, had recently become the dean of studies at Henson Community College.

"What a delightful surprise, Rose, to think of bringing him along," Deirdre exclaimed.

"Right full of them I am tonight," Rose said, blushing. "Go ahead, Jason, tell them yours."

Less tongue-tied than before, the young man said he'd been accepted for a couple of courses at Henson in math and computer science.

"What else should you mention?" Rose prodded him.

"Oh, it's all thanks to Dr. Tremayne here for helping me get in. And Uncle Rowan."

Dylan and Zach poured out champagne for a toast to Jason and then another to celebrate Dennis's promotion. Over a buffet dinner, the professor inquired after Deirdre's research and her plans for returning to Klimpton. She elaborated, no doubt encouraged by the wine, and the laughter in the house. Her mother made a point of not interrupting the two of them, corralling Caitlin and Nasreen to help out in the kitchen.

"I always knew you'd go far once you found your niche," he said, lighting up a final pipe before the midnight hour.

"The challenge in the Humanities, Dr. Tremayne," she explained, using his honorific to make her academic point, "is to find relevancy for today's undergraduates while never disregarding the texture and tone of the past. Not an easy task, as you doubtless know."

Dennis drew in the tobacco, exhaled slowly, sending a bluish plume in the air, and nodded satisfyingly. Something about the way he performed this ritual reminded Deirdre of Ashton. For an instant, she wondered why their long-ago study partner had never married.

"Anyway, not to bore you, Dennis," she continued, wanting to wrap up her thread, "but I have, finally, alighted on three women, who, I believe, epitomize key facets of the Middle Ages, but also herald changes to come."

"Well, I cannot wait to see this all in print. And, were the opportunity to arrive, we'd be honored if you found time to lecture at Henson. We could put together a little package and have you around for as long as you'd care to be stay."

Deirdre was touched to realize her old friend was practically offering her a job, though, as she hurried to explain, she was contracted for the next two years at Klimpton. "That's more than generous, Dennis. And I'd be delighted to, if warranted. I'm not due back in Ohio until the summer."

"To be continued," he smiled, briefly laying his hand atop hers. "This is all so serendipitous, *n'est-ce pas*?"

"*Absolument*," she concurred.

At precisely a quarter to midnight, the house phone rang. This time Mrs. Durrell answered. From the set of her mother's jaw, Deirdre guessed it was Ashton. After a minute of pleasantries between ex-son-in-law and ex-mother-in-law, Deirdre motioned to her mother that she'd continue the call out in the vestibule.

"Sorry I waited so late to do this, but Happy New Year, Deirdre. The kids, both OK, I take it," he began. "And your mother sounds peppy."

It sounded eerily quiet on Ashton's end.

"I trust all is well up there. Cold, no doubt." She felt a pang of remorse that her ex-husband had nothing better to do than ring her up on New Year's Eve. Where were his wife and child, friends, colleagues? "Were you out? I bet Winslow puts on quite a party." For a moment there was no response. "Hello, Ashton? Are you still there?"

"I'm guessing Dylan or Caitlin didn't tell you," he stated, notes of both resignation and exasperation in his voice.

"Tell me what?"

"Not exactly a subject for celebration but Jennifer and I are no longer together. She's gotten a divorce; her father sped things up."

Knocked for a loop, Deirdre lowered herself onto the stool next to the phone table. "Now that that's out of the way," he rushed on exuberantly, "I'm at home, with Sierra, who's in bed, of course, as is her nanny. Lovely woman. A refugee from Syria. A godsend, actually."

"I cannot believe after everything we've been through, Ashton, you didn't tell me this. Yourself," she berated him, despite herself—despite its being a quarter to midnight on New Year's Eve.

"Tried to. Couldn't."

Deirdre let out a long breath. There was a lot to absorb, but she didn't have the focus to process it all. Not on this night. "So, you left it to the children."

"Not on purpose. They visited, saw the situation, met Amira the nanny, but no. It never came up whether you knew or not, and I never said they should or shouldn't mention it. They're our kids, remember? They don't think like we do."

"I'm not convinced we still think like we once did either, Ashton," Deirdre replied ruefully, now feeling more deflated than disapproving.

"Anyway, in case you think I called to ruin your party, that was not the plan. Got a weird call from Roxane a couple of hours ago. Wondering, she was, if Dylan was back at Princeton yet. She couldn't get hold of him and so was worried, or whatever."

Deirdre exhaled loudly. "More the *whatever*," she replied. "Dylan and Nasreen are both still here, Caitlin and Ray, Zach too for that matter."

Comparing what she imagined was the sadness in his home that evening with the laughter in her mother's house, she felt momentarily remorseful, and surprised at herself for feeling so. No need to rub things in. "So how is Sierra? You should send us a few photos."

"She's a charming child. I'll write soon, bring you up-to-date," he wound up, sounding tired or despondent.

"Yes, do that, and may 2014 be a happier year."

"Tell the kids I love them."

Hanging up the receiver, Deirdre remained slumped over, running her hands through her hair. For however many years she had nursed her grievances against her ex-husband, the call brought home how much time had been wasted, how many tears futilely shed, how many unkind words spoken, how much happiness squandered.

Once through that wringer is quite enough, she told herself.

However dejected, she returned to the festivities in time to mingle with her mother's friends before the countdown, promising to come over to inspect the spinster teacher's assortment of quilts and to drop by the widowed teacher's place to sample her herbal teas.

Glasses of bubbly were raised high as the clock struck the magic hour.

Deirdre hugged her son extra tight, resolving a sit-down to discuss Roxane was in order before he headed back. Zach, she noticed, managed to give Caitlin a kiss before she was cordoned off by Ray. Guests departed an hour later, Rose making a show of taking Dennis's arm on their way to his car, a Lexus, Deirdre observed. Their former school chum had done well.

The next morning as mother and daughter drank extra strong coffee and chatted about their guests, the doorbell rang. On the threshold stood Rowan with a bouquet of red roses—for both the Durrell ladies, he specified—and was apologetic lest he disturb anyone on the first day of the year. It was Mrs. Durrell who had gone to the door, insisting he come in and have a proper breakfast. Deirdre considered escaping the kitchen to get dressed and put on make-up but changed her mind.

"I only have a few minutes as I'm on to Memphis to catch a plane," she heard him explain, and her mother reply, "Then all the more reason for coffee and toast to warm you up. DeeDee and I are doing the same."

The two lovers both blushed when he was ushered in, but both recovered as Mrs. Durrell bustled about, bringing out her homemade muscadine jelly and fig preserves to the table.

"Why ever didn't you come over last night?" Mrs. Durrell asked, placing a cup of Cafe du Monde coffee in front of their guest.

"I only managed to get here around 11:30 last night, Clarissa, and there were papers to fill out, questionnaires and things, to do for Jason. It didn't seem right to barge in," he said sheepishly.

"A shame," Mrs. Durrell replied, looking pleased to have been called by her first name. She poured him a tall glass of orange juice. Rowan then sampled the jelly, declaring it delicious, and downed the juice in short order.

Before he could elaborate on where he was next headed, the young people appeared at the door, bleary-eyed but newly hungry.

"This is Rowan Kleinfeld, guys, Rose's brother. He's an engineer and passes through now and again," Deirdre said, trying to keep a neutral tone.

Caitlin and Dylan exchanged a quizzical glance but then raised their hands in welcome mode. "You're Jason's uncle, right?" Dylan asked.

"He's cool," Caitlin added.

Mrs. Durrell handed each of the five a mug, with coffee and a little cream.

"Oh, and these are the twins' friends, Ray, Nasreen and Zach," Deirdre added.

"Nice to meet all of you," Rowan replied, quickly checking his watch and stealing a glance at Deirdre.

"I'll throw something on since it's cold, and walk you out," she said.

Upstairs, she rifled through her closet and pulled out a pair of black wool slacks and a red sweater. Then she ran a brush through her hair and dusted her face with powder.

Once the two of them were outside and out of earshot, Rowan spoke first. "I wanted to call you from Vicksburg, but things only came together late yesterday. I made Rose promise—"

"It's all right, Rowan. We don't have to explain anything to each other." He looked dismayed. "It's enough to lay eyes on you," she added more warmly.

Rowan cast about to see if anyone in the neighboring houses were out and about. An old man was making his way along down the street, but he had his back to them. "Get in the car with me for a minute," he said, taking her arm. Deirdre looked bemused but didn't object. "I need to kiss you properly, on this first day of the year," he went on, his voice modulating register.

It was one of the things about him that made it hard to resist, the way his tone amplified his feelings. She did as he asked.

Once in the SUV, he started the engine to warm it up and then leaned over to kiss her. His other hand slipped under her sweater and caressed her breasts. "Jesus, Deirdre." He tore himself away and grasped the steering wheel with both hands, his head bowed. "I must have forgotten how much I have missed this—you, us—whatever you want to call it."

"We don't have to call it anything," Deirdre replied softly, adjusting her clothes and wriggling her body upright. She refused to let herself inquire about his plans or when they might see each other again. He had met her children; he had eyed her unadorned. That seemed enough for one day. She ran her hand along his arm and got out. "Drive safely and may this be the happiest of years for you."

Late in the spring, an unusually wet season in the Delta, Deirdre, and Rowan found themselves once again in his suite at the Park Hotel, albeit *suite* might be an overstatement for the two modestly furnished rooms he paid for to accommodate their encounters. While both Rose and Mrs. Durrell had come to accept that the two were engaged in a serious, if sporadically prosecuted, affair, and that whatever complications arose from it, these two were no longer teenagers. Entanglements came with being adults—: it was not up to them to harp on the dangers.

Besides. Rose still carried a torch for their erstwhile schoolmate, who was making more of an effort to spend time in Riverton; she was content to know that Deirdre's attentions were elsewhere.

For her part, Clarissa Durrell knew only too well how hard satisfying male companionship, be it platonic or sexual, was to acquire and sustain for a divorcée, or for a widow. Not long after her husband had died, she had her own fling—on that first Viking Cruise down the Rhine—but eventually, her paramour had drifted away, finding safe harbor in the arms of a much younger woman. Only then had someone closer to hand begun to have a positive effect on her life. At sixty-six, she was too private a person to confide any of this to her daughter, nor did she reckon Deirdre needed to be told that a relationship with a married man brought its own challenges, vastly upping the odds of heart-break. Her daughter appeared happy and energetic, never more so than when Rowan showed up. *Is that not all that matters?* she had asked herself, and answered in the affirmative.

Lying together in the queen-sized bed that dreary April night, Rowan lit two cigarettes, passing the first to Deirdre. They both inhaled deeply, their heads against the pillows, the snarled sheets haphazardly covering their torsos.

"Funny how I only have the taste for this sporadically—avidly but sporadically," she mused aloud.

Rowan looked startled. "You mean the sex?"

"No, silly. Smoking," she laughed. "When Caitlin had her accident, all I seemed to do was pace hospital corridors, waiting to accost doctors or waylay a nurse. Bumming cigarettes off whomever." She took another puff and shut her eyes in memory of that fraught year.

"Obviously, Caitlin came through it in spectacular shape, though when I glimpsed her at Easter, she seemed on edge. Her face was all acute angles."

Deirdre absorbed his words before responding, aware once again of how observant he was. Must have something to do with being an engineer, being able to deconstruct the landscape one is confronted with, she had concluded. "For my daughter," she responded with deliberation, "everything is a drama. Dylan, on the other hand, is hard to ruffle."

Rowan nodded, stubbed out his cigarette and reached over to pour them a second glass of the *sauvignon blanc* he had brought up from Vicksburg.

"But to your point, she has split up with Ray—the one who came down with her at Christmas—and is involved with some other band member. Or another band altogether."

"I see," he said, touching his glass to hers. "Lots of young males around in that profession. She doubtless has the pick of the lot."

"Doubtless," Deirdre deadpanned, wishing for a moment that her daughter would confide in her, however little that had ever been the case.

"You don't look thrilled that she can pick and choose," Rowan ventured.

"I don't want her to end up with a drug addict, and lose herself to that scourge again," Deirdre shot back. "If she had her head about her, she'd recognize there's a young man in their orbit, hers and Dylan's, who is crazy about her. If only she—"

At that moment, Deirdre's cell phone rang. Her face tensed. She threw off the sheet and reached for the device on the night stand. One glance at the number on the screen, she tumbled out of bed and headed to the window, her back to Rowan. (So he had done, a couple of times when Sophie had rung up unexpectedly.)

She tapped the icon to take the call.

"Is something wrong with Caitlin?" she asked, her voice thin, reedy.

"I didn't know where you were and I know it's late"—(Deirdre could hear faint cries of a child in the background)—"but yes, something's happened."

"Is she all right, Ashton? That's all I need to know," she repeated vehemently.

Sensing that something was wrong, Rowan approached and gently draped a robe around Deirdre's shoulders. Distractedly, she pulled it over her exposed torso.

"I'm trying to tell you. Not Caitlin. Dylan. He's in the hospital, but Zach says he's going to be OK."

"What are you talking about? They're at Princeton, for God's sake!"

"Calm down a minute and I'll explain: it's Roxane," Ashton persevered, his voice enunciating every syllable. "She went down there to see him Sunday, but he had gone to Baltimore to visit what's-her-name. Sorry, Nasreen. She waited around all day, worked herself up. When he got home, they apparently argued. Zach, who has the adjoining apartment, could hear them going at it. Dishes flying and such."

"I don't understand, Ashton. Why is our son in the hospital?"

"Roxane must have grabbed a kitchen knife and slashed at the air; he tried to stop her, but she lunged at him, catching his arm. Don't know which one. At that point, he must have howled in pain. Zach banged on the door but had to retrieve his spare key. When he got the door open, so he told me, Dylan was lying on the floor; she pulled a piece of paper out of her pocket, flung it at him, then slit her wrist. As though it were some kind of fucking performance."

Standing at Deirdre's shoulder, Rowan could only intuit the account from her questions, but her face had gone white, her legs wobbled. Rather than touch her, he pulled up the only armchair in the room and helped her collapse into it.

"Are you saying Roxane tried to kill my son, Ashton? For what earthly reason?" she wailed, her voice reverberating off the walls of the room.

"Zach called an ambulance and both were taken to the ER, where she expired. Dylan's had stitches put in and is sedated."

Rowan retrieved a kleenex to wipe away the tears that began to streak Deirdre's face. She grasped his arm and squeezed it. "Some water would be good," she rasped.

"Deirdre, are you still there?"

"Of course."

"Caitlin has taken the train down from the City and will call or text once she sees Zach and Dylan. Naturally, the police will be involved, the university too. It'll be a mess."

"I'll fly up right away," Deirdre mumbled.

"No, no. I'm canceling classes and will get there tomorrow afternoon. You should give yourself time to digest all this. Think about Wednesday or Thursday. We can overlap but divide up what needs to be done." There was a pause at the other end. "I knew Roxane was an odd bird, Deirdre, but I never imagined..."

"Of course not, Ashton. Neither did I," she replied, trying to reassure him.

"OK then. It's the middle of the night. We both need to sleep. Sierra too," he said, his tone now a bit lighter.

"What did Roxane's note to Dylan say?" Deirdre asked.

"No idea," Ashton answered. "Zach has it. It's in French."

Sleep did not come to either Deirdre or Rowan for the rest of the rain-soaked night. They finished the wine, but rather than talk, they held each other close, their fingers intertwined, knowing that their world had been turned upside-down.

Chapter Twenty-Five

T he New York tabloids had a field day with the scandal. *Spurned teacher slashes student lover, slits own wrists,* blared one; *Princeton scholar at center of deadly love triangle,* trumpeted another.

Deirdre could not bring herself to read beyond the lurid headlines. In the *Times*, however, she did notice something else. Apparently, the school where Roxane had been teaching found out that she had "misrepresented" herself in her résumé, including a discovery that her degree certificates from Paris were fraudulent, this, despite "glowing" recommendations from college professors Stateside. One of these last was purportedly from a Midwest professor of Medieval Studies, which distressed her even more, if such were possible in the circumstances.

There would be an inquest, which no one in the family looked forward to. But before that ordeal, Deirdre had her son to attend to.

When she arrived at the hospital in Princeton, Dylan was propped up on pillows and eating a bowl of cherry-flavored jello. Nasreen was sitting in the only chair in the private room, her head bent over a textbook. She immediately rose when Deirdre entered and moved toward the bed. Dylan handed the bowl of jello to her and made an effort to sit up straighter.

"Mom, you didn't have to come all this way. Dad went down to talk to the doctors, and they're going to discharge me later today," he went on.

Trying to keep her face composed, Deirdre put her arms around her son's neck, gingerly, not wanting to disturb his bandaged right arm or the left hand, which was encased in a cast. "I'm so sorry, sweetheart. We had no idea about—she couldn't bring herself to say Roxane—*her*, or what she was capable of doing," she burbled.

A dark cloud flitted across her son's face but he forced a wan smile.

Deirdre reached for a kleenex on the table next to a water glass and a cell phone, presumably her son's. "All that matters now is you're OK. "She dabbed at her eyes and then turned her attention to Nasreen. "So glad you're here. I know it means a lot to him, to all of us." The young woman remained stone-faced and did not speak.

"We wanted to tell you, Mom, before all this happened. I had gone to Baltimore over the weekend but I had forgotten my cell phone, so I didn't know..." Dylan trailed off, unable still to express his thoughts cogently. Deirdre darted her eyes from one to the other. "I asked Nasreen to marry me on Saturday night."

Both the young people blushed, but Nasreen kept her gaze on her textbook.

"That's wonderful news. The best there could be. Have you told your dad?"

"I had talked to him before I left for John Hopkins, Caitlin too," he said, watching his mother's face. "Sis has been great, by the way. And, if it hadn't been for ..." His voice quavered and he looked away to get hold of himself. "Zach. When he got back to our house that evening, Roxane was pacing outside the building, so he invited her in. They drank some wine, though not a lot, he said. Somehow, during the wait for me to show up, he let on that I had gone to Baltimore to propose, which must have, well, set her off." Dylan sank back down a few inches into his pillows, unable to continue the account.

In the silence, Nasreen stared vacantly at the far wall. For the first time, it hit Deirdre that her son might have had sex with Roxane, perhaps as far back as high school or as recently as—she didn't want to imagine, and it wouldn't be any of her business, except that the woman had one way or another taken advantage of her son and, for whatever desperate reason, taken her own life.

A lot was bound to come out in the investigation, her too careless academic recommendation the least of it.

What was clear to Deirdre was that her son had been shaken to the core, and that, like his sister before him, he would be knocked off course, as it were, albeit his physical injuries were not life-altering. It had taken Caitlin several years to right herself after the car crash, and to get right with the world remained an ongoing battle; what had happened to Dylan was of a different order but arguably as traumatic. Glad as she was that her son would have the support of friends, she was also relieved that Ashton was making an effort to be on top of things. She needed a sounding board, something that Rowan, a married man and constantly on the road, had not been in a position to become, and something that she missed from poor Howard, who, in his lawyerly fashion, had weighed in so judiciously on the kids.

Once the doctors had looked in on their patient, they took the Coles aside to suggest a delay in discharging their son, as his blood pressure was still high and, his cognitive responses still erratic. The neurosurgeon who had reattached the severed nerves in his left hand counseled that another forty-eight hours in the hospital would be beneficial. Not only did he want to observe how the affected fingers were responding to stimulation—"He told me he plays the violin, so there's added incentive," a Dr. Marsh pointed out, but the team also wanted to monitor his psychological state, as what had happened had been, in their collective judgment, "highly disturbing."

Upon hearing this assessment and seeing his ex-wife's stricken face, Ashton put his arm around her. Once the doctors dispersed, he suggested they head to a nearby restaurant for a proper meal, and, in his words, "come to grips with the facts."

They shared baked sea bass in the half-empty restaurant, the other customers looking similarly worn-out as though they too were distressed relatives or friends of patients in the hospital. Eventually, they broke their own silence. "Do you think they...?" were all the words necessary to signal the crucial question, and which was sure to figure as a focus of the police investigation into what transpired between Roxane and Dylan.

It had been a long time since the two ex-spouses had read each other's minds.

"Go on," Ashton said quietly, inviting her to extemporize as he poured them more wine. Women were, to his mind, better at tackling such an indelicate subject than men were, and, in any case, he was finicky about discussing sexual matters with the opposite sex. He took a swallow of the expensive *sancerre* and tilted his head expectantly.

"It's easier to see signs that something was amiss or unsavory in retrospect," Deirdre began, thinking of the New Year's Eve she came home to find the two watching that French movie. "But back then my preoccupations were—what can I say?—elsewhere, and, as regards the children, more centered on Caitlin. It never hit me that..." she trailed off, bewildered by the puzzle she never pieced together of what might have been motivating her friend to seek out the children nor how vulnerable her son might have been to her blandishments.

She too took a swallow of the crisp wine, it helping to squelch the desire to hold her husband to account (yet again) for not being in the picture at such a crucial stage in his son's development. By her calculations, Dylan must have been fifteen or sixteen when first exposed to Roxane's attentions. The idea of his being sexualized at that age by an older woman—*that* woman: her supposed friend—

made her squirm. Reaching for her water glass, she downed half of it.

"What about you? Before you left us, did you notice anything suspicious?"

The muscles in Ashton's face twitched, but he allowed the reference to abandonment dissipate in the air. The last thing he wanted, or had the energy for, was an argument.

"Dylan had become moody, but that seemed normal for a teenager," he hazarded, looking up toward the ceiling of the restaurant, as though trying to pull down more remote recollections. A waiter walked by their table but seemed to determine it was not an apt time to interrupt.

"As with Caitlin. Except that she acted out rather than internalized—pouting, provoking me, painting her nails that ox-blood red," Deirdre reminded, shaking her head as though still in disbelief.

"Dylan kept a lot of things under lock and key," Ashton concurred. "However," he went on, his tone shifting. Deirdre raised her eyebrows in a question mark. "On one of our fishing trips, he asked me, out of nowhere, how many years separated you and me, and whether it would matter if the woman rather than the man were older. Something to that effect."

"How did you respond?" Deirdre asked drily, the calculus of their age difference, not to mention the chasm between her ex-husband's and Jennifer's, not something she had forgotten.

"A huge perch took his hook, pulled it under and we had to fight to land the damn thing. We never got back to the subject, though, as you say, in retrospect perhaps I should have..."

"Quite," Deirdre replied, not needing to finish her sentence.

After another pause in which each rummaged again through their memories of Dylan's awkward age, Ashton suggested they split a *tiramisu*, a dessert they had both relished in their courtship days. Although she no longer had a sweet tooth, Deirdre acquiesced: anything to be *picked up* in spirit, as it were.

"The main thing," Ashton emphasized, as she unobtrusively slid the plate of cake toward him, "is that our son tell the truth.

Whatever was the—(here, he hesitated)—extent of their intimacy and whatever the hell could have explained her going off the deep end."

"Of course he should. Still, they're going to go berserk with this." She stared at the dessert, bewildered by the circus that was already setting up camp around her son's off-campus building and her dead friend's school back in Manhattan.

"They?"

"Oh, you know, Ashton. The media...*social* media. Dylan and Caitlin, Zach and Nasreen, all are going to be rattled, if not raked over the coals—not to mention the annoying fact, which I learned from a reporter who rang me earlier today, that I'm apparently the closest contact for Roxane, as far as Dorset High is concerned."

"How is that possible?"

"I wrote her that recommendation, remember? And, as Roxane blithely told us on innumerable occasions, she has—*had*—no immediate family."

Ashton signaled for the waiter, ordered two cognacs, and handed the young man a credit card.

After the cordials, the ex-spouses agreed that it was imperative that Dylan regain use of his arm and hand, the cost of physical therapy be what it may, and that they would jointly support whatever decision he made about continuing his studies, or taking time off to recuperate.

The inquest into the suicide brought to light several disconcerting contours of the relationship between Roxane and Dylan. It had only turned sexual, according to a signed affidavit from the injured party, after he had matriculated at Penn and then only for "the briefest of periods." He would have been nineteen, she thirty-four at the time—eyebrow-raising but not illegal.

In preparing his statement, Dylan did not discuss the particulars of the affair with either Deirdre or Ashton, nor did his parents talk about it to each other. The revelation of the heretofore undisclosed intimacy nonetheless did cause Nasreen to back out of, (temporarily, she was quick to aver), her plan to marry and caused Dylan to take a leave from Princeton and return, (temporarily, he too was quick to aver), to his childhood home in Ohio.

If there were any good news, it was that the whole sorry mess caused Caitlin to draw closer to her brother, having never seen him to be so vulnerable.

For her part, Deirdre found herself under scrutiny to justify how she could have been taken in by, if not bamboozled, by her friend of many years, and how negligent she might have been for penning "such a laudatory appraisal," as one of the lawyers put it, of the aforesaid. "I can only say that Roxane had an enormous gift since, despite coming from such difficult circumstances, she managed to construct a credible narrative and to immerse herself so totally in it that few were ever led to question it or her."

Or, as Ashton put it when Deirdre ran her preliminary statement to the authorities by him, "In a way, she had become her own avatar, although, as we are only now learning from the newspapers, her past did eventually come back to haunt her."

He was not wrong. Roxane's mother had behaved just as violently against her own spouse, and, per the report in the *New York Times*, had only been released from prison several months before the tragedy. Whether Roxane knew about her mother's getting out, which might have been an aggravating circumstance, could not be determined.

In the final summation from the authorities, it was concluded that Roxane had acted out of a jealous rage when she discovered that Dylan planned to marry the young woman he was dating. As they argued in his apartment that evening, she had, in the heat of passion, lashed out with the nearest implement to hand; he, in turn, had tried to defend himself and to disarm her. To little avail, since he quickly sustained cuts and was bleeding profusely when fellow Princetonian, Zachary Rutherford, managed to open the door and intervene to succor both.

Adding to the distress that likely underlay Roxane's paroxysm, was, according to several of her colleagues at the high school, her agitation over having been fired for brazenly misleading the school authorities—from the get-go. So flagrant were her misrepresentations, it could not even be verified that she had ever lived in Paris, despite the fact that a number of students, especially males in her class, attested to her talents as a teacher of French.

As Deirdre prepared to leave Princeton two weeks later, taking Dylan back with her to the Delta and then on to Ohio, Zach knocked on her door in the off-campus boarding house. "I have something for you," he said, holding out a folded piece of paper. "Look at it when you're up to it. Lines from a poem, something about dead leaves. Didn't seem right to toss it."

PART THREE

2018

Sumer ist y-comen in
Well singest thou, Cuckoo
Ne swik thou never no.

Anonymous
(thirteenth century)

Chapter Twenty-Six

T he call came late on a summer evening while she was fiddling with the Reminders app on her iPhone. Things like letters of recommendation to write, research notes to organize, honor students to advise, an anti-Trump rally to attend on campus, and real estate agents to vet. Not to mention boxing up the rest of the children's books to send to Sierra, a set of dinnerware to mail to Dylan, and random CDs to pack up for Caitlin.

The landline rang four times before she got up from her desk and hurried to the hall to pick up.

"The job is yours if you want it, Deirdre. Everyone would be honored to have you here," a male voice announced, without preamble or other niceties. They were, after all, old friends and the subject had been broached months ago. Not one to oversell his offer, Dr. Dennis Tremayne paused, took a deep breath and waited for a response. And just like that Dr. Deirdre Durrell decided to sell the house in Oakville and move back to the Delta.

She had her reasons.

Clarissa Durrell, who in her widowhood had blossomed, had suffered a fall the previous winter, the hip operation had not gone well, and the seventy-five-year-old, despite her assertions to the contrary, could plausibly no longer get by solely on her own.

As an only daughter, Deirdre had put out feelers from afar for available sitters in the area but without success; subsequently, she had scoured the state of Mississippi for a teaching position in one or another institution of higher learning, one which would not make for a difficult commute to and fro Riverton. When nothing materialized, she had let her intention to relocate be generally known the last time she had flown down for a long weekend. Rose had duly passed the proposition on to their mutual high school friend.

With the twins now on their own and managing reasonably well, and she having risen as far as possible in the Klimpton firmament, there was no compelling reason to keep her rooted (if that were the right word) in the town where she had spent the better part of twenty years as a college professor and, more recently, divorced mother of two.

Dylan, after a couple of years back in Oakville, doing volunteer work at a women's shelter, working a few hours a week for pay at the campus library, and otherwise helping his mother with the house and yard, he had righted himself sufficiently to return to Princeton. He completed his Ph.D., took up again, tentatively at least, with Nasreen, and settled into a job at a think tank in New York City. For her part, Caitlin had limited her time performing on the road, ditched the latest in her series of boyfriends, and flew out to Ohio regularly to spend time with her brother and mother.

"I could not have gotten through this without you, sweetheart," Deirdre had told her at one point, grateful for her daughter's unexpected competence. It was almost as though her two children had switched personalities, Dylan now the fragile, needy one.

Sometimes, Zach tagged along on these visits, including a break-through weekend in late 2014 when the two jointly cajoled Dylan into bringing out the violin for the first time: since. The three played trios for an entire evening, their only audience Deirdre, Cookie curled up in her lap, and Margery, with the golden retriever, a rescue of indeterminate age, lying at her dainty feet. If Dylan's fingers did not move as deftly as before his injuries, only a highly trained ear would have been aware.

Such good times with her children came more frequently for Deirdre after that. The three attended Margery's staging of *The Tempest* (the professor having sworn it would be her last hurrah), hiked the mountains in Michigan, and drove to Chicago to hear the symphony—all of which also helped her cope with her loneliness, even if she refused to call it that. (Ever since what they tacitly agreed to call the "incident" at Princeton, guilt had persuaded her to relegate sex to the past, as compatible as she and Rowan were in bed.)

She had her work, and as the years went by, she received sufficient encouragement to want to expand her palette.

For one thing, Margery made an off-hand suggestion that shifted the course of her efforts. "To hear you talk about the period, Deirdre, I sense the drama behind these lives. Why don't you pull back the curtain and write a play about these women?"

At first, Deirdre dismissed the idea out of hand, as though it might devalue the research she had done to paint an accurate picture of that epoch. Slowly, however, she warmed to the task. It might be a way to make these figures less remote and more accessible to modern minds. (Klimpton's classes devoted to the Middle Ages had continued to dwindle after the recession was declared over, and she, like many instructors, had been obliged to handle additional courses, for little extra pay and not all of them to her taste.)

Above all, Deirdre did not wish to become a dried-up prune. A change of venue might be invigorating on several fronts.

Naturally, she would miss certain colleagues, especially Margery and Stella as well as Dr. Beauchamps, now semi-retired and blatantly ignored by his inveterate flirt of a wife. But other than these, and the initial enthusiasm she felt each term at the fresh faces she was called upon to engage, there were few other people she would miss. Caedmon had died while Dylan was still in Ohio recovering from the scandal—the two had buried him near the pond; Deirdre's hairdresser Erica, with whom she had exchanged confidences of a sort she'd never shared with anyone else she could think of, had recently returned to Chicago to work in some fancy salon; and Rowan, still married, still traveling for the Corps, had only ever shown up twice. (It was Erica who, while wielding her scissors above Deirdre's head, had jokingly insinuated that he might very well have a lover in every damn town that sat near a dam. The beautician then caught her client's dismayed expression in the mirror. "Anyway, he's married, so there's that," she added, afraid she might have gone too far, and lost a regular customer.)

Not that such an offhand comment needled Deirdre unduly. As far as she was concerned, the relationship with Rose's brother had run its course—Dylan's troubles had seen to that—and other preoccupations had tamped down her enthusiasm to pursue the affair. She had her son to tend to as well as the loose ends of Roxane's life to tie up. (To her consternation, she had been called upon by the probate court to assist in handling the deceased's assets, a duty she discreetly complied with, if for no other reason than to get the thing over with as quickly and painlessly for her son as possible.)

That chore entailed a visit together with a harried lawyer hired by Dorset High to Roxane's Upper West Side walk-up, where, to her further consternation, photos of Dylan were on display. (She stuffed them in her briefcase while the lawyer was taking notes in the kitchenette.) Several dozen books in French would be donated to the school library. (She did not saddle the lawyer with her suspicion that some of the volumes, rare editions of Balzac and Hugo among them, might have been stolen.) Once the clothes, jewelry and knick-knacks were boxed up, and, once all stipulations of the court were met, they were FedExed out west to one Winifred P. Johnson. The meager balance in Roxane's Chase bank account did not cover all the legal bills; Deirdre wrote a check for the balance and tried to consider the whole sorry affair closed.

As for Rowan, he had tried his best to stay in the picture, but Deirdre had begged him to get on with his life when he phoned shortly after the inquest. At her insistence, he refrained from calling or writing as long as he could.

Or until he couldn't.

Shortly after Labor Day of 2014 he had shown up unannounced in Ohio, reserved a hotel room at the Elm St. Arms, and rung the Cole house. Dylan had answered, sounding to Rowan's ear uncertain, and thus the visitor essentially invited himself over. The two were out in the back throwing a frisbee to the retriever, which they had named Topsy, when Deirdre got home.

For the first time since their return to Ohio, she heard her son's laughter.

The three had pot roast for dinner, which in turn called for the bottle of Brunello the guest had brought along. To keep the conversation on neutral ground, Rowan distracted them with the government's plans to come to grips with climate change, the which was already making flood control all the harder.

"I may be traveling more, not less, up this way," he had let on, winding up with a description of the vulnerable farmland and river towns dotting the Midwest. He failed to catch Deirdre's eye, however, at the mention of his travel plans, and she did not accompany him back to town.

A few letters, all affectionate but not overly personal, and postmarked variously Sacramento, New Orleans and Albany aside, did not induce Deirdre to reciprocate. Rather, she sent her former lover Christmas cards each year, to his work address with only cursory comments, mostly about Dylan's progress and Caitlin's singing engagements.

In short, Deirdre had stared into the mirror, and had determined that time for "all that," as she now termed it, had passed her by. Her limbs were still strong, but the flesh appeared less taut; there was a thickening around her middle and a thinning over her cheekbones. When those things had happened she did not know, nor whether others had made it their business to notice.

Had Rowan? Perhaps not; he had only ever complimented her, in bed too (something Ashton had never done). Even in front of Dylan, Rowan had exclaimed at how "well" she looked. She had smiled, accepted the wrapped bottle of wine and changed the subject.

Not that there weren't nights when she lay in bed wishing to hold and be held by someone, but she was thankful that her erstwhile husband was no longer someone she would want to awaken next to. And, she was relieved that she no longer ached for Rowan nor longed for her body to be entwined with his.

At least most of the time.

Shortly before the sale of the house, Margery and Stella came over for one last celebratory evening with their colleague. The former brought a fresh sourdough loaf and an assortment of fancy cheeses the local farmers market had begun to stock; Stella brought along a bottle of red and a white wine—and a secret she had never shared with anyone. Deirdre had whipped together a salad to go along with the last of the frozen casseroles she pulled from the freezer. She had pretty much given up on desserts, especially after that critical assessment in the mirror. As for the cheeses, they too would have to be savored in moderation.

"I guess there's no way to talk you into staying with us?" Margery began as soon as they were comfortably seated on the patio and the wine poured. "We didn't see your departure coming or we'd have—"

"I know it's all about your mother, but I'm sure I could prevail upon Louis—Dr. Beauchamps—to better the offer from down there, and even scrape a course or two off your plate," Stella jumped in. For some reason, she reddened. "Especially since you're now writing a play, and that will further enhance your chances."

"Thanks to Margery's urging—the play, that is," Deirdre responded. "And, if I can get it done." She tossed a few biscuits out in the yard for the dog and then sliced the loaf of bread. "But, ladies, the move to the Delta is a *fait accompli*, as you can see from the disarray in the house."

The three women tried the various cheeses and sipped wine for a few minutes, watching Topsy chase squirrels up the oaks.

Eventually, Stella returned to the subject. "Perhaps you'll get back around the holidays, your kids too—: Margery is threatening that *Henry IV* will be the last ever production she mounts, and Louis has been enticed to play Falstaff."

Stella's eyes shone brightly in the late afternoon sunlight as she spoke. To Deirdre, she appeared unusually vivacious, a description she had never associated with her otherwise reliably dour friend.

Something's going on with her, she thought, but declined to ask. Instead, she turned toward her other friend.

"I've come to think of you, Margery, as the Barbra Streisand of Klimpton. The next concert or stage production will avowedly be your last, but the world would wobble on its axis were that actually the case," she said.

Margery laughed appreciatively. "To return the compliment, my dear, I would say that I misread the tea leaves." Deirdre and Stella's eyebrows both arched up in a question mark. "When Ashton left us, I thought Klimpton would take a terrible hit—I don't mean only the donor money—but, as it's turned out, your contributions to the college have been more long-lasting."

Deirdre reddened, thinking it the nicest thing anyone at the college had ever said to her.

"We just hope you will find someone with whom to share all these gifts of yours," Margery added parenthetically but, to Deirdre's ear, also pointedly.

"As I have," Stella of a sudden piped up, her voice high-pitched. "I mean, without all your gifts, of course, Deirdre, but nonetheless. Louis and I, we're in love. As hard for me to imagine as for anyone else. He's going to be leaving his wife as soon as, well, as soon as he can."

Gobsmacked by this revelation, Deirdre proposed a toast to the (unlikely) lovers. Before the evening was over, the threesome had consumed both bottles.

That night in bed as she went over the evening, she did wonder if she'd ever have another lover herself—and, if she'd have to give up cheese as well as sweets in order to make that happen. *Stella of all people*, she murmured as sleep overtook her.

Within a week of that get-together, the contents of the house in Ohio were auctioned off or otherwise placed on consignment with the town's top antique store. Only the Globe-Wernickes would be moved to her mother's home; the grandfather clock would be shipped to Ashton in Pennsylvania.

Topsy, along with several boxes of books, would travel with Deirdre by car all the way to the Delta.

Chapter Twenty-Seven

A lashing rain impeded the last sixty miles to Riverton, forcing Deirdre to pull off and wait out the worst. A few eighteen-wheelers whizzed by as though oblivious to the slick asphalt that late summer squalls left in their wake. A flock of fat crows swooped over a nearby stubble field. For a few minutes, she closed her eyes to calm her nerves. As Margery and Stella had both intimated, she was about to embark on the biggest life change since Ashton had left her—a return to her childhood home, a job she was overqualified and underpaid for, a paucity of friends, and a mother who was fast-fading, with neither of her children around to take the pressure off, or distract her from what were likely to be mounting challenges.

"That's one way to look at things, right, Topsy?" she murmured aloud as she ruffled the dog's fur. The canine appeared to yip in sympathy.

As the storm let up, she stared out at fields of soybeans to the west and corn to the east, an abandoned barn with a rusty tractor adjacent, a nondescript box of a church with a flat corrugated roof, and nearer to hand, steam coming off the pavement. At 6 p.m. the outside temperature was still in the 90's, judging from the gauge in the car. She pulled out a couple of dog biscuits for Topsy and then lowered the driver's seat window. A faint odor of wet wool mixed with gasoline rose to her nostrils. Still, she needed to stretch her legs and the dog to do her business. Hot coffee would help.

At the next exit, for a town called Rosedale, she veered off. The main street was not hard to find: two blocks of rundown storefronts, crab grass having cropped up between and widened the cracks in what remained of the sidewalk. A convenience store was attached to the gas station at the far corner. She filled the tank and drank half of the acrid-tasting brew described by the attendant as Columbian Supreme. She scrunched the styrofoam cup and got back in the car.

Such places as this, Deirdre thought, have been abandoned by progress itself. It was as though everything that could happen in the town had already occurred. She flicked on the radio to drive away her sense of desolation.

 Back out on the highway, traffic was picking up. Mealtime had always been sacred in the Durrell home, and 8:15 had been agreed upon when she rang up early that morning from the outskirts of Memphis. An unfamiliar voice had picked up, one Lorraine, who described herself as a nurse's aide.

"Just here looking in on the missus. Miss Pattie Lee from the church sends me over. Now and again."

It was the first time Deirdre had considered how her mother's meals were being put together, and by whom, since the hip replacement. Whenever they had spoken, Mrs. Durrell had been evasive about her condition and what help, if any, she needed or had herself engaged.

Not knowing what to expect, Deirdre determined to swing by the local Piggly Wiggly for basics before arriving at the house. (Was the store even open after 5:30? She couldn't recall.)

It was also the first time she had thought of her former classmate in ages, though apparently, she was now even more a force to be reckoned with. Pattie Lee had become the most unapologetic Trump supporter and Tea Party zealot between Memphis and Vicksburg, as Rose had once put it—and that was before he was swept into office.

"The very idea of her," Deirdre muttered, clutching the steering wheel tighter. Her jaw set, she picked up speed, passed a couple of slow-poke pickup trucks, and prayed that patrolmen were not in plentiful supply along that stretch.

When she did arrive at the house, the first thing Deirdre noticed on the front porch was a wheelchair. Her heart sank. Regaining her composure, she carried the two bags of groceries to the front door. Then she returned to the passenger's side and coaxed Topsy out. "You behave now, or we'll have to build a doghouse for you in the back yard," she said, putting her key into the lock and ringing the doorbell at the same time.

"Mother, it's me. I'm here, with Topsy, the golden retriever I told you about."

She held the door open and scooted the dog inside. Hearing no response, she brought in the grocery bags and headed to the kitchen. Sniffing her way, the dog followed. Still no sign of her mother, Deirdre slipped several Lean Cuisines into the freezer and put a quart of milk, a bottle of V-8 juice and two filet mignons in the fridge. She filled a large bowl with water and put it on the floor. Over the dog's slurping, she could make out voices coming from the living room. Automatically, she brushed loose strands off her forehead, straightened her back and headed toward the sounds.

Talking heads on CNN were jabbering about senators who didn't have the wherewithal to stand up to Trump, but no one appeared to be in the room to hear. That is, until Deirdre noticed a walker next to a recliner in the corner. The chair was upholstered in dark green, and looked a bit tattered. In it, indeed swallowed up in it, was Mrs. Durrell, slumped over, her legs covered by a shawl.

Deirdre stood stupefied for an instant, then tiptoed over. "Mother, it's me," she said, laying her hand on the older woman's arm. It was dry as parchment.

Slowly, Mrs. Durrell's eyes flickered and opened.

"Ah, DeeDee. I wasn't expecting you. Tomorrow, didn't you say?" her mother murmured, wriggling to sit up straighter.

"Actually, it was today, but not to worry," Deirdre responded, determined to be cheerful. "How are you feeling, with the new hip and everything?"

"Not bad, all things considered," she responded vaguely, looking around the room as though she didn't know quite where she was. Her gaze came to rest on her daughter's face. "You look tired, DeeDee. Your hair. Was it a long drive you made?"

"From Ohio, but I'm fine," Deirdre replied, resisting the temptation to correct her mother's misconception or to appear disconcerted by how considerable her mental lapses might be. "And I'm hungry, which I imagine you are too."

"They've gotten me this contraption," Mrs. Durrell then mumbled, fumbling under the blanket and retrieving the TV remote. "Oh, not this," she went on, feeling to her other side. She raised a small gadget with two buttons for inspection. "If I press the red button, the foot stool disappears and the chair lifts me up." Deirdre nodded her head. "It's from the Baptist Church."

"Why don't you show me how it works and we'll go have supper," Deirdre replied, lifting the shawl off her mother's knees. Mrs. Durrell pressed the button and the chair responded, slowly tipping her to the front edge. She then maneuvered the walker in position and heaved herself up.

It took Deirdre all her self-control not to intervene. *She needs to do these things on her own for as long as she is able,* she silently told herself.

In the kitchen, Deirdre rustled about, heating up leftover field peas and sticking two Lean Cuisines in the microwave.

Mrs. Durrell did not object nor offer to help; rather, she appeared taken with Topsy, declaring that she had "always and forever" wanted such a dog, especially one with floppy ears that you could stroke. (Deirdre could not recall a single instance in her childhood in which she heard her mother mention such a desire, or ever use the expression *always and forever* about anything. The family *had* had a succession of cats—a tabby, then a calico, then a siamese, then a manx—and it was only ever Mr. Durrell who looked after them, petted them, buried them in the back garden.)

Whatever.

"So, tell me about the children. How is school going?" Mrs. Durrell asked once they had finished the meal, and Deirdre had placed two scoops of Häagen Dazs strawberry ice cream in front of her mother.

Again, she had to deconstruct the question and what it implied about her mother's sense of time.

"As you know, Dylan has wrapped up graduate work at Princeton and is working in New York. Caitlin is performing, singing in clubs, and also living in New York. They're both hoping to come to visit during the holidays."

"Like the last time. With those interesting friends. Such fun we had."

Blinking her eyes in rapid succession, Mrs. Durrell appeared to be trying to pull up the names of Zach and Nasreen, or perhaps even Rowan, but Deirdre decided not to complicate the picture by supplying them. Things had, after all, not turned out as she might have wished with those friends. Nasreen had never managed to get over the episode that led to her breakup with Dylan; Zach had never managed to profess his feelings for Caitlin; and in the interim, if Deirdre interpreted the twins' texts correctly, Zach and Nasreen were spending lots of time together.

Regarding Rowan, there had been too much water under the bridge. She wouldn't know what to say.

That night after she had helped her mother settle in in the converted bedroom downstairs, Deirdre retired to her room upstairs. Despite her exhaustion, she slept fitfully, alternately castigating herself for having neglected her mother these last few years, and anguishing over her new challenge: how to juggle her new role as a caregiver with teaching chores, ongoing research, and, selfish though it might be, a desire to have a life that was her own. In such a place as Riverton, she feared too many Pattie Lee Pattersons to butt in, and not enough Kleinfelds to take comfort in. She fought off images of her times together with Rowan but vowed to search out Rose as soon as she got her feet on the ground.

She didn't have to wait long. In such a small town, word of her return had already seeped out. While bringing in her boxes of books the next morning, Rose stopped by, bringing a cured ham and potato salad in a huge picnic basket. And hobbling less.

"I could get Jason to come over and unload your car, Deirdre. No point in injuring your back," she said, an open smile on her face. The two women embraced warmly.

"They're not that heavy, the boxes, but nonetheless, the rest of them can wait," Deirdre exclaimed, holding her friend at arm's length and examining her. "Those Facebook pictures don't do you justice. You look wonderful." She didn't add how much she thought her friend resembled her brother, something she had not remarked in the past: same laughing gray eyes, something sardonic about the mouth. A sudden rush of regret swept over her, but she shook it off. "And no cane. Good for you."

Rose smiled broadly, but ever self-deprecating, added, "Dennis has gotten into photography. When he aims the camera, the shots enhance their subject. And, well, I did try a new hairstyle since I was being immortalized so regularly."

"And how is he? You do know how appreciative I am of the chance—"

"Stop, Deirdre. You're a catch for any college. They're over the moon to have you. Dennis will be around come the weekend. We should all have dinner."

Later, after Jason had been commandeered to unpack the trunk of the Volvo, Rose returned to the kitchen and pulled out the ham and potato salad, retrieved plates from the cabinet and cutlery from the drawer next to the sink. She seemed to know her way around.

"Since your mom makes the best mayonnaise in town, I made this batch differently, with stoneground mustard. I'm thinking she might like to try something new."

"You went to a lot of trouble, what with the store and everything," Deirdre replied, racking her brain to remember what extended family that might require help her friend still had, or whether Rose had now taken it upon herself to minister to some among Dennis's relatives. "But Mother will be pleased."

"We'll fatten her up yet. Don't you worry," Rose averred. They sipped the tea Deirdre had made earlier in the day from mint leaves in Mrs. Durrell's herb garden. After a bit, Rose added, "As for the store, you wouldn't believe what people are willing to spend online. I've had to hire someone to do the mailing and shipping. But with Jason managing the website, I have more free time than I ever did when I ran the place!"

"Splendid. And that you've found time to cater to my mother is beyond fabulous."

For a few minutes, both women appeared lost in thought, Deirdre wondering if Rose's solicitude toward her mother had something to do with Dennis, or with Rowan, or even with Pattie Lee, Rose wondering if Deirdre's reappearance on the scene had to do with more than filial devotion. They both had been competitive in high school, each believing that the other still was. Neither, however, felt it proper to probe further, so early in the day, so early in their renewed friendship. Besides, they heard the click of the wheels on Mrs. Durrell's walker.

Within half a minute the older woman appeared, her hair bobby-pinned in place and her expression more alert than the night before.

Deirdre was ecstatic, and relieved.

The three women made a meal of it, Deirdre carving the ham and setting out the potato salad and slices of tomato, Mrs. Durrell pouring tea from her pewter pitcher without making a mess of it, and Rose rattling on about Jason's transformation into a computer whiz, thanks largely to her brother's ongoing oversight.

"Can you imagine, putting him through junior college and then getting him into a summer course at MIT. Connor—that's Rowan and Sophie's daughter—had just graduated from there. God only knows how much had been lavished on *her* education," the young man's proud mother went on, as she doctored each of the ham sandwiches with slices of pepper jack and dill pickles.

"Rose tells me Jason has turned the store into a success across the country. People order right on their computers, Mother, and the store does the shipping," Deirdre further explained.

"It's all about algorithms, and Google rankings, my son keeps telling me. And having the right merchandise. Real antiques and curios of quality. Things that speak to customers, as my father used to say," Rose added, as she refilled her glass with sweet tea.

Mrs. Durrell nodded politely, not catching the technical jargon Rose threw out but content to be sitting with the two younger women and talking about something other than her ailments. "So, Rose, do you think Jason can be persuaded to settle down here?"

"Hard to say, Clarissa," Rose replied, "but it won't do to push him. Never does with a man…," she wound up, her expression suddenly more solemn.

Deirdre wondered if she were thinking of Dennis, of all the years she had carried a torch for him, and he not yet seeing the light, or whether she was referring to Rowan, which was unnecessary since she had no intention of pushing him in any direction. Or even thinking about him.

"And how is Rowan?" Mrs. Durrell then asked, munching one of the oatmeal cookies Deirdre had picked up at the Piggly Wiggly. "I can't remember the last time we saw him. Would have been that Christmas, when the kids were here, right, DeeDee?" she continued, looking across the table at her daughter. "Or, more recently…?"

"That's right," Rose replied. "When Jason graduated, a year or so ago. The four of us came over—Dennis and Rowan, too. My son wanted to thank you for the gift, Clarissa. That lovely briefcase that had been your husband's."

Deirdre looked flabbergasted but quickly stood to retrieve the ice cream. A blast of cold air from the freezer made her skin tinkle. She lowered the power from five to four and set the half-gallon on the sunlit counter to thaw. That leather briefcase had been Stephen Durrell's pride and joy, what with its burnished gold latch and its secret pockets inside. Ashton too had admired the workmanship, aloud to his father-in-law and profusely, before the two of them got into that awful argument on the porch. Rightfully, it should have been bequeathed to him, she thought, staring into the kitchen sink, astonished at how indignant on her ex-husband's behalf she felt. Still, she hadn't remained in Riverton for the reading of the will, given that her father had died in the middle of the term at Klimpton, and everything would have passed to his widow. There must not have been a codicil indicating specific gifts to particular persons, like to herself or her husband. She had never thought to ask her mother about it.

"Are you looking for something, dear? Things have been rearranged to make things easier for me," Mrs. Durrell said to her daughter's back.

"Just something for the ice cream," Deirdre replied distractedly, rummaging in a drawer for the scoop she had washed and put away the night before. "And I'm making coffee, if that's what you two would like."

"Excellent," Rose said. "And then I shall be on my way."

Late in the afternoon as a breeze took the edge off the heat, Deirdre attached Topsy's leash and took her for an introductory walk through downtown. She had decided not to take stock of her mother's medicines until she had a better idea of her overall condition and her level of pain, but she did want to tend to immediate needs. Few locals were about at that hour, a wizened old man with a cane doffed his hat as he passed her on the sidewalk but did not speak; several others darted in and out of the Rite Aid and ducked back into their cars without so much as a how-de-do.

Deirdre tied the dog to the lamp post outside the drugstore and went inside. It was icy cold and the muzak loud, something with lots of strings, a movie theme she couldn't identify. Hurriedly, she bought pressed powder and pink lipstick, several night lights, and a bag of Purina dog chow.

The sole clerk on duty ambled over to ring up the bill. She eyed her customer suspiciously. "Don't I know you?" she managed to ask while smacking her gum.

"I dare say you don't," Deirdre replied flatly.

Quickly then and while an orchestral version of "People" blared from the amplifiers, she handed over a twenty and a ten and stood glaring at the clerk until she came up with $2.25 in change.

Outside, Topsy had gotten her leash tangled up around the post and was frantically trying to get free. "We've got to get used to things here, Topsy, though not too used to them. OK? However, I won't leave you like this again. Promise," she said, reaching down to unfasten the leash.

They crossed the street to complete Deirdre's other errands. She had wanted to browse the windows of the Fashion Plate, the only decent dress shop, hoping to spot a suitable lightweight outfit to wear to orientation at the college but it too had been transmogrified into a thrift shop. However, several buildings further down was Grace Notes, which had been there since after the war, and was owned then by the only other Jewish family in the area besides the Kleinfelds. She went in, Topsy in tow.

A young woman behind the counter smiled in her direction. "Let me know if I can help you," she said.

"Could you point me to the sheet music? Things have changed so much since, well, years ago," Deirdre replied, while eyeing the cases of guitars—many, many guitars—and left out in the open, drum sets, cymbals and a xylophone, which looked to be gathering dust.

"If you mean music for piano, we've stopped carrying anything other than holiday stuff. Not so many players anymore, and those that do come in, copy what they need and bring the books back for a refund. It hasn't been worth it to stock much. For a while now," the young woman explained, shrugging apologetically.

"I see," Deirdre said, flipping through the few items that remained in the bins—basic finger exercises for piano, an album of Christmas carols, and a few graded pieces for guitar or ukulele. "Such a shame," she murmured, more to herself than to the clerk.

"We could order something, if you'd like...if you're from around here, staying around here," the young woman persisted, albeit without much conviction.

Deirdre turned and smiled, remarking for the first time the clerk's silky-slinky black hair and her almond-shaped eyes. A pretty girl, perhaps home from college, stuck catering to pimply-faced boys wanting to start a band. Like Lou, or Ray, or who knows who among her daughter's friends. (Still, sad about the former young man, dying from an overdose, Caitlin flying in to Oakville to console Claudia, Stella reportedly beside herself but never able to talk about her nephew thereafter.) She fished in her mind for the name of the family that founded the music store but couldn't come up with it. She would have inquired of the girl, but Topsy started to tug at the leash.

"No bother, really, but thanks for letting me browse—my dog too, for that matter."

"*Nada problema*. Enjoy your evening here. And, by the way, there *are* concerts around here, mostly country-style music. You can check online."

"Appreciate it. And you too, enjoy your evening."

Outside again, the wind had strengthened, and a few clouds scudded across the sky. The traffic, such as it was, had died down, the only sound a calliope on the ice cream truck turning down the near side street. It was the corner where the Park Hotel stood. Seeing it, looking more imposing than anything else on the block, made her heart skip a beat.

"Come on, Topsy. We're going to move past everything, as it were, and then turn around and go home."

And they did, scurrying past the façade of the hotel, not turning to look through the French windows nor glance at the upper floors, and on past the bingo hall, the shoe repair shop, Kleinfelds, Scully's Sporting Goods, the Merchants Bank, another thrift shop, and a new liquor store called Last Serve. Past this last, they took a left and headed home.

Chapter Twenty-Eight

O rientation at the college was nothing if not disorienting. So Dennis had intimated when he came over the prior weekend, with Rose on his arm, and a basket of fresh peaches for Mrs. Durrell.

"I remember what great ice cream you used to make, Clarissa, you and your husband with that machine out on the back porch—Louisiana strawberries in May, Georgia peaches in late summer—so I'm hoping you'll teach Deirdre how to do it," he said, placing the basket on the kitchen table.

"We'll have to check the attic, DeeDee, but I do believe I never got rid of the maker. It would be a good thing to get back to, though Stephen did most of the churning," Mrs. Durrell replied, clearly pleased that Dr. Tremayne had remembered her culinary gifts.

After Mrs. Durrell had gone to bed, Dennis suggested the three go out for drinks, ending up at the Park Hotel. To Deirdre's dismay, the same bartender as years before brought them a bottle of wine and a platter of nuts and olives. Allen, if she recalled correctly, hesitated, eyeing her curiously, but she did not acknowledge him. As soon as her glass was filled, she took a sip, wishing they had gone elsewhere.

Within a few minutes, several other customers ambled in, arranged themselves at the counter and proceeded to command the bartender's attention.

"Funny we never think to come here," Rose ventured, smiling over at Dennis, "but Rowan almost always stays here when he comes to town. Says it relaxes him, or holds fond memories, something like that," she chattered on, as though she couldn't recall what specifically her brother had said of the place. She, with such a prodigious memory, and having always hung on every word of her sibling.

Deirdre bit her lip.

Glancing from one to the other of the two women, Dennis raised his glass and cleared his throat. "I'd say this calls for a toast, to Deirdre, for accepting our offer at Henson."

The two women raised their glasses in response.

"Thanks, Dennis. I just hope I can be of service. I do have a lot of questions but many can wait, or will get answered soon enough."

"Feel free to fire away," Dennis said, putting down his glass.

"OK, preliminarily. Is there anything I should know about the school, or the student body, before things kick off?"

"Well, you're not in Kansas anymore, Deirdre," Rose said drily.

"Or Ohio," Dennis chuckled, before assuming his more professorial posture. "First and foremost, do not fret. We need you more than you need us, but yes, there'll be adjustments from what you're accustomed to."

"Do go on," Deirdre encouraged him.

"The good news: Enrollment is up. We've been able to upgrade the science lab, hire a head of the computer programming department, and acquire dulcimers for the music dept. The bad news is that many kids haven't gotten the education they deserve, or their family life is crap. Basic skills often have to be honed."

Deirdre nodded, not in theory unhappy with the idea that she'd be helping worthy students who simply needed consistent guidance to get ahead in life rather than trying to inspire bored

Midwesterners who were at Klimpton only because their parents insisted they go through the motions. Only a few, like that lovely young man—what was his name?—really ever sparked to the pleasures of medieval literature. Most were more like Jennifer, if not as pretty or privileged. How could Ashton have been so predictable, so priapic...?

Her mind beginning to meander, she reached for her water glass.

"What Dennis is trying to say, Deirdre, is that things have deteriorated since we were in high school. These kids have less preparation than we did. Which means—wouldn't you agree, Dennis?—that teachers have to have lower expectations and greater resolve than ours did."

In his diplomatic way, Dennis demurred. "The idea is not to demand less from students. If you insist, firmly but fairly, that students rise to the occasion, then often they surprise us."

The three munched a while longer on nuts and finished off the wine, chatting about this and that. Once Dennis had paid the tab, they stood to leave.

"Anything else you need to know before the gathering? I don't want you to lose sleep."

Deirdre paused to adjust her shoulder bag. "I was wondering: dulcimers?"

He laughed. "Oh, you'll see. In due course."

Some things Deirdre wouldn't have guessed.

For one, the first faculty meeting that late August morning started with a prayer and ended with buckets of fried chicken, mashed potatoes and buttermilk biscuits from a nearby KFC franchise, even though the college had no religious affiliation, and no one of her past academic circle ate anything fried, certainly not at 11:15 in the morning! Deirdre said nothing, and was partially reassured that not everyone bowed their head during the benediction nor partook of the greasy drumsticks.

Not to appear aloof, she nibbled at a biscuit and mingled, trying to be extra cordial to those who came up to introduce themselves. She was glad not to have gone overboard by buying a new outfit, having opted at the last minute to wear the beige linen skirt and jacket that had languished in the closet for the last five years. Looking around, she saw that most teachers, male and female, were wearing khakis or cotton slacks with shirts or blouses that didn't bother to match. Half of the two dozen instructors looked to be older, grayer and dustier than Dennis, life or teaching having presumably beaten them down.

If Deirdre did not want to stand out in this new arena, she also did not want to quite fit in.

"We were darn excited when we heard Dr. Tremayne had lured you here. Ph.D., published author and all. Most of our students could use a little literary polishing," a rough-hewn sort who described himself as an agronomist accosted her to say.

"That's true about students pretty much everywhere," Deirdre replied airily.

The agronomist remained planted in front of her, holding his paper plate of chicken bones and unabashedly raking her body head to toe. Especially the toes, whose nails she had painted a bright pink, and which were easily visible in her medium-heeled Italian sandals. She wished to be rescued from this man whose name she had already forgotten but didn't know where to turn. She gulped the rest of the iced tea and racked her brain for something neutral to say.

The agronomist rubbed his nose and snorted. "Might want to rethink the shoes," he said, before raising his eyes to her chest. "There's a lot of walking to do around campus, and you wouldn't want to wear out those pretty feet, or jostle yourself overmuch."

While Deirdre was considering whether to take his behavior as rude or simply clueless, a striking woman wearing a sarong and jade earrings sauntered over. Smiling at Deirdre and ignoring the other teacher, she held out a long slender hand.

"I'm Pippa Perlman, the head of the music department. Such as it is," she began. "We're glad to have you onboard, Dr. Durrell." There was confidence in her bearing, and in her voice. Deirdre instantly relaxed.

The agronomist, however, looked peeved, as though interrupted in whatever game he was working himself up for.

"So—Dwayne—" the woman in the sarong continued, pronouncing the instructor's name with bemused disdain, "someone made that lemon meringue pie you're always going on about. Better get some before it's gone."

Hers was not a suggestion, Deirdre thought, and, whatever it indicated about the relations between the two, she was grateful for the intrusion. Both women waited purposefully for the agronomist to react.

"Whatever floats your boat, Pippa," he replied. He eyed his colleague closely too, but she did not flinch. "So, again," he added briskly, turning back toward Deirdre, "welcome to our tight little circle. Trust you'll find your footing."

"That will be my goal," Deirdre replied.

Once he had shuffled off, Pippa rolled her eyes conspiratorially. "Don't worry about Dr. Sutter. He tries it on with every woman. Essentially, he's harmless, however much a bore."

"So I figured. And nice to meet you. I had heard the college had a music department. The more arts, the better."

"Since you grew up down this way, you'll know there's musical talent all around, much of it untapped or underdeveloped."

Deirdre nodded, enjoying the other woman's easy aplomb and the deft way she sidled up to people. "And you, are you originally from here?"

"Memphis, but I did my degrees at Indiana. Been here for a decade. Family still in the area, including, for the moment, my daughter."

"Oh, is she a student here?"

Pippa laughed, and pushed her coal-black hair off her forehead. There was a kind of knowingness in her expression. "Myra's already graduated, Bryn Mawr. Identity issues, though."

"That's what she studied?"

"No, no. It's what she's going through! Her generation, I guess."

Deirdre nodded in tacit agreement, though she wasn't sure about what.

"Anyway, Dr. Durrell, I understand you have grown children yourself—one at Princeton, the other, I can't recall. Dennis did put all of this in a memo, but it was a while back."

At that point, having heard his name, Dr. Tremayne weaved his way over. "I see you two have met," he said. "You'll find you have much in common, including a few students. Plus, Deirdre, you'll be bowled over by Pippa's place. Counts as an oasis around here."

"He exaggerates. But indeed, I'd love to have you over as soon as you settle in." Turning back to the dean, Pippa added, "And, Dennis, the workshop. You wouldn't believe what Lance has done with it."

Not until her drive home did it dawn on Deirdre. Pippa Perlman must have married into the Jewish clan that owned the music store—and the young woman who was currently running it looked too much like her not to be the daughter. Of all the people she had met that day—leaving aside Dr. Sutter and one snotty woman who explained that she was the head administrator, and still awaited unsigned forms from Deirdre—none appeared as intriguing as the head of the music department.

Chapter Twenty-Nine

T he next few weeks were rocky. Although Dennis had warned her of the challenges, Deirdre had relegated them to the back of her mind, thinking he had overstated the lack of preparedness she would find. It wasn't just *what* students hadn't learned in high school—no Chaucer, little Shakespeare and only a smattering of novelists or poets that they could even name; in numerous cases, they didn't know *how* to learn. Either their family life was too fraught, their jobs too time-consuming, or drugs and gangs hampered their efforts.

On the first day of class, described as devoted to Modern Literary Classics, Deirdre began by asking students to name their favorite book, one that had moved them, not one that prior teachers had thrust upon them. She was met with blank or bored stares.

Finally, from the back of the room a young man piped up, "Stephen King, anything by him." Several of his friends tittered, one of them snickering, "You can't even read, dude, so who you trying to impress?" loud enough for her to hear.

She ignored the joshing. Searching faces closer to the front, she settled on a young woman with neat bangs and wide-framed glasses.

"What about you, Miss...?"

"The name's Jenkins and I don't much cotton to books. But my sister left one behind last year when she ran off with her boyfriend, '*Fifty Shades of Gray*.' They made a movie of it, with lots of sex." A couple of the boys in the back row guffawed.

Deirdre decided not to ask Miss Jenkins to elaborate on what she liked about the book, or the movie. Rather, she spoke briefly about the pleasures of reading, what can be learned about character, about time periods not lived in and places never visited, and about the many versions and purposes of life explored in fiction. As she warmed to her subject—and the students remained docile, if not rapt—she extolled the virtues of language itself, and how the ability to wield it well, speaking and writing, became one of the great tools in making us *homo sapiens* more, well, *sapiens*. (The word *sapiens* seemed to go over their heads, but she decided it was wiser not to enlighten them on that score. As yet.)

With forty-five minutes still to go, and no hands raised, she reached into her briefcase and pulled out a copy of *The Gathering Storm*. "This is one of the many books that Winston Churchill—you will have heard that name: prime minister of England during World War II." A few heads nodded tentatively. "In any case," she went on, "many people believe that it was Churchill's speeches that got his country through the war against the Nazis. To give you an idea of the power of the pen as opposed to the sword, I'll read you a brief passage from one of his speeches to the British Parliament."

A few eyes rolled and a couple of students checked their cell phones (something she would interdict going forward), but, clearing her throat, she plowed ahead in her clearest diction with an excerpt steeling his countrymen for the sacrifices ahead.

Another young man, sitting off to the side and chewing gum (another thing she would ban from her classroom), finally raised, or rather, waved, his hand.

"Yes, Mr....?"

"Randy, Randy Thomas," he called back. "How many books are we going to be tested on, and is this Churchill going to be one of them?"

"Actually, ilt's good you asked, as I was going to get around to that," Deirdre said self-mockingly, though it was likely not a tone her students were good at recognizing. "As the course description indicated, we'll be focussing on ten works, none of them as long and dense as Churchill's, mind you, but all with something to commend them. I'm going to read out today a list of nine novels, which you should write down. Following which," she added, more dramatically, "for the next thirty minutes, you will need to rack your brains for a tenth book that you think we should also tackle together. Of your choices, we'll vote to add one of them to our assignments."

Again, blank stares or vague befuddlement.

"And, yes, you can use your cell phones to google 'great American novels,' if you must. After today, phones will need to be turned off in my class."

Grumbling aside, the students took out pen and paper and copied down the following: *Ulysses, The Great Gatsby, The Sun Also Rises, Light in August, To the Lighthouse, 1984, The Age of Innocence, The Catcher in the Rye* and *Catch 22*.

During the next twenty minutes, some students conferred with one another, laughing, disagreeing, or shrugging off the request; others scrolled through their mobiles or stared off into space. Deirdre busied herself pencilling through her course outline, scaling back certain requirements and underscoring others. (Already, she reckoned James Joyce would be a bridge too far; *Ulysses* would be scrapped.)

When the students began to pack up, she asked them to file past her desk and drop their selections in a bowl. Half obliged.

One young woman did linger to say, "I'm glad to be here, Dr. Durrell. I never get around to readin' much, in school, I mean, but, well, I know it's important."

That's quite alright, Miss...?"

"Sharon Simpson. And I didn't put down a title because I couldn't think of any, off-hand like that. Right now, I don't have a cell phone."

"Not to worry. That's why we're all here, so we can get back to, or get to reading," Deirdre replied, sensing her own eyes way too bright. "We'll see you next Tuesday, Miss Simpson. Perhaps by then, you will have thought of something you'd like us all to read."

Once all of the students had cleared out, Deirdre plopped down at her desk and pulled her water bottle from her satchel. She felt deflated, wishing there were someone around who could empathize. Not Ashton, she thought, who has his own academic headaches to deal with at Winslow; not Dennis, who probably has to buck up a discouraged teacher every week; not Rowan, nor Margery, nor Stella, whose lives were unfolding elsewhere, and no longer included her. And not her mother, upon whom she would never permit herself to heap another burden. She took a few swallows of the lukewarm water, and then closed her eyes. One of Ashton's early dicta popped into her head: *Feel for your students but always keep your distance*, he had cautioned her when they first started teaching at Klimpton. Funny how she had followed the advice, while he...*Oh, forget it*, she scolded herself half-aloud, rapping the desk in disgust.

Walking across campus a few minutes later, Deirdre breathed in the fall air to clear her mind and lighten her mood. It worked. She would take the initiative and invite Pippa Perlman to meet up.

An oasis sounded enticing.

By the middle of October, Deirdre and Pippa were getting together regularly at the campus coffeehouse as, however coincidentally, they had classes on the same two days. These were the encounters she most looked forward to, a chance to talk to someone who not only took the arts seriously (and believed they could enhance life more than money, power, and iPhones), but whose life experiences had seemingly left her serene rather than embittered, and blessed with a delightfully bemused sense of humor.

On a rainy afternoon after they had ordered, Deirdre confided that she might have overloaded her students: some of them were balking, a few of them no longer showing up or refusing to do the homework.

Pippa listened attentively, sipped her herbal tea (she brought her own leaves along in her handbag), and then brushed a lock of hair off her forehead.

"It's not too late. You can rethink this, and likely get them back on board. As you've discovered, some are overburdened outside of class and some have never acquired basic skills. Proceeding slowly is sometimes the best way to get to a place."

Deirdre nodded for her to go on.

Among other things, Pippa advised her to divide the assignments among her students—letting each read two or three, say, of the books on the syllabus rather than force-feeding them all ten. (*To Kill a Mockingbird,* which the shy Miss Simpson had come up with, had been chosen from among the students' entries.)

"That way, they can report back to the class and help each other, reviewing what they've read aloud. What you're hoping, and what we're striving for here, is for them to want to read more, or to play more music, or to grow better crops after they've left here—you, me, Dwayne, all of us."

"The thing is, I don't want to be branded as a push-over," Deirdre countered.

"If I had to guess, I'd say you're a harsh critic—of yourself. Give yourself the benefit of the doubt and don't demand too hard. That way, they're more likely to step up rather than push back," Pippa suggested in her relaxed but persuasive way.

Deirdre managed a smile and nodded in acceptance of the criticism.

"No one's ever told me that, but it may be true. I was always trying to compete with, or compare myself to, my ex-husband," Deirdre confided, not knowing if Pippa had any inkling of her past. "Academically anyway. In other ways too, I may have vied, pointlessly, with my husband: for the kids' attention or affection, or whatever." She took another swallow of the coffee and bit into one of the lemon cookies Pippa had brought along from home.

"We've all compared ourselves to men, unfavorably," Pippa replied. "The trick is to break the habit and learn to compete only with ourselves. Collaborate with others, like musicians are taught to do."

"You are right. But there's more to my failings than meets the eye," Deirdre said, her expression newly pained. "But that'll be for another time."

"Go on. It's raining cats and dogs out there. Let's take advantage of the quiet."

"Well, for one thing, I have been too easily blind-sided." Pippa gave her a disbelieving look. "As a cultural historian, I'm supposed to be attuned to subtle shifts in human behavior, but for years I was oblivious to the fact that my daughter was hooked on drugs or that my son was inveigled—I'm using a euphemism here—by an older woman, who happened to be one of my close friends."

Pippa's eyebrows went up briefly at this last admission, but she downed the remainder of her tea before looking up to speak.

"Surely, you know it is with children, particularly our own, that we make the most mistakes," Pippa responded, "though not beating oneself up over them is easier said than done." She munched one of the cookies, looking out over the room in an effort to let her viewpoint sink in. "Hard to change ourselves; even harder to change others. I, for example, tried to mold Daniel, Myra's father, but people will do what they yearn to do. In his case, it was *wanderlust*."

"Did he fall for someone else?"

"Not that kind of *wanderlust*! He wanted to see the world: an *artiste*, he fancied himself, though he practiced no particular art. So after college—we married way too young—he set off for India, the Far East, South America. Still lives a peripatetic existence, as far as anyone can determine."

"I didn't realize you had brought a child up on your own."

"There were men in my life, now and again—I do enjoy them in small doses—and now that my daughter is older, I can experiment with other things I'd like to do, people I'd like to spend time with, and so forth," Pippa wound up, smiling enigmatically.

Unsure what precisely her friend was signaling, Deirdre scanned the coffeehouse to gather her next thought.

"Whatever you want to do, you should go for it. As for me, I find it hard to envision another romantic relationship, for myself, that is."

"And why is that?"

"I'll soon be fifty. After my husband and I divorced, I had two subsequent relationships, fulfilling in their own way, but well, without boring you, they each ended. Abruptly. And now, the field of available men is slimmer. I suspect there are a lot of Dwaynes around, boorish if harmless, but who wants them, right?"

"Indeed. The idea is not to search, at least not openly—that's what young people do, with few parameters, even online. For us, the idea should be not to rule out anything, however unconventional. Be open, discreet but flexible."

Deirdre couldn't stifle a giggle. "I'm sorry. I don't believe I'm as fearless, or spontaneous, as you, Pippa. And anyhow, I'm focused on other things: these classes, my mother, the kids (to the extent they need me), and a play I'm writing."

"All worthwhile. You'll have to tell me more, another time." Pippa looked at her watch and motioned for the check. "However, regarding what we've been dancing around, don't closet yourself. You're a beautiful woman, with brains. You have much to give, and no doubt much that would be fun to receive," she concluded, then cocked her head as though making a quick calculation. "In fact, why don't you come out to the house next weekend? You can try out my piano—and I can show you the dulcimers."

Pippa was, Deirdre decided, a person *bien dans sa peau*. Simply being with her had soothed her spirits.

Chapter Thirty

Pippa's place did not disappoint in its quirkiness. The front door gave right onto the kitchen, where copper pots dangled over a sturdy oak island and a wood furnace squatted in the corner. Tomatoes overflowed a bowl on the counter; bananas, red apples, and apricots hung in a wire contraption near a window. A handgun lay on top of the microwave.

"Oh, that's Myra's. Never know where she'll leave it. Thinks women on their own should have one. Says it's about 'empowerment.' "

Pippa rolled her eyes. Deirdre, who had never in her life touched a weapon, declined to comment. Her friend proceeded to fill two glasses with ice-cold *sauvignon blanc* and handed one to her guest. "We'll eat later but before dark, I thought you'd like to take the tour." A cuckoo clock on the wall chirped the half-hour. "See, it's already 6:30. We've got an hour at best."

The rest of the house was similarly *sui generis*, its warped floors creaky, its layout haphazard. At the end of the house was a huge library lined with overstuffed bookcases. A baby grand held court in the corner.

"Such a lovely room, so lived-in," Deirdre said evenly, not wanting to appear overly complimentary. She wanted very much for Pippa to like her, but she had come to believe her friend did not need, or care for, flattery.

"It's in here we occasionally have a pickin," Pippa threw out, gesturing toward a table in the corner with a couple of banjos and what looked from a distance to be a zither.

"And what exactly is that—some kind of picnic?"

Her friend laughed heartily. "OK, you're not the first person not to know the expression, but you'll find out soon enough. There'll be one in a few weeks. There always is."

Deirdre paused to touch the piano keyboard, noting that it was a Steinway, likely from the 1920s, but, despite a couple of stained ivories, seemingly in excellent condition.

"You can play it later, but I want you to see the grounds and the workshop before dark."

Pippa then led Deirdre through the other downstairs rooms of the house, pointing out this or that painting or sculpture. "Some of them are Daniel's. I did forget to say, once settled in Europe, he turned himself into a pretty good painter."

Moving down a long hallway, Deirdre noted a series of framed photographs, mostly southern scenes, which Pippa said her daughter had taken during her camera craze in college. "Myra inherited her visual instincts from the Perlman side."

A door at the end of the corridor opened into a cozy room dominated by a canopied bed—and a large cat of indeterminate breed curled atop a stack of pillows. The feline opened her emerald eyes but did not bother to move.

"I take it she reigns over the place," Deirdre said drily.

"Found her at the side of the road. We've slept together ever since," Pippa said. "I gather you like cats."

"Dogs too. Brought my retriever Topsy with me."

"This here is Grace, named after Daniel's mother, a lovely woman who played divinely. But, she responds best to Gracie, when she deigns to respond."

They lingered in the bedroom while Deirdre silently admired a large canvas on the wall opposite the bed. It was of a young woman plucking an old-time instrument. She walked up close.

"Oh, that's Grace Perlman, done by Daniel's father. He only dabbled, but in this one he really caught her luminosity. There's a sheen to it, don't you think?"

"Yes, it's quite accomplished. What is that she's playing?"

"It's a psalter, which went out of style centuries ago, but Grace did play the dulcimer, which is similar in some respects." Deirdre nodded, thinking how much more inviting to have such a portrait on the wall than those of Ashton's haughty ancestors. "The psalter reminds me. I want to show you the workshop. All these glorious instruments are being made there—some for the department, some for sale elsewhere, a few I give away."

"And who is making them?"

"We'll do a quick walkabout. He may still be there."

Once outside and her eyes having adjusted to the fading light, Deirdre took in an elliptical pond full of exotic fish. Water flowed briskly into it from a man-made waterfall. Around the area, Pippa had placed a number of metal chairs and gliders. A pair of wooden swings hug from the oaks that outlined the pond.

"It's enchanting," Deirdre said, taking in several stone sculptures scattered about and a totem pole of enameled cats, all with jeweled eyes, all staring down at the scene below. With feline insouciance.

"Everyone admires the totem," Pippa explained. "It was Daniel's gift to Myra when she graduated, but where else was it going to live if not out here? Anyway, they, the enamel cats I mean, seem happy enough," she went on, moving past the sculptures and down a gravel path lined with azaleas.

A couple of dogs of mixed breed joined the two women as they made their way toward a barn-like structure with huge windows. As they approached, a lanky man emerged, shut and locked the double doors, and then turned to toss something into the back of a truck. Deirdre could make out a chiseled profile as he opened the driver's seat door and started to climb in.

"Lucky you're still here, Lance," Pippa called out. The man hesitated, perhaps startled, and turned his head their way. "I've brought along my friend Deirdre. She doesn't know much about dulcimers, but she does, about a great many other things," Pippa said.

"You do have a way with introductions, Pippa," Lance responded, hopping off the runner and extending his bare arm toward Deirdre. Taking a deep breath, she held out hers.

"Pleased to meet you," she mumbled, feeling her throat tighten. She did not allow herself to meet his eyes, but she did register the firmness of his grip, the warmth of the fingers over hers. She decided the wine and the surroundings had gone to her head.

The dogs sniffed around Lance's trousers, enticing him to bend down and rough their fur. "Sorry fellas, no biscuits this time. Go catch a rabbit. Show us what you can do," he challenged them. Then, straightening up, he wiped his hand on his trousers and glanced from one to the other of the women.

"I'd show her around now, Pippa, but I've got things to do—Sue Ellen and all," he explained, twirling his hand as if to suggest something difficult, or boring, or obligatory, it not being clear to Deirdre which. And none of her business.

Nonetheless, she felt a thudding swipe across her breastplate.

"It'll be for another time. Deirdre grew up in Riverton, moved away but *voilà*—is now back. Sorta like you."

Lance did not pick up this thread. Instead: "I did want to tell you. The rosewood we ordered is superb. I'm using it for the soundboards as well. You're going to love the tone."

"Can't wait," Pippa said. "You're a genius."

At this remark, he let out an infectious chortle. "I wouldn't go that far, but I'm getting the hang of it." After a pause, he circled back to the guest: "And nice to meet you too, De-ir-dre," pronouncing her name in three syllables as though he hadn't gotten the hang of that name before.

She liked the thought of that.

The two friends watched in silence as Lance climbed into the pick-up—an older model Dodge Ram—deftly turned it around and headed up the incline toward Pippa's poplar-lined front driveway. Neither woman said more about him, Deirdre hurrying to ask about this or that corner of the garden, river rocks in one, herbs and spices in another, blueberry bushes along a fence in yet another, and trying all the while to slow her racing thoughts. She had felt her heart leap up, for no reason other than the sight of this Lance fellow, who struck her as a concentrated version of a man, whittled down, spare.

Driving home that Saturday evening she could barely remember what she and Pippa talked about over salad and fresh bream. What if she'd been sprinkled with fairy dust?

Any supposed enchantment would have dissipated except for a chance encounter.

Deirdre had been lunching with Rose at the local diner, the one that advertised fresh seafood, having insisted that would be more fun than drinks at the Park Hotel. Whether Rose picked up on the hint or simply wanted to be polite, she did acquiesce, digging into her shrimp étouffée with enthusiasm, while Deirdre enjoyed stuffed crabs, which she declared as tasty as any in New Orleans. Rose had prattled on about all the things she and Dennis did on weekends, and what trips they'd be taking together during the breaks from Henson. If she were somehow rubbing it in, as Deirdre first suspected, or trying to make clear that their mutual friend was off-limits (however closely they worked together at the college), it didn't bother her. She had always liked Dennis, but there was nothing more to it than that.

"It's splendid, Rose, that you two have rediscovered each other. And, you should know, he's a marvelous administrator. Henson is fortunate."

"I've heard good reports about you too, Deirdre. 'Demanding yet fair,' Dennis said, and that your students are starting to read and write way beyond their initial assessment."

"A work-in-progress," she replied diplomatically, not wanting to suggest that the students attending the college were woefully unprepared.

Over dessert, which Rose insisted they order despite her diabetic flare-ups, she switched topics. "By the way, I know it's none of my business as to what happened between you and my brother, but— (Deirdre kept her face focussed on her key lime pie.)—he and Sophie have split up." Deirdre bit her tongue to keep from betraying any emotion. "Some time ago, actually. I guess they waited until Connor got through MIT."

"Makes sense," she said, her tone flat.

"Well, that's out of the way," Rose declared, looking vaguely disappointed that she had solicited so little a reaction. She probed in another direction. "How are things with *your* ex, and your children? I did read about what happened with your son."

Of course, Deirdre sighed. In a small town, all it took was one person to spread the news or share an article online. "Things are good. Ashton is teaching in Pennsylvania and the kids are both working in New York—: Caitlin teaches music in a grammar school and sings with different bands; Dylan completed his doctorate and is working at a think tank."

"Like Connor, who is also in Manhattan, working at a similar firm. Though I have no idea what a think tank does."

"Likewise. But we can query Dylan. He and Caitlin will be here during the holidays. Mother and I will throw another party. You're our first *invitée*! Jason second."

"Sounds like fun. By the way, Connor should be here too round about New Year's, with her dad..."

"Ah," Deirdre responded, determined not to take the bait. "That will make it more fun for the kids, getting to know her."

On their way out, the two friends agreed to make their get-togethers a regular thing, though neither attempted to spell out what time frame that would mandate.

As Deirdre walked along Main Street, she took out the list she had scribbled for Rite-Aid—her mother's three prescriptions, a few cosmetics, and some melatonin. She had been tossing and turning more than usual, still struggling to engage all her students—and still unable to get that Lance fellow out of her thoughts.

Then, while passing Grace Notes chance intervened. She literally bumped into a man coming out the door, backing out rather, with two instruments in his arms. He turned about, and smiled, his laugh lines clearly visible and his eyes flashing with amusement.

"It's you, isn't it? De-ir-dre?"

"It's really only two syllables but you can pronounce it however you like. Lance, right? Pippa's friend."

"You remembered." Lance paused long enough to make sure the door had shut behind him and then eyed her anew. "I can't exactly shake hands as I've got these instruments to repair, but hope I didn't step on your foot."

Deirdre shook her head in the negative but found she couldn't move on. Standing there in front of her he appeared even more concentrated, his virility undeniable even though his features were oddly feline. His long fingers were wrapped around the neck of a guitar, and another instrument was secured by his muscular arm. She could detect tiny blue veins in his wrists.

"Looks like you have your work cut out for you," she said lamely.

He rubbed his lips together in concentration. She glanced up and down the street. Rose was no longer to be seen.

"How about tomorrow afternoon, Deirdre, if you'd still like to see the dulcimer shop? I should be working away on these until 6:00 or so. Myra needs them back asap for her customers."

"Of course, yes, but I'll need to check, with my mother. Also with Pippa," she stammered, her cheeks flushed.

He cracked a wry smile. "You still clear these things with your mother?" For an instant, his hooded eyes seemed to bore into her.

"I take care of her. It's what I came back here for, more or less. Anyway, it should be fine. She's doing better."

"Excellent. You needn't worry about Pippa. She does her own thing. We may see her, or we may not," he teased, something mischievous in his voice. "Anyway, if you're still in the mood tomorrow, come around 5:00."

Nodding noncommittally, Deirdre willed her body to move along the sidewalk toward the drugstore. Before long, she found herself at home, her mother napping in front of the TV. Some old movie with Robert Mitchum was playing. She tiptoed over and switched the set off, not before thinking that Lance, whatever his last name was, projected a similar, sleepy-eyed sexiness. She went upstairs, took a shower and worked on lesson plans for the coming week. After an evening with her mother, playing two-handed bridge and drinking Bloody Marys, she doused the light around 10 p.m., popping a pill in hopes of sleeping soundly. It did not help.

A light drizzle had begun to fall as Deirdre maneuvered the Volvo down the gravel incline. She edged the car next to the Dodge Ram and adjusted her hair in the rearview mirror. Having put on a blue silk skirt with a flared ruffle hem and a matching blouse—which to her mind fell short of calculated—she added a strand of pearls but no ear rings. Still, the ensemble was enough to cause her mother to use the word "fetching" to describe the effect. And to quip: "I'm guessing it's not church you're headed to."

"I'll only be a couple of hours. Going to see how dulcimers are made. At Pippa Perlman's place. There'll be other people there."

Her mother nodded and went back to reading yet another of the novels being studied in her daughter's course at Henson: Virginia Woolf's *To the Lighthouse*, which Deirdre had suggested, both because it was short and because it was focused on family dynamics. It's probably where her mother snagged on the word "fetching," something of a British-ism, and something Deirdre had not been called for some time.

Adjusting the clasp of her necklace to the side, she gathered up her purse from the passenger seat, got out and rapped on the double wooden doors to the workshop. From within, a machine quickly shut off.

Lance studied her closely as he ushered her in. "You look more like you're on your way to a concert than to a place where the instruments are put together," he said. Her face fell. "Hey, I meant that as a compliment. You look lovely."

"Thanks," she murmured matter-of-factly, as though his approbation was not necessary or sought after. To hide her embarrassment, she deposited her handbag on a nearby stool and moved toward a case of instruments of different sizes and shapes and in various stages of completion. After a couple of minutes, she said: "These must keep you busy. I hope this isn't too much of an intrusion."

Lance approached her from behind and pointed over her shoulder to a finished instrument to her right. "That's the latest one I've worked on, experimenting with the woods. It's all in the hardness or the softness—maple, cedar and now this latest batch of rosewood."

She nodded, feeling the warmth of his breath. Unwarranted thoughts beat wildly in her head. She moved sideways to scour other instruments on display. Lance remained in place.

"Pippa tells me you play, the piano, that is." Deirdre nodded and took a deep breath. "If you like, I'll take one of these out and show you how they're played, or rather plucked."

Without waiting for a reply, he moved around to the back of the case, unlocked it and retrieved a smallish instrument. "Let's sit over here, and I'll demonstrate the basics," he went on, motioning her to join him on a leather couch, with a coffee table in front and a small fridge next to it.

For the next half hour, Lance was all business, describing the woods that went into the sound box—mostly spruce or cedar—and the harder ones that went into the back, sides and neck. "I had been working with mahogany, but this latest shipment of rosewood has turned out to be excellent. Such a beautiful burnish, such a rich sound," he enthused.

Deirdre studied the holes in the sound box. "These are heart-shaped, but I think several others have—what is it called?—an *f* hole, like a violin," she ventured, hoping she didn't sound suggestive.

He looked impressed. "You *do* know music. The tone can vary depending on the shape of the hole and how many are carved. Sometimes the shapes are at the player's request. We make some on commission, and some we sell here and there."

For a few minutes they sat in silence, the rain having picked up, the room lighting up with flashes of lightning. Lance retrieved a bottle of mineral water from the fridge and poured them each a glass. Deirdre drank readily, hoping the cold liquid would clear her head.

"I find that water helps me concentrate when I'm doing delicate work," he offered. "Not like in Japan. You wouldn't believe how many craftsmen imbibe saké while they labor away," he added off-handedly.

"Whatever were you doing over there?" she asked, wondering if he knew that she didn't yet know his last name, let alone his life's story.

"Lived there after I left the Navy. A number of years..." he replied, his gaze lifting toward the rain-soaked windows, his expression not inviting further questions.

"I see," she said, not seeing anything but wanting him to know she understood all about privacy.

Minutes ticked by. Gusts of wind rattled the door of the workshop and the front windows were battered by sheets of water.

"I guess there are worse things to do in a storm than to stay inside and play the dulcimer," Deirdre remarked, eliciting a chuckle from Lance.

As if on cue, he straightened up, uncrossed his legs, and took the instrument back into his lap. Exaggerating his motions, he demonstrated a few folk tunes on the instrument, *Swanee River* and *She'll Be Comin' Round the Mountain*, among them, she watching his hands as he plucked the strings. "As you can hear, I'm not very good at this. I build them; others play them."

"Don't be modest."

"OK, your turn. I'll guide your hand. Keep it firm but relaxed," he said, starting to hum *Shenandoah*. Handing her the plectrum, he placed his hand over hers and got the tune started. With a few repetitions, she managed to reproduce the tune on her own, with only a couple of wrong notes.

"Well done," he said when she desisted and handed him back the plectrum. He placed it and the instrument on the coffee table.

"Like so many things in life, playing the thing is easy to do, just not easy to do well," she replied, her voice strangely low.

In the near darkness, he turned to hold her gaze. "Things take practice," and after a pause, he added, more quietly, "but you must begin somewhere."

A thousand objections flew through Deirdre's head, but she batted them all aside. She plucked at a line of poetry, *none do there embrace*, and let that be her justification.

For the next hour, until the rain ceased, they played each other, softly, as one would a dulcimer.

What Deirdre learned in the wake of making love to a man whose last name she did not know did nothing to make her regret that Sunday afternoon. She had not felt so in harmony with herself, as it were, since the times she had spent with Rowan all those years ago. It is true she had resigned herself to the notion that sex after a certain age would be inappropriate or ludicrous or too awkward to engage in, but Pippa's sense of things was more perceptive than she had realized.

Desire can overtake one in a heartbeat. And Lance had made getting naked with a virtual stranger seem the most natural thing in the world. Perhaps it was. Perhaps we all wait too long, require too much, reproach too easily, when all we should do is lie back and

298

enjoy what there is to enjoy. So what if she was fifty? Her body still responded to touch, and her mind was now freer to let things happen than it had been for—how long would she have said—: decades?

However rustic he was in appearance, there was also, as she had intuited at first sight, something exquisite about Lance's manners. He pleasured her as he might have played one of his instruments, treating her with carefulness, and timing his own excitement to crescendo along with hers. Neither said much during that hour of transport, but as it came to an end, they both gasped in ecstasy.

Lance eventually fumbled around on the coffee table for a pack of cigarettes and pulled two out. "I rarely smoke, but this has arguably taken us both by surprise. Would you like one?" She had nodded. He lit hers and handed the Winston over.

They lay in the darkness blowing smoke rings and collecting their thoughts. She spoke first.

"I needn't tell you how lovely that was, but I must be going."

He had slowly rubbed out his cigarette and turned toward her. "For me too. But I understand." Without further elaborating, he stood up and made his way toward an unobtrusive side door. A light from within went on. "This is the bathroom. I'll be out in a minute and you can dress in here, if that's more agreeable."

While gathering her clothes, she heard water running and the humming of a snatch of *Shenandoah*. What a strange amalgam of a man, she had thought.

As she got into the car fifteen minutes later, he planted a soft kiss on her forehead. "Be careful, Deirdre. Things are slippery."

The question she kept mulling in the car was whether she would want this thing, whatever it was, to continue, and whether she (or he?) would do anything to make it so.

Such a question naturally led to other quandaries: should she confide in Pippa as to what had happened or at least mention the visit to the shop? (She had seen lights on in the house when she passed by, which meant her friend may have seen her Volvo pass by.) And wouldn't it be prudent to know this man's last name, and who this Sue Ellen might be? She could only imagine what would pop up if she googled Lance.

The idea made her smile. She felt buoyant, like an overfilled party balloon.

The very next day she did google the name, and up came Lance Bass, the musician, also from Mississippi, as well as a number of football players named Lance, who might or might not have been from the state. A pointless search. For whatever reason, *her* Lance was more or less off the grid.

"How was the party last night? Did you have a good time?" her mother asked that Monday afternoon as they shelled peas at the kitchen table.

"I did. You wouldn't believe how beautiful those instruments are, mainly dulcimers, and how hard they are to play well."

"Hmm." Mrs. Durrell pulled off the strings of a large legume and, though her hands trembled, slowly dumped the peas into the bowl between them. As she had become accustomed to doing, (when she managed to be patient), Deirdre slowed her own shelling to remain in sync. Her mother picked up another legume and then asked, "Did you find out who makes these instruments?"

"Turns out, a local named Lance something-or-other," she replied, as though too disinterested to summons a surname. "He cuts the pieces and carves the neck and soundboard from scratch—with rosewood, maple, and so on. The strings too. He's very adept at it."

Mrs. Durrell held the legume aloft, looking as though she didn't know what to do with it. "This one's discolored," she said, tossing it into the small pile of rejects.

Deirdre slid another handful over in front of her mother, keeping the bulk for herself. "You'd be amazed at the rich tone of the thing. That song you like, *Shenandoah*, sounds lovely on that instrument," she said, to her own ear, a little too ardently.

Again, Mrs. Durrell plied open a casing and dumped the contents into the bowl, one little pea at a time. Deirdre sipped her tea, so as not to sit idle.

"You say this Lance is from around here? Got a family?"

"I don't rightly know, Mother. He's forty-five or so, but lived away for some time. So Pippa said." She started shelling the remainder of the pile.

"Might be a Tatum. Poor white trash that woman was, but her husband was quite a carpenter. Did all kinds of woodworking back in the day. Scrawny kids running around bare-foot, getting into trouble. The mother upped and ran off with someone. Stuck him with the raising of those kids."

Mrs. Durrell shook her head in remembered disapproval; Deirdre marveled at her mother's memory, intermittent but vivid, and like most Mississippians', pre-programmed to recall other families' roots, not to mention their various trials and tribulations.

"Could very well be, from what you recall, a Tatum. Lance Tatum," Deirdre said, liking the sound of the words as she spoke them.

They worked in silence for a few minutes. Mrs. Durrell finished up her pile and rested her hands on the table.

"I'll heat up your tea and then we'll watch the news. How's that?"

"Fine, dear." Mrs. Durrell massaged the joints of one hand with the other, tilting her head in thought. "Your father would have better recall. Seems they both got into regular trouble, all around the county...Some kids get raised, and some get jerked up. 'Twas ever thus."

"Who are you talking about, Mother?"

"Lance Tatum, the son. After some brawl or other, the judge gave him a choice: six months in the pen or the armed forces."

That did make sense to Deirdre, the stint in the Navy and the tiny scar. Only when Lance switched on that table lamp had she noticed the mark, pale against his jawline, him standing there at ease in his nakedness.

She put the bowl of peas in the fridge and heated the refilled teacups in the microwave. When she placed the cups back on the table and sat down, her mother took a couple of sips, the warm liquid stimulating her memory further: "But the girl, she was a handful. Been in and out of jail several times. Not having a mother and all."

301

Mrs. Durrell shook her head at the sorry lot of others.

"Do you remember her name?"

"Not rightly. Been in the papers though when she got sent up. Unlike her brother's, a common name: Ellen or something."

Chapter Thirty-One

B efore the dean caught up to her coming across campus on a bright November morning, Deirdre had decided it might be best to decline the invitation to the pickin that arrived at her mother's house.

The invite featured a hand-drawn sketch of folks strumming banjos with the particulars typed below. *An evening of music and mingling. Bring your instrument if you play or bring your best voice if you don't. It's potluck. You know what to do. Saturday, November 18 from 8:00 pm until...Pippa's Place. Regrets only*. On hers, Pippa had scrawled in blue ink: *Looking forward to having you there, Deirdre. We sometimes do a singalong to Irish folk tunes on the Steinway. No pressure! We're all in this together.*

Reading it made Deirdre realize she hadn't crossed paths with her friend for the last three weeks, not since her encounter with Lance in the workshop. Admittedly, classes had become more consuming as they moved toward quarterly exams, and students who were lagging behind or worried about their performance were lining up at office-hour to speak to their professors. She reckoned Pippa's were no different from hers.

Still, there was no denying something had cooled between them.

"Hello there," a voice called out, interrupting her reverie. "You will let me know if any of your students are at risk or need special counseling, right? We want to salvage any who are borderline before it's too late."

"Thanks, Dennis. I'm concerned about two or three, a Mr. Thomas and one other. I'll know more by the end of the week. Most, however, appear to be buckling down. I did as suggested—scaled back the workload as much as I could."

"Come by on Friday and we'll go over the problem cases," he said, accessing his cell phone calendar. "5:30 should work."

"Absolutely."

"Not to change the subject, but Rose and I will see you at Pippa's on Saturday night, right? Folks of all kinds pop out of the woodwork—or even out of the woods!" he added, chuckling at his own joke.

"It sounds amazing. I'm going to try," she replied, faltering. "I'll have to see with Mother."

"I trust she is OK?" Deirdre nodded. "Until Friday then."

When she pulled up around 8:30 that Saturday evening, two dozen cars or trucks had already parked haphazardly along Pippa's long driveway. Carrying a vegetable casserole she had tossed together that afternoon, Deirdre made her way toward the house, as she did so, passing a silver Dodge Ram, a bunch of tools in the back. *So be it,* she murmured. Since Lance had not bothered to make contact, she would act as though nothing had transpired between the two.

The first person she encountered as she took the tin foil off her dish and placed it on the table along with other platters was Dwayne, who, along with several other guests she dimly recognized, had already filled a plate.

"Haven't spotted you in a while, Deirdre. Looking good, though. Students haven't worn you down a bit."

"Pay no attention to his shenanigans," another teacher, who, if Deirdre recalled rightly, taught computer programming, interrupted. "But he is right. You look well. I think you'll find a few of your students here. A couple of them play or sing."

"I didn't know that."

"Randy Thomas and his father both showed up—with their guitars. Sharon Simpson, who's becoming a bang-up coder, has a beautiful voice. You'll hear it once things get underway." As if on cue, they could hear instruments being tuned in the library, several fiddles and banjos, even an accordion.

Another wave of guests, most of whom Deirdre did not know, soon crowded into the dining room and began to fill their plates and pour drinks. Deirdre did likewise and then wandered through the house, stopping to chat with whoever addressed her. At one point she caught a glimpse of Pippa, glass in hand and deep in conversation with her daughter, whose expression suggested she was being taken to task for something.

Not to interfere, Deirdre backtracked, following a few people to the patio in the back, where Japanese lanterns had been strung and the waterfall had been turned on. In the late November breeze, the smell of rosemary and mint rose to her nostrils.

"Ah, there you are," a voice reached her from across the lily pond. "Quite a place, don't you think?"

It was Rose, dressed in a Land's End-inspired sheath, her hair gathered with colored clips up on her head. To Deirdre, she looked country-chic, a style she had never associated with her friend. For his part, Dennis, who was positioned on a bench next to his lady-friend's chair, sported cowboy boots and a plaid shirt. She imagined they had thought long and hard about their outfits, and had been accustomed to doing so for some time. To be so in sync as to have coordinated attire was something she had never done with anyone, not even with Ashton.

"You were right. It *is* an oasis," Deirdre concurred, taking a seat on the wooden bench.

"And the music is a hoot. Sometimes they go on until 3:00 in the morning," Dennis chimed in.

"Not that we stay that late. However, if *you* play the piano—Pippa doesn't ask just anyone—we'll remain for the singing," Rose said.

While others wandered up to chat, Deirdre sipped her wine, wondering if she was supposed to have taken the idea of playing Irish tunes seriously. Or to have brought along her own music. Presumably, Pippa was merely being polite.

A few minutes later, the music started up in earnest with old-time folk tunes, some of which she had never heard. It was, Deirdre thought, the kind of music Zach would recognize, if he were still interested in such things. Were the twins still hanging out with him in New York? (She would make sure to inquire when she called to firm up the holiday plans.)

"Shall we go in?" Dennis asked. "If we don't, we'll never find a seat."

Once they maneuvered their way into the library, several of the younger people, likely students, got up to allow Dr. Tremayne and his two companions to take their places on an overstuffed couch.

By Deirdre's estimate, forty-odd people were crammed into the room, some sitting, some standing, some poised on arm rests or stools or table tops. Guests called out numbers now and again, which the musicians sometimes picked up on and sometimes ignored. Several different performers took turns singing, including Sharon Simpson, who belted out her rendition of *The Night They Drove Ole Dixie Down*, everyone in the room joining in the final chorus, and Randy Thomas, who, along with his father, performed *The City of New Orleans*, also to warm applause.

Another of the players, an older woman, who looked as though she could be part-Indian, sang a plaintive version of *Shenandoah*, during which Deirdre's eyes scanned the room. In the far corner, seated on the piano bench was Lance, together with a youngish woman, pasty-faced and pouting. At one point, he put his hand on her shoulder and whispered something. Deirdre darted her eyes away.

Around 10:30 the musicians took a break, helping themselves to food or walking about the back yard.

"So, what do you make of all this?" Pippa, who had meandered in from another room, asked of Deirdre.

"I hardly have words."

"Great. But don't forget, we're hoping you'll play a few pieces that we can join in on. We never break up until someone bangs out *Danny Boy*." Several nearby guests joined in the request. "And don't worry, the Folk Songbook is over there on the piano."

Reluctant but not wanting to appear precious, Deirdre rose to make her way across the room. Seeing what was going on, Lance and his companion also got up. He reached his hand for Deirdre's as she approached. His face had flushed.

"I had hoped you'd be here, Deirdre. By the way, this is my sister, Sue Ellen."

The younger woman held out a fidgety hand. Whether bored or disinterested, Deirdre couldn't tell, but clearly, she had not been mentioned by Lance as someone his sister needed to know.

"Nice to meet you," Deirdre replied, as perfunctorily as she could. Her eyes then searched the top of the piano for the songbook.

"Thank you for doing this, Deirdre, " Pippa whispered to her, before calling for (relative) quiet and introducing her friend as "an accomplished pianist as well as an esteemed professor of English Literature and other things I don't pretend to know about." Turning back to Deirdre, she added, "Two or three pieces would be fine. Everyone loves to start with *Shule Aroon*."

Five or six songs later, Deirdre desisted though pleased enough that folks had sung along to three or four. Although she flubbed a few notes, no one paid any attention, the rich sound of the Steinway masking the missed notes. As she stood to take a modest bow, she noticed that Lance and his sister no longer appeared to be in the room.

The noise picked up and people re-arranged themselves as more musicians crammed into the room, including a couple of older men with scraggly beards and wizened faces. Too much sun or too much moonshine, or both, Deirdre thought.

"You play well. Even under duress," a young woman commented as she worked her way through the crowd. It was Pippa's daughter, who held out a glass of white wine to Deirdre. "Mom says this is what you like to drink at parties."

"Thank you. Myra, right?"

The young woman nodded her head, looking, as did many young people when having to interact with their elders, both deferential and dismissive. "Anyway, I think they're out in the back." Deirdre looked non-plussed. "Lance and his crazy sister."

Albeit dumbfounded by the remark, Deirdre tried not to betray any reaction. "A little fresh air sounds good. Nice to see you again, Myra."

Outside, other fragrances had come to the fore—lavender and thyme, she intuited, thinking she ought to replenish her mother's garden, another little thing she could so easily do to make her parent's life more pleasant. No reason to demur, she murmured, wandering over to the herb and spice plot to see which plants looked hardy and happy. She stooped to take in the odor of the thyme, and then broke off a twig from another plant, which was even more aromatic, but which she couldn't identify. Placing it in her jacket pocket, she felt footsteps behind her.

"You play better than you had let on," Lance said, automatically extending his arm to help her up from her crouch.

"Thank you. I was admiring Pippa's spices, thinking I might try to grow a few in my mother's garden," she replied, determined not to appear put out that he had not called in all these weeks.

"In case you doubt me, that really was my sister I brought along, but, true to form, she got antsy. She took off in the Dodge."

"I see," Deirdre said flatly, not seeing anything, and not letting on that she'd be interested in seeing.

"Look, I did want to explain a few things. It's just that—"

"You needn't trouble yourself. We'll agree nothing ever happened," she interjected, cutting him off in mid-sentence. "Next time I see a dulcimer it'll be as though for the very first time," she added, unable to keep a note of bitterness out of her tone. She started to walk off but he grasped her wrist.

"Please don't," he said, looking perturbed. "Or rather," he continued, glancing this way and that, "walk with me a bit."

Not wanting to make a scene, Deirdre accompanied Lance down the path that led past the cat totem and toward a grassy nook bordered by camellias in full November bloom. "Sit with me here," he indicated, taking a seat on a metal glider.

For the next half hour, Lance filled out the portrait that Deirdre's mother had sketched of the Tatum family, how their mother had abandoned them when Sue Ellen was only eleven, and how Lance, seven years her senior, had become her de facto protector and champion. Not, as he readily admitted, that he'd done a particularly good job of it, given that this last was her third stretch in the pen, this time for selling meth and possession of an illegal firearm.

"Right after I saw you that Sunday, I drove to the coast to pick her up and get her home in one piece. Not to mention set her on a better course: training for something, or getting a job, avoiding that no-good crowd she was running with. One day she promises to fly right and the next she cusses me out. It's been a roller-coaster..."

"What about your father? Can he do nothing?"

"While I was in the Navy, Dad managed to ride herd on her. She graduated high school and was planning to move to Jackson for cosmetology school. That's when he had his accident at the sawmill. Tore his left leg clean off. From then on, he mostly sat on the porch, playing the fiddle, drinking and, when he could summons the energy, yelling at her. From Japan, I sent home what I could spare but it got squandered, one way or another."

Lance took a swallow of his drink and shook his head in dismay of it all. "I don't mean to unload on you, but I did want you to know why I haven't been able to focus on much else."

Deirdre gave him a faint smile. "I do see. It's never easy when people are bent on self-destruction. My own daughter for a while..."

They rocked silently in the glider for a few minutes, sounds of strumming still coming from the house.

"Anyway, things got worse while I was abroad. Instead of going on to learn a trade, Sue Ellen got tangled up with the Wiggins—: if you don't know, they're low-lifes who've terrorized the county for years. Drugs, guns, prostitution—you name it, they've got their finger on it. In fact, if it hadn't been for them, she'd not have been nabbed. One of the sons of bitches ratted her out to save his own skin."

Inadvertently, Deirdre's left hand came to rest on Lance's arm, his evident devotion to his sister striking a chord within her. "Well, I'm glad she's out. Does she have a place to live and what-not?"

"Dad willed the house we grew up in to the two of us, and, as soon as I got back from Japan in '14, I began to make improvements on it. After he died, I bought acreage closer to the river and built my own log cabin. I've turned the house over to Sue Ellen, though I've kept my name on it in case she ever goes off the deep end again." He shook his head as though not convinced that she wouldn't.

"So, what's the next step? Any way to get her into a job that leads somewhere?"

"One reason I've wanted to stay connected to Henson, and to Pippa's workshop. Hoping maybe that Sue Ellen could be persuaded to take some courses. Born with a good ear, for one thing, like our parents."

"Like her brother too, from what I heard," Deirdre said more tenderly than she meant to, but this man had bared so much that her resentment melted away.

Lance laughed softly. "All four of us used to sit out on that rickety porch, playing and singing deep into the night. We had diddly-squat, but until my mother left us, I had never noticed."

Again, he shook his head and kicked the ground with his foot to swing the glider a little higher. ""And never was I so happy again until—oh, never mind. I've presumed way too much."

"No. Please. Do go on."

He eyed her sideways and brought her hand to his lips. "Here's the thing, Deirdre. You and I started off ass-backwards. I don't regret what happened, but the prior steps need to be filled in with more deliberation. If that is what we both want."

If there were a question in this last statement, Deirdre did not respond to it. Instead, she squeezed his arm and gently withdrew her hand from his. "You will let me know if I can do anything, like

310

speaking to Dr. Tremayne on your sister's behalf. And, by the way, where did she go off to?"

"So like Sue Ellen. Said she had people to see. She sometimes tends bar at that juke joint up on 61." He rolled his eyes, clearly exasperated. "Now that I think about it, if you came here in your car, I'd be obliged for a ride home. My log cabin isn't more than a few miles from town."

Back in the library, the pickin' had picked up steam, even though it was past midnight, with newly arrived players bringing out their instruments and an assortment of soloists taking turns. After a performance of *Folsom Prison Blues* by two of the old codgers in the room, Deirdre took her leave, telling Pippa this was the most-fun-ever event. Lance separately said his goodbyes, joining her in the Volvo a couple of minutes later.

They rode mostly in silence, except when a deer darted out in front and Deirdre had to swerve to avoid it, and again, when they had to take a minor detour because of a tree blocking the main road. Lance pulled out a pack of cigarettes, first offering one to Deirdre. When she declined, he asked if she minded. "It's something of a habit, ever since Japan, but only one or two a day."

"There are worse things," Deirdre said.

"Yes, there are."

Minutes went by as she wondered what else to Lance's story might account for the sadness in his voice. Perhaps it was life's ups and downs, which something in his face—not wrinkles, nor a scowl, more like a haunted look—suggested he had already experienced a number of. (He had to be younger than she, but how much so, she couldn't pinpoint. Nor did she care.)

Out of the blue, he blurted out: "I googled you after that night, which means a couple of the first steps I mentioned can be short ones. Still, there's a lot more I'd like to know."

She laughed. "OK, so you know, I wouldn't have been able successfully to google you, because I didn't know your last name."

He sat in silence for a moment, mulling her admission. "That's a brave thing to say, given what took place between us."

She blinked a few times, unprepared for the overt reference to their lovemaking. They had come up to the first stoplight on the eastern edge of town. Deirdre slowed to a crawl as several pickup trucks sped through the intersection, radios at full blast. "You're going to have to direct me as I have no idea where a log cabin might be found around here."

"It's not hard. Go the length of Main Street and take a left on Sassafras. A mile or so further, there's a gravel road, narrow but navigable, where we'll take a right."

It took only ten minutes to get to the gravel road, which, from what she could make out in the darkness, sliced through a cow pasture on one side and a fallow or abandoned cornfield on the other. As it curved its way down an incline, she spotted a light.

"That's my front porch up ahead. Slow down so my dog doesn't get spooked," Lance said, indicating a flat expanse where she could pull up and park.

With the high beams on, Deirdre could make out the entire structure, which included a wrap-around porch and a chimney jutting from the roof. Pots with what looked to be bonsai in them dotted the steps. Several dark-leaf but delicate trees, barely taller than crepe myrtle, stood at the corners of the house.

Before she turned off the ignition, a lab bounded out of nowhere, barking at the unfamiliar car. Lance opened the passenger-side door to calm the dog. "Steady Inu," he said, rubbing the animal's ears in welcome. "This is Deirdre. She might or might not come in to see the place."

"At this hour it's *might not*," Deirdre replied, "but it looks inviting. I'll take a raincheck."

"Good. It's supposed to pour tomorrow, so come in the late afternoon and I'll show you around. Built it myself. And, from the ridge in the back, you can see the river."

She started the engine but before she could put the car in gear, Lance leaned over and touched her cheek with his hand. "Thank you for hearing me out as well as for the lift."

"What will you do without the Dodge?"

"In a pinch, I can walk through the fields to the Tatum place. She'll have parked it there. But do come. Promise?"

Despite herself, Deirdre nodded.

Chapter Thirty-Two

For Clarissa Durrell some days were better than others, but ever since Deirdre's arrival, the good ones had begun to outweigh the bad. Not only did her hip ache less as she hobbled around, but she had become more energetic, thanks in part to having more interesting things to think about. Like her daughter's newfound friends and her more active social life. The name Lance Tatum popped up now and again in conversation, but Mrs. Durrell made it a point not to inquire too deeply into whether "the woodcutter," as she referred to him, had something to do with her daughter's nocturnal comings-and-goings.

For her part, Deirdre was not desperate to keep her relationship with Lance a secret—but she was uncertain as to how much such a revelation might upset her mother. Whenever she did bring up his name, her mother found a way to mention "that lovely man who used to be so taken with us," and then feigned forgetfulness before coming up with the name.

"I take it this Lance fellow, unlike Rowan Kleinfeld, is not married," she once mused aloud.

Deirdre ignored the invitation to elaborate, searching around for a wire brush to use on Topsy's unruly coat. "She prefers your gentle strokes, Mother. You do that while I water the garden."

On the days of classes at Henson, Deirdre went out of her way to make a healthy breakfast for them both, engaging her mother by reading from the Greenville newspaper or summoning what little town gossip she picked up when during errands or lunching with Rose. *Pattie Lee had taken the Greyhound to Wisconsin for one of Trump's rallies, and came back with all sorts of MAGA paraphernalia, which she proceeded to pass out in the Baptist Church parking lot. As though she herself were running for office, folks had snickered.* Things like that...

When weather permitted, Deirdre coaxed her mother into the wheelchair ostensibly to take Topsy for a walk up one side and down the other of Main Street. Occasionally, an old acquaintance would engage Mrs. Durrell in conversation, which did her more good than the pills she was still prescribed to take. The old woman would sit up straighter in her conveyance and suggest they indulge in ice cream cones sold at the stand at the end of the block. (By the beginning of December, Deirdre had poured all the salt out of the shaker and replaced it with a no-sodium substitute. Mrs. Durrell's blood pressure improved; from there, she began to cut her mother's pills literally in half with a kitchen knife, which brought her read-out down even more.)

Still, there were occasions when Mrs. Durrell appeared listless, which prompted Deirdre to hire a sitter for the afternoons: Elwood Harrison's granddaughter, Sandra. The job, as she described it to the youngster, would have little to do with sitting. Instead, she was instructed to read to her mother or to get the patient to read out loud herself. Several of the novels from Deirdre's class as well as collections of poetry were strategically arranged on the coffee table in the living room as was a stack of CDs for the stereo. Under no circumstances, she made clear to the girl, was the television to be turned on.

During those afternoon sessions, Deirdre sat at her desk upstairs with the door ajar, in case something downstairs was amiss, and worked on her play. The opus had begun to take shape, it being a three-hander in which the women protagonists meet by chance in the year 1412 and use the occasion to assess their lives, taking strength from the trials and the triumphs of the others. Her plan was to finish a draft by Christmas and rehearse it aloud to her mother and then to Pippa and Dennis for their feedback. Also, in her iPhone was a reminder to send a copy to Ashton, whose opinion she still valued, and to both Margery and Stella back at Klimpton.

Pushing back from her desk after one such stint, Deirdre rose to splash water on her face and join her mother for the evening. When she came downstairs, patient and caregiver were bent over a book. They appeared engrossed. "These are the last two pages," Sandra mouthed in a whisper.

Quietly, Deirdre took a seat across the room and listened. Her voice full-throated, Mrs. Durrell read the final passage: *"With a sudden intensity, as if she saw it clear for a second, she drew a line there, in the centre. It was done; it was finished. Yes, she thought, laying down her brush in extreme fatigue. I have had my vision."*

For an instant, all three women sat in silence, it finally hitting Deirdre that they had tackled *To the Lighthouse*, which—she now calculated—she had first read around the age of fourteen, with her mother seated at her side helping her through Wolff's denser passages.

And here they were now, their circumstances so altered. Her eyes became liquid.

"That was beautiful, Mrs. Durrell," Sandra said, clearly moved. "You read the ending like you could visualize what Lily's painting represented."

Mrs. Durrell hummed softly. "The fact is, my dear, I'm much older than you. I was acquainted with the book, years and years before."

Over dinner, Deirdre reminded her mother of the time they had read the novel together, but that memory had faded, or coalesced with another.

"I had the sensation I was familiar with the story, that my own mother, there in New Orleans, read it to me out on the veranda. All those ferns in their pots, and she was drinking a glass of sherry. Could it be so, DeeDee?"

"Absolutely. Mrs. Dupree, your mother, probably did read it to you, and later, you and I went through it together when I was old enough. For that reason, it has always been a favorite of mine—and you did read this evening so beautifully."

Picking at her pear salad, Mrs. Durrell surprised Deirdre further, mentioning a poem she and Sandra had apparently been reading in the last few days. "Sometimes, dear, I too have fears that I may cease to be. Do you know the lines I'm referring to?"

"Yes, Mother, I do," bracing for she knew not what.

"Well, I want to make sure loose ends are tied down. The house will be yours, but I have bequeathed the other assets—it's the term your father's firm uses instead of the word *money*—to Dylan and Caitlin. They're young, and it's harder to be a young person today. I realized that the years when I taught."

"They will be hugely appreciative. But regarding any other..." Deirdre returned, hoping to loosen whatever else was rattling around in her mother's mind. Especially if it were troubling her.

"Perhaps I never said, but your father left more assets than he ever let on to us."

"What do you mean?"

Mrs. Durrell took a sip of the one glass of white wine they allowed themselves when they had cooked something special.

"It's not so much the amount left in the bank, in his name only; it was all the years he had cried poverty as an excuse not to do much, with me, or go anywhere, or see much of anyone."

A cloud passed over Deirdre's face, but she refrained from jumping in to fill the void. Too often, she was finding, words fluttered sideways and struck their destination inches too low.

"In short, DeeDee, there came a time I took comfort elsewhere. With your father, I always moved in the background, which I had come to believe was the nature of things. But nothing is necessarily the nature of things. We have to shape our own lives and so, eventually, I did. As best I could, without—" (Here Mrs. Durrell appeared to search for the right expression)—"without upsetting the apple cart."

Although disconcerted by what her mother was circling around, or what behavior she was trying to confess to, Deirdre didn't disagree with the sentiment, nor did she want to stifle further revelations. As far as she could recall, this was the most sustained, and intimate, conversation that the two had fallen into since her return to Riverton. She hadn't felt so gobsmacked by anything regarding her mother since she happened upon that Viking travel brochure.

"I'm telling you all this, DeeDee, so that you won't be in the dark when the time comes."

"Oh, Mother, please. You're doing way too well to talk like that."

Mrs. Durrell smiled sweetly. "My will is in the top drawer of your father's desk. As I say, a million or so dollars to be divided between the kids; also my obituary, which you will see refers to 'a special friend' I leave behind. I wanted you to know, because wonderful things can happen to you too. Like me, you may find a soul mate, or someone with whom you play beautiful music, as it were. Or, maybe more than one such person."

Deirdre fixed her eyes on the table top, too flabbergasted to interject. Had she not just been told that her mother may have had a lover whom, for whatever reason, she believes it's important for me to be aware of? The world had tilted a little more on its axis.

"By the way, DeeDee, love expands. And it expands us, making us able to embrace more in life. Our job is to seize upon it. Isn't that what the great poets say?"

"Yes, it is what they say."

"Don't get me wrong. I loved your father as I'm sure you once loved Ashton. But I tend to think we had, and have, a lot more to give than they, or any one man, is able to receive."

At that point, Topsy came bounding into the room and nuzzled Mrs. Durrell's feet. The old woman reached her arm down to pet the dog's head. "She and I have become quite the pair—haven't we,

Topsy?—especially the nights you are out, DeeDee, and she curls up next to my bed."

Whether this comment was a subtle invitation to talk about her wild nights in the log cabin with Lance Tatum, Deirdre wasn't persuaded. She was, however, relieved that her mother appeared less critical of her behavior than she had feared. She regretted that she was not as clear about her feelings for this man, or how enriching the relationship with him could become, as her mother was about what had happened to her.

Until I am certain, better not to go there, she told herself.

That evening, Deirdre helped her mother prepare for bed, leaving the night-sitter downstairs to watch cable news. She marveled at her mother's still pellucid skin, which she washed with nothing more than Dove soap and warm water, but despaired at the shaky hands with which she did so. As she tenderly spread a throw that Sandra had knit across her feet, Mrs. Durrell suddenly mused, "I'm having trouble with names of late..."

"You're not alone. It's natural as we get older."

"That writer we were talking about earlier."

"Ah, you mean Keats, the Romantic poet."

"Perhaps so. You are the college professor."

Deirdre smiled and reached to switch off the lamp on the night table.

"I wanted to tell you another thing, DeeDee, before you shut off the light," Mrs. Durrell whispered in an altered voice, raising her head off the pillow. "There's a strange dog in the house," she mouthed under her breath.

Reminding herself not to contradict anything outright, Deirdre responded matter-of-factly: "Yes, that would be Topsy. I brought her with me from Ohio. She's very friendly."

Mrs. Durrell allowed her head to sink back down. "Ah, then I hope you both stay a long, long time."

"That's the plan, Mother," Deirdre whispered, placing a kiss on her smooth forehead. She turned out the light and tip-toed out, tears in her eyes.

The next day Deirdre texted both Dylan and Caitlin to make sure they were in the process of booking flights for the holidays. *I can pick you up, but don't wait too long. Your Grandmother and I will be thrilled, however long you can stay. Bring friends if you like.* She did not mention Zach or Nasreen by name, having sensed that things among the four had devolved, or dissolved.

Inviting Lance to come over was a stickier proposition. He had on several occasions—those being almost exclusively at his log cabin or in the workshop behind Pippa's place: they rarely were seen in public together—hinted that he was not in Deirdre's league, and though it didn't bother him, he didn't wish for it to complicate her life. For one thing, he had not, when younger, been encouraged to pursue any higher education or had any exposure to what was still called in rarefied circles *high culture*.

Such comments had embarrassed her, partially because there was truth to them. Lance had had his rough edges chiseled off, but that, she had concluded, had more to do with the discipline that the Navy had drilled into him, and the years he had spent in Japan.

When he went on like that, minimizing his worthiness, Deirdre would dismiss such contrasts between them as unimportant. But she didn't outright contradict them either. Rather, she would stress his skills as a craftsman, the gentleness of his soul, and the generosity of spirit he displayed to those in need. (First and foremost to his exasperating sister, whose crassness, she privately came to believe, Lance would have shared had he never had the gumption to get up and get out of town. She had little patience for Sue Ellen, who did at odd times show up at the cabin to ask for money, or borrow her brother's pick-up, or spend the night because she was spooked by this or that.) When Deirdre did go on in this way, praising him, however, Lance's face would constrict as though something was caught in his throat which he couldn't expel.

"What else did you want to tell me?" she once ventured, but he shook his head, and took her in his arms. The sex between them was so good, so unencumbered by the outside world, that neither pressed to let other things jeopardize it.

But with the holidays looming, it seemed to Deirdre only fair to indicate that various friends would be congregating at the Durrell home for New Year festivities. To get this off her mind, she drove out to the cabin late on a Thursday straight from Henson. A dusty Corolla was parked next to the pick-up. Before she got out of the Volvo, she could hear raised voices. The two siblings were arguing next to the bonsai in their assorted pots. She was gesticulating wildly; he was staring off into space.

"Don't think I don't have your number, or know what an imposter you are," she heard Sue Ellen menace.

With no way to backtrack gracefully, Deirdre got out of the car, approached the steps, and cleared her throat.

Looking irritated to be interrupted in the middle of her rant, Sue Ellen turned on the intruder. "It's really all your fault. Yours and Pippa's. Always going on about my gittin' some education. Hell, I got all the learnin' I need right there in that prison."

Deirdre looked up at Lance for a clue how to react. He shrugged, then said: "My sister was about to leave."

Sue Ellen spit into one of the bonsai pots.

"Nice," Lance said resignedly. "And, just to repeat, I'll send you what I can when I can but only if you promise."

"What is she supposed to promise, Lance?" Deirdre asked, trying to back him up.

"Just because you're fucking my brother doesn't mean you can butt in," Sue Ellen hissed, jerking her head in Deirdre's direction.

"My sister has promised to leave her job up at that place on 61 and move to Jackson. Take that cosmetology course," Lance said evenly. "Get away from—" he gestured with his arm as if to indicate, *all this*.

Sue Ellen mumbled something in response, but Deirdre couldn't make it out. She stepped aside as the other woman, still furious, stomped off the porch and sped off in her Corolla, the tires spitting up gravel in their wake.

Lance and Deirdre sat on the porch swing in silence, Inu coming out of hiding to join them. Off to the west the sun, huge and purple, was preparing to set.

"We could walk up to the ridge and watch it sink into the river, if that would make you feel better," Deirdre ventured.

Lance tapped her arm. "Wine might work as well," he replied, getting up and heading into the house. There was something despondent in his tone she had never picked up on before.

While he was inside uncorking a bottle, Deirdre noticed an opened letter on the table to her left, strange stamps on the envelope.

"I put a couple of ice cubes in yours, as I know you like it ice-cold," he said, handing her a glass of chardonnay and putting the bottle on the table next to the letter.

She smiled, and took a couple of sips. "Some might say you are as patient as Job. Your sister is a piece of work."

"I tried to tell her that working tips at that speakeasy is not, at age thirty-seven, a wise career move, but that made her blow her top. Sorry she went after you like that."

"As I've mentioned, my own daughter could be as vile when she was on something, or simply mad at me," Deirdre responded in commiseration.

"But your daughter was a teenager. I'm dealing with someone on the verge of middle-age who can't break away from her bad habits or the people who got her into them," Lance countered with more vehemence than usual.

As the strumming of insects picked up, Deirdre sat wondering if this was the right evening to talk about her plans for the holidays or to mention the lovely conversation that her mother had managed to conduct recently. She didn't want to rub her good fortune in.

Perhaps it wasn't even the right evening to make love, though up until now it had been the panacea for anything that ailed them. She reached down to rub Inu's ears, suddenly intuiting that the letter might be from someone in Japan. She eyed it as though for the first time and so that Lance would take note.

After a long drink of the wine, he seemingly took the hint. "I had been meaning to talk to you anyway, but today this letter came. Brought it all back—not that it had ever, or will ever, leave me."

"Whatever it is you want to talk about is fine with me. Whenever you like," she said, suddenly grasping that he did indeed have something bottled up inside. She leaned back in the swing and waited.

"I'm only telling you so that you'll know why I am such a hollowed-out person, with no core left, really, and so little to give. To anyone."

Deirdre could hear her heart pounding, but she sat stock-still. If she reached out to stroke her lover's arm, it wouldn't work because Lance put his glass down and rose from the swing, picking up the envelope and waving it. She thought his hand trembled in the act. Still, she remained silent, and increasingly alarmed.

"It's to tell me there will be a plaque to the victims. With all their names…They were inviting me to come back to Ishinomaki for the commemoration in March."

He telegraphed these facts without hesitation, but he looked blank, as though sleepwalking.

"What victims are we talking about?" she asked with deliberateness, wondering if this had anything to do with Hiroshima or Nagasaki. Seventy years ago: surely not.

"You will have heard about that tsunami nine years ago? The Fukushima nuclear reactor. All the devastation. I had taken the train to Tokyo for the day, to order some wood and to pick up a musical instrument they both wanted. I can't even remember what it's called now in Japanese. Like a zither, more or less…"

Here, the veins in his temples stood out against his skin as he tried to conjure the word. Deirdre made a movement with her head to indicate her bewilderment and that he should go on. He seemed to be in deep contemplation for a long, agonizing minute. And then: looking out over the yard past the dark-leafed Japanese maples, Lance blinked a few times and gathered himself.

"My wife, Michiko, and my eight-year-old daughter, Mia, both perished that day—swept away, along with many, many others in the village school."

Hearing this, almost parenthetically, the blood drained from Deirdre's face. How could such a thing be true? Hurriedly, she fished through her mind, dredging up a few images. A huge tidal wave had washed over a shoreline, sweeping boats, piers, cars, buildings all before it. The same pictures over and over had been shown on the TV news but, it had not occurred to her to think of it ever again. Another natural disaster far away: how could it have devastated someone so close to her?

"I wasn't at home, you see," he persevered, his voice ardent in its adamancy, "or I could have done something. Most of the kids in the school drowned, a few teachers too. Many of the bodies were never recovered. It was days before I could even travel from Tokyo to what was left of the village. Barely a trace of Okawa Elementary School..." he trailed off.

Lance had begun to pace the porch, his breathing labored enough for Deirdre to register the effort. He went on, detailing the efforts of the community to search for survivors, days dragging into weeks, limbs aching, hearts breaking, desolation descending over everything. The salvage operations went on for months, the Japanese citizenry doing their collective best to tend to the injured, relocate the dispossessed, and rebuild what they could of their towns and their lives.

"I stayed on, Deirdre, because I was too numb to do anything else, and because they called on me to help with reconstruction throughout Miyagi prefecture. It was the only thing that saved me—hammering, and nailing, and hoisting, and hoping—"(Here he shook his head as though to suggest the pointlessness of such wishful thinking, and then completed his thought)—"and helping others."

He leaned against one of the posts holding up the porch ceiling. With his back to Deirdre, he ran his hand over his face, stifling a sniffle or drying his eyes. Inu padded his way over, whimpering at his owner's feet. In the fading light, a whippoorwill started up in one of the Japanese maples. And still, Deirdre remained rooted on the swing, unable to imagine anything she might say or do to help.

Eventually, Lance squatted to pet the dog, burying his face in the animal's fur. Deirdre stood and walked over, placing her hand on his shoulder. "Such pain as you have suffered is unspeakable. I can only thank you for letting me know about them, Michiko and Mia."

She too stooped to run her fingers through Inu's thick coat, their attention to him a much-needed diversion.

That night, Deirdre held Lance extra tight as he cried himself to sleep.

Chapter Thirty-Three

P ippa's advice did not fall on deaf ears. The two friends met up at the coffeehouse on the last day of classes to compare notes and, though not spelled out between them, to thaw out the chill that had settled on their relationship.

"You were right, Pippa. In the end, most of them came through and did the work. The three books each of them had to both write and speak about will hopefully remain with them." Deirdre looked pleased but not completely convinced that this was enough.

"So: what? In the end, you're only concerned about holding back two of them, two out of twenty-two? That's an excellent percentage. Dennis is going to pat you on the head, or try to cajole you into taking on an additional course!" Pippa calculated, fishing in her bag for her mint leaves and motioning to the waitress. "This is on me. Let's share a slice of coffee cake, and you can order your cappuccino."

Encouraged by her friend's assessment, Deirdre went on to inquire about the two students which the two women shared, Randy

Thomas, who had done decently enough in the novel class but had of late stopped showing up, and Sharon Simpson, who had impressed everyone with her review of *To Kill a Mockingbird*—the book that she herself had recommended.

"Both Randy and Sharon could go further on the English literature track. Unless you have different plans for them, Pippa. I don't want them to be torn in different directions."

They sipped their drinks and nibbled at the cake while Pippa went over in her mind what conclusions she had drawn about these two kids. "Here's the thing, Deirdre. The music business is a tough game—as your daughter has doubtless found out—so, only if I'm convinced I have a Leontyne Price or a Muddy Waters in front of me, do I steer them toward a career in music."

"And neither Randy nor Sharon is in that camp?"

"They each have talent. Randy plays the fiddle—the dulcimer too—like a charm, but so do a lot of folks around these parts. Sharon has a good voice, with more training it would evolve into an even better voice. But is that really enough? I say this because I don't believe it's fair to be color-blind. They're both black, they're going to have to get real jobs in the real world, and we're in Mississippi. Yes, they have smarts and are motivated to please, if not to succeed, but in my opinion they're not going to be musical megastars."

Pippa took one final sip of her tea and placed the cup back on its saucer with conviction. "In short, I don't subscribe to the theory that kids can realize whatever dream they have in their heads."

Deirdre turned these thoughts over in her mind. "I understand what you're saying, and to an extent, I agree. However, I am convinced—however delicate the subject is in today's world—for kids, especially for black kids like Randy and Sharon, learning to read, write and speak properly in the King's English or American English— will give them a leg up, whatever they end up doing in life."

"To be sure," Pippa concurred, looking around the cafe to see who else might be in hearing range. Then she patted her companion's hand. "We are two very privileged, very white and arguably very myopic middle-aged women, Deirdre. But I do believe we see eye to eye on this. My *modus operandi* at Henson is to pass all those I in good conscience can, encourage the others to take on as much as they can handle, and steer only the most gifted toward a career in my own field. Make sense?"

"Eminently," Deirdre agreed, gratified that she and her friend had eased back into camaraderie instead of having to thrash through whatever thicket had grown up between them.

"Still, if you needed an example of what I'm talking about, you need look no further than our mutual friend." Deirdre looked puzzled before assuming she meant Dennis.

"From what I understand, his high school teachers tried to steer Lance toward books and music, ignoring the shambles that was his family life and the fact his real gifts lay elsewhere. Hell, the kid was whittling at his father's knee at age four!"

Deirdre scrunched her toes to keep from reddening.

"He is a master craftsman, and has done very well at it. Not everyone has to have a Ph.D., wouldn't you agree?"

"Of course not, Pippa. And no one should be saddled with a sibling who takes such advantage."

"Yes, there's that. Sue Ellen needs professional help which, obviously, she won't submit to."

Deirdre took a deep breath. "Speaking of which, Lance spoke to me recently about his time in Japan." Pippa's eyebrows arched in preparation for what was to come. "Losing his wife and child, and so on."

"I didn't say anything, because it was up to him, or not. Not many people around here ever knew, and fewer remember."

"I was at a loss to comfort him. Still, it is nine years on. Has he had any professional help?"

"Doubtful," Pippa replied, before adding, "However, I've never seen him so happy as of late. Take that for what it's worth." At this point, Deirdre did blush but said nothing. "And, in case you're hesitating, you might want to invite him to your New Year celebration."

Deirdre nodded, they hugged, and each headed off in a different direction across campus, final written exams stuffed in their satchels.

The highlight of the holidays came on New Year's Eve as everyone that had been invited managed to put in an appearance.

If Deirdre had been nervous about how Lance might be received, she needn't have feared. There was too much going on for anything or anyone to be awkwardly received. Caitlin and Dylan had arrived, gifts in hand for their grandmother, on Christmas Day itself (having waited too long to book their flights). Within hours they had taken up again with Jason as well as with his cousin, Connor, who had flown in from New York City. Myra came over briefly on Christmas night, bringing with her songbooks she had ordered from the store, including Christmas carols and Appalachian folk tunes, and insisted all the young people come over to Pippa's the next night.

Thus, by the time December 31 rolled around, the young people had all gotten acquainted, including Zach, who surprised them all with his unannounced arrival, and Randy and Sharon, who brought along their instruments. Even Ray managed to fly in for the evening "on my mate's private plane," as he put it, sporting his trademark (but now much more expensive) sunglasses and blowing a kiss across the table in Caitlin's general direction.

Also at the table for dinner were Elwood and the two teachers Deirdre had met years ago, the one who knit and the one who grew herbs. The former presented Clarissa with an exquisitely designed shawl; the latter placed on the back porch a couple of flats of parsley, rosemary and coriander from her own garden. Rose brought along a couple of vegetable casseroles, Pippa made one of her signature salads, and Dennis, who prided himself on his buttermilk biscuits, arrived with two dozen ready to pop into the oven.

Mrs. Durrell rose to the occasion by delivering up a strawberry cake she had made from scratch that morning—"It's always been my daughter's favorite and since it is also her birthday..." (Deirdre had begged her mother not to make such an announcement but it's possible she forgot.)

Hence, a toast was called for and she was obliged to open a couple of presents, including a ticket to New York for the fall, when Caitlin would be performing somewhere in the West Village, and a beautifully carved dulcimer, which Lance said was the only one he knew of made solely of rosewood. "Now you'll have to learn to play," he said half-jokingly.

Shortly thereafter, another guest appeared at the entrance-way. He stood quietly while those at the table passed around the dulcimer or finished up their desserts.

"Hi, Dad, come on in," a voice at the table called out. It was Connor and her summons made Deirdre look toward the front door. Rowan was standing there, in a light overcoat, not quite as ramrod-straight as she remembered him. He was holding a bag, awkwardly. She pushed her chair back and went to greet him.

"Why didn't you let us know you'd be here? Let me take your coat," she said, noticing the gray at his temples.

"I did not know it was your birthday, Deirdre. I don't think you ever told me."

"The new year is enough to celebrate—especially as one gets older," she replied. As she turned to face him, they both blushed. He took her hands in his, but gave them only a cursory squeeze.

"You look splendid. I only arrived a few hours ago. Wasn't sure if—"

"Well, you're here now. And your daughter is charming. You know how young people are. They're already bff's and all that."

His lips formed a smile, the tautness in his jaw relaxing as Deirdre chattered away. He deposited the bag next to his coat and followed her into the dining room. Mrs. Durrell insisted he try a slice of strawberry cake. While he munched, Deirdre went around the table introducing him to the guests he did not already know.

Rowan and Lance eyed each other with curiosity but neither spoke.

Later, Dylan and Caitlin rearranged the living room so that musicians could form a semi-circle around the piano. Deirdre and her mother played a few of the carols from the songbook Myra brought over, and then turned the instrument over to others, including Sharon, who played and sang a couple of Gospel hymns.

Once the fiddles, clarinets, and dulcimers got in on the act, guests called out their favorites from the floor. Lance pulled up a stool next to Pippa, following her lead on the dulcimer through a few numbers, but then came to sit next to Deirdre on one of the sofas. Rowan took a seat between Mrs. Durrell in her lift chair and Connor on a nearby stool. "Did you know, Dad, that Dylan and I both work right near the Flat Iron building? You're going to have to come visit," Deirdre heard her say. There was something about the sparkle in her eyes that mirrored her father's.

Eventually, Dylan, Caitlin, and Zach performed a few of the medieval pieces they had played together at Princeton, including a jaunty version of *The Cuckoo Song*, which the latter explained was the oldest surviving song in English. Ever prepared, he passed out copies of the piece so they could sing it as originally intended, as a round, with everyone joining in.

Closer to midnight, Deirdre observed Zach and Caitlin deep in conversation at the back of the room. The exchange went on for a good while. (Ray appeared oblivious to or disinterested in their huddle; Myra, on the other hand, kept darting her eyes their way.)

All Deirdre herself picked up was her daughter's final plea: "Now is as good a time as any, Zach. He won't be that surprised." Young people, she thought. Impossible to know what goes on with them, and yet, she surmised, something serious might have finally firmed up between Zach and her daughter.

She would soon be disabused.

As Elwood poured champagne for everyone and the television was turned on to watch a repeat of the ball drop in Times Square, Caitlin tapped on her glass with a fork. "Everyone: Zach has an announcement to make."

He had, only days before, asked and received formal permission of Nasreen's parents to marry her.

Everyone applauded. Several of the men shook Zach's hand, including Jason and Ray, but Dylan hovered near the window alongside Sharon and Randy. Fortunately, Connor soon rose from her stool and wandered over next to him for the ball drop, placing a soft kiss on his cheek at the stroke of midnight. Elwood took the vacated seat next to Mrs. Durrell and took her hand in his. Having noticed Lance lay his hand on Deirdre's, Rowan got up and stood next to Jason.

The evening had been full of surprises, no one more stunned than Deirdre.

The next few days brought more. Ashton rang up the next afternoon to extend his greetings and to let his ex-wife know he had decided to remarry. "This time," as he tellingly put it, "more commendable a choice than the last."

"And who is this lucky person?" she asked, bent on keeping any hint of sarcasm out of her voice.

"Actually, it's the wonderful woman who's been caring for Sierra—for both of us, now that I think about it."

Deirdre rolled her eyes, remembering how little her ex-husband ever noticed who did all the caring for him. But she did not wish to be uncharitable. That the little girl had someone she could call mother would be a good thing.

"So, what is her name—and when is this happening?"

They would marry in the late spring, after her own son finished up his medical studies. "As you might imagine, Amira's had a tumultuous life. Her husband ended up in the hands of Assad and was never heard of again, one son joined the rebels and was killed, she and her other son emigrated here to avoid the worst."

When they hung up, Deirdre returned to the kitchen and finished washing the dishes. She felt disoriented, but to her relief, no bile rose as she dried and put away the champagne flutes. She didn't even feel envious of Ashton's enthusiasm for another go at marital bliss. Without making too harsh an assessment of it, she assumed he wanted to remarry mainly because of the child. (For one thing, he had sounded proud to declare, Sierra had become fluent in both Arabic and French thanks to her nanny's tutelage.)

She poured herself a cup of coffee and sat down at the kitchen table to take stock. Mrs. Durrell was sleeping in, having stayed up past 2 a.m., and having been fully engaged, chatting away with

Elwood until almost all the guests had left. The twins had gone over to visit Jason and Connor at the Kleinfeld home.

She wondered if Rowan would be staying around for a few days, he having kept his distance from her for the better part of the evening. Only at the last minute, when making his exit with Rose and Dennis, did he search in the bag at the hat rack and pull out two beautifully wrapped gifts, one for her and one for her mother.

"You really needn't have," she had insisted, flushing at the gesture.

"It's not about need, Deirdre," he had replied softly.

"Well, I know Mother will be pleased," she had wound up, extending her hand to him but not meeting his gaze. She sensed that Lance had come up behind her and was retrieving his jacket from the rack.

Once the front door closed upon Rowan, she turned back with a smile. "Do you really have to go?" she had asked.

"I need to check on Sue Ellen at the house. Grover Wiggins and his brothers have been coming around, giving her a hard time," he explained.

"I hope she finally appreciates what a good brother you are."

Lance sniffed dismissively at the idea and proceeded to zip up his jacket. "This was fun," he added, "the food, the music, your friends."

Despite herself, Deirdre had blushed. There was something off in his tone. Perhaps Rowan's appearance had rattled him, or he felt the disparity between her family life and his, or, as he had so adamantly declared, he *was* a hollowed-out person who would never be whole again.

Later that very day the phone rang again, while Mrs. Durrell was leafing through the book of *Paintings from the Delta* which Rowan had chosen for her, and Deirdre was planting the herbs from the widowed Mrs. Stennis in the back garden. She ran in to answer, thinking it might be from Lance, or from Rowan.

Instead, it was a call from Margery and Stella on speaker-phone—with a proposal.

Once they finished exchanging New Year greetings, Margery came to the point. "Presuming, my dear, that you will have finished the play, I'd like to propose that its first staging be here at Klimpton, both because we know it will be good and good for the students, but also because"—(Here she faltered and Stella jumped in.)—"because Margery, after a gazillion years, is going to be leaving us, and she wanted to go out with something special, theatrically, as it were. Does that make sense?"

"Not the part about Margery's leaving, as it's incomprehensible to imagine the place without her. But, yes," Deirdre said, deeply touched, "I would be honored. I'm close to having it finished."

"The point is, Deirdre, a staging here could be a springboard for further runs elsewhere. Best to get the kinks out first," Margery said.

"Indeed," Deirdre replied. "When exactly would I need to get the text to you—and when would be the staging?"

"I'll be leaving at the end of the spring term"—("There's to be a celebration for her right on the heels," Stella interjected.)—"so we were thinking, Beauchamps and I, to book it in for Friday and Saturday, May 17 and 18. How does that sound?"

"Doable. I will talk to the dean here at Henson, but I suspect we can work around that weekend. I should have the completed play mailed to you by mid-March."

"Wonderful, my dear. And we want to see Dylan and Caitlin too, if they can come," Stella added. She sounded as excited as Margery.

"Do know, too, Deirdre, that Ashton will naturally be on the invitation list for my retirement party. If he were so inclined, and you were comfortable with it, perhaps he'd come to the performance as well," Margery added.

"You needn't fret. We're on good terms. He's getting married again—someone, well, reasonable. Anyway, I'll discuss it with him."

"And naturally, bring along whomever else you would like," Stella hastened to throw in.

Chapter Thirty-Four

W ithout undue effort, Deirdre put the final touches on her play, taught her classes and managed a weekend jaunt to New Orleans with her mother, all by mid-March. The day she took hard copies to mail at the post office she ran into Rowan and Jason on the street.

"I'm going to leave you two to chat while I get a couple of things at the drugstore," Jason said, demonstrating more sensitivity than she imagined he possessed.

"Looks like something important if you're going to stand in line for twenty minutes," Rowan said, his mouth upturned in a wry smile.

"It's a play. I'm sending it to colleagues at Klimpton. They're going to do a dramatic reading in May, provided, that is, they can make sense of it."

"Impressive. I thought you were still teaching over at Henson."

"I am. This was something I've been working on for a while," she replied, then shifted gears. "And you? Here for a visit or...?" which she instantly knew to be a ridiculous question, since why else would he be standing in front of her.

"I've been on the river, given all the flooding, and otherwise coordinating things at headquarters, either in Vicksburg or in St Louis. Depending."

She nodded her head as disinterestedly as possible. "And Connor? How is she doing in New York?"

"Loves it. I believe she sees Dylan, and even Caitlin once in a while. And Jason's landed a job at a digital start-up in Brooklyn, handling their computer needs and so forth. He's relocating next month."

After several shoppers passed them on the street, he added, "It's a new world, isn't it?" in a tone that suggested he was posing this last question as more than a throw-away line. He looked intently at her face.

Deirdre forced herself to return his gaze. "For some people it is," she replied, thinking it best to remain on solid ground, and not wanting to be led where she wasn't prepared to go.

"I wasn't referring to some people, Deirdre. I was referring to us," he responded more forcefully.

While she was preparing to explain that her life had taken an unexpected turn, as his purportedly had, Jason wandered back with a shopping bag in one hand and a diet coke in the other. "You two still jabbering? Post office closes in ten minutes," he reminded, jerking his head at the adjacent building.

"Right. I need to get this done. By the way, congratulations on your job," she said, holding out her hand to the young man. Blushing, he switched the bag to his other arm and took her hand in his, shaking it vigorously. "And, Rowan, do come by to see us when next you're in town," she added as cheerily as she could.

Without waiting for a reply, she walked determinedly into the post office.

By the time she got home a little after 5 p.m., Mrs. Durrell and Sandra were finishing up a chapter of *The Age of Innocence*, another of the selections Deirdre had added to her modern novel course for the spring term. On her way out, the girl confided, "I'm starting to be way ahead of the others in my English class, Dr. Durrell, all because of spending time with your mother."

"How lovely of you to say. I know it does Mother good, so if it helps you, even better."

"My grandfather says your mom is the smartest person he ever met, and so I guess that explains why you..." the teenager went on before losing her train of thought.

Over dinner, Mrs. Durrell remembered to mention the phone call that came in. "I had forgotten because Sandra and I were reading that Edith Wharton book, but Rowan Kleinfeld rang up shortly before you returned. Wanted to invite you to the Main St. diner for lunch tomorrow. Said he's only here fleetingly or would be coming by to see me. Anyway, I told him it shouldn't be a problem, as you don't have classes on Wednesday."

Deirdre didn't know whether to be pleased or irritated, but since Rowan did have the decency, and the delicacy, not to invite her back to the Park Hotel, she would acquiesce and go.

As luck would have it, the two ex-lovers were seated directly opposite Pattie Lee and two other women who looked to be fellow Tea Party enthusiasts. They wore political buttons of some kind on their jackets.

Being at such close quarters with Riverton acquaintances, Rowan and Deirdre limited their conversation to their respective jobs and family members. The name of her play: *Their World, Their Way,* which he politely reacted to as "intriguing." (She instantly decided to change the title.)

Once their stuffed crabs and steamed vegetables arrived, the two spoke even more softly. About Sophie, Rowan remained vague except to say she had moved on with her life; about Ashton, Deirdre said that he was planning to remarry. About Lance, neither was inclined to comment.

For Rowan's part, he had told himself that her affair, if that's what it was, was none of his business, and he sensed that Deirdre herself was conflicted about it. Still, he had done enough digging to unearth his disadvantaged upbringing, while Rose filled him in on Lance's reputation as a woodworker and the burden of his troubled sister. Nothing had he uncovered about the twenty years Lance spent away from Riverton, and nothing popped up on social media except the workshop website.

For Deirdre's part, she had come to the conclusion that something had shifted inside her, whether as a result of Lance's revelation about the tragedy in Japan or something more intangible. From what she could determine, Lance had expended all the love he had to offer on his wife and child, and more recently on his sister. What he had stressed might very well be the truth: there was a void in him that left others unfulfilled, however much they might have warmed to him.

Thus, she wouldn't bring up Lance's name, not only because she would be at a loss to articulate her feelings for him, but also because Pattie Lee kept eyeing them, occasionally shaking her curls to regal her lunch companions.

After splitting a slice of key lime pie and the bill, Rowan and Deirdre parted company at the door, with whatever eyes upon them, and she, for lack of something else to say in taking leave, off-handedly invited him to Ohio for the play, were he up that way at the time.

The rains intensified toward the end of March. The Mississippi had overflown its banks further north and by mid-April was threatening vast acreage from Memphis on down through the Delta and all the way to New Orleans. An unspecified number of students at Henson had dropped out or skipped classes in order to help with flood relief or with family businesses that depended on agriculture. Most of the students in Pippa's and Deirdre's classes remained enrolled, but a few requirements were dropped because of what locals began calling "the emergency."

The Trump administration eventually signed off on disaster relief but not nearly enough to offset the ongoing devastation. Crops were ruined, livestock drowned, houses inundated, jobs lost. The Army Corps of Engineers dispatched emergency teams to deal with flood control up and down the river and its bulging, alligator-invested backwaters, Rowan among them. When he finally managed a rare couple of days off, he flew to New York City to see Connor, treating her, Jason, Dylan and Caitlin to dinner in the West Village. From that locale, they rang Deirdre on her cell phone, but she didn't pick up.

Instead, on that very Thursday in late April, she had determined to drive over to the workshop after classes, knowing that Pippa had gone to Jackson for a concert. In the campus coffeehouse, she had the waitress wrap up two slices of coffeecake and pour three hot cups of coffee into her thermos. On the way over, she rehearsed what she would say: she had been inordinately busy, what with the play and all, and Pippa had told her his orders for instruments on the website had skyrocketed. So obviously he had been busy too.

We shall see, she told herself as she maneuvered the car down the thinly graveled road. A hundred yards out, Inu shot out of nowhere, running alongside the car. She slowed to a crawl, lowered the window and called out to the dog. When she got out, her satchel over her shoulder, Lance was leaning against a post on the porch, looking oddly disheveled. Inu sniffed at her sandaled feet as she approached the house.

"This is a surprise," he said, whether pleased or not she couldn't tell.

"That was part of the idea," she replied, "as was bringing you coffee and cake to keep you focused." He was holding a lit cigarette in his hand, which she rarely remembered him doing except in bed, after sex. "I hope I'm not interrupting," she somehow felt bound to add.

"We were just winding up," he stated, turning his head back toward the screen door. Behind it, Deirdre could barely make out a figure, the late afternoon sun shining directly on the house. She blinked in confusion. "Myra and I. We were filling orders on the computer. She's much more adept than I am."

Torn between retreating to the car or barging inside, Deirdre remained fixed in place at the bottom of the porch steps. Lance took a puff on the cigarette and slowly exhaled.

At that point, the screen door creaked and Myra, dressed in a short red skirt and blue tank top, emerged. Even without a shred of makeup, she was an arresting creature, her almond eyes larger even than Pippa's, her coal-black hair shinier. In the silence, Inu padded his way toward the girl and sniffed her feet. They were clad in blue flip-flops, her toenails painted a matching shade.

"I thought you worked," Deirdre found herself saying in a tone bordering on accusatory.

Myra tilted her head languidly before responding. "Not much business of late. I closed up early."

Lance took another drag on his cigarette and flicked it away. He looked preoccupied, as if to say, *you ladies figure it out. I've got other things to think about.*

Deirdre tried to get hold of herself, so as not to turn this encounter into a scene. Especially since Lance and she were no longer, if they had ever been, committed to each other in any public way, and because Myra was the daughter of her friend and colleague. "Well, since this thing is heavy and I did bring it for you, Lance, you two can enjoy this treat. The campus coffeehouse is one of the best things about Henson," she said as blithely as she could, fingering inside her satchel for the goodies.

"That's what Mama says about that place," Myra interposed. "Anyway, Lance, I've got to go. Text me next time you're in a jam. With the computer, not with your crazy sister."

With that, the young woman sashayed off the porch in her flip-flops and started to walk back up the path to her mother's house. Without turning her head back around, she called out to Deirdre, "Tell Caitlin I said hello, OK?"

"Yes. Of course," Deirdre shouted back.

Later, over the coffee and cake, Lance made an effort to be apologetic, if not affectionate, but it came across as just that, an effort. Not that Deirdre, sitting stiffly, her lips pursed, made things any easier. Finally, he came up with a classic rejoinder: "I know what you're thinking, Deirdre, but you'd be wrong."

"So, enlighten me. What would be the right way to look at this?"

Despite himself, Lance reddened, but he took his time to fashion a response. "Myra's a funny kid, still trying to figure out who she wants to be—what she wants to be, for that matter."

"Aren't we all, " Deirdre replied drily. "But that doesn't answer my question."

"OK, to be blunt about it, she doesn't know if she likes men or women."

"I intuited that from Pippa some time ago," Deirdre shot back, "but what I'm asking is how much *you* like *her.*"

Here, Lance got up, walked across the room and switched on the stereo. "Thought you might like this," he called out. "It's the Waverly Consort—lots of recorders and other plaintive instruments. Soothing, not too taxing."

For a moment, Deirdre wondered if the last phrase was a hint to her to be less taxing, but quickly decided she was reading too much into his every utterance. How is it, she further asked herself, that this man has become so aggravating, even as he remains so appealing. And possibly not just to her. And how much should she even care.

On his way back to the sofa, Lance stopped at the fridge and brought out a bottle of wine. "The coffee was great," he said, pouring a little into each of two glasses, "but this, at least in small quantities, stiffens my spine." He handed her a glass, clinking his against hers. Deirdre took a sip and waited. He reached over and stroked her hair, but she did not react. Sighing heavily, he lowered himself back down next to her.

"I did have sex with Myra, if that's what you want to know. Before I met you, more than a year ago when she first got back to town. Believe it or not, I tried to ward her off: me forty-five, she twenty or so, but (hesitating, he closed his eyes and shook his head ostensibly at the memory) she wouldn't take no for an answer." He took another sip and plowed on. "Mind you, I'm not flattering myself. The girl was throwing herself around to all and sundry, including a couple of low-lifes that my sister knows."

Deirdre could feel her stomach beginning to churn but took a few deep breaths to settle it. "So, what happened?" she finally asked, her voice thin.

"Nothing. This went on for a couple of weeks but that was it. I wasn't into it, and she could sense that. Not to mention she had other things to figure out. Like with other girls and all. In case you're also wondering, she and I have never talked about it, because there was nothing to talk about," Lance went on, more emphatically.

Feeling a little faint, Deirdre put down her glass.

"I've told you before. I don't feel things like other people. They've all been washed out of me."

His vehemence left her torn between wanting to berate him and wanting to console him. "This thing is not for me to judge, Lance. Your pain, however, that's what makes me sorry."

He took a final sip of the wine, put down his glass, and took her hand in his. "Whatever else you may think, it is you who have come closest to making me feel whole again, and it's you whom I have enjoyed having in my life, however different we are. And we are— different. I know that."

Blinking to hold back her own tears, Deirdre got up to walk around. He had not lied about being busy for the last couple of months. Twenty to thirty dulcimers and several other string instruments in various stages of completion lay on the counter or behind glass. Piles of differently shaded woods stood in the rear of the shop next to a table laden with tools.

Eventually, Lance ambled over. "A few of these I'll be taking to the Ozarks in a month or so. There's a folk festival there and, rumor has it, a market for these things. Perhaps, well, we'll see—" Deirdre nodded noncommittally. "And, I'd ask you to stay, but Sue Ellen needs to spend the night. People are harassing her, so she says. Hard to get away from the past."

"Of course," Deirdre said. "I hadn't planned to stay."

As she was getting into the Volvo, she extended the invitation to her play at Klimpton. "It would be nice to have you there," but even as she said it, she knew it not to be the case. Lance would be out of his depth, and she would be newly sorry to see it so. What they had was what they had, each to give what they could, and no more.

Turning onto the road back to Riverton, she spotted a Corolla speeding in the direction of Pippa's place, a woman with blond hair at the wheel. Hard to ever know what is true and what isn't, who is and who isn't an imposter, she mused.

Chapter Thirty-Five

T he performance of *The Wonder Women of 1412* went over better than Deirdre could have imagined, the sassy title bringing in a larger proportion of the student body than she would have predicted. Or, as likely, they came out because it was Dr. Willingham's last turn as stage director and three of the most popular seniors at Klimpton had been chosen to play the characters.

Either way, she was happy enough to bask in the limelight for two successive evenings and to share that recognition with her old friend.

Fortunately, too, she had arrived in time for the dress rehearsal on the Thursday evening, and during a break, supplied the performers with the backdrop to the characters' lives, especially since none were history or literature majors. The Humanities department had continued to shrink over the last five years as more students switched to business administration or computer science.

"What I was trying to do in setting up a fictional encounter was to dramatize why these three figures, whose actual lives did overlap were harbingers of things to come. Their world was circumscribed, their lives predetermined by happenstance of birth, the limitations of marriage, and the dictates of the Church. As Margery's stage lighting suggests, theirs was a world lit only by fire and, dare I remind you young women, controlled exclusively by men."

"It kinda still is, Dr. Durrell," one of the girls interjected, causing the other cast mates to chuckle.

"Indeed," Deirdre replied. "That's partially why I fashioned this piece, to provide a sense of how far we've come and how far we still need to go."

"Dr. Willingham told us the characters are, like, you know, the suffragettes of their century," another of the three actresses said.

Deirdre mulled this over. "Margery's not wrong to think of them in that way, the major difference being that there were, to our knowledge, no mechanisms available for women collectively to do anything about their treatment by society. Each had to make an individual choice, thwarting authority outright, circumventing it subtly, or in a few cases, renouncing the world of men altogether, which in that period could only mean the convent."

The three young women nodded politely. A number of the stage hands, who were also female, had gathered around to hear the discussion. Margery encouraged Deirdre to elaborate further.

"All you can do, ladies, is give voice to my inadequate text, but remember, if it helps, each of these figures displayed an act of rare courage. After her young husband died and left her with huge debts and three little children, Christine de Pizan spent the better part of her life arguing that women had much to give to society, and, in so doing, became the first-ever woman to make a living as a writer. After marriage and many children, Margery Kempe threw off her shackles and became an astute business woman, even though she hadn't been taught to read; when that wasn't enough, she transformed herself again, traveled extensively on her own, sometimes as a religious zealot, sometimes for the pure fun of it. She also found time to write the first-ever autobiography in English. As for Juliana of Norwich, she too had married but eventually secluded herself in a convent where she wrote exquisite works of spiritual enlightenment."

Before the cast and crew broke for the evening, the two professors between them treated the cast and crew to an informal summary of the entire period, leaving one of the stagehands to exclaim that the hour seated on stage was more useful than the entire course on the Dark Ages she had just completed. "Plus, tonight, I don't have to worry about a grade!"

On the Friday night, Deirdre arrived early in Margery's company. Several students came up to introduce themselves or mention that they had taken one of her classes. To her delight, an easily recognizable John Burnham made his way over. "My parents still live around here, so when I heard it was your play being performed, I had to come." He turned crimson but recovered enough to explain he had gone on to graduate school and was now an instructor at Northwestern.

Once the auditorium had filled to capacity, Dr. Landry, who now used a cane, hobbled onto the stage and tapped on a live microphone to insist Margery and Deirdre stand and face the assembled.

"In these two women you have two of the most gifted, and giving, of our professors," he announced in his most stentorian voice. "Dr. Willingham has dedicated herself to Klimpton for forty years, and Dr. Durrell made her own unique contributions here for two decades. She is now giving back by teaching down in the Delta and continues to publish in her chosen field." He paused to let a few late arrivals find seats. "And, as many of you also know, Dr. Willingham has tirelessly overseen the staging of countless productions here at the Taft, giving innumerable students their first taste of the limelight."

Scattered applause broke out. The president appeared to search the front rows for someone. "Have I left anything out, Stella?" he called out, having located the college administrator next to Dr. Beauchamps. "Ah, of course. You're all invited to linger for refreshments in the foyer after the performance. The celebration of our esteemed colleague's career will be tomorrow at lunchtime in the quad. No rain allowed!"

Looking out over the audience, Deirdre spotted Ashton on the aisle ten rows back. Next to him was a child with straight blond hair and a bright face and on her other side a woman with dark hair. After she and Margery were seated, the lights were dimmed and a hush fell over the audience. She took a deep breath, wondering if her jitters were more to do with her play or with seeing her ex-husband for the first time in years, and in that very theater where...

Margery patted her hand. "Enjoy your accomplishment, my dear. It took imagination and determination. You should be proud."

"As should you, Margery."

And the performance did go off smoothly, with only a couple of flubbed lines, and the sound system which faltered during the musical interlude between the two acts. Whatever else anyone thought, Deirdre was delighted to hear her words brought to life by the three amateur thespians. If there were something static about the piece—more a tableaux of characters than a drama with beginning, middle and end—so be it. That was, after all, the way she saw the entire period of the Middle Ages, as a pageant of successive still-lives.

At the end, the applause was more than polite, if less than thunderous.

Deirdre didn't have time to mind. She was dragged out to the foyer and surrounded by well-wishers, hugged by several of her former colleagues, and even asked to autograph a few playbills. With a brightly made-up Stella on his arm, Dr. Beauchamps marched over and with Gallic gallantry raised her hand to his lips, pronouncing her one of the most discerning talents who had ever graced his department. Perhaps he had imbibed too much of the cheap champagne being dispensed. He had, after all, resisted raising her salary every year until the end. About that too, she no longer minded.

Finally, one of the stagehands thought to bring her a goblet and she took the time to look round the room as the crowd thinned out, most of the students still having final exams to prep for. Scouring the remaining guests, she spotted her ex-husband in a group with several former colleagues as well as the dark-haired woman now holding the hand of the child.

She would have made her way over, but a determined-looking young woman with a reporter's notebook waylaid her with questions for the school paper and website. "Did she think the country under the current administration was going backward with respect to women's rights?" "Did she consider her play a protest piece in the mold of Margaret Atwood's *Handmaid's Tale*?" and "Was sexual harassment as rampant in the Middle Ages as it is today?"

To do any of these queries justice would mean more than yes or no answers, Deirdre thought, though she had not considered that her opus could withstand that kind of analysis. Plus, she wanted to speak to Ashton and to meet Sierra and what must be his future wife. "Could we do this tomorrow morning on the phone? Your questions deserve more thought than my brain is capable of right now. It's been a long day."

By the time the two finished exchanging cards and scheduling a phone chat for 9:00 a.m., Ashton and his party had extricated themselves and circled around the foyer over to his ex-wife.

"The play was marvelous, Deirdre. And you look the same—marvelous, that is." He leaned in to give her a clumsy hug, before pulling back and extending his hand toward his daughter. "Sierra, this is the lady I was telling you about. She and I were married before, and she is Dylan and Caitlin's mother."

Wide-eyed, the little girl studied Deirdre's face but was too tongue-tied or shy to respond.

Deirdre bent down to speak to her. "I'm very happy to meet you, Sierra. You and I can talk more tomorrow, OK?"

The little girl nodded, but then blurted out, "And this is *my* mother. Tell her, Amira."

"Yes, soon-to-be officially so," Ashton interposed, his cheeks infusing with color. He took the dark-haired woman by the arm. "Amira Jaafar, Deirdre Durrell."

"Honored to meet you, Deirdre. I have heard many good things. And you have wonderful children," Amira replied in nearly flawless, if noticeably accented, English.

Touched by such a kind response, Deirdre squeezed the woman's hand. "I trust the two of you, rather, the three of you, will be very happy together."

Ashton inclined his head as though blessing this exchange. "We can catch up tomorrow at the lunch, but I didn't want to leave here before they had a chance to meet you. Oh, and I've been instructed to relay messages from the kids: Dylan had to fly last-minute to London for some conference, and Caitlin couldn't get out of a performance. Both send kisses and wanted to know if the play's being taped."

That night lying in Margery's guest bedroom, Deirdre's brain snagged on the word *bile*, which had figured in the play when one of the characters lamented her marriage. No such humor had risen through her body upon seeing Ashton: for whatever reasons—the passage of time, tragedies to deal with, other lovers to alleviate the pain—she no longer felt anger or resentment. All that remained was a vague regret that they hadn't managed to keep their marriage on track, despite all the things they had shared. Or did she exaggerate? Perhaps her current sadness had more to do with the realization that Lance Tatum, as much of a tonic as he was and as much as she cared for him, could never be her, or by his own admission, anyone else's be-all and end-all.

Perhaps no one is ever anyone's be-all and end-all, she whispered to herself.

Still, standing there next to that beautiful child and the next Mrs. Cole, so gracious and seemingly devoted to Ashton, she had felt a twinge of envy. She had come back to Klimpton entirely on her own, with no one to share the festivities with. And likely no one thought to tape the thing.

Around 1 a.m. Deirdre fluffed her pillow, turned on her side and willed herself to sleep.

The celebration for Margery in the quad brought a sizable influx of alumni, former colleagues and old friends, as well as most of the student body. Despite the encomia and general warmth shown toward the departing professor, Deirdre sensed that things had been scaled back since she last worked at Klimpton. Aside from Dr. Beauchamps, there were few chairs of departments, Ashton's position, for example, having never been refilled, and many more young instructors without their doctorates were spread across the various disciplines. Likely paid as poorly as she had been, she reckoned.

As if she had read Deirdre's mind, Stella leaned over to say discussions were underway about merging with one of the colleges "down the road," which she took literally to mean one of the other struggling liberal arts institutions in eastern Ohio. "You did well to leave, Deirdre. I only ever stayed because of Beau," she confided proudly.

Another of the unlikeliest of relationships, Deirdre thought, but did not voice.

Once the speeches were over and music came blaring through the loudspeakers, Deirdre got up from the head table—the only one where wine rather than lemonade was served—and weaved her way toward the cluster that included Ashton. He was seated with a few of what she imagined were his former students (perhaps even from the same class as Jennifer) and with a dyspeptic older professor, whom she faintly recalled seeing around campus but couldn't identify. Sierra and Amira were listening patiently as this latter rambled on about the cutbacks and the lack of wine on the tables.

Ashton was fiddling with his cellphone. "I just glanced at the review of the play, Deirdre, and it's not half-bad. Actually, it should have been kinder, but reviewers these days, especially younger ones, clamor to be snarky," he said. Deirdre smiled.

"Anyway, here's what the Klimpton critic had to say: '*If the plot was sketchy, the characters were well-drawn. One could rest assured such women existed in the Middle Ages, as the playwright had painstakingly modeled these characters on historical figures. Charlotte Robertson, who impersonated Christine de Pizan, brought a crisp intelligence to the role of the French courtier turned literary sensation; Sarah Tish, who portrayed the English matron Margery Kempe, brought an ebullience to her interpretation, reminding us of a real-life Wife of Bath; and Deborah Olson, a theater arts major, was cast perfectly as the mysterious Juliana of Norwich—about whom historians do not even know her last name—into a sympathetic, if slightly neurasthenic, nun.*' "

"I'm content with that," Deirdre interrupted him. "They were splendid, the actresses, and I have no illusions. I will not be leaving my day job!"

They chatted amiably for the next half hour, Sierra relaxing enough to demonstrate her French and Amira making a point of praising Dylan's grasp of Middle Eastern politics.

"So, have you set a date for the wedding?" Deirdre asked.

Amira deferred to Ashton, whose face clouded over. "You know how it is, Deirdre. Mother and Father are doing poorly. Not to mention Adeline, who will soon have to be institutionalized. In short, we're working around all that." She nodded sympathetically, but made a mental note to call her ex-mother-in-law. "Plus, since it's Mother's Day tomorrow, we're flying straight to Boston this evening, so we'd better get a move on," he added, eyeing his watch.

As they gathered up their belongings, Ashton suddenly paused. "As we were checking out this morning—from the Silver Creek Inn— the strangest thing." Deirdre looked at him expectantly. "A man checking in next to us. He looked somehow familiar. And then I heard his last name."

"Which was?"

351

"Kleinfeld."

Deirdre thought she misheard.

"Connor's father. She's a friend of Dylan's. You obviously know her from Riverton. Small world, huh?"

The trip back home went like clockwork, thanks to Rowan's thoughtfulness in driving Deirdre all the way to Cincinnati to catch the non-stop to Jackson in time to celebrate with her mother. So long the two had talked into the night, she had never turned her cell phone back on since the Saturday night performance started. Only once the plane landed in Mississippi did she switch it out of airplane mode. Pippa had texted to say "break a leg" with an appropriately goofy GIF, the kids had sent kisses and regrets they couldn't be there, and Lance had left two phone messages.

She retrieved the voicemails while driving to Riverton and played them twice. He would be headed to Mountain View, Arkansas, first thing Monday morning in case she wanted to come along. Great music, great food, great vistas. "So say yes," the message had ended. Deirdre smiled. He was childlike in his exuberance.

The second call was to say he'd swing by around 7:00 in the morning, no need for her to make or bring anything other than a jacket. "I'm running around like crazy now and my phone is dying on me. I've got to pack the dulcimers, check on Sue Ellen, and get some sleep. No need to call back. Oh, and Happy Mother's Day. Your mom too."

Going away so soon again would all depend, she told herself. It was close to supper time when she got home, Sandra and her mother were seated in the living room watching *Wheel of Fortune* and sipping iced tea, Deirdre having banned all sodas from the house. With relief, she noticed nothing that had changed in her absence other than the fresh flowers in the vase she had bought at Kleinfelds.

"Those are beautiful, Mother," she said, planting a kiss on Mrs. Durrell's forehead and smiling over at the girl.

"Elwood always did have a way with pretty things," she said.

"So sweet of you to bring them over, Sandra," Deirdre said.

"Oh, I didn't. Grandfather came himself yesterday. Stayed the whole afternoon. You don't have to pay me for that day, or even for today. Your mother is teaching me how to play bridge. It's complicated."

"Nonsense. You could have been doing fun things with your friends. But hopefully, we will see you tomorrow afternoon, right?"

Already, Deirdre was racking her brain to think who else she might get to come over to sit with her mother if indeed she did go to Arkansas.

Sandra began to collect her things, putting a notebook back in her backpack and the near-empty glasses on a tray.

"A few more lessons, Sandra, and perhaps the four of us can play a rubber or two," Mrs. Durrell told the young girl in something of an aside, patting her on the arm.

Deirdre wondered what foursome her mother was thinking of but decided not to inquire. She herself hadn't played in twenty years, not since she and Ashton had briefly belonged to a club—a time, brief though it was, when they did things together, had friends, socialized. She shook off the memory.

Over dinner, Deirdre recounted her weekend, how pleased she was the play had gone over well enough and so many people had shown up. She mentioned Ashton, who, she was quick to stress, came equally for the retirement party of a fellow professor, but she did not have the energy to bring up Amira and little Sierra.

"And the children?"

Deirdre looked flummoxed. "Oh, you mean Caitlin and Dylan. Both super-busy. Neither could make it."

Mrs. Durrell stirred the bowl of homemade vegetable soup that one of the sitters had left in the fridge Saturday night. "You haven't said anything about Rowan Kleinfeld, DeeDee."

Deirdre reddened.

"He called here the other day because he didn't know where you might be staying and where the play was being performed. I believe he wanted to surprise you. Anyway, Sandra and I found the note you had left me, with all the details."

Trying to sound nonchalant, Deirdre replied, "Oh yes. He did find the place—enjoyed it, so he said, and was nice enough this morning to drive me back to Cincinnati for the plane."

She turned her attention to the biscuits in the oven, bringing them out piping hot and buttering a couple. She placed one on the rim of her mother's plate and another on hers. For a few minutes the two ate in silence, Deirdre happy to see that her mother seemed more on top of things than she had months before.

"Well, my dear," Mrs. Durrell eventually said, "it comforts me when you're here, though I suspect I am quite a burden."

"Not in the least, Mother," Deirdre replied, a tad too adamantly.

"You must not let me hinder you. You have your own life to live."

Blinking to keep a tear from falling, Deirdre reached out and patted her mother's arm. She would sleep on Lance's invitation.

Chapter Thirty-Six

S everal insistent knocks woke Deirdre out of a dream. A swathe of faint light bathed her bedroom. She grabbed the alarm clock. It wasn't yet 6 a.m. Throwing on a bathrobe and slippers, she hurried downstairs and to the front door. Pippa was standing there, white as a sheet.

"What on earth?"

"Something's happened, Deirdre. Come out here and close the door."

"I may be leaving soon. Why are you here?"

Pippa took hold of Deirdre's arms, to steady herself as well as her friend. "It's Lance. He's been shot. Last night."

"That can't be. We're going to Arkansas this morning."

"He didn't make it."

Her breath shallow, Deirdre looked past her friend at the car parked at the curb. Someone was in the front passenger seat, her head buried in her hands. "Myra. She did it?" her voice unearthly, her cheeks beginning to drain of blood.

"What are you talking about? The police think it was an accident."

"How could she do such a thing? Lance, of all people...someone she—"

Deirdre felt her legs start to give way as she lurched forward, apparently in an attempt to get to the car. Pippa held on to her arm and lowered the two of them onto the front steps.

"I'm trying to tell you. It was Sue Ellen, not knowing she was aiming at her brother. Says she was holed up, expecting gang members to come after her. She shot through the bedroom window thinking she was under attack."

"That doesn't make sense. He has a key to their house," Deirdre said almost proudly, as though this fact put paid to any notion that a shadow on a window could lead to a fatal accident. Pippa shook her head and hugged her friend. "How could anyone do such a thing, to one of the sweetest people in the world," she wailed.

"Because Sue Ellen's a fucking junkie or a paranoid idiot, that's why," Pippa exploded, unable to keep the rage out of her voice.

Deirdre buried her face in her hands, sobbing uncontrollably. Her own skin gave off a peculiar odor, like an animal *in extremis*.

Pippa motioned to Myra to get out of the car and come help. The young woman did so, mother and daughter practically hoisting Deirdre into the back seat.

"Where are we going? To see him?" Deirdre eventually asked.

"To the police station. They have questions that we might be able to shed light on."

Before they got past the scanner at headquarters, they could hear the cries. It was Sue Ellen, in hysterics, unable to explain what happened in what order. She was seated across the way from the police captain but without handcuffs. "Where did they take him? Where did they take him?" she was wailing when the three women entered. Deirdre had to resist the urge to slap her across the face.

Another policeman ushered the three new arrivals to the back office where he took notes on what they knew about Lance's last movements and motivations, the phone calls to Deirdre on Sunday afternoon, and Myra's account of an argument on the street between Sue Ellen and one Grover Wiggins.

Later that morning, three of the Wiggins gang were brought in for questioning. They had alibis, having drunk themselves silly up at the speakeasy on 61 the night before. A court-appointed lawyer for Sue Ellen was soon roped into service.

That same afternoon, Pippa swung into action, herding both Myra and Deirdre out to Lance's log cabin to retrieve whatever was likely dear to him before the police, vandals or flood waters interfered.

And also, to keep all three of them busy.

Inu came out of hiding under the porch, barking plaintively. Myra and Deirdre carried several bonsai plants to the car and put them in the trunk. Inside, they collected wood carvings, a couple of photos in a drawer which Deirdre had never seen before, and a cache of letters tied with string found in an old desk. Several musical instruments and an antique Japanese gong they placed in separate cardboard boxes and laid on the back seat of the car.

"These things are not material to anything the cops might need, and Lance would not want outsiders pawing over them. Better with us," Pippa wound up in justification of the illegal raid. "I'll come back again once, well, once all is said and done."

In the car, Myra and Deirdre took turns burying their faces in the unsuspecting dog's fur.

Surreal days followed.

Those closest to Deirdre clung to one another, Rose making herself useful by looking in on Clarissa and bringing over a different casserole every night. Sandra and Elwood came over every afternoon for cards, tea, and sympathy.

"He had seemed like a nice enough young man," Mrs. Durrell commented at one point. "A very unlucky family life, those Tatums, however," she had appended once she thought her daughter out of earshot.

Deirdre ate and said little, though she tried to put on a brave face. On the Wednesday, she had enough strength to carry the bonsai plants to her mother's back garden where they sat at either end of the spice and herb patch. The gong, which Lance had occasionally struck in her presence, she placed on its own shelf in her mother's curio cabinet.

For their part, Pippa and Myra returned the musical instruments to the workshop and Inu soon made himself right at home with the Perlmans' other canines.

Several days after the cremation—an event at which Sue Ellen displayed unwonted empathy by insisting that the urn be in possession of his closest friends, handing it off without demurrals to Pippa, Myra and Deirdre. "You three will figure out what to do."

As for the accident itself, it was soon investigated and adjudicated.

Sue Ellen, it was established, had been harassed by the Wiggins gang ever since she got out of prison, their particular beef being over a missing AR-15 that they claimed was theirs, and which she insisted was no longer in her possession.

Myra's statement included a conversation overheard in front of Grace Notes between what she called "a bantam chicken of a man" and Lance's sister. She remembered it distinctly because she was having trouble closing up the storefront, and neither of those two volunteered to be helpful.

"I heard the tone and it was menacing," she told the lawyers. " 'You'd best come up with something more convincing, you bitch, or cough up the dough for that gun.' Sue Ellen tried to explain herself, saying, 'I told you, Grover, I ain't got that gun. Cops confiscated it when they nabbed me, and I ain't got the dough either.' The man then spat on the sidewalk, in broad daylight, paying no attention to shoppers or anything," Myra further testified. "His final words sounded like a threat: 'You think hard, Sue Ellen. You think real hard 'fore Lester hisself shows up to get his due.' "

Throughout Myra's recitation, Sue Ellen sat bobbing her head catatonically.

That exchange in front of Grace Notes took place on a Friday some thirty hours before the shooting, and led Sue Ellen to purchase a dead-bolt for the front door, and to position a loaded shotgun next to her bed. It turned out too, as Lance's phone message to Deirdre indicated, he didn't have enough battery power to alert his sister he'd be dropping by to retrieve a few things for his trip. (She *had* had the wherewithal to make an extra key for the new lock but hadn't yet given it to him.)

Presumably, per the police report, when he finally showed up around 10 p.m., he had tried the door and then came around to check for an open window.

"When I seen that shadow and heard the rattling of the screen, I didn't think. I just unloaded. Bang, bang, bang," Sue Ellen managed to say before breaking down on the stand.

As for the role of drugs in this sorrow affair, the lab report came back clean except for a small amount of alcohol in the shooter's system. A small glass, half-empty, smelling of whiskey, was spotted on Sue Ellen's night table by the cops when they did their sweep. They bagged it, along with a photo of her and her brother in happier times.

Most town folks shook their heads in weary resignation over the Tatum tragedy and went about their business.

For a month or so, Deirdre went through the motions, doing her best to be cheery around her mother and whenever the twins rang up. Part of her was relieved when they explained work was too intense in the summer to make it down to the Delta. "Plus, don't forget,: you've got a round-trip ticket for the fall. We'll see you then, Mom," Caitlin had reminded her.

Rowan too had rung up in the aftermath of the shooting, Rose having waited a discrete amount of time before telling her brother what had transpired.

Their exchange was brief. "I am thinking about you, Deirdre, and I realize this is a great loss. It being so unexpected no doubt doesn't make it any easier."

"No, it doesn't," she had replied, her voice flat. "But you are thoughtful to call," she added, as if by rote.

"You do know how to reach me, if ever, or if I can do anything. What I said there in Oakville has not changed."

"Thank you for calling, Rowan," she responded and replaced the receiver.

On a steamy afternoon in late July, Pippa drove into town to see Deirdre and make further arrangements. To inch closer to closure couldn't be a bad thing, she reasoned, if closure actually were a thing. The ache around one's heart though *was* a thing and she was determined to help mitigate it, for all three of them.

She found her friend out in the back garden, watering the herbs and spices.

"You've gotten adept at this. Keeping these things alive through the summer is a challenge," Pippa said.

Deirdre turned and smiled, her eyes less filmy than before. "Note the bonsai. They appear to have made the move unscathed."

"Like Inu. He has managed to calm the others. So serene that dog."

"Like his former owner," Deirdre remarked, replacing the watering can on the work table and wiping her hands on her overalls. "Anyway, perfect timing. I was about to make a pitcher of iced tea to have with the cookies Elwood brought over. That man is a godsend, for me as well as for Mother."

"I passed them walking arm in arm at the end of the block, he the only one with a cane."

"Hmm," Deirdre nodded. "Nine months ago, I would never have expected Mother to make any improvement. With him, or *for* him, she rises to the occasion. And I had no idea..."

In the silence that fell softly between them, each thought fleetingly of Lance. Both enjoyed invoking his name now and again, but neither needed any longer to voice their sorrow or to wallow in their grief.

Deirdre gathered up the mint leaves she had cut and placed them on a saucer; Pippa stooped to pick up and return a trowel and clippers to the table alongside the watering can.

"Anyway, since you asked, I will stay for tea and to see your mom, but I have a couple of things to run by you first," Pippa soon announced in her take-charge voice.

Deirdre turned toward her friend.

"I was thinking that it makes sense for me to keep one of the photos of his wife and daughter, and you the other. Both taken apparently in 2013. Mount Fuji is in the background."

Deirdre looked away, perplexed, but said nothing.

Pippa went on: "As for his personal correspondence, I've sorted through the stack. Apparently, there were no letters between Lance and his wife that survived, but those from Sue Ellen or their father should rightfully go back to her, don't you think?"

Deirdre nodded distractedly. She had wrinkled her forehead, seemingly making some calculations.

"Other things, like his discharge papers from the Navy, an expired passport, and a certificate, in both Japanese and English, from some woodworking academy in Tokyo—: what would you say about burning them, then scattering the ashes along with his in the river? With the water so high, it's only a quarter- mile from the log cabin."

"I'd say it is the best thing I can imagine," Deirdre replied.

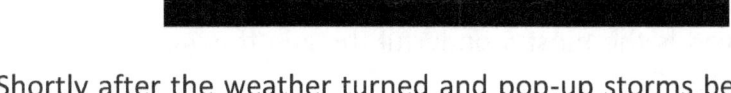

Shortly after the weather turned and pop-up storms began to tamp down the worst of the heat, Pippa organized a pickin' to celebrate Lance Tatum's life. Both she and Deirdre were stunned at the number of cars that lined the long driveway, the number of musicians who came from up and down the river to participate, and the sizable contingent of current or former students from Henson that showed up. Invitations that Myra had printed up on the computer had gone out, but word-of-mouth had obviously spread much further.

To Pippa's astonishment, her daughter had also scouted around to locate where Sue Ellen was living in Jackson, and sent her a handwritten note. *"Be there. He was your brother. And you'll be the better for it. Myra Perlman,"* it had read.

"Lance, in his unassuming way, would have been touched by all this, even if he would have begged us not to do it," Pippa remarked to the assembled guests crowded into the library or standing outside at the open windows in the September evening. "In particular, I'd wager there are more dulcimers gathered here than any other place in the world," she added to applause as the musicians tuned up.

With the help of Elwood and his granddaughter, Deirdre organized things so that her mother could come along and enjoy being in company. Performers took turns but with so many on hand the music went on until long after midnight. Sharon Simpson belted out one of Lance's favorite hymns, *Morning has Broken*, Pippa played a haunting version of *Shenandoah* on her dulcimer while Myra, whose voice was reedy but affecting, sang the words, and Deirdre performed *Danny Boy* on the piano, everyone joining in on the chorus.

When she looked out over the crowd, she spotted Sue Ellen standing in a far corner, her hair neatly bobbed, her face brighter, singing along with the others.

After they dropped Elwood and Sandra off at their home—it must have been past 2 a.m., though no one had bothered to check—Mrs. Durrell eventually turned toward her daughter.

"To be loved is the most wonderful thing in the world, wouldn't you say, DeeDee?"

Epilogue

W hether earlier intervention could have improved quality of life for Adaline Cotton Cole remained an open question after the deaths of her parents. Richard and Zenobia had passed quietly away within a week of each other, having just come home from a holiday performance by the Boston Symphony.

"As if they had arranged it themselves," Ashton had suggested when he called Deirdre in Riverton. "And, can you imagine, Brahms had been on the program that evening. What more could anyone have wanted?"

"Indeed," she had replied, her own sadness for the passing of her erstwhile in-laws surprising her, as did so many unexpected feelings of late.

After catching her ex-husband up with goings-on in the Delta and asking after Amira and Sierra, she returned to the bridge game in the parlor. (Thanks to Clarissa and Elwood's tutelage, Sandra had picked up quickly. She rarely misplayed a trick.) With so much laughter at the table and a roast baking in the oven, Deirdre would wait until the next day to tell her mother the news from Boston.

Dutifully, she did fly up for the funeral, pleased to see that Caitlin and Dylan had managed to come up together by train from New York. As she suspected, Adaline was reckoned too fragile or confused to be subjected to the obsequies. She did not argue with her ex-husband about what might be best for his sister. Ashton was distraught enough, despite his quip about Brahms and despite his being comforted by Amira.

Medical personnel at the Harvard-backed institution where Adaline would now be consigned were diplomatic when Ashton brought her to the clinic, the requisite paperwork on behalf of his sibling already filled out. But privately, they too were shocked. Autistic Adaline had been since early childhood, but with so little exercise or exposure to sunshine over the years, she had developed other ailments, some treatable, some less so.

Should the elder Coles have been held accountable for such benign neglect? Ashton preferred to emphasize the meticulous provisions their parents had made for her upon their deaths: all the proceeds from the sale of the house and its furnishings would go toward her care. (Only the family portraits in the gallery were earmarked for Ashton.)

Fortunately, the value of the Beacon Hill home had continued to rise, albeit the Coles' liquid assets, entrusted alas to Bernie Madoff, had been substantially depleted. However, given the family's centuries-long association with the university, Adeline's care for the remainder of her life would be top-of-the-line.

Ashton returned to Rolling Hills with the sense that a burden had been lifted, and was amazed by his own feeling of lightness. (The Coles had not warmed to Amira the sole time they had met her—having determined that Aleppo was even more alien a place to come from than Riverton, Mississippi. Thus, he no longer had a need to be embarrassed or defensive on her account.) He left the portraits of the Mathers and the Mores boxed up in the attic.

Despite the passing of his formidable parents and Adaline's decline, Ashton had much to be sanguine about. Sierra was not only precocious but openly affectionate with her new mother. So much so that Ashton marveled, and blushed, that there ever had been Jennifer in his life. However much her blonde physicality had overwhelmed him, his second wife was becoming more like the fantasy apparition in Donne's "The Dream." How sadly apt the poem, he thought.

Back in Riverton, Deirdre and Pippa continued their coffeehouse conversations at Henson, occasionally inviting students to join them to discuss music and books or whatever else seemed to be the subject du jour. One thing the two friends did not discuss: Deirdre's lingering suspicion that the photo of Lance's presumed wife and child belied his account of what happened to them—: the tsunami hit Japan in 2011; the photo was developed and stamped 2013 and the penciled inscription on the back read *M and M, spring 2013*.

Some nights she did lie awake, puzzling over the discrepancy and trying to reassemble the fragments of what he had confided so convincingly that afternoon in the workshop. Was her former lover an imposter after all, as Sue Ellen that day had shouted out, and which accusation had seemed so odd to Deirdre? She waited for Pippa to allude to Lance's need to fabricate things, as it were, but she never did.

As the autumn unfolded, however, and other, more immediate things clamored for attention, Deirdre decided the matter should remain a mystery. More important would be to hope that the beautiful woman and child with the snowy mountain behind them were indeed still alive.

Occasionally too the two friends got together for dinner with Rose and Dennis, who had tied the knot in a private ceremony six weeks after the memorial pickin for Lance.

"Something about his senseless death made us newly recognize that life is both fragile and fleeting," Rose had confided the week before the newlyweds headed to New Orleans for a short honeymoon stay in the Garden District. Turned out to be the very weekend Deirdre and Pippa flew together to New York to take in a play and visit their children.

To Pippa's delight, Myra had righted herself enough to apply successfully to NYU Law School and was sharing Caitlin's apartment in Soho. Nor could Deirdre be happier about how her daughter's career was progressing. Her performance with a jazz band in the West Village got good reviews and was sold out during its two-week run. The entire contingent of family and friends showed up on the final Saturday night, securing front row seats and applauding loudly. Zach too put in a brief appearance, but on his own. Four months pregnant, Nasreen had pleaded fatigue and a headache.

All of them, including Zach, headed to a nearby Italian restaurant afterwards, one the younger set apparently frequented. Walking in front of her, Deirdre noticed Dylan and Connor holding hands, and not because the sidewalk was treacherous. Caitlin and Zach, however, seemed ill-at-ease with each other, their days of easy camaraderie long past. Over the food and drink, not to mention the noise, Connor rang her dad to recount the evening's events. Although she heard her name mentioned a couple of times, Deirdre remained engaged in conversation with Jason and Myra, ignoring the moment Connor held out the cell phone in her direction.

If Rowan wanted to speak with her, he'd have to ring up expressly. And even then…

Such an occasion did eventually arrive. On Valentine's Day, Deirdre had made a strawberry cake, and together with Sandra, at home for a long weekend from Vanderbilt, decorated it with hearts on top. It was to be a surprise for Clarissa and Elwood after a rubber of bridge. However, Deirdre and Sandra ended up the ones most surprised: once the cake was ceremoniously placed on the table, Elwood spoke up. "Before it becomes the talk of the town, Clarissa and I wanted to let you two know the news: we are going to marry—sooner rather than later."

"Well, it's about time," Sandra piped up, rising from her chair to hug her granddad and then Mrs. Durrell.

Deirdre beamed from the other end of the table at her mother. "I can't think of anything that could make me happier."

Not an hour later, while the foursome was back in the living room sipping the latest specialty tea Pippa had sent over, the phone rang.

Sandra scurried to the hall. "No, no, we've already had dinner. Hang on a moment." Putting the receiver down, she called out: "Deirdre, it's for you."

"Hello?"

"I hope I'm not disturbing you, but they told me I could be the one to tell you. You know how young people are."

"Whatever are you talking about, Rowan, and where on earth are you?" Deirdre asked, happy, despite herself, to hear his voice.

"I'm in New York. Had dinner with Dylan and Connor: they've just gotten engaged. I believe I'm the first to know—my daughter flashed a gorgeous ring in my face—and they wanted you to be the next." Deirdre sat down on the stool and took a deep breath.

"I don't know what to say except that it's wonderful news. And serendipitous."

"I was hoping you'd say something like that."

"No, no. What I mean is Mother and Elwood Harrison—I believe you met him at one gathering or another—are planning on doing the same."

"No kidding. That's great," Rowan replied. After a considered pause, he added, "And for the life of me, dearest, I don't see why we don't make it a hat trick."

However many misgivings she might have mustered, Deirdre decided not to. "In that case, you should get yourself down here and do it properly. Time is fleeting."

The End

Other Works from Elizabeth Guider

The Passionate Palazzo (2013)
Milk and Honey on the Other Side (2016)
Connections (2018)

About the Author

Elizabeth Guider is a longtime entertainment journalist who has lived and worked in Rome, Paris and London as well as in New York City and Los Angeles. Born in the South, she holds a doctorate in Renaissance Studies from New York University. Currently, she divides her time between Hollywood, where she does freelance writing about the media business, and Vicksburg, MS, where she grew up and where she focuses on her fiction. *Our Long Love's Day* is her fourth novel.

More from Foundations Book Publishing

Pity's Prelude
By Creighton Halbert

Stephen Bates is desperate. Paid by a foreign superpower to leave Earth and sacrifice his life, he finds that ritual suicide isn't that simple when the planet he lands on erupts into civil war. He and local war hero, Titus Sirocco, struggle to discover who's trustworthy and who's gunning for them. As two different wars rage around them, will Stephen and Titus find what's worth dying for, or will the rebels choose their fate first?

Paved with Good Intentions
Dick Denny

Hold onto your scotch and taquitos, this one's another wild, supernatural ride..."When you do a job for Hell, Heaven expects the same.

When Archangel Gabrielle shows up at the door of Decker Investigations offering home kick-ass cars in exchange for a job, Nick takes it just to keep the peace.

www.ingramcontent.com/pod-product-compliance
Lightning Source LLC
Chambersburg PA
CBHW072341020726
47506CB00004B/953

*9 7 8 1 6 4 5 8 3 0 2 9 0 *